OUT OF THE FRYING PAN

Michael was in the wardroom, deep in the middle of a subdued discussion of the morning's extraordinary events with Aaron Stone, when a quiet voice interrupted.

"Helfort. Come with me." It was the provost marshal. The man's tone was quiet but firm.

"Yes, sir. What's up?" Michael asked, climbing to his feet.

"You'll find out. Come on, let's go."

When they left the wardroom, one of *Ishaq*'s marines was waiting outside, the man falling in behind them as they made their way up two decks to the ship's regulating office. When they got there, Armstrong waved Michael into his office, telling the marine to wait outside.

"Sit!"

Armstrong looked right at Michael while he gathered his thoughts. He had been a cop for a long time. He had more experience than he cared to think about, and every bit of that experience argued that the business at hand wasn't right. Sadly, for the moment at least, his hands were tied. There was a process to follow even if that meant trampling all over two officers who, by all accounts, had always tried to do their duty and—in Helfort's case at least—had the scars to prove it.

"Right, then." Armstrong's voice was flat, unemotional. "I'm going to comm you a document. It's a preliminary charge sheet alleging that you and Lieutenant Commander Fellsworth entered into a conspiracy to mutiny."

By Graham Sharp Paul

HELFORT'S WAR
Book I: *The Battle at the Moons of Hell*
Book II: *The Battle of the Hammer Worlds*

The Battle
of the
Hammer
Worlds

**HELFORT'S WAR:
Book II**

Graham Sharp Paul

BALLANTINE BOOKS • NEW YORK

A Del Rey Books Mass Market Original

Copyright © 2008 by Graham Sharp Paul

Published in the United States by Del Rey Books, an imprint of The Random House Publishing Group, a division of Random House, Inc., New York.

DEL REY is a registered trademark and the Del Rey colophon is a trademark of Random House, Inc.

ISBN 978-0-345-49572-3

Printed in the United States of America

www.delreybooks.com

OPM   9 8 7 6 5 4 3 2 1

To my parents, from whom I inherited my love of books.
Wish you could have been here to read this one, Pa.

Acknowledgments

As ever, my thanks to my wife, Vicki, for her encouragement, tolerance, and support. Thanks also to my agents, Russ Galen and Tara Wynne, without whom none of this would have happened, and to my editor, Liz Scheier, for her drive, unsparing advice, and commitment to deadlines.

"Cargo's stowed, Captain. Just doing my final walk around now."

The flat, uninterested voice of the *Constancy*'s first officer dragged Captain Curtis Karangi away from a review of the options he'd have if the Feds discovered the containers the *Constancy* had just loaded. Karangi was not a happy man; it had been a depressing exercise. The plain fact was that if the Feds did intercept his ship, being neurowiped was probably the best offer he was going to get.

Karangi picked up the old-fashioned hand mike. "Captain, roger. We'll get under way shortly."

"Righto," the first officer replied dismissively.

"Righto! Righto! I'll give you righto, you disrespectful son of a bitch," Karangi muttered as he smashed the mike back into its cradle.

Karangi sighed despairingly as he patted the stun pistol that never, ever left his hip. If the damn Feds didn't get him, his crew probably would, every last one of them an insubordinate, money-grubbing ratbag. And if his crew didn't get him, *Constancy* would. The bloody ship was clapped out, a death trap, her every transit through pinchspace a roll of life's dice. But he was trapped. He owed money—mountains of money—to a Hammer-backed finance company, and until it was paid off, he would do exactly what they wanted him to do.

Goddamn the Hammers. A more evil bunch of people he hoped never to meet. If it were up to him, he'd have nuked them all to hell years earlier. After all the grief the Hammers had dished out over the years, why the Feds hadn't done just that he would never understand. Anyway, it mattered not— they had him by the balls, so if they wanted him to captain a blockade runner, that was exactly what he was going to do. Besides, they might be complete assholes, but they paid their blockade runners handsomely. He would keep slipping contraband past the Feds and into Hammer space—something he fancied he was very good at—until he had repaid every cent he owed.

Well, Karangi consoled himself. Look on the bright side. Two more runs would see his debt paid off in full, with interest. Then, finally, he would be off the hook, and the Hammers could go screw themselves.

Five decks below the bridge, *Constancy*'s first officer gave the brilliantly lit cargo bay a last look-see. Satisfied that all was as it should be, he slipped behind a wall of contraband containers. Safely out of sight of the ship's surveillance holocams, he concentrated on the task at hand. He would not get another chance; if he wasn't on the bridge for *Constancy*'s departure out of the Korovin system, Captain Karangi would want to know where he had been and what he had been up to.

It was the work of moments to connect a thin cable into the ship's emergency data network. Impatiently, the first officer waited as the covert access routines loaded into his neuronics burrowed their way through the layers of security that protected *Constancy*'s master AI. Finally, he was in. Disguised as a diagnostic logging subroutine, he downloaded the ship's navigation plan buried in a mass of other ship data. Moments after that, the entire plan—now an anonymous collection of heavily encrypted data packets—was on its way via the ship's communications hub down to Korovin's planetary net.

Where the data packets had gone, the first officer did not know, nor did he much care. He would be well paid for what amounted to less than a couple of minutes' work, and that was all he cared about.

With a final check to make sure nobody else was around, he was on his way up to the bridge.

At 17:23 Universal Time, the massive bulk of *Constancy* began to accelerate slowly away from Korovin planet. According to the flight plan lodged with Korovin nearspace control, its destination was the obscure planet of al-Harrani, 425 light-years distant.

Wednesday, June 23, 2399, UD
Federated Worlds Warship Ishaq, *berthed on Space*
Battle Station SBS-44, in orbit around Jascaria planet,
Federated Worlds

Junior Lieutenant Michael Helfort's posting to the Haiyan class heavy cruiser *Ishaq* started badly.

Michael's left leg was on fire. He swore under his breath as a white-hot sliver of pain cut its way through his thigh. It had been months since a razor-sharp piece of titanium blasted off the hull of the light scout *DLS-387* by a Hammer rail-gun slug had ripped into him; his leg was still not right. Stubbornly, the pain refused to go away despite the best efforts of a host of Fleet surgeons and their prodigious armory of medical geneering, targeted drugbots, psychotropic pain inhibitors, and neuronics blockers. The pain stayed, a dull ache in the background until provoked into the open to explode in snarling fury.

Like now, and fool that he was, he had not bothered to get his drugbots replenished.

Rigidly at attention, Michael stood in front of a tall, sourfaced man. He had been there for a good five minutes. His weight drove down into a thigh muscle that protested every second it was held immobile. He kept his eyes locked in approved Fleet style on the man in front of him, unmoving because that was the last order he had been given.

Michael's tormentor was *Ishaq*'s officer of the day. The man was turned out in immaculate dress blacks; medal ribbons, unit commendations, and combat command hash marks were conspicuously absent. The name tag read LIEUTENANT XING. Michael wondered what the man's problem was. He sure as hell seemed to be having a bad day, though why Xing seemed so determined to take it out on him was a mystery.

Michael needed every ounce of self-control to stand in silence while he let Xing's tirade run its vitriolic course. He tried to explain that he was late because the up-shuttle had suffered a main engine defect. Xing had not been interested. He had cut Michael off with a contemptuous order to speak only when instructed to do so. You pompous, stuck-up moron, Michael thought, his face a frozen mask, eyes on his tormentor's face.

"You haven't heard the last of this, Helfort. Let me see . . . yes. The executive officer is expecting you at 10:00, so try not to be late. The ship's administration office will comm you the rest of your induction program. Now get out of my sight." With a dismissive flick of the wrist, Xing turned away.

For a moment Michael stood there, unsure what to do. He might be only a lowly junior lieutenant, but long-standing Fleet tradition dictated that one member of the duty watch be detailed by Xing to carry his gear to his cabin. God knows, there were plenty of duty spacers to call on; they stood ranged against a bulkhead. To a spacer, they avoided Michael's eye. He suppressed a sudden urge to smile at the sight of the long line of spacers, apparently all engaged in studious examination of the air lock's overhead wiring. He realized that no order was going to come from Xing, to whom Michael seemingly no longer existed.

Bugger it, Michael thought. The time had come to show Xing and the rest of *Ishaq*'s crew that he was not going to take any more crap than he absolutely had to.

He turned to the quartermaster. Throughout Xing's tirade, she had not moved a muscle.

"Leader, when you get the chance, can you arrange for my gear to be dropped off? My cabin is down in, let me see—"

The quartermaster—Leading Spacer Petrovic according to her name tag—did not let him finish. "Not a problem, sir, not a problem." Petrovic smiled warmly. "I know where you're billeted. I'll have your stuff there in five. Oh, and welcome aboard, sir. Leading Spacer Bienefelt and I went through basic training together. She's told me all about you."

Michael smiled, pleased to find that he had at least one ally onboard *Ishaq*. "All good, I hope?"

Petrovic's face crinkled into a broad grin. "Not for me to say, sir. Matti would tear my arms off if I did."

Michael laughed. He knew she could; Leading Spacer Matthilde "Matti" Bienefelt was big enough to tear the arms off a geneered gorilla. Out of the corner of his eye, he saw Lieutenant Xing's spine stiffen. Clearly, the man was undecided as to whether Michael was best ignored or a challenge to his authority that needed to be dealt with firmly on the spot.

Michael decided to save Xing the trouble of choosing. The man was a complete jerk—probably that was being generous—but it was not a smart move to upset him even more. He should go.

With a quiet word of thanks to Petrovic, Michael walked out of the personnel air lock. He could only hope that the rest of *Ishaq*'s officers were not like Xing.

Thursday, June 24, 2399, UD
Federated Worlds Warship Kapteyn's Star, *in deepspace*

"Okay, ops. Let's go to general quarters."

"Sir!"

Lieutenant Commander Marco Gianfranco, captain in command of the Federated Worlds Warship *Kapteyn's Star,* sat back and watched as the combat information center dissolved around him into controlled chaos, combat spacesuited spacers hurrying into their positions, chased along by the urgent demands of the ship's klaxon. He had a good team; in less than a minute, chaos had been replaced by the low murmur of a combat information center crew bringing the ship to full combat readiness.

"Captain, sir," Gianfranco's executive officer and second in command reported formally moments later, "the ship is at general quarters in ship state 1, closed up to airtight condition zulu."

"Roger. Boarding party?"

"Loaded; assault lander is at immediate notice to launch, sir."

"Good. Let's hope we see some action this time."

"Oh, please, let it be," Gianfranco's executive officer said with a grimace. "I'm going walkabout."

"Off you go," Gianfranco said, waving the man away. "All stations, this is command. Depressurizing and shutting down artgrav in two minutes." They might be up against only a couple of smugglers, but Gianfranco was not one to take chances. If anyone started shooting back, he would rather not have them punching holes in a hull under pressure, and leaving his artificial gravity on would make him vulnerable to detection even by commercial gravitronics sensors.

"Command, Mother. *Kruger, Markeb,* and *Alioth* report ready in all respects."

"Roger." There was nothing more Gianfranco needed to say. If Mother—the AI that ran *Kapteyn's Star*'s mission-critical systems—said the four deepspace heavy scouts that constituted Task Unit 950.5.3 were ready, they were ready. And so they should be. To a spacer, everyone knew exactly what had to be done, and he was not going to waste their time and his going over it again. He sat back, content to let Mother and his two senior warfare officers—operations to his left, threat assessment to his right—attend to the details of what some creative genius in operations planning had called Operation Final Blocker.

For the umpteenth time that long morning, Gianfranco

scanned the massive holovid screens that curtained the combat information center in front of him. Nothing had changed. Passive sensors from the four ships of the task unit, relentlessly crunching data sucked by the terabyte from billions of cubic kilometers of space, reported nothing unusual; this particular blob of interstellar deepspace was completely empty and had been that way for a very long time.

Gianfranco suppressed a sigh. The *Kapteyn's Star* had been part of the Federated Worlds' blockade of the Hammer Worlds for six long months now; he had lost count of the number of times they had been dispatched—always in response to reliable intelligence, of course—to some featureless point in deepspace to intercept blockade runners that never turned up.

He reckoned he had good grounds for thinking that this time would be a bust like all the rest. Though as an optimist at heart, he could always hope he might be wrong.

The minutes dragged by. Gianfranco cursed under his breath. This was shaping up to be yet another wild goose chase. He shifted restlessly in his seat, his combat space suit stiff and uncomfortable. He turned to his operations officer.

"Well, Tamu, what do you reckon? Another bu—"

The matter-of-fact voice of *Kapteyn's Star*'s sensor officer cut him off. "Command, sensors. Positive gravitronics intercept. Estimated drop bearing Green 25 Up 5. One vessel. Grav wave pattern suggests pinchspace transition imminent. Designated hostile track 885001."

Well, well, well, Gianfranco thought exultantly. Finally. "Command, roger. Okay, folks, let's do this right. Threat! I want confirmation of this one's identity as fast as you can."

"Roger that, sir."

"Mother, anything from the other ships?"

"Triangulating now. Stand by . . . consensus drop datum is at Green 23 Up 4, range 50,000 kilometers."

Bingo, Gianfranco thought. Close but not too close. For once, the intel they had been given was on the money. "Roger."

"Command, sensors. Track 885001 dropping now. Confirm drop datum at Green 23 Up 4 at 45,000 kilometers."

Gianfranco watched the command holovid intently as a fleeting flare of ultraviolet betrayed the inbound ship's drop out of pinchspace. Yes, he said to himself exultantly, finally.

"Command, sensors. Hostile track 885001 confirmed as *Constancy,* Holterman system registration."

"Threat concurs."

"Command, roger." Gianfranco breathed out a sigh of relief. Game on.

Ten long minutes later, the second piece of the puzzle dropped into place. Gianfranco and the rest of the combat information center crew watched with bated breath as the task unit's sensors tracked what should be an incoming Hammer ship as it dropped out of pinchspace in a flash of ultraviolet radiation. And then the ground underneath Operation Final Blocker shifted.

"Command, sensors. Hostile track 885002 is the Hammer Diamond class deepspace light patrol ship *Adamantine.*"

"Threat concurs."

"Oh, shit," Gianfranco murmured. This was definitely not standard operating procedure for Hammer blockade runners. The *Constancy*'s cargo had to be something the Hammer really, really wanted for them to send a light patrol ship to pick it up. This operation was not going to be the walk in the park he had planned. Diamond class ships were rail-gun-armed, and rail guns could do his ships some very serious damage.

"Mother! To all ships," he snapped, "maintain current vectors, stand by revised tacplan."

Gianfranco watched the command holovid intently, the two blockade runners now marked by blazing red icons. His rules of engagement were crystal clear. It might be utterly improbable for two ships to be in close proximity in the middle of nowhere, but he could not fire so much as a peashooter at them without unequivocal holocam evidence that *Constancy* had transferred cargo to a Hammer ship contrary to the flight plan her captain had lodged with Korovin nearspace control. Well, Gianfranco consoled himself, at least this time no smart-ass lawyer was going to stand up in court to argue that the *Adamantine* was anything but a Hammer ship.

Here we go, he said to himself as the first container crossed the gap between the two ships to disappear slowly into *Adamantine*'s cargo bay, the handlers visibly struggling with the container's awkward bulk. Gianfranco had seen enough.

"Mother. To all ships. Weapons free. Acknowledge."

"Stand by . . . all ships acknowledge weapons free."

"To all ships, execute to follow, Kilo Tango 45, I say again, Kilo Tango 45."

"Mother, roger."

"Ops! Ready?"

"As we'll ever be, sir," Gianfranco's operations officer replied, teeth behind the plasglass visor of his combat space suit bared in anticipation.

Nerves jangling, Gianfranco waited until *Constancy*'s second container was making its final approach to the *Adamantine,* a third and a fourth close behind. Now, he thought, let the damn lawyers argue their way out of this one.

"Mother. To all ships. Kilo Tango 45, stand by, stand by . . . execute!"

As one, the four ships of Task Unit 950.5.3 fired their main engines, pillars of white-hot flame driving them toward the two blockade runners. A second later, the rip-buzz of missile dispensers announced the deployment of a warning salvo of Mamba antistarship missiles, the ASSMs accelerating hard away from the incoming ships and toward the hapless smugglers.

"Constancy, Adamantine. This is FedWorld Warship *Kapteyn's Star.* You are in violation of the Allied Declaration of Embargo. Do not attempt to jump. Maintain current vectors. Stand by to be boarded. Failure to comply will result in the use of deadly force. No further warnings will be given. Acknowledge."

Constancy's captain needed no more persuasion. With her massive cargo hatches wide open and the better part of his crew outside handling containers, his ship was a long way from being pinchspace jump-capable. Voice trembling with shock, he capitulated on the spot. Mother wasted no time, the missiles targeting the *Constancy* command destructing in a massive wall of white-hot flame.

The *Adamantine*'s captain had other ideas; Gianfranco knew he would. There wasn't a Hammer captain alive who would allow the Feds to board his ship, and *Adamantine*'s skipper was not going to be the exception. Ignoring the in-bound missile salvo, *Adamantine* fired her main engines barely seconds after Gianfranco had sprung the ambush, the ship slewing to bring her rail-gun batteries to bear on the *Kapteyn's Star* even as she worked frantically to close the cargo doors that stopped her from jumping safely into pinch-space. The bodies of her cargo handlers were abandoned to spin away into space, their orange distress strobes marking vectors to oblivion.

"Making a run for it," the operations officer said, "but not before he drops a rail-gun swarm on us, I think."

Gianfranco grunted. He didn't need to say any more; blockade standard operating procedures were clear. Any attempt to run invited the use of deadly force, and his ships were already responding.

Gianfranco watched intently as the four Fed ships, their antiship lasers flaying *Adamantine*'s hull, sent a full salvo of Mamba ASSMs on their way, the missiles masked by active decoys and a blizzard of jamming to baffle and confuse *Adamantine*'s sensors. The *Adamantine* treated everything thrown at her with disdain. Slowly, inexorably, she came bows on to *Kapteyn's Star* and fired her forward batteries, her bows split from side to side by the brilliantly white pin-pricks of a rail-gun salvo.

"Command, Mother. Rail-gun launch from *Adamantine*. Target is *Kapteyn's Star*. Time to impact 54 seconds."

"Command, roger. All stations, rail-gun attack imminent. Brace for impact." Gianfranco swallowed hard, his stomach knotted into a hard ball of fear. This was a first for him; he had never been on the receiving end of a Hammer rail-gun swarm, and he wasn't enjoying the experience. Somehow, all those hours in the sims beating back Hammer attacks just like this one did not quite convey the pitiless horror of a rail-gun swarm.

The swarm—thousands of tiny platinum/iridium slugs seeded with thousands of decoys to confuse *Kapteyn's*

Star's defenses—leaped across the gap between the two ships at close to 3 million kilometers per hour.

"Command, Mother. Swarm geometry is good. Slug impact certain. No time to maneuver clear."

Gianfranco swore as he checked Mother's assessment. She was right. Whoever the Hammer commander was, he was no slouch. *Adamantine* had dropped into normalspace closed up and cleared away for action, and her rail-gun crew was good. Taking full advantage of the close range, the thousands of slugs that made up the swarm were tightly grouped and perfectly synchronized. Ripple fired into the shape of a cone whose pointed end was coming right at *Kapteyn's Star,* the swarm left her nowhere to run. Bows on to the threat, *Kapteyn's Star* could only wait.

Hands slippery with sudden sweat, Gianfranco sat and stared at the command holovid, with the incoming swarm, an ugly rash of brilliant red icons, closing in at frightening speed. There was nothing he could do, nothing any human could do. The fate of Gianfranco's ship and crew now rested with Mother; dumping noncritical tasks, her massive processing arrays worked frantically to weed out the decoys strewn at random through the rail-gun swarm, the better to direct the lasers, missiles, and chain guns that made up *Kapteyn's Star*'s close-in defenses as they worked desperately to blow the incoming rail-gun slugs out of existence.

All things considered, Mother and the *Kapteyn's Star* did a good job—but not good enough. The swarm geometry was too good, and there were too many slugs for the ship's close-in defenses to deal with. In less than a microsecond, five slugs, all wrongly classified as decoys and ignored until too late, slipped through the defenses, their enormous kinetic energy transformed into enough thermal energy to blow massive craters in the ship's armored bows. The *Kapteyn's Star* staggered under the weight of the slugs, their impact momentarily overwhelming the ship's artgrav. Gianfranco was snapped hard against the safety harness that locked him into his chair as the ship bucked and heaved under the shock. He ignored it. It would take more than a few Hammer slugs to get through *Kapteyn's Star*'s frontal armor. Thank God, he

thought, the attack had not been beam or stern on. The result
might have been very different. A quick check of the ship's
damage-control status board reassured him. The *Kapteyn's
Star* had suffered a serious loss of forward armor but was
otherwise undamaged.

"Our turn now, so suck this," Gianfranco hissed venomously as the task unit's first missile salvo fell on the Hammer ship. In desperation, *Adamantine*'s defenses clawed
missile after missile out of the attack, her successes marked
by searingly white-hot flares as missile warheads and fusion
drives blew. In the confused melee, a single missile made it
through, driving into a slowly closing cargo hatch to punch
deep into the ship before exploding, the warhead driving a
white-hot lance of plasma deep into the Hammer vessel. It
was all to no avail; the warhead's blast was absorbed in the
bunkers that fed driver mass pellets into *Adamantine*'s main
engines. Gianfranco cursed softly; the Hammer ship barely
registered the blow. Then, seconds before the second missile
salvo fell on her, the *Adamantine* jumped into pinchspace;
the briefest of brief flashes of intense ultraviolet provided
the only record that she had ever been there.

"Son of a bitch," Gianfranco said, bitterly disappointed.
The *Adamantine*'s scalp would have looked good on his service record. Around him, the *Kapteyn's Star*'s combat information center crew was silent, their unspoken frustration
obvious.

"Hang on, sir. Have another look." The operations officer's
voice crackled with excitement. "The cargo hatch. Still
open. Must have been jammed open by the missile impact.
Unless they recomputed their mass distribution, and I don't
think they had the time, their chances of making it home
safely would not be good. We might have a kill to our name,
after all. Well, a quarter share at least," he concluded hopefully.

"You know what, ops? I think you might be right," Gianfranco said, cheered by the thought that *Adamantine* might
not have gotten away cleanly. "When the dust has settled,
have Mother take a good look at it. I'd like to know what she
thinks. Okay, how long before we can get the boarding party

away? I really want to see what was so damned important that the Hammers would send a Diamond class deepspace light patrol ship to pick it up. Oh, yes. Ops! Detach *Markeb* and *Alioth* to recover the people the Hammers left behind. I have a feeling the boys and girls at Fleet intelligence will want to talk to them."

Thursday, June 24, 2399, UD
FWSS Ishaq, *berthed on Space Battle Station SBS-44,*
in orbit around Jascaria

Michael's first two days on board *Ishaq* passed in a blur. Harried from one place to another by the AI—artificial intelligence—that managed the ship's administration, he had found the pace relentless.

"Getting near that time, I think." Michael was exhausted. His guide for the day, Cadet Aaron Stone, was good company, but Michael had another long day to look forward to. He needed a good night's sleep.

Stone nodded. "You might be right. One for the road?"

Michael's determination to call it a night crumbled. Being alone in his cabin did not seem so attractive all of a sudden. "Oh, go on, then."

Stone walked off to the bar. Michael commed his neuronics to bring up the news. It had been a while since he had checked what was going on in humanspace, and this was as good a time as any to catch up. Moments after the World News Network popped into view, he wished he had not bothered.

The news was bad. Talks with the Hammer over the hijacking of the Fed Worlds mership *Mumtaz* had collapsed; the Hammers were pulling out of the negotiations.

Stone was back with two new beers. "Check out WNN," Michael said. "Looks like the Hammers have pulled the plug." He sighed. Suddenly he was a million years old. "Well, Aaron. I think the shit is going to hit the fan."

"Bastards." Stone frowned. "Beats me how that new chief councillor . . . what's his name?"

"Polk. Chief Councillor Jeremiah Polk."

"Yup, him. How can he try to pin the *Mumtaz* hijacking on someone else? Do the Hammers ever take responsibility for anything?" Stone took a long pull at his beer. "Man's a total idiot," he said dismissively.

Michael shook his head. Jeremiah Polk was many things—devious psychopath sprang most immediately to mind—but Michael was damn sure he was not an idiot.

"Don't know about that, Aaron. He's a very dangerous man, that Polk. This doesn't look good."

A gloomy silence fell over the two young officers.

Intently, Michael watched Polk being interviewed. He had read pretty much every word written about—and by— Jeremiah Polk. He struggled to think of a more amoral man. Christ! To call Polk a psychopath was being unkind to psychopaths, but a few things were clear. True to his Hammer bloodlines, Jeremiah Polk was a man who never forgave. He was a man who never forgot. He was a man unable to let an insult pass unavenged. He was a man whose preferred solution to most problems was violence. He despised intellectuals; smart-assed thinkers, he called them. On the basis of those traits alone, something was brewing. He would stake his life on it.

"So, Michael. What does it all mean?"

Michael had been asking himself the same question.

"Hard to tell . . ."

Michael's voice trailed off as he contemplated the terrible prospect of another full-blown war against the fundamentalist Hammers. It was not a happy thought. Nothing but nothing could ever convince the Hammers that their so-called religion was the invention of one man, that everything they thought and did was based on one giant lie. He shook his head in despair. The curiously shaped rocks discovered on Mars by Peter McNair were no more relics of an ancient civilization dedicated to the universe's supreme being, Kraa, than his toenail clippings were. The whole thing was an elaborate charade on which the Hammers had erected possibly the most viciously cruel society known to humankind. But like all fundamentalists down the ages, reason and logic had no weight with the Hammers. They understood only one thing: brute force, so brute force it would have to be. Maybe this time, Michael thought, the Federated Worlds would go for the throat, not stopping until the entire rotten edifice that was Hammer society lay crushed into dust.

"Now," he continued, "exactly what does it all mean? Well, I hate to say this, but I think we're in for a fight. I think that's what it means. So stand by for a fourth worlds war."

Stone's eyes opened wide in shock. "You sure of that?"

Michael shook his head. "No, I'm not. There's no way I can be. But Polk's got to do something. Look at the problems he's got at home. The Hammer's falling apart at the seams. Remember your Politics 101: When things at home are going to shit, fight a foreign war. Distracts the peasants; keeps them in line. Anyway, I think force is the only thing the Hammers really understand, so force is what Polk will turn to."

Stone ran his hands through his hair. His face hardened. "So what? Bring it on. We'll kick those Hammers back to the Stone Age where they damn well belong."

Michael shook his head. "Be careful what you wish for, Aaron," he cautioned.

Stone stared at Michael. He looked guilty. "Oh, yes. You've been there. Sorry. Forgot."

"That's all right. Anyway, there's nothing much we can do about it. We are junior officers, nothing but low-life bottom-feeders. So drink up. I need a decent night's sleep."

Monday, June 28, 2399, UD
Offices of the Supreme Council for the Preservation of
the Faith, city of McNair, Commitment planet,
Hammer of Kraa Worlds

Chief Councillor Jeremiah Polk sat back in his chair,
stretching in yet another vain attempt to ease the kinks out of
an aching back. His mood was foul. "Kraa's blood," he muttered. For once it would be good to have a day without crisis
after crisis crashing onto his desk.

"Chief Councillor?" The diffident tones of his secretary
broke into his thoughts.

"Yes, Singh."

"Fleet Admiral Jorge is here, sir."

"Ah, good. Send him in."

The man ushered into his office was tall, his looks well
served by his Spanish forebears. Once his face must have
been classically handsome. Now it was deeply lined by the
long hours and stress that went with every senior position in
the Hammer Worlds.

Jorge looked nervous, his forehead slicked with a telltale
sheen of sweat. That was not surprising, Polk thought as he
waved Jorge into a seat. The man should be nervous. After
all, it was only a matter of months since Polk, in the wake of
the Hammer fleet's pathetic response to the Fed's attack on
Hell's Moons, had personally ordered the deaths of thousands of Jorge's fellow officers, their bodies even now rotting
in DocSec lime pits. Truth be known, Polk was reassured by
fear. He liked being feared—very much.

Once Jorge was settled, Polk pinned him back in his chair
with a long, unblinking stare. Polk was pleased to see the
man actually push back a fraction as if trying to escape.

"So, Admiral," Polk said eventually. "Let's get on with it.

The last time we met, I asked for a firm date for the start of Operation Cavalcade."

Jorge nodded in agreement. "You did, Chief Councillor. I've scheduled a full Operation Cavalcade presentation for next week's Defense Council, and I'll be asking for formal approval to proceed with the operation then. If I get the go-ahead, the ships assigned to Cavalcade—"

"Those ships. Where are they now?"

"The shipbuilder handed over the converted ships on schedule. They are now in a Keradiniyan black weapons yard having their rail-gun systems fitted. We expect to take delivery of all six q-ships in late July."

Polk looked pleased. "Good. I just hope your man . . ."

"Monroe, Commodore Monroe."

"Yes. Monroe. I just hope he can do the job."

"He can, sir, and he will. I have every confidence in him."

Polk stared at Jorge. "Yes," he said. "I certainly hope so, for your sake. Continue."

"As I was saying, provided I get approval to proceed, the ships assigned to Cavalcade will start interdicting FedWorld mership traffic to and from the Old Earth system from the end of August."

Polk waved a hand dismissively. "You'll get your approval, Admiral."

Jorge sat back a bit; he looked relieved. For all his powers as the commander in chief of all Hammer defense forces—and those powers were huge- –the Hammer was at heart a bureaucratic beast. Without the right bits of paper signed by the Defense Council, there were always limits to those powers.

"Okay, what else?"

"Nothing immediate, sir. I'll have the plan for Operation Damascus. You'll recall that's the operation that will follow on from Cavalcade"—Polk nodded—"from Rear Admiral Keniko and his team next week. I'm happy with what I've seen so far. I'll be looking to brief you within the next two weeks before going to the council."

Polk was not able to restrain himself; a broad smile split

his face wide open. Damascus was all about taking the fight back up to the Kraa-damned Feds. This time the Hammer would be on the offensive. This time they would win. "By Kraa, Admiral, I shall look forward to that. Make a time with Singh as you leave."

"Thank you, sir."

Wednesday, June 30, 2399, UD
FWSS Ishaq, berthed on Space Battle Station SBS-44,
in orbit around Jascaria

The command training simulation had been a complete and utter shambles. A simple sim, but Captain Constanza had managed to make a complete mess of it, ignoring her staff, short-circuiting the chain of command, and overriding her subordinates until the whole debacle ground to an embarrassed and disastrous conclusion.

Michael, along with every other spacer in *Ishaq*'s flag combat data center, did his best to melt into the background. In full view of all present, Captain Constanza was flaying the man she held responsible for the shambles, her second in command and *Ishaq*'s executive officer, Commander Jack Morrissen.

Michael watched in horrified fascination as Constanza tore Morrissen to shreds—in public, in front of *Ishaq*'s officers, and without restraint. The public humiliation of *Ishaq*'s second most senior officer was an appalling sight.

Constanza might be captain in command and supreme under God and all that, Michael thought, but he would not have blamed Morrissen if he had strangled her on the spot. Nobody watching would. Thankfully, Constanza's second in command was too smart to do anything. Silent and unmoving, he refused to respond in any way. Michael watched as Morrissen weathered the storm. In the end, something must have told Constanza that she had better call a halt as, with a final spray at Morrissen, she stalked out of the combat data center.

Michael could only stand there, wondering just what sort of ship he had been posted to.

Michael lay in his bunk for a long time. His earlier optimism had all but evaporated. Sleep eluded him. He cursed. Not sleeping was beginning to become a habit.

His mind churned through all the complexities and unknowns facing him. The worst and most immediate of his concerns was *Ishaq* herself. In one short week, he had seen more than enough to convince him that it was a ship in trouble.

Outwardly *Ishaq* was the very embodiment of the Federation's awesome wealth and technology. She was big, she was impressive, and she radiated raw power, but to Michael, form had triumphed over substance. Michael could see past the ship itself and did not like what he saw: carelessly stowed equipment, safety racks short of gear, untidy compartments, more dust and dirt than he had ever seen in any Fleet unit, large or small. But worst of all was the crew. Their attitude, with some honorable exceptions such as Leading Spacer Petrovic, largely ranged from sullen through uncooperative to downright hostile. As for the officers, Michael was even more confused; without exception, they acted as though all were well, as though this were how Federated Worlds warships were supposed to be. And Michael was under no illusions that he was going to be voted *Ishaq*'s most popular officer. So far, he had been given the cold shoulder by almost everyone he had met; the resentment, the envy, the bitterness were all too obvious.

The more he thought about things, the more he felt alone and the more his thoughts kept turning back to Anna. With a few short breaks—largely the product of adolescent stupidity and mostly his fault—he and Anna had been together throughout their time at Space Fleet College. Despite the relentless pressures of college life, the bond had deepened to the point where Michael believed with all his heart that Anna was the one for him. He liked to think that she felt the same way about him.

But even if she did, there was a fly in the ointment. There always was, of course.

There was the old adage: Space Fleet College made relationships for Fleet to break. Michael knew it was an adage founded on years of bitter experience. In his case, it was beginning to look dangerously prescient. He and Anna had seen little of each other since graduation. No surprises there; the chances of two frontline heavy cruisers being in the same port at the same time were vanishingly small. He knew. He had done the math.

True, the chances of his arranging leave at the same time as Anna were better, but they still were not good. If he and Anna were lucky, they might spend a month a year together until they got senior enough to pull staff jobs ashore, but that happy state of affairs was a long, long way off, and even a month a year did not allow for random acts of stupidity by those Hammer dickheads. God only knew what they were up to. Knowing the Hammers, anything was possible.

The thought of what the Hammers might do if they cut loose made his heart skip a beat. Much as he hated the Hammers—and he did with relentless, cold-burning intensity—the thought of facing the murdering swine again was almost too much to bear. The bowel-churning fear he had felt working with Matti Bienefelt outside the light scout *387* to fix battle damage, all the while knowing that there was nothing but hard vacuum between him and an oncoming Hammer rail-gun salvo, had been seared into his memory. The pain he had felt as *387*'s battle dead left the ship after the Battle of Hell's Moons was with him for life. Did he want to go through all that again? Did he really want to be a Fleet officer? Maybe he should quit. He could marry Anna and set up a home while she pursued her Fleet career. After all, Dad had always hinted that there was a place for him in the family flame-tree business, so a job would not be a problem.

For an instant he was tempted, but it was only for an instant.

"Bugger that," he muttered. Flame-tree salesman. Christ! What a depressing thought. Salesman or Fleet officer? He snorted. That was no contest. Besides, he had a debt to settle with the Hammer. The thought of what he might have to go through to settle that debt made him feel physically sick. Still, the debt would be settled in full. The ghosts of 387's dead crew would not settle for anything less.

Even as he repeated a promise already made countless times, something deep inside, something cold and dangerous, started to pull him down into darkness. Abruptly, the urge to curl up and shut out the world and all its fear and pain started to overwhelm him.

Panic engulfed him; Michael started to slide over the edge into the black pit of depression. For a moment he let himself go, unwilling to stop the fall, but then his training kicked in, the routines ground into him by the combat trauma counselors after the Battle of Hell's Moons taking over. Slowly, he pushed the tide of hopelessness back. Bit by bit, he recovered his mental balance; it took another ten long, hard-fought minutes to bring a racing heart and heaving lungs back under control. Shakily, Michael took a deep breath, almost defeated by the sheer physical effort it had taken to claw his way back to normal. Well, as normal as he could be under the circumstances, he thought wryly, if a flat, sick tiredness was normal.

Michael pulled up the holopix of his last visit with Anna. He knew full well that the sight of her would do nothing to help his mood, but he did not care. Then there she was, and for the umpteenth time Michael marveled at her beauty, wondered at the luck that had made him the man she wanted in her life. Well, he reminded himself, so he hoped.

Anna's face was beyond striking. It was breathtaking. Dominated by large green eyes, her geneering-enhanced face drew its classic beauty from every one of Old Earth's major gene pools. The mix of Asian, Chinese, African, and European bloodlines had produced a result that was all of them and none of them at the same time. Michael forgot everything as he stared at a face the color of dark honey, his whole being falling helplessly into eyes framed from above by fine black hair cut unfashionably short at the sides and set wide over sharply defined pink-dusted cheekbones.

No two ways about it; Anna Cheung was some work of art.

Michael commed his neuronics to stop the holopix. If he watched any longer, he would feel even worse than he already did. With a heartfelt prayer that things would work out for the two of them, he turned over, determined this time to get to sleep.

Friday, July 2, 2399, UD
FWSS Ishaq, *berthed on SBS-44,*
in orbit around Jascaria

The *Ishaq*'s conference room was packed. A murmur of conversation washed over every officer not on watch while they waited for the captain to arrive.

Michael, Aaron Stone, and the rest of *Ishaq*'s junior officers were seated where all prudent junior officers sat: right at the back of the conference room, well to one side and out of the line of sight of prowling senior officers, of which *Ishaq*, being a capital ship, had a depressingly large number.

Everyone was stumped. Nobody knew why the meeting had been called. Something was up, that much was clear, but Captain Constanza was not acting normally. It was no secret that Constanza did not like face-to-face meetings; in particular, she did not like groups as large as the one that waited for her now. She much preferred to use her neuronics for virtual conferences. Why Constanza was breaking the habit of a lifetime had been the subject of an energetic debate conducted in carefully hushed tones.

Thus far, the most popular theory was that Constanza's time as *Ishaq*'s captain was finished and that Morrissen would take over.

Michael—and many more in the conference room that day, he suspected—wanted this to be the reason so badly that it hurt, if only for *Ishaq*'s sake. Sadly, he was not convinced that Constanza had convened this meeting to announce her own demise. Why would she endure such public humiliation?

There had to be another reason. From the little he knew—mostly secondhand from his father—Fleet was more than willing to chop nonperforming captains if it had to, but it liked to do so quietly. Announcing a change of command at a three-ring circus, which was what they had here, was not Fleet's way. So what the hell could it be?

Michael had a leaden feeling in his stomach. He thought he knew even if his peers had howled down his theory. Please, God, he thought, not a program change; anything but a program change. He and Anna had booked a weekend away, and more than anything else, he wanted that weekend. He would give anything to get away from *Ishaq* for a few days. That was how badly he wanted to see Anna again.

"Attention! Captain on deck." The executive officer's crisp tones snapped Michael and all the others to their feet.

Captain Constanza strode into the conference room and went straight to the lectern. She ignored Morrissen.

"Sit down, everyone." Constanza paused for a moment, looking around at the mass of *Ishaq*'s officers arrayed in front of her. Michael could not help himself. He shrank down into his seat.

"I'll make this as short as I can." Constanza paused again.

"Doesn't look too comfortable," Michael whispered to Stone, who nodded.

"The reason for this briefing is to let you all know that we have been retasked by Fleet in response to new intelligence . . ."

A barely audible sigh swept through the room. No spacer liked program changes.

". . . suggesting that mership traffic on the trade routes between the Old Earth Alliance and the Federated Worlds is to be the target of significant pirate activity over the next few months. Our task will be to provide enhanced security for all ships using those routes. We will be part of Task Group 225.2 under the tactical control of Rear Admiral Chavez in *Recourse*. However, in accordance with antipiracy standard operating procedures, the *Ishaq* will operate independently. The program change is effective on completion of our formal visit to Kelly's Deep. How long these patrols will last is anyone's guess. Fleet tells me they are open-ended at this stage, but they have assured me that *Ishaq*'s docking for scheduled maintenance next June still stands. Before I hand over for the intelligence briefing, are there any questions?"

Constanza was met by a stunned silence. The personal plans of *Ishaq*'s entire crew lay in ruins, and the officers present would have to clean up the mess.

"No? Okay. Commander Nandutu?"

"Thank you, sir. Now . . ."

Michael tuned out. He would look at the detailed intelligence summary in his own time. One thing was for sure: He would not be asking any questions of Constanza, Nandutu, or anyone else. He cursed softly under his breath. His long-planned and much-anticipated weekend with Anna had been flushed down the crapper. Damn, damn, damn, he thought despairingly.

Finally Nandutu finished and sat down. Michael had taken in not a single word. Constanza came to the lectern again.

"That's all I want to cover right now. The operations planning group will have the preliminary operations order out by Monday . . ."

Bang goes their weekend, Michael thought.

". . . so I think that does it. Before we close, are there any questions?"

"Yes, sir."

Michael peered around the officer in front of him to see who the brave soul was. "Foolhardy idiot" might be a better description. According to his neuronics, it was some lieutenant commander from navigation. Jenkins was his name. Michael had not met him yet.

"Go on," Constanza muttered. Her body language was unmistakable. She was not interested in questions.

"Thank you, sir. As a member of the ops planning group, I had a chance to study the intelligence summary before the meeting, and I must say that while it is long on the blood-stained history of these pirates, it is short on the tactical detail we need to put together an effective operation: their order of battle, ship types, weapons systems, likely tactics, logistics arrangements, that sort of thing. Now—"

Constanza was not having any of it.

"Thank you for your insight," she spit venomously. Jenkins blanched and quickly sat down. "I think you'll find we have all we need to deal with what are another bunch of undisciplined, murdering crooks. If these pirates really are the Karlisle Alliance as Fleet intelligence is telling us, we whipped them back in '92, so I don't think we'll have any problem doing the same thing again. In fact, I look forward to meeting them. A bunch of pirates should give us some useful live firing practice." Constanza looked pleased at the thought.

Michael leaned over to Stone. "She should be careful what she asks for," he whispered.

Stone nodded. "I know, I know. She might get it."

Michael smiled. By now, Stone knew it was one of his favorite sayings, knew it well enough to finish it for him.

Constanza did not wait for more questions. "That will be all for now," she declared, and left the room. Behind her, the meeting broke up in a welter of small talk.

Michael sighed, a long and heartfelt sigh of frustration. Stone patted him on the shoulder. "Michael! You are one unlucky boy. Anna is going to rip your balls off." Stone looked positively cheerful at the prospect.

Michael nodded. "She surely will. If she gets close enough, that is, which I doubt she ever will. Christ, what a life we lead. I'd better go and get a vidmail off to her."

Stone shook his head. "No. Don't do that. Wait for the revised program to come out. You never know your luck. We might get a few days off somewhere, and maybe the relationship fairy will arrange for *Damishqui* to be alongside at the same time."

"Or maybe the relationship fairy will keep you apart," an unfamiliar voice taunted. "A true test of the bonds of luuuuuve." Everyone found this highly amusing; Michael's love life—or lack of it—was turning into an enjoyably soft target.

"You are all bastards," Michael responded without rancor. "Heartless, scum-sucking bastards."

"What crap you all talk." Stone shook his head in despair. "Michael! I'm sure it'll turn out okay. Stop feeling sorry for yourself. Check the ship's program, then write the vidmail.

Oh, and in case you've forgotten, before we go chasing pirates, we have a long weekend to look forward to. Kelly's Deep, here we come!"

Michael had to laugh at Stone's infectious enthusiasm. Stone was right to be fired up, and he was not alone. In fact, everyone was practically drooling at the thought of *Ishaq*'s long-planned formal visit to Kelly's Deep, and for good reason.

When it came to foreign ports, Kelly's Deep would rate in the top five in all of humanspace. The planet was a great place to spend a long weekend. Not quite up to the standard of Jackson's or Scobie's, but damn good nonetheless. Great scenery, great beaches, cheap booze, some of the best food in the cosmos and—not that he would be interested, of course—some of the friendliest people known to humankind.

Michael slid out of his seat. Everyone senior to him finally had left, so the chance of being ambushed by a senior officer on the lookout for some poor sucker to do some shitty little job or other was now minimal. He had things to do. True to form, Stone's advice had been good advice, and he intended to take it.

"I'm off. See you all later."

Tuesday, July 6, 2399, UD
FWSS Ishaq, *berthed on SBS-44,*
in orbit around Jascaria

"All stations, this is command. Stand by to drop in ten minutes."

Well, thank God for that, Michael thought. Finally! The wait had been a long one. His still-painful left leg did not appreciate it when he sat around doing nothing; low-impact exercise was what it liked, and lots of it. Not that he had much say in the matter. With *Ishaq* firmly berthed on SBS-44, the job of assistant sensor officer responsible for passive intercepts was a nothing assignment. And all in all, it had been a bad morning;

things had not gone well. The *Ishaq*'s scheduled departure time had come and gone; despite the crew's frantic efforts to get the ship under way, what could go wrong had gone wrong.

First there was a glitch with the forward maneuvering system. Then there was a main engine problem, quickly followed by another with one of the auxiliary fusion plants. All the while, the command holocam feed through to the sensor management center showed Captain Constanza pacing up and down the combat information center in frustration, her face blotched red with barely concealed rage. Michael tried not to smile at the obvious efforts everyone was making to avoid her mounting anger, heads well down, eyes locked firmly on holovid screens. Inevitably, not everyone succeeded, and the unlucky ones earned an earful of abuse and threats, with Commander Morrissen as ever bearing the brunt of her spiteful anger.

The growing sense of relief was almost palpable as the minutes ticked away without any more setbacks. Finally the moment came. The time-honored phrase "All stations, this is command. *Ishaq* is go for launch. May God watch over us this day" was broadcast throughout the ship. With a faint tremor, hydraulic locking arms pushed the massive heavy cruiser away from the space battle station. *Ishaq* was at last on its way to its designated departure pipe en route to Kelly's Deep.

He turned his attention back to the data feeds from *Ishaq*'s passive sensors, looking for anything his operators and the sensor AIs might have missed. He was so absorbed in the feeds that he jumped when Constanza stood the crew down from departure stations as *Ishaq* settled down for the long low-g haul out-system. Thankful that *Ishaq* was on its way, Michael began to relax a little as he handed over the duty to his relief and slipped out of the sensor management center.

Michael put Constanza out of his mind as he threaded his way through the training office's maze of workstations before settling himself into his tiny cubicle. He sighed. Fellsworth had given him a mound of things to do, all of them undemanding and none of them even remotely interesting. He sighed again as he commed his neuronics to bring up the first job on the list, an analysis of the sims used to train *Ishaq*'s junior spacers in basic sensor drills. Constanza was not happy about the results the trainers were getting, and Fellsworth wanted him to make sure the problem did not lie with the simulations her department produced.

He did not get far.

"Michael! Job for you."

It was Fellsworth.

"Okay, sir."

"You know *Ishaq*'s annual operational readiness evaluation is scheduled for late January?"

"Yes, sir. I do." How could he forget? *Ishaq*'s ORE was perhaps the single most important event in the ship's year. Substandard OREs had destroyed more than a few Fleet careers; he could only hope that Constanza's was one of them.

"Right. I want you to produce one of the command exercises we need to get ready. I'll comm you the specs so I won't have to waste any time explaining precisely what I want. It'll all be there. I want an initial outline of what you plan to do by . . . um, let me see, yes. Friday, 16:00. Nothing too detailed. Just an outline of what you think the COMEX should look like from the Hammer point of view. Geopolitical script, rough concept of operations, order of battle, time line, that sort of thing. You know the drill. Okay?"

Michael nodded. "Yes, sir! First cut of the COMEX by 16:00 Friday."

"Good. Now, it's a big job, so I've detailed Chief Petty Officer Ichiro and Petty Officer Bettany to help. Make the most of them. They are very good people."

Fleet Admiral Jorge left the fast courier ship and brushed past the small gaggle of officers who made up the formal welcoming party. A casual salute was his only acknowledgment.

Professor Wendt was waiting for him by the door of the conference room.

"Professor," Jorge said curtly. "Ready?"

"Yes, sir," Wendt replied, ushering Jorge into a cramped room that was brilliantly lit and sparsely furnished. Jorge ignored the rest of Wendt's team, a mixed bunch of men in white lab coats, their faces a mix of fear, tension, and exhaustion. Professor Wendt and what he had to say were the only things that mattered to him. He took his seat. "Let's go."

"Right, sir. The purpose of this meeting is—"

"Professor! I know why I'm here, so get to the point," he snarled.

Wendt gulped. "Yes, sir." He took a deep breath before continuing. "As you know, the only thing delaying operational deployment of the Mark-48G warhead was the unacceptably high failure rate of its antimatter container."

Jorge's eyes narrowed. He knew that. Why, he wondered, did people like Wendt find it so hard to cut to the chase?

"Now," Wendt continued, "we know we cannot make a fail-safe antimatter warhead. So our design objective has been to develop a warhead with an acceptably low risk of accidental detonation, even though that risk can never come even close to zero."

Jorge nodded. There was no avoiding it: Antimatter warheads were much more dangerous than the fusion and chemex warheads fitted to the missiles now in frontline service with Hammer warships. He waved for Wendt to continue.

Wendt reached into a plasfiber box on the table in front of him. "And here it is." He pulled out a metallic object the size of a shoe box. Its mirror-finished metallic surface was deeply scarred, and at some point it had been subjected to intense heat; one end was badly discolored by blue-black streaks.

"This is the antimatter container from a Mark-48G warhead," Wendt said, unable to keep the pride out of his voice. "This is a live operational container. It's fully charged with antihydrogen, there's no external power, and it's still maintaining full containment. We recovered this one from a missile we test-fired last night, and as you can see, it has survived not only launch but impact with the target."

"Holy Mother of Kraa, Professor," Jorge said finally. "Well done. All of you. By Kraa! Well done!" Then Jorge was on his feet, his face split side to side by a huge grin, his arm across the table to shake the hands of Wendt and his team. "By Kraa! This is great news, Professor." His voice hardened. "This is for real? This is the real thing?"

"Yes, it is," Wendt said triumphantly. "Now, if you would like to look at the holo—"

Jorge's hand stopped Wendt in his tracks. "One second. Give it to me."

Wendt pushed the lump of metal across the table. Jorge picked it up. It was surprisingly heavy. He turned it over in his hands, marveling at the ingenuity of Wendt and his engineers, shocked that something so small could contain so much destructive energy. He shook his head in wonder. Then, without any warning, his arm went back, and he hurled the object into the rock wall behind Wendt, the heavy metal shape barely missing the man's head. As the object crashed to the floor, Wendt and every member of his team flinched instinctively away from the threat, their faces white with shock.

"Kraa!" one of them hissed softly. Wendt just stared in horror at Jorge as he struggled to recover his equilibrium.

Jorge laughed out loud at the sight of grown men cringing in front of him. He nodded slowly as he sat down. "You know what, Professor? I think I believe you. I think it really is a live container from a 48G."

"It is, sir. Trust me, it is."

When the fast courier unberthed, Jorge allowed himself the luxury of a smile. It had been a good day, one of the best for a long time.

But Wendt's success told only part of the story. Ironically, the Feds—Kraa damn them—had played their part, and an important part, too. Jorge had no illusions about the Feds. Fed warships would thrash Hammer warships in most head-to-head fights. Their ships were too good, their sensors were too good, their weapon systems were too good, their people were too good, and they were not afraid to use their Kraa-damned AIs to devastating effect. Any way he looked at it—it pained him to have to admit the fact—the Feds were better than good. When it came to space warfare, they were the best in humanspace, and by a very respectable margin.

Sadly for the Feds, there was a catch. Yes, the Feds were good and they knew it, but over time, that knowledge was highly but insidiously corrosive. After a while, success sapped the will to do better. Success blunted the urge to try harder. Success stifled innovation. Success encouraged politicians and politicking. Success made hard decisions easy to avoid, and why not? After all, with the best space fleet in human-space, there was always time to stab your peers in the back before fixing things later. Wasn't there?

So, for a raft of reasons, antimatter had never been a high priority for the Feds, and Jorge had seen the intelligence reports to prove it. Even better, the Feds had no idea how successful the Hammer's work on antimatter had been. That work was buried so deep that only a tiny handful of people outside the project knew of its existence; many of them had no idea how close the project was to success. Jorge had seen the internal security reports to prove that, too. He was pleased to know the Feds had not the faintest suspicion that tucked away on an obscure planet-sized asteroid in deep-space many light-years distant from the settled Hammer

Worlds, antimatter labs and a production plant were working flat out to make the Fed's much-vaunted military technology obsolete.

Well, Jorge thought, trying not to feel too smug, those Kraa-damned Feds were about to find out what a terrible mistake that had been.

Operation Cavalcade was on.

Monday, July 19, 2399, UD
FWSS Ishaq, *Vijati Reef*

"Sensors, gravitronics."

"Sensors," the duty sensor officer replied. She sounded bored.

"Sir, we have a positive gravitronics intercept. Estimated drop bearing Red 5 Up 2. Designated track 775101. One vessel. Grav wave pattern suggests pinchspace transition imminent. Vector is nominal for Earth-FedWorld transit. Traffic schedule indicates the vessel is the Fed cargo ship *Treaty of Paris* en route Old Earth to Terranova, mixed cargo and passengers."

"Confidence?"

"It's 99.99 percent, sir."

"Helfort?" the duty sensor officer asked, looking to Michael for confirmation.

"Confirmed, sir." Michael was confident. The *Treaty of Paris* was on schedule to the minute.

Satisfied, the duty sensor officer nodded. "Roger. Red 5 Up 2. Watch track 775101."

"Aye, aye, sir. Watch 775101."

The duty sensor officer looked as bored as she sounded. "Well," Michael grumbled under his breath, "fair enough—maybe." It was some ungodly hour in the early morning, the middle watch had dragged interminably, and the intercept would be the latest in an unbroken and utterly predictable succession of merchant ships. One by one, they had dropped out of pinchspace in a brief flash of ultraviolet to cross Vijati Reef, a rip in space-time hundreds of light-years wide and high but less than 800,000 kilometers deep, the gravitational anomaly creating a barrier in pinchspace no ship could ever cross.

Michael pushed his holovid range scale out to a billion kilometers, well past Vijati Reef. The sight of the two hundred or so merchant ships making the crossing was breathtaking. Michael failed to understand how anyone could be bored with such a spectacle. Well, okay, he conceded. It might be a slow-moving show, but it still had a fascination, even a magic about it. The ships' positions were a mass of green diamonds painted onto black emptiness, their vectors probing out into interstellar space. Well beyond them, thrown out in a protective shell, were ranged a small array of tiny surveillance satellites, their simple optronics suites keeping an eye on the proceedings. Michael patched his neuronics into the master surveillance AI. All nominal, he noted. He turned back to the ships.

On they came, one after another. Ships of all sizes—always spherical to maximize internal volume—from a hundred different planets of registration. They carried every material good known to humankind, along with thousands of people shuttling endlessly between the planets of humanspace.

Of all the grav anomalies that infested humanspace, the Vijati was the most active, with tens of thousands of ships dropping out of pinchspace each year to make the crossing. It was nothing short of a miracle that accidents around the Vijati were so rare. Some merchant ship captains seemed to regard accurate navigation as an optional extra, something to do when more important problems—like scratching their asses—had been taken care of.

"Sensors, gravitronics."

"Sensors."

"Track 775101 is about to drop. Stand by . . . there she is. Drop confirmed nominal for Earth-FedWorld transit."

Michael's holovid brightened for a second with the ultraviolet flare of a starship dropping into normalspace. Within seconds, the sensor management center's AI had integrated the information flooding in from *Ishaq*'s active and passive sensors to confirm that the latest arrival was indeed the *Treaty of Paris*. Michael had nothing more to do than listen in as the duty sensor officer made the ritual report confirming the drop to *Ishaq*'s combat information center.

Michael stretched. In fifteen minutes, he could hand over the watch. That done, he would head straight for his bunk. What with the COMEX project given to him by Fellsworth and a twenty-four-hour duty as second officer of the day starting at 08:00, not to mention all the other crap junior officers in large capital ships were burdened with, sleep had been in short supply lately. He intended to make the most of the three hours he would get.

Well, time to get his handover brief sorted out.

Tuesday, July 20, 2399, UD
Hammer Warship Obsidian, *interstellar space*

From the combat information center of the deepspace light patrol ship *Obsidian,* Commodore Monroe watched the proceedings, his eyes fixed on the holovid tracking his six new q-ships. He would be damn glad when they got back to Kasprowitz. Hanging around in deepspace had never been his idea of a good time. Worse, the *Obsidian*'s ability to defend her new charges was limited. Yes, their new rail-gun systems worked, but he did not have the people to operate them. Until he did, his new acquisitions were big fat sitting ducks.

The latest additions to the Hammer order of battle, their spherical bulk marking them out as merships, hung in interstellar space 70 light-years out from and due galactic south of Damnation's Gate. With all navigation lights off, their anonymous dirt-gray hulls were barely visible as black cutouts etched from millions of stars scattered in all directions with

dazzling extravagance. The only activity was the steady shuttling to and fro of *Obsidian*'s four space attack vehicles and
two landers. Monroe's fingers tapped out his impatience;
transferring the q-ships' Hammer crews was going well, but
he could not help himself. He just wanted to be done and on
his way.

Monroe pushed away a momentary pang of anxiety. He had
to admit that the chances of running into anyone else were
tiny. The small sphere of deepspace they occupied was a long
way from anything even remotely interesting to the rest of
humankind. That, of course, was why it had been picked in the
first place, and operational security had been tight.

So far, so good.

"Commodore, sir."

It was his chief of staff. "Yes, Captain?"

"Just to let you know, sir. We're ahead of schedule on the
crew transfers, and I have confirmation from the engineers
that all ships are online. We'll be ready for vector realign-
ment to set up for the jump back to Kasprowitz Base at
06:15."

"Good! The sooner we're out of this Kraa-damned place,
the better. Send to all ships. From commodore, stand by to
execute ops plan Kilo Yankee Five at time 06:15."

"Roger, sir. Stand by to execute ops plan Kilo Yankee Five
at time 06:15."

Monroe sat back as his small staff got things moving.
Things were going well, though he wondered how long that
would last. He hoped Fleet Admiral Jorge and his political
masters knew what they were getting the Hammer into. The
Feds were going to be awfully, awfully pissed when his ships
started to rip the guts out of their interstellar trade routes.

The forenoon watch had been pretty much the same as all the other watches Michael had stood, though he had been promoted. Deemed competent, he now ran the entire sensor management center when—somewhat to Michael's surprise given that they were supposedly out hunting pirates—*Ishaq* was at cruising stations, two full levels of readiness below general quarters. He would have been more than happy with the promotion had it not been for the fact that it put him firmly in the firing line when Constanza came looking for someone to kick. Still, he consoled himself, at least he did not have to defer to officers who did little to conceal their lack of interest in the job at hand.

By Michael's rough calculations, he had watched well over four hundred merchant ships go through the routine of dropping out of pinchspace. The endless procession of spherical ships transiting this or that reef before jumping back into pinchspace had been interrupted only by the other ships of Task Group 225.2 as they and the *Ishaq* patrolled the FedWorld–Old Earth trade route. Michael sighed. Antipiracy patrols in response to a threat as vague as the one supposedly posed by the Karlisle Alliance—pirates nobody thought actually existed—were boring, and it was becoming a real struggle to stay keen and enthusiastic.

Things on board *Ishaq* were not getting any better. On any other ship, Michael's latest stint as second officer of the day would have been just a matter of trailing around behind the officer of the day. In theory, it gave him the chance to observe firsthand how more experienced officers skillfully defused the minor crises that beset ships as large as the *Ishaq*.

That was the theory, anyway. To be fair, most of the day had been routine enough to allow Michael to put in some serious time on his COMEX project. That had all changed in a hurry. Michael, tired of work, had been passing the last dregs of the evening away in the wardroom with Aaron Stone when an urgent comm from the officer of the day had dispatched him to take charge of the ship's internal security patrol. A vicious brawl had broken out on one of the junior spacers' mess decks, and it had to be stopped before half the ship joined in.

Order had been restored eventually, but it had been one hell of a job, with Michael twice calling for reinforcements. When the dust settled, eight spacers were in the ship's sick bay, another ten had been dragged to the cells struggling like wildcats, and thirty were subject to further investigation. It took the internal security patrol well over two hours to get to that happy state of affairs, another hour to clean up the damage, and Michael another three hours to debrief the patrol, review *Ishaq*'s internal security holocam footage, and write up the official report for the executive officer. All in all, it had been a horror night. Michael had the bags under his eyes and the wandering concentration to prove it.

"Sensors, gravitronics."

"Sensors." Michael started. Had he been asleep on watch? Christ, he hoped not.

"Don't like the look of this one, sir. Here. It's only just painting on gravitronics and the AI's making a mess of it, but it looks to me like inbound on Green 10 Down 2."

"Not on the traffic schedule, I take it."

"No, sir."

"Okay. Call it in."

Michael's heart began to pound as the gravitronics operator formally reported the suspect contact. No ship should be joining the traffic stream from that angle. That would put it on the wrong side of the traffic lane running galactic north toward the Federated Worlds. Depending on the new arrival's vector, it could mean chaos as fully loaded merchant ships, probably the most sluggish things in deepspace, made desperate attempts to avoid a collision. "Unbelievable," Michael muttered. Billions of cubic light-years of space to work in, yet here was some clown looking to get up close and personal. The son of a bitch should be shot.

The sensor management center was no longer the relaxed place it had been. In seconds, Michael had every available sensor on the task of working out what was about to drop and, much more important, what its vector was. If the ships transiting Karovic Reef were to have any chance of avoiding a rogue crosser, they needed good vector data, and fast.

The tension rose and, as quickly, ebbed away. To Michael's relief, the bearing of the gravitronics intercept started to move across *Ishaq*'s bows, dropping as it did so. It was a rogue for sure, no doubt about it. The ship had no flight plan logged into the traffic control AIs and was about to make an illegal entry into restricted space. Thankfully, it was not a dangerous rogue. All Michael could hope for was that eventually the ship would fall into the hands of the International Admiralty Court, though there was not much chance of that. According to the sensor AI's best guess, the ship was probably in transit from the Rogue Worlds across humanspace to one of the Marakoff Consortium Planets. Because neither system paid much—if any—regard to the institutions of international space justice, he did not think the ship would ever be caught.

"Sensors, gravitronics. Track 781553 is dropping. Estimate drop datum at Green 5 Down 15, range 55,000 kilometers."

Ouch, Michael thought, 55,000 kilometers was safe but still way, way too close. "Sensors, roger."

Track 781553 dropped in a short-lived blaze of ultraviolet light. Michael went through the routine of reporting the new arrival's identity, but it was a short report. Apart from confirming the ship's vector and noting that the starship was a small, spherical high-speed courier, there was little more the sensor team could add.

The ship carried registration marks recorded in no database held by *Ishaq*—probably false in any case, Michael thought—squawked the same unknown identity, transmitted nothing else on any frequency, and refused to acknowledge *Ishaq*'s strident requests to stop and be boarded.

For a moment, Michael wondered if Constanza would launch one of *Ishaq*'s space assault vehicles to get close enough to have a better look. When he worked out the vector needed to intercept, he realized that although it could be done, it would be pretty marginal. In the end, the *Ishaq*'s log recorded the rogue crosser as yet another of space's little mysteries.

The watch ground its predictable way to an end. Michael handed over to his relief; after a quiet word of thanks to the gravitronics operator, he was on his way to grab a quick lunch.

He had a lot to do, and the previous night's fracas had added to the load.

The debate got quite heated. It was surprising, Michael thought, that two people who normally were so controlled could get so worked up, and Ichiro and Bettany were pretty worked up. Each was clinging like a limpet to the rock of a well dug-in position. Michael waited until logic started to give way to emotion before interrupting.

"Okay, guys. Enough. Can I have a go?"

"Be my guest, sir," Ichiro replied with a wave of her hand. "I'm not getting anywhere with Petty Officer Bonehead here. Maybe you'll have more luck."

Michael laughed. He knew as well as Bettany did that there was no malice in Ichiro's invective. "Yes, thanks for that, Chief." He paused to gather his thoughts. How the debate was resolved would decide the Hammer strategy Michael and his team were putting in place for the COMEX. With a mountain of small details to be worked out before uploading the exercise parameters into the AI running the COMEX, time was getting short.

"If it were left to the Hammer's admirals, I would agree with you. They hate nukes because in the end war is about territory, productive territory. Keeping theirs, taking ours. So what's the good of an irradiated planet? It's just another lump of useless, slag-encrusted dirt. God knows we have trillions of those to choose from, whereas there are precious few terra-standard planets. Left to the admirals, there'd be no nukes, but it's not up to the Hammer's admirals, not this time. We've been through all the intelligence summaries analyzing what's changed with Polk's takeover. Merrick was a hard man, no doubt about it. Until he went solo with that damn stupid *Mumtaz* hijacking, he would at least listen to his military staff. Polk won't. He's put the best part of the Hammer's brass into DocSec lime pits, so who in their right mind is going to stand up to him? I'll tell you. Nobody! It's too dangerous."

"So it's Polk's call," Ichiro said. "Is that what you're saying?"

"Exactly! In the end, Polk will tell the military what to do."

Ichiro sat back, hands behind her head. She took a while to think it through. Patiently, Michael and Bettany waited until Ichiro, mind apparently made up, came back to the table. She nodded her agreement. "Okay, I agree. Dirtside nukes it is. Of course, there'll be hell to pay, sir." Ichiro looked troubled. "You know that?"

Michael nodded. "Yeah, I do."

Thursday, August 26, 2399, UD
FWSS Ishaq, *pinchspace*

Ishaq's flag combat data center was hushed as the opening moves of the COMEX played themselves out on huge holovids arrayed all around Captain Constanza and her command team. From the back of the compartment, Fellsworth and the rest of her directing staff watched the proceedings, a noticeably nervous Michael among them.

Fellsworth leaned over to him. "For Christ's sake, Michael, relax," she whispered. "It's an exercise."

"Wish it was only an exercise, sir," he whispered back. He was more nervous than he'd expected. Putting together a COMEX was a serious intellectual challenge, and he did not want the work he and his team had done to be found wanting. More than that, he wanted Constanza to do well. He wanted her to make an obvious and public success of the COMEX. Sadly, he had a sinking feeling that he was going to be very, very disappointed.

Without being too obvious about it, Fellsworth had worked hard to position things for Constanza. She had made damn sure that the flood of background information setting up the COMEX's political and military context would give Constanza every opportunity to see that this Hammer attack would not—could not—be like every other attack. The clues had been there—lots of them—but Constanza had refused to take them despite the best efforts of the rest of her command team to make her do that. Michael shook his head in frustration. To a spacer, Constanza's team had drawn the right conclusions from the intelligence provided, but Constanza had not.

In the end, she had rejected the possibility that nukes might be used dirtside out of hand. It was "something the Hammers would never do," she had declared forcefully. So that had been that. From that point on, her forces were always positioned to deal with a nonnuclear planetary attack. The possibility that she might be wrong had no place in her thinking. Sadly, that meant that there was little in the way of fallback planning. Worst of all, to allow her ships to engage the attackers right down to the edge of Terranova's atmosphere, the bulk of her long-range Merlin missiles, the backbone of any FedWorld space fleet, would not be nuclear-armed.

In the absence of any nuclear threat, Constanza had adopted what space warfare strategists called the shell. She withdrew the bulk of her forces to be close to Terranova in planetary nearspace, concentrating her ships where they could best support one another. Out deep along the most likely attack vectors were smaller groups of ships made up of heavy escorts with a scattering of light escorts to fill in the numbers. Constanza was hoping to get lucky. If she did, the escorts would get close enough to ambush the Hammers as they dropped out of pinchspace. Luck was not all she was relying on, though. Constanza would use a far-flung network of remote sensors to give her enough warning to allow her to move her ships within the shell around Terranova to meet the oncoming attacks head on. All standard stuff and fine so long as one was facing a standard attack.

Oh, well, Michael thought resignedly, Fellsworth and the

warfare training department had done their best. Now it was up to Constanza.

All of a sudden, things began to happen, and fast.

"Command, sensors."

"Command."

"Multiple positive gravitronics intercepts, Sector 2. Grav wave pattern suggests pinchspace transition imminent. Vector appears nominal for grazing run past Terranova."

"Command, roger."

Michael watched, fascinated. Constanza and her team began the intricate game of three-dimensional chess that was space warfare. She would assume this first attack was not the major attack. Most likely, the ships would drop and unload every piece of ordnance they could, their fire control solutions based on targeting data acquired from surveillance drones loitering out in farspace. Then, before the forces converging on them got close enough to pose a problem, the attackers would jump back into pinchspace. Standard operating procedure for a Hammer attack and intended to sound out the opposition, so no surprises there. Chief Ichiro had pointed out that one of the great weaknesses of the Hammer was its military commanders' fondness for standard operating procedures, an assumption that Constanza had been more than happy to accept without challenge.

"Command, sensors. Multiple ship drops Sector 2, range 250,000 kilometers. Thirty-five ships. Stand by identification."

Within seconds, sensor AIs on hundreds of FedWorld ships began turning terabytes of raw data vacuumed out of space by their active and passive sensors into useful tactical data. It was a quick process; the result was an ugly mass of bright red vectors painted on the flag combat data center holovids. The Hammer attack quickly took shape; feverishly, Constanza and her team worked to make sure *Ishaq*'s fleet battle management AI had the situation under control. Orders poured out across laser tightbeam tactical networks to move ships into position, coordinate missile and rail-gun salvos, integrate radar and laser jamming, and manage the flood of decoys on their way to baffle and confuse the incoming Hammers.

"Command, sensors. Multiple positive gravitronics intercepts, Sector 3. Grav wave pattern suggests pinchspace transition imminent. Vector is nominal for grazing run past Terranova."

Michael could almost see Constanza relax.

Hammer standard operating procedures would have this as the main attack, though one of their more creative commanders might have thrown in a few more diversionary attacks to keep the opposition under pressure and off balance. So far, Constanza had not gone too far wrong. For once, her usual urge to override her subordinate commanders seemed well under control, and, with the usual chivvying all AIs needed to get it right, the fleet battle management AI had the right ships going to the right places to deal with the two attacks now driving hard toward Terranova.

"Command, sensors. Multiple ship drops Sector 3, range 260,000 kilometers. Seventy-five ships. Stand by identification."

By then, Constanza's body language was easy to read. "This has to be it," she announced confidently to one of her team as the holovids arrayed around the combat information center blossomed with a new set of red vectors. "This is the primary attack."

Ship sensors were tracking upward of a hundred Hammer ships as they ran planetward, wave after wave of missiles and decoys behind walls of rail-gun slugs driving on ahead. Their ceramsteel armor was beginning to boil off as FedWorld antistarship lasers flayed their hulls.

In response, *Ishaq*'s external holocams showed the hundreds of FedWorld Merlin long-range heavy missiles on their way to meet the attackers, the mass of searingly white-bright shafts of fire driving the Merlins onward, punctured by yellow-red blooms of ionized gas as Hammer lasers and area defense missiles began to rip missiles out of space. Closer in, Hammer missiles began to die, too, as Fed missiles started to chop the Hammer attack to pieces.

Slowly the tide began to swing in favor of the Feds. Missiles and rail-gun salvos clawed their way through the storm of defensive fire put up by the Hammer ships. The Hammer's close-in defenses—short-range missiles, antimissile lasers, and chain guns—were being overwhelmed by a combination of speed and coordination overlaid by carefully crafted jamming and spoofing to blind and confuse them.

Then the Hammers began to lose ships. The first to go was a Jackson class light cruiser. A single Merlin missile tore a gaping hole in the ship's ceramsteel armor left damaged by an earlier rail-gun salvo, the warhead's plasma jet striking deep to reach a fusion power generator. Milliseconds later, the generator lost containment. Half a second after that, the hull gave way under the enormous pressure and the aft end of the ship blew wide open, spewing ice-crystal clouds out into the vacuum of space. The ship was dying now. As it died, it began to spit lifepods in all directions.

More Hammer ships began to die as the Fed response ground the Hammer attack into ionized gas, the counterattack relentless. The space around the Hammers became a mass of shattered ships surrounded by lifepods, like so many fireflies with their double-pulsed orange strobes. Constanza could not contain herself. Getting out of her chair, she overrode the fleet battle management AI. "Too cautious," she muttered, "too damn cautious. Time to go in hard for the kill."

Without a moment's hesitation, without any attempt to consult her team or the battle management AI, she threw her reserves in the attack and ordered the last of her heavy units to engage. Her fist punched the air. Every shred of body language betrayed her conviction that this was the time to destroy the Hammer attack.

Michael leaned across to Fellsworth. "Even though she doesn't know what we know, surely that's a mistake, sir? She's committed all the forces she needed to deal with the Hammer attack. There's no need to assign more. Now she's got very little in reserve."

Fellsworth nodded, her face impassive.

With her remaining heavy cruisers accelerating hard toward the incoming Hammers, the sensor management center crashed Constanza's party.

"Command, sensors. Multiple positive gravitronics intercepts, Sector 6. Grav wave pattern suggests pinchspace transition imminent. Vector is nominal for grazing run past Terranova."

Constanza stiffened. "Sensors. Confirm Sector 6."

"Confirmed. Sector 6."

Constanza shifted to a private circuit. Michael would have to access the voicecomm datalogs after the COMEX to see what was said, but it was clear from the command team's body language that nobody could work out what the new attack meant. Coming from below Terranova's orbital plane, it was developing at right angles to the attacks that were in progress. Confusingly, whatever this attack was, it was not consistent with normal Hammer operating procedures.

Constanza had a big problem. She had committed her reserves to meet an attack that already had been well contained. Now those forces were heavily engaged, pinned down by the incoming Hammer ships, and unable to disengage without presenting their relatively thin stern and flank armor to Hammer missile, rail-gun, and laser attack. Constanza did what she could. She threw the last of her ships, none of them heavier than a light escort, into the breach, with the fleet battle management AI pumping out the orders to position her limited assets to meet the new attack. Time to start praying, Michael thought.

"Command, sensors. Multiple ship drops Sector 6, range 160,000 kilometers. Forty-five ships. Stand by identification."

Constanza's confusion visibly deepened. Michael sympathized. Forty-five ships was too small a number for a primary attack. If this was not the primary attack, what was the point of another diversion? The main attack was well developed already. More confusing still was the fact that by dropping into Terranova's gravity well only 200,000 kilometers out, those ships soon would be inside the 150,000-kilometer threshold for a jump back into pinchspace. Unless they jumped inside twenty minutes or so, they would be in Terranova nearspace for at least two hours, more than enough time for them to be mopped up.

None of it made any sense to *Ishaq*'s command team, and Michael watched with a heavy heart as they began to thrash around looking for answers.

Then the game changed. The Hammer went nuclear.

Constanza's face turned ash-gray as she watched her defense of Terranova fall apart. Earlier, her task force AI had highlighted the fact that a surprisingly large number of the Hammer's Eaglehawk missiles seemed to be going nowhere in particular. A quick discussion among the command team had put it down to poor Hammer technology. One even had gone so far as to say that the useless pricks could not hit a barn door at five paces. Constanza had made her decision. Missiles without targets were missiles without a job to do, so they were to be ignored. And they were; the missiles were left untouched to continue their drive toward Terranova.

It soon became clear that the Hammer's missiles were doing exactly what was asked of them. One by one in blindingly quick succession, the multimegaton fusion warheads fitted to the missiles detonated. In seconds, an immense wall of gamma radiation was expanding toward Terranova. *Ishaq*'s alarms screeched as sensor after sensor shut down to minimize damage from the electromagnetic pulse that washed over the Fed ships.

The combat information center went quiet as alarms were muted. "Oh shit," Constanza muttered, her voice hoarse with stress, before her training kicked in, driving her into a desperate attempt to cope with a situation that was past saving.

Moments later, it was the turn of the third and last wave of Hammer ships to fire. Their first salvo destroyed Terranova's six space battle stations. The huge mass, immensely thick armor, and multilayered missile and laser defenses of the stations were no match for an overwhelming flood of hardened fusion warheads detonating in waves until the stations had been irradiated into blackened submission. Terranova stood alone, and only ground-based antiballistic missiles and satellite-mounted lasers were standing in the way of the oncoming Hammer attack.

With Terranova's space battle stations silenced, the Hammer ships launched a second salvo, their hybrid solid fuel/pinch-space generator engines accelerating the missiles at more than 200 g. Seconds later, thousands of Eaglehawk missiles dropped onto Terranova at more than a million kph. Seconds before they were ripped apart by Terranova's upper atmosphere, fusion warheads began to explode directly over Terranova's major cities. Two minutes later a third salvo followed. Two minutes after that, a fourth. Then a fifth. Finally the sixth, seventh, and eighth salvos were on their way, but this time the missiles had been throttled right back to ensure that they could survive entry into Terranova's atmosphere. These missiles would be ground bursts targeted on every known high-value target on Terranova, starting with Foundation, its capital. A handful of missiles were kept back until the end. Their target was Terranova's oceans. The missiles plunged deep into the sea before detonating to drive tsunamis into Terranova's low-lying coasts and columns of ionized, superheated steam high into the air.

Two minutes before they would be locked into Terranova's gravity well, the Hammer ships, swatting aside the incoming missile and rail-gun attacks with contemptuous ease, jumped.

It had taken less than twenty minutes to destroy an entire planet and most of the ships tasked with its defense. Terranova no longer was habitable by humans or by any other species known to humankind. Now it was a shattered, charred, radioactive ruin of a planet. Its atmosphere was a seething, roiling mass of flame-shot cloud punctured by huge black hammerheads climbing out of the murk into nearspace as ground bursts drove millions of tons of earth and water kilometers into the air.

Terranova was finished.

Leaving the shattered wrecks of their casualties behind, surrounded by swarms of lifepods, the rest of the Hammer ships jumped out of Terranova nearspace. There was a long, long silence as every spacer in the combat information center absorbed the awful sight of Terranova writhing in agony, a planet dying a slow and terrible death. "Holy Mother,"

Michael muttered. Even though it was only a simulation, he felt sick.

The soft voice of the AI running the COMEX broke the silence with the pointless observation that the exercise was over.

Flanked on either side by *Ishaq*'s executive officer, Commander Morrissen, and the head of the warfare department, Commander Pasquale, Fellsworth stood rock solid. Her eyes were focused on the bulkhead as a ranting, nearly demented Constanza, her face red with anger, spittle-flecked lips working furiously, struggled to get her words out.

"How dare you? How dare you humiliate me like that! By God, Fellsworth, I'm going to break you for this; you can depend on it. And I know it's not only you. I know you had that arrogant, self-serving shit Helfort do the legwork. That makes it a conspiracy, Fellsworth," she screeched furiously, "a conspiracy against your legally appointed captain. I can put you away for twenty years and that little worm Helfort and the rest of your lickspittle team if I want."

"Sir—"

The executive officer's attempt to intervene was stillborn; Constanza cut him off with an angry wave of the arm. "No, Commander Morrissen. I do not want to hear from you. I wouldn't be surprised to find that you're part of this."

She turned back to Fellsworth. "Well, it won't work. I'm taking formal action against you, Fellsworth. Conspiracy. I'm charging you with conspiracy to mutiny. That'll do it. You are confined to your cabin. Morrissen, get the provost marshal in here. I want the ship to see this woman in custody. I want them to see what happens to people who conspire against me."

"Sir!" The executive officer's voice was thick with protest.

"Be quiet, Morrissen! I won't tell you again."

"No, sir, I will not be quiet," the executive officer replied firmly. "I should not have to remind you that under Fleet regulations I have a duty to speak."

"Sir!" Commander Pasquale waded into the fray. Constanza's appalling behavior—her intemperate language, her arrogant disregard for subordinates, her refusal to take counsel—went against everything she believed in. "I must tell you, sir," she protested, "that you have no choice but to hear Commander Morrissen out. Fleet regu—"

Constanza's face was a cruelly contorted mask of vicious, uncontrolled anger. "Shut the fuck up, Commander Pasquale, or I'll have you arrested as well."

Pasquale could only gape at Constanza in amazement. Captains did not swear at commanders—well, not in front of witnesses at any rate.

The executive officer put his hand on Pasquale's arm; he shook his head. This was his fight. Morrissen tried again. "Sir, I really must—"

One last thin shred of sanity forced Constanza to take control of herself. "Go on, then. If you must," she muttered bad-temperedly.

"Sir. I have to tell you you are making a very serious mistake. An officer who does her duty cannot be conspiring to mutiny. Fellsworth was doing her duty, and I will attest to that fact when asked."

"So will I, sir," Pasquale interjected.

The executive officer plowed on. He wished Pasquale would stay out of it. A first-shot commander, Pasquale was young, talented, and ambitious. She had a career ahead of her; as for him, he was beginning to be pretty damn sure he did not. "So, under the circumstances, I think—"

Constanza lost it. In seconds, she was incandescent with rage; her voice crackled with uncontrolled fury. "Think! Think? I don't care what you think, Morrissen. I don't give a damn what you think." She paused for a second, noticeably struggling to get her voice under control. "Listen to me, all of you . . . ah, wait!"

The door opened to admit Lieutenant Armstrong, *Ishaq*'s provost marshal.

"Armstrong!"

Armstrong, a thin, wiry man with the watchful eyes of a policeman, looked puzzled. Something bad was happening here, that much was obvious, but it was clear he had no idea what. "You wanted me, sir?"

Constanza waved him in. "I do. First, I want you to witness the order I am about to give."

"Yes, sir."

"Good." She turned back to look her second in command right in the eye. "Commander Morrissen! I am giving you a direct order to take Lieutenant Commander Fellsworth here into custody pending the completion of investigations into the charges I will be laying against her. She is to be confined to her cabin under close arrest until further notice. Now, Commander, is there any part of that order you did not understand?"

Morrissen shook his head; he knew when he was beaten. "No, sir. I understand," he muttered unhappily.

"Good," Constanza crowed triumphantly. "Now that that's out of the way, I am also giving you a direct order to take Junior Lieutenant Helfort into close custody. He is to be confined to his cabin under guard until further notice. Now, Commander," she declared looking right into his eyes. "Did you understand that?"

"I understood the order, sir," Morrissen replied dejectedly. This was turning into a clusterfuck of serious proportions, and there was nothing he could do to stop it.

"Pleased to hear it. So good of you to comply." Her voice dripped sarcasm. "Now get on with it. Dismissed!"

Morrissen tried one more time. Pasquale tried one more time. Their protests were to no avail as Armstrong took Fellsworth by the arm and led her out of the captain's office.

Michael was in the wardroom, deep in the middle of a subdued discussion of the morning's extraordinary events with Aaron Stone, when a quiet voice interrupted.

"Helfort. Come with me." It was the provost marshal. The man's tone was quiet but firm.

"Yes, sir. What's up?" Michael asked, climbing to his feet.

"You'll find out. Come on, let's go."

When they left the wardroom, one of *Ishaq*'s marines was waiting outside, the man falling in behind them as they made their way up two decks to the ship's regulating office. When they got there, Armstrong waved Michael into his office, telling the marine to wait outside.

"Sit!"

Armstrong looked right at Michael while he gathered his thoughts. He had been a cop for a long time. He had more experience than he cared to think about, and every bit of that experience argued that the business at hand was a gold-plated crock of shit. Sadly, for the moment at least, his hands were tied. There was a process to follow, even if that meant trampling all over two officers who by all accounts had always tried to do their duty and—in Helfort's case at least—had the scars to prove it.

"Right, then." Armstrong's voice was flat, unemotional. "I'm going to comm you a document. It's a preliminary charge sheet alleging that you and Lieutenant Commander Fellsworth entered into a conspiracy to mutiny."

Michael looked stunned. "What?" he finally stammered. "Mutiny? I don't understand."

"Just read the charge sheet, Helfort."

Minutes later, Michael looked up, his pain and confusion plain to see. "Sir," he said, shaking his head, "I've read this thing five times over, and it still makes no sense, none at all. How can developing a COMEX be construed as mutiny? This is a complete load of crap—"

Armstrong's hand went up, stopping him in his tracks. "Now's not the time to respond, so—"

"Sir!" Michael protested. "It's wrong. It's—"

"Stop right now! Goddamn it, Helfort! That's an order!" Armstrong barked. His voice softened as he continued. "Now. Listen to me. This is what's going to happen. You'll be confined to your cabin until further notice. You'll eat there, have an hour's exercise twice a day under escort, and be able to have visitors at my discretion. Maximum two at any one time. The ship's legal AI will act as the accused's friend, and let me tell you it will do a better job of it than anyone I know, so don't waste your time looking for any amateur lawyers on board. When I have the brief of evidence, I'll pass that to the AI, and it'll tell you what it thinks of the case against you." And what a no-brainer that'll be, Armstrong thought savagely.

Michael sat openmouthed, obviously not taking any of it in. Armstrong felt for him. The whole business must be like a bad dream, some dreadful black comedy, a bizarre tale of a mad captain crossing swords with a young officer too dumb not to know when to keep his head down.

"Helfort! Are you listening to me?"

"Sorry, sir."

"Hmm," Armstrong grunted. "Okay. Where was I? Oh, yes. Accused's friend, use the legal AI, brief of evidence. I think that covers it all, so that's it for now. Any questions?"

"Fellsworth, sir. Has she been charged, too?"

"She has."

"Can I see her?"

"No, not at the moment. If I decide both cases can be dealt with jointly, you will. Be patient."

"Not much choice there, then, sir," Michael muttered with a twisted half smile.

"No, I suppose not. Right, let's get you to your cabin. I've got work to do. Lance Corporal Johannsen!"

Friday, August 27, 2399, UD
HWS Quebec-One, *Xiang Reef*

Hammer Warship *Quebec-One* dropped into normal-space a safe 2 billion kilometers and 2 light-hours out from Xiang Reef. The ship's registration proclaimed her to be the independent merchant ship *Nancy's Pledge* from one of the more obscure planets of the Pascanici League. Her hull had the space-dust-worn blues and yellows of the real thing, which at that point in time was in pinchspace somewhere between two of the Far Planets and a long way from Xiang Reef.

Commodore Monroe sat oblivious to the usual postdrop

buzz of activity around him in *Quebec-One*'s combat information center. He studied the command and threat plots intently while *Quebec-One*'s sensor teams brought order methodically out of the chaotic mass of data pouring into the ship from the surveillance vehicles surrounding the anomaly.

In front of him, the plot showed the merchant ships making the six-hour crossing of the Xiang, a confused mass of orange vectors turning to green as ships were downgraded to no threat. When the command plot stabilized, Monroe grunted in satisfaction. Things were as they should be.

The plot in front of him matched the ship and vector data that had streamed in from the Hammer pinchspace comsats standing off Paderborn Reef to the north and Vijati Reef to the south. More reassuringly, the comsat data were consistent with the traffic schedules broadcast by an ever-helpful FedWorld traffic coordination center on Terranova.

Monroe smiled broadly. He liked what he saw. To make sure that no witnesses were left behind, what he now called Force Quebec would attack when Xiang Reef was clear of all but transiting FedWorld merships. There could not be too many merships, either; Force Quebec had to be able to eliminate every mership crossing the reef in a single brutal strike. Nor could there be too few to make an attack profitless. In a concession to the bleeding hearts—even the Hammer had a few of them—Xiang Reef had to be clear of passenger liners. Operation Cavalcade's rules of engagement were very clear. They prohibited any attacks on liners, FedWorld registered or not.

Most important of all, there had to be no chance of running into a passing FedWorld warship. The thought of a FedWorld heavy cruiser doing to him what he was about to do to the FedWorld merchant ships made him shiver.

It had taken some doing, but finally his staff had identified a number of windows in which all the mission constraints would be met. Based on the traffic reports, the earliest was in seven days' time, but he had to be sure. Each attack depended on all the conditions being right. It would take only one Fed heavy cruiser to be in the wrong place at the wrong time, and Operation Cavalcade would be over before it had started. To make sure that did not happen, he had to get a better handle on what the Fed starships were up to.

Thus far, the indications were good. It was beginning to look as though the monotonous grind up and down the trade route was taking the edge off the Feds. In fact, things were beginning to slip to a point where few of the patrolling ships were making random changes of vector, and even then not as often as they should. Things had gotten so bad that predicting where individual warships would be was getting easier and easier. It was sloppy stuff, Monroe thought, and not at all what he had come to expect from the Feds.

Even as he congratulated himself on his good fortune, Monroe gave himself a mental kick. No Hammer commander ever won an engagement by underestimating those Kraa-damned Feds, and he was not going to start now.

Until he was sure that he had identified the right time to strike, Force Quebec would sit and wait and watch.

Sunday, August 29, 2399, UD
FWSS Ishaq, Paderborn Reef

It had been a long three days since Constanza had ordered his arrest, and the bulkheads of his cabin were beginning to crowd in on Michael.

At first, being confined to his cabin had not been so bad— the exact opposite, in fact. It had been wonderful. For one thing, he had been able to catch up on some badly needed sleep; like every other junior officer on board, Michael had been running a serious sleep deficit. For the first day and a half, he had been so tired that he had slept more than he had been awake. But with the problem of sleep deprivation overcome and with him unable to concentrate on the entertainment accessed through his neuronics, boredom had set in, made worse by the nagging, stomach-churning worry that Constanza might get away with her lunatic proposition that

Michael and his boss were part of some conspiracy to mutiny. Early on, the idea of a conspiracy had sounded so far-fetched that he'd laughed out loud at the thought. Now, as the hours and then days dragged by, the idea was beginning to look less and less absurd. After all, captains of FedWorlds Space Fleet starships were powerful people, and it did not take much of that power to break the careers of two officers.

He decided that he would make another attempt, the latest in a long line of failed attempts, to write a vidmail to Anna. He did not get far. There was a knock, and Marine Murphy stuck his head in, his massive frame filling the doorway.

"Visitor for you, sir," Murphy announced with a cheerful smile.

Michael smiled back. "Ah, good. Hang on a sec. I'll just check my diary to see if I'm free."

Murphy's smile broadened into a grin. "Don't waste your time, sir. It's Lieutenant Armstrong."

"Oh, right." Michael scrambled to his feet as Murphy pushed the door open to admit Armstrong. "Afternoon, sir. To what do I owe the honor?"

"Dangerous trait being a smart-ass, Junior Lieutenant Helfort," Armstrong replied, cheerful eyes contradicting a stern voice. "Not career-enhancing at all."

"And what career would that be, sir?" Michael responded, the sudden bitterness in his voice ill concealed.

"The one you've got in front of you, so pay attention." Armstrong pulled up a seat. "Sit! We've got a bit to talk about." He waited patiently as Michael perched himself awkwardly on the edge of his bunk. Junior officers' cabins were cramped spaces and certainly not designed for meetings.

"Ready?"

"Ready, sir."

"Okay." Armstrong was all business. "This meeting comes in two parts. The first bit is the formal part. You may record it if you wish."

Michael nodded. *Ishaq*'s legal AI had briefed him well. Its avatar—a cheerful, late-middle-aged man with a no-nonsense fatherly attitude to life—had made sure Michael knew his rights.

"The second part I would rather you didn't, so please enable me to access your neuronics to block recording."

Michael looked at him in surprise. The capacity of Fleet officers to do and say things that completely baffled him seemed endless. "All right." There was a small pause as Michael commed the necessary authority to Armstrong's neuronics. "Done, sir."

"Good. Let's get on with it." Armstrong cleared his throat. "Junior Lieutenant Helfort. As required by law, I am required in my capacity as investigating officer to keep you informed as to the progress of the investigation. You and Lieutenant Commander Fellsworth are still under arrest. I've just received the formal brief of evidence. It's now up to me to review that. Once I have reviewed the brief and if I am satisfied that no further investigation of any matters relevant to the charges made against you is required, I then have to decide whether the evidence supports a case with enough merit to proceed to court-martial. With me so far?"

"I am, sir," Michael replied.

"Right. Now, until I have made that decision—whether the evidence warrants a court-martial—nothing changes, so you will have to be patient."

"Thanks, sir," Michael said bitterly, "I'm good at being patient."

Armstrong ignored him. "That concludes my formal report to you. Do you have any questions?"

Michael shook his head. "None, sir." What was the point? The process was the process.

"Good . . . neuronics stopped recording?"

"Stopped, sir."

"Let me check . . . right, that's done. Okay, Michael. Now for the unofficial part."

"Hope it's better than the official part."

"Oh, yes, I think it is. First, the brief of evidence. How can I put it? 'Useless' is probably the most charitable description, and cert—"

Michael's eyes opened wide in shock. This he had not expected. "Useless? You mean it won't support the charges?"

"Got it in one try, Michael. No, it won't, and that means

the chances of this business making it to trial are nil. And by the way, the legal AI agrees. Took him five minutes to rip it apart."

"So no trial?" Michael asked hopefully.

Firmly, Armstrong shook his head. "No. No trial. Ever. I'm briefing the captain as soon as I've finished here."

Michael sat back to think about that, the enormous weight bearing down on him gone. "Well, what can I say? Thanks for that. It'll be good to get things back to normal."

Armstrong's hand went up. "Not so fast, young man. I will be briefing the captain shortly and will recommend to her that the charges be dropped. However . . ."

Michael's heart sank. Why was there always a catch?

". . . it is up to Captain Constanza to withdraw the charges—"

"Or not?" Michael interrupted flatly.

Armstrong nodded. "If she wishes, she can refer the matter up the chain of command when we return to port. If she does, I stand relieved as investigating officer."

"Jesus, sir!" Michael protested. "That could be weeks and weeks away. What do I do? Just sit in this damn cabin and rot?"

"Michael!" Armstrong said sharply. "Settle down. Be patient and let us work on sorting this mess out. Getting angry and upset is not going to help!"

"Sorry, sir," Michael said contritely. He could see that Armstrong was doing his best.

The provost marshal stood up. "That's it for now. I'll keep you posted." With that, he was gone.

Michael sat for a while wondering how Constanza had allowed herself to get into such a mess. He felt a fleeting stab of pity for the woman. She must have been a good officer once. Fleet made mistakes—all big organizations did—but on the whole its record in appointing warship captains seemed pretty good. Michael sat there wondering what had gone wrong, when, and why. What on earth had tipped a competent officer with successful commands of smaller Fleet units behind her over the edge?

His moment of charitable concern was fleeting. She might

have been good once, but it was the here and now that mattered. The sooner all this was over and *Ishaq* got the captain it deserved, the better. The thought that a change of command might come sooner rather than later cheered him up immensely.

There was another knock on the door, and Marine Murphy's head reappeared. "Sir?"

"Jeez, Murphy. You lonely or something?"

Murphy smiled broadly. "Got to do something to keep amused, sir."

Michael laughed. He liked Murphy. Even though Murphy was relaxed and friendly, Michael knew full well that the nearly cyborg-sized man would be on him in a split second if he tried anything. Not that he would. He was not that stupid. Michael was small by FedWorld standards, and Murphy easily outmassed, outmuscled, outreached, and overtopped him by margins he did not even want to think about. The bloody man was huge. Any bigger, Murphy would be classified as an illegal cyborg and either reengineered or deported. The FedWorlds were strict about that, but that did not stop people like Murphy—and let's not forget Leading Spacer Bienefelt, he reminded himself—trying to get within a hairbreadth of the limits.

"Yeah, yeah. You've told me. Standing in front of a closed door isn't the most exciting thing to do of a watch."

"True enough, sir. Anyway, it's coming up on 16:00, so my relief will be here shortly. Will you be going to the gym?"

"Too true I will. Try and stop me," Michael declared forcefully. He would take any chance he could to get out of the box he was confined to, and today's gym session was one he was not going to miss. "Who's your relief?"

"Corporal Yazdi, sir. I'll be back for the middle watch."

"Lucky you. See you then."

"Will do, sir."

The door closed, and Michael busied himself digging out his gym gear. The two hours of gym time he was given each day was the one chance he got to burn off the unholy mix of ennui, anger, frustration, and fear that churned through his body. He meant to make the most of them. No sooner was he ready than there was a knock on his cabin door.

It was Corporal Yazdi. "Afternoon, sir. Ready to go?"

"Hi, Corporal. Yup, ready."

Small and sinewy, she did not look capable of taking on a granny in a wheelchair. Michael knew better, much better. Corporal Yazdi was not a woman to be underestimated. Michael would willingly bet a year's pay that Yazdi was every bit as dangerous as Murphy, her lethally fast reflexes and precision more than making up for what she lacked in height and mass. He liked the marines who had been posted to make sure he did not try to blow up the *Ishaq,* and Yazdi and Murphy in particular. To while away the endless hours stuck in his cabin, he had talked at length to both of them, the two marines a mine of information on the Marine Corps. Contrary to the popular view held by most spacers, Michael included, that most marines were mindless grunts, Yazdi and Murphy were as sharp as anyone with whom Michael had served.

Yazdi looked cheerful. Michael knew she would have arranged for a couple of marines to back her up so that she could get some time on the mats with him doing basic drills. Despite his three years at Space Fleet College, Yazdi had not been impressed with his unarmed combat skills. In her professional opinion, they were barely up to the job of fending off a bad-tempered drunk on a Saturday night, a situation Yazdi thought was criminally irresponsible and one she had made it her business to do something about.

Monday, August 30, 2399, UD
FWSS Ishaq, *Paderborn Reef*

"Now, get out! Get out, Goddamn it!"

"Sir!"

The door to Captain Constanza's day cabin hissed shut behind Commander Morrissen. For a moment he could not move. He felt sick. He wiped a forehead greasy with sweat.

What a mess. *Ishaq* was a ship in all sorts of trouble. And what was he doing? Trying to get his captain to see that no matter how much she ranted, how much she raved, nothing would change the fact that the charges of conspiracy to mutiny against Fellsworth and Helfort would not stand up. Never, ever. Why could she not see that?

If that wasn't bad enough, now she was threatening to have him arrested as well. Christ, he thought as he set off back to his office, what a bloody joke. He was the executive officer of a FedWorld heavy cruiser, for God's sake, and he couldn't even talk to his captain without being accused of treachery. So much for the fearless provision of advice so heavily stressed in his training. One thing was for sure: His career was over, so none of it mattered. Constanza could rant and rave all she liked; he was finished. Not that he cared anymore; any organization that tolerated people like Constanza was not an organization he wanted to work for. The bitch would have his resignation on her desk as soon as he could find the time to write it.

But that would have to wait. Somehow—he had no idea how—he was going to have to find a way to undo some of the damage Constanza had done. He owed Fellsworth and Helfort that much. And, as much as he hated the idea, that meant another confrontation with Constanza.

"I'm warning you, Commander. One step out of line and I'm charging you."

"I understand, sir."

"All right, then. Continue."

"Right, sir. Clearly, Lieutenant Armstrong no longer has your confidence."

"That's an understatement," Constanza muttered.

"So I think the best thing to do would be to pinchcomm a summary of the brief of evidence to the Fleet provost marshal. If Fleet agrees with you, then we can off-load the two officers at our next driver mass replenishment for transfer back to Terranova. Fleet can hold them until a court-martial can be convened. It would be good to put the problem behind us, to allow *Ishaq* to move on."

Morrissen held his breath as Constanza, eyes narrowed, considered his suggestion. If she agreed, Fleet would see exactly what was going on on board poor old *Ishaq*. That meant there was a chance—a slim chance—that they would do something about *Ishaq*'s crisis of command.

It took a while, but eventually, much to Morrissen's relief, Constanza nodded her agreement.

"Right, Commander," she said. "For once, you've done the right thing. It's a good suggestion. When can you get the draft pinchcomm to me?"

"Give me an hour, sir, if that's okay."

"Make it so, Commander."

"Thank you, sir." Morrissen started toward the door but stopped. "Oh, sir. One thing. Since we're in effect passing this matter on to Fleet, I would like to put Fellsworth and Helfort under open arrest. We can manage, of course, but close arrest is a serious drain on—"

Constanza's hand went up. "Say no more, Commander. I know where you're going, and I agree," she said expansively. "Open arrest it is. They won't be with us for long."

"Thank you, sir. I'll take it from here."

"You do that. Get that report to me. Now go; I've got work to do."

"Thank you, sir," Morrissen said to the top of Constanza's head.

You're a damn fool, Captain Constanza, if you think for one second that Fleet's going to back you up on this one, Morrissen thought as he left. The beauty of it all was that the facts—or, more accurately, the lack of facts—would speak for themselves. Fleet would throw the whole pathetic business out the window, of that he was absolutely sure. He would bet what little was left of his career on it.

Ishaq's executive officer coughed. "Thank you all for coming." He looked acutely uncomfortable.

"Our pleasure, sir," Lieutenant Commander Fellsworth replied sardonically. Michael grinned. He liked the exec. Despite everything, Commander Morrissen was a decent guy. Sitting beside him was Commander Pasquale, Fellsworth's boss. Pasquale looked angry. She glared at Michael; dutifully, he wiped the smile off his face.

Michael knew that Morrissen had reason to look uncomfortable. Morrissen had not covered himself in glory over his handling of what was now called the COMEX affair. Well, that was what the polite members of *Ishaq*'s crew called it. The impolite preferred "COMEX screwup," the rude liked "COMEX fiasco," and the insubordinate were going with "COMEX clusterfuck." That was Morrissen's choice; apparently he had been overheard saying it in an unguarded moment. Michael had to agree. It was probably the only label that even came close.

"Forgive me, Jack, but for God's sake get on with it." Commander Pasquale's impatience was obvious. She had a busy department to run, and none of this made that job any easier.

"Yes, please do, sir," Fellsworth said.

"Right," Morrissen muttered. "Well, I can tell you that the charge of conspiracy to mutiny will be withdrawn, so that's good news."

"Thank you, sir. No surprises there considering it was a complete load of nonsense in the first place," Fellsworth exclaimed angrily.

Morrissen looked embarrassed. "Er, yes. Quite so."

"When, sir?" Fellsworth's tone was angry.

"Well, that's the problem. The provost marshal has formally advised the captain that the charges are unsupported by the available evidence and must be withdrawn, um, er . . ." Morrissen's voice trailed off into an uncomfortable silence. Fellsworth sat back, arms folded. Michael stepped up to the plate.

"Sir, is there a problem? Surely all the captain has to do is sign a piece of paper." Michael leaned forward, a look of innocent inquiry on his face even though he knew full well what the real stumbling block was.

Morrissen nodded. "That's correct, Helfort. That is all she has to do. The problem is that until we return to port and the matter is formally taken over by the Fleet provost marshal, she is the only one who can withdraw the charges. That's her right under military law, and I'm afraid it's a right that I cannot, umm, well, er . . ."

Michael finished the sentence for him. ". . . persuade her not to exercise?"

Morrissen nodded glumly. "Yes."

Fellsworth leaned forward to look Morrissen full in the face. "So that means we're still under close arrest?"

Morrissen's hands went up as if to fend her off. Before he could speak, Pasquale got in first.

"I have told the captain that would be inappropriate, and she has agreed. Right, Jack?"

"Correct. You will be under open arrest. A formality. You are free to go anywhere you like on board, though for the time being you'll not be standing watches."

"Some good news, then, sir." Michael grinned, happy that his run of unbroken nights would not be ending.

Morrissen ignored Michael's feeble attempt at a joke. He looked at Fellsworth. "I know you aren't happy about any of this, but believe me, neither am I. You'll have to trust me, Karla. I know I could—should—have done more. Believe me when I say I regret that bitterly, but I can assure you that standing between a captain in command and her rights is a bad place to be. So, unless there is—"

Fellsworth's hand went up to stop him. "Sir! I know that," she interrupted, her voice softening. "I don't think I can judge you—or anyone else involved, come to that—without being in the same position as you all were in. So why don't we leave it at that? What more is there to say?"

"Not a lot." Morrissen shook his head. "So thanks. I'll keep pushing, but in the end Fleet will have to step in. Oh, talking of Fleet, I forgot something. I think I can safely say that there will be a formal apology from Fleet once this is all sorted out. Okay. I'll see you all later. I've commed the necessary orders to Armstrong. You'll lose the marines effective immediately."

"Thank you, sir," Fellsworth and Michael chorused.

Morrissen nodded, stood up, and left without another word. Michael thought he looked terrible; the stress of the COMEX affair on top of all the shit Constanza had piled on him would have made anyone look terrible.

Pasquale started to get up but thought better of it. She sat back down.

"You two okay?" she asked.

Fellsworth and Michael both nodded.

"Hang in there. So there are no doubts, I can promise you this: The charges will be dropped. You will get the formal apology from the commander in chief personally. There will also be—" Pasquale stopped abruptly. Michael looked at her curiously. She had been about to say something but must have thought better of it.

Pasquale gathered her thoughts before continuing. "That's it. Let me know if you have any problems. You shouldn't. Word's out. That's it. I'll see you both in the wardroom: 12:30 sharp. I want you both to have lunch with me." She stood up. "Think of it as rehabilitation if you like," she added with a small smile. "I'll see you then."

"Sir."

Once the door closed behind Pasquale, Fellsworth let out a long sigh. "Well, Michael. There it is." Her voice was flat, emotionless.

"Never a dull moment, sir."

Fellsworth looked curiously at Michael for a moment. "You haven't picked up on it, have you?"

Michael was baffled. "Picked up on what?"

"Oh, Michael!" Fellsworth complained despairingly. "For a bright boy, you can be awfully thick sometimes. Think!"

He thought long and hard, but whatever Fellsworth was talking about, he did not get it. "Sorry," he murmured, hands held out wide in an embarrassed apology.

"Well, please do not repeat this, but I think we're in for a change of command."

"Oh!" Michael sat stunned. He had wondered what Pasquale had been about to say. Now he knew.

Michael was jerked awake by the ship's main broadcast.

"What the f . . ." he mumbled as he struggled to get his sleep-clogged brain back in gear.

"All stations, this is command. Stand by for unscheduled drop in ten, repeat ten, minutes. Command out."

Strange, Michael thought. Something had gone wrong with one of *Ishaq*'s mission-critical systems, or the ship had received a pinchcomm with a change of plans. Which was it?

Michael patched his neuronics into the ship's management system. A quick check told him that all *Ishaq*'s systems were nominal. So, he thought, no systems problems; it had to be a pinchcomm. Now, that would be most unusual. Getting through to a ship in pinchspace was a difficult and uncertain business involving multiple slaved pinchcomm transmitters sending at maximum power. If the beam formers were good enough to focus the message—essentially a coded modulation of pinchspace itself—onto the same piece of pinchspace occupied by *Ishaq,* she would get the message, a laboriously transmitted four-letter group repeated over and over. Nine times out of ten, pinchcomm messages sent to ships in pinchspace did not get through; that was why Fleet doctrine reminded planners emphatically not to rely on them at any time. Any way one looked at it, *Ishaq* had been lucky to get it. Must be damned important for Fleet to go to all that trouble, he thought.

With no duty to attend to, Michael thought briefly about getting out of his bunk to see what was going on. On second thought, he decided, he might as well stay right where he was. He lay in the half darkness, neuronics patched into the ship's holovids to see what was going on, until the ship duly dropped out of pinchspace.

For a while, nothing much happened. Getting the full pinchcomm message, Michael thought. Then furious jets of reaction mass began to roll the ship slowly end over end. They were turning back, Michael thought. What in God's name was going on?

Once positioned, what started as a gentle trembling grew into a ship-shaking rattle. *Ishaq*'s main engines came up to full power, the aft holocams whiting out in the face of a glare as bright as any sun as driver mass accelerated at 40,000 g blasted out of *Ishaq*'s two main engines, the ionized driver mass ripping its way through space. *Ishaq* decelerated slowly, but the main engines stayed at maximum power even as she came to a dead stop. For a moment, *Ishaq* seemed to hang motionless in space. Then, her fabric groaning under the 5-g acceleration, the main engine burn started to drive the ship back to jump speed.

Twenty-three minutes and a lot of driver mass later, *Ishaq* was ready to jump on a vector back the way she had come. Michael was impressed. Must be one hell of a set of new orders to justify something so drastic, he thought.

"All stations, this is command. Stand by to jump in five minutes."

While *Ishaq* settled down after the ordeal of jumping, Captain Constanza came up on main broadcast.

"All stations, this is the captain. As you are all aware, we have reversed vector and are now on our way back toward Terranova. We have orders to rendezvous with a deepspace fast courier, *DFC-667*. We'll be meeting her once we transit Paderborn Reef. I have no other information to give you at this stage, so bear with it. I do not know why we have been retasked, but all will be revealed when we rendezvous. Captain out."

Michael turned Constanza's words over in his mind. He might have been imagining it, but Constanza's voice did not seem to be the usual self-assured mix of arrogance and confidence.

Suddenly light dawned. *Ishaq*'s orders were brief because

they involved Constanza. Fleet was relieving her. There could be no other reason. He sat up so quickly that he cracked his head on the built-in cupboard above him. Cursing, he hopped out of his bunk, forcing himself into a tangled, recalcitrant shipsuit. He had to see Fellsworth. This was too good not to share.

Friday, September 3, 2399, UD
HWS Quebec-One, *Xiang Reef*

Commodore Monroe's mouth tightened into a bloodless slash. Face grim, he stared at the command holovid. When his final rail-gun salvo ripped into the FedWorld merchant ship *Betthany Market,* he bared his teeth for a second. Satisfied, he sat back.

Monroe had to give credit where credit was due.

The captain of the *Betthany Market* had tried his best to escape from the trap. With merships exploding all across Xiang Reef, he had pushed his main engines far beyond their manufacturer's limits; Monroe had expected the mership's fusion power plants to lose containment. By some miracle of Fed-World engineering they had not, but nothing was going to help the doomed *Betthany Market* and her ill-fated crew. Fully loaded, sluggish, and unwieldy, the mership had no chance of evading a rail-gun salvo fired at close quarters, and *Quebec-One* had been so close that her optronics had picked out every last dent and scratch on the hard-worked mership's hull.

In the end, *Betthany Market* died like all the rest of the merships ambushed by Monroe's ships that bloody morning. Rail-gun slugs sliced through her thin plasteel hull. Punched deep into the ship, two slugs reached the engine room to release the enormous energy bottled up inside her fusion power plants. Microseconds later, the ship exploded into a gigantic ball of incandescent plasma that writhed away into the emptiness of deepspace.

The command team of *Quebec-One* sat silent around Monroe. They stared in horrified fascination at the command holovid. The mership had vanished. Only a gas cloud and a few shattered fragments of the ship remained; the cloud twisted away into nothing, cooling fast, its dance of death a fading memorial to mership and spacers now dead.

Monroe's ships had executed the operation with brutal efficiency. Most of their victims knew nothing of the attack before death engulfed them. The hellish fires of runaway fusion plants consumed the few lifepods launched. The last witnesses to the latest in a long line of Hammer atrocities survived only a few seconds before they, too, were wiped out.

The operation had been easy. No, Monroe thought, it had been too easy. Twenty-seven merships destroyed in less than an hour. Cold-blooded murder was what it was.

Monroe broke the spell when the last traces of the *Bethany Market* disappeared. He had pushed his luck far enough; they should have been long gone by now. He turned to his chief of staff. "Time we were on our way. To all ships, immediate execute—"

The sensor officer's voice broke in, urgent with alarm. "Sir, we have a positive gravitronics intercept. Designated track 220547. Stand by . . . estimated drop bearing Red 3 Up 1. One ship. Grav wave pattern suggests pinchspace transition imminent. Vector is nominal for Earth-FedWorld transit. Sir! This one's not on any schedule. Military, sir. It has to be military."

Monroe wasted no time. Every instinct told him his sensor officer was right. The new arrival must be a FedWorld warship. The Old Earth Alliance never patrolled deepspace this far out; the Xiang Reef gravitation anomaly was too remote. If it turned out to be an Alliance warship, bad luck; he needed to survive before he worried about that possibility.

"Designate track 220547 hostile," Monroe barked. "Immediate to all ships, stand by rail-gun salvo. Targeting data to follow. Kraa's blood! Sensors! Get me the drop data . . . come on, sensors, come on! I need a drop time, position, and vector. Now, Kraa damn it!"

The sensor officer's voice shook under the stress. "Stand

by . . . okay, sir. Here it comes. She's close. Confirmed Red 3 Up 1 at 85,000 kilometers. Stand by . . . targeting data confirmed and passed to all ships."

"Roger."

Monroe checked the command plot. Impatient, he drummed his fingers on the arm of the chair. The rail-gun crews were taking too long to reload. He forced himself to sit still. Nothing he said or did was going to speed things up.

"Sir! All ships confirm valid firing solutions on the drop datum, full rail-gun salvos loaded, ready to engage." His chief of staff's voice cracked in the heat of the moment.

Monroe wasted no time. "Command approved to fire!"

"All rail-gun salvos away, sir."

"Roger that," Monroe snapped. He forced himself to breathe normally, to ignore the iron bands that crushed his chest with sudden force. If his ships failed to destroy the new arrival the instant it dropped and it really was a FedWorld warship, they were all dead. He buried the thought. You ought to have more faith, he chided himself. A six-ship rail-gun attack would overwhelm the unfortunate ship.

Monroe allowed himself to relax a little. *Quebec-One* and her sister ships might be fitted with obsolete Buranan rail guns, but the engagement geometry weighed heavily in favor of the attackers.

Crucial to their chances, the target would drop close and broadside on to three of his ships; it would be the perfect ambush. Provided that his ship's firing solutions were accurate, the tightly grouped swarms of platinum/iridium alloy slugs should sweep through the drop datum only seconds after the target dropped into normalspace. True, most of the slugs were destined to disappear into the void. That was the fate of almost all rail-gun slugs, but proximity had allowed his ships to tighten the swarm grouping to put more slugs on target. Monroe checked the command plot again. He liked what he saw. *Quebec-One*'s warfare officer predicted a first strike of more than three hundred slugs. Monroe smiled. The raw numbers looked good. Where the slugs might impact looked even better.

If the attack went according to plan, slugs from the first

two salvos would hit where the armor thinned back from the bow. Seconds later, slugs from the third salvo should smash into the target toward its stern, the most vulnerable part of any warship. After it was hit there and hit hard, its chances of survival were close to zero. If everything went well, the final salvos would be redundant, their contribution limited to finishing off an already dying ship.

The seconds melted away with glacial slowness. Monroe struggled to keep his breath under control. The atmosphere in *Quebec-One*'s combat information center thickened until it threatened to choke him. Monroe cursed under his breath. He had seen action throughout the last war; he should be used to combat by now.

"Sir! Track 220547 is dropping. Confirm drop data nominal." The sensor officer sounded ecstatic. He deserves to, Monroe thought. The man had done well under intense pressure. Targeting data from commercial-grade gravitronics were unreliable at best, but this time the system had worked and worked well. Monroe's ships had solid firing solutions; the new arrival was condemned to drop right into the path of the oncoming rail-gun salvos. Without a miracle—and Monroe put no faith in miracles—the hapless ship was trapped. She would have little time to react before the massive rail-gun attack fell on her.

Commodore Monroe sat back and waited.

Friday, September 3, 2399, UD
FWSS Ishaq, pinchspace

Under strict instructions from Commander Pasquale, Fellsworth had wasted no time getting the warfare training department back on its feet. The routine weekly team meeting had been in full swing for over an hour when it was interrupted by the main broadcast announcing five minutes to the drop for the transit through the Xiang Reef.

Fellsworth knew when to quit. From long experience, she knew she could never compete with a pinchspace drop, and so she was not about to try. "Okay, folks. Take a break. We'll reconvene once the drop's over."

Michael stood up, stretching. It was strange to be back at work, to sit around a table for the weekly team meeting, with everyone acting as though nothing had happened. To make things even more uncomfortable, Fellsworth had reverted to her normal standoffish self. Any and every attempt by Michael to talk things over was rebuffed politely but firmly. It was as though Fellsworth had forgotten that they were still under open arrest and that the charges had not been withdrawn by Constanza even if she and the rest of the ship knew they would be. With a mental shrug of the shoulders, Michael went to the cooler to get some water. He was going to need it. God, he hated pinchspace drops.

"Sir?"

It was Bettany.

"What's up, Morris?"

"There's something to see you. Too big to be human, so it must be either a cyborg or a marine. Oh, and a small marine as well."

Michael laughed as he went to the door. Had to be Yazdi and Murphy. Who else could it be?

It was. Christ, Murphy is huge, Michael thought. His neck ached trying to look the man in the face. "Corporal Yazdi, Marine Murphy. Come to arrest me?"

Yazdi's face reddened. "Hell, no, sir," she muttered. "Just wanted a word."

"Okay. Can't be too long. I've got a meeting after we drop. Got your bag? Don't want you chucking all over the table."

Yazdi waved a bag in silent reply. The two marines followed Michael through to one of the small meeting rooms. "Take a seat, guys."

"Thank you, sir."

"What can I do for you?"

"Well, sir." Yazdi stopped; she looked faintly embarrassed. "Well," she continued, "we wanted to say that we're pleased it all worked out for you in the end. I know it's not official yet, but it seems pretty clear what's going to happen."

"Thank you. You're right. It has all worked out in the end. Oh, shit. Hold on, guys." With that, *Ishaq*'s alarms sounded and the universe turned itself inside out as the ship dropped into normalspace.

After the drop, Michael and the marines cleaned themselves up quickly.

"Right, where were we? Oh, yes. I was—" Michael was stopped dead by the strident urgency of the ship's klaxon driving the crew to general quarters.

"What the hell?" Michael shouted. Acting on instinct, he and the two marines erupted from their seats to join the crowd of spacers trying to get out of the department's one and only door at the same time. With maddening slowness, the jam cleared.

When Michael got to the door, with Yazdi and Murphy close behind, the world erupted around him, a sudden tornado of smoke and flame ripping the ship apart around him before disappearing as fast as it had come. Oh, shit, Michael thought despairingly. Rail-gun slugs; it had to be. God above, he prayed, not again; please, God, not again. For a moment, he did not think he could take it, his hands turning cold and clammy when he remembered the last time. Desperate now, he knew that duty was his best defense against the bowel-churning panic threatening his tenuous grip on reality. Michael clawed his way to a survival station, with Yazdi and Murphy following. With frantic energy born of a desperate hope that somehow *Ishaq* and her crew were going to survive, Michael tore open the doors and began to hurl skinsuits into the mass of people behind him. Murphy's huge mass forced some semblance of discipline on what was close to a panic-stricken mob. When there were only three suits left, Michael threw two to Murphy and Yazdi before grabbing the last one for himself. In a matter of seconds, he was secure inside it, the plasglass helmet sealing onto the neck ring with a satisfying *sssssssffffffit* as the shapeskin molded itself to his body. He watched carefully as the suit ran its start-up diagnostics. Thank God, he thought. All green. He had a good suit.

Michael looked around, cold sweat beading on his face. He wondered what the hell he could do that would make the slightest difference in a situation that seemed to be going from bad to catastrophic faster than he could think and faster than *Ishaq* seemed able to react. Hesitating, he stood there, and then another rail-gun salvo hit home. This time there was serious damage. All of a sudden, the air around Michael was a tortured mass of smoke and flame. The shock wave from a close pass by a rail-gun slug punched him hard against the nearest bulkhead. We're dead, he thought as he staggered back to his feet. Whoever was attacking was good enough— and close enough—to have the *Ishaq* on toast.

In seconds the smoke was so dense, Michael could not see an arm's length in front of him. Underneath him, the deck bucked and heaved as more slugs smashed home. He cursed silently, pushing the fear and panic that threatened to overwhelm him back down where they had come from. Secondary explosions were beginning to rip *Ishaq* apart; massive shock waves were hammering through the ship, and the artgrav was losing the unequal struggle. Around him, skinsuited shapes came and went, looming out of the smoke before disappearing to God only knew where, the spacers staggering and slipping like drunks. Frantically, Michael patched his neuronics into the ship's main AI only to find to his horror that it was dead. That meant one thing: *Ishaq* was in serious trouble. No matter which channel he tried to patch his neuronics into, there was nothing. The calm, rational voice of authority, of someone— anyone—who knew enough to take charge of the situation and mobilize the *Ishaq*'s crew was completely absent.

For a moment he was baffled. He stood, with an arm wrapped around a stanchion the only thing keeping him on his feet as *Ishaq* bucked and heaved like a mad thing under his feet. He did not understand it. How could a ship the size and power of the *Ishaq* become a useless wreck in the space of a few minutes? The massive shape of Murphy appeared out of the gloom with what looked like Yazdi close behind. Murphy's massive hand came out of the murk, clamping his and Michael's helmets together. "What do we do, sir? What do we do?" Murphy yelled hoarsely.

"I don't know. I'm trying to find out what—"

The voice booming out of his skinsuit speakers came as a complete shock. "All stations, this is command. Abandon ship, I say again, abandon ship. All stations, this is command. Abandon ship, I say again, abandon ship. Sitrep on neuronics channel 45 Bravo. Sitrep on neuronics channel 45 Bravo. Go with God. Command out."

"There's your answer, Murphy. Go. Go now." A frantic check with his neuronics showed him the way to the nearest lifepod station. "8-November's our best bet, so let's go."

Michael and the two marines began to run, making their way to the nearest lifepod station. Michael patched his neuronics into channel 45 Bravo, apparently the only one of *Ishaq*'s hundreds of internal comm channels that was working. Whoever was responsible deserved a bloody medal, Michael thought as finally he got access to channel 45 Bravo. It was not what he expected. No situation reports there. The channel accessed the *Ishaq*'s event log, raw data from hundreds of ship systems, all chronicling *Ishaq*'s catastrophic fall from operational warship to dying hulk. He pounded along, the vast bulk of Murphy forcing a way past smashed bulkheads, wrecked equipment, and fallen cables; hydraulic pipes were spewing fluid onto decks already slippery with the blood of broken bodies awkwardly twisted across the passageway. He kept running with the event log scrolling in front of him, his neuronics skimming through each of *Ishaq*'s major systems in turn. He began to get some sense of the calamity that had befallen the *Ishaq,* and it was grim reading.

There was far too much unprocessed data for him to get any real understanding of it, and so it would have to wait. Comming an order to dump the entire event log into his neuronics for later, he turned his mind back to the more pressing matter of survival. From what he had seen so far, it was only a matter of time before *Ishaq*'s main fusion plants blew, and if they were not a long way clear when that happened, that would be it.

Murphy skidded to a halt. Turning with surprising speed for such a large man, he shot his arm out to grab Yazdi and Michael before hurling them unceremoniously into the access hatch of one of the few lifepods still left at station 8-

November. Michael offered up a quick prayer of thanks. He had missed the hatch, and without Murphy he would have wasted precious seconds finding it.

"Stay there!" Murphy barked. "I'll make a final check, and then we'll go. If I'm not back in one minute, go without me. I'll get the next bus." He disappeared back into the filthy gray-black murk that choked *Ishaq*'s passageways from deck to deckhead.

Michael did as he was told, clawing his way across the sill and as far into the pod as he could get. Huddled at the far end were three spacers, two women and a man, all still alive from what he could see, but barely. The man looked to have been caught without a skinsuit too close to an explosion. His face and upper body were a mass of reddish-brown blisters streaked with black charring, and his mouth a hideous grinning parody of a smile with white teeth against blackened lips; his one-piece shipsuit was a tattered wreck, ripped and torn almost to his waist. The other two were unconscious. Michael could get only a quick look at them before Murphy returned. He hurled two more spacers bodily into the pod, then climbed in, dragging two more after him. Michael watched openmouthed as Murphy reached back out of the air lock to grab another two. The pod was now full, and without hesitating, Murphy flipped the black-and-orange safety cover on the launch panel, put the selector to automatic, and mashed the red jettison switch with a fist the size of a large ham before collapsing onto the deck, chest heaving.

A second later, the lifepod's solid fuel motors ignited with a thudding jolt. The pod's artgrav trembled as it struggled to compensate for the massive acceleration pushing it clear of the doomed ship. Even as the lifepod's artgrav stabilized, a second giant blow smashed into it, picking it up and hurling it into space.

It was a blast wave.

Ishaq was gone.

Michael and the two marines, the only occupants of the lifepod who were not injured, had managed to restore a semblance of order.

The three worst casualties—two weapons techs and an ordnance petty officer—were beyond help. It had been the work of moments to strip them before bundling them into one of the emergency regen bags secured to the lifepod's bulkheads. There was nothing more Michael or anyone could do for them. They would live long enough to be rescued or they wouldn't. It was as simple as that.

The rest of the lifepod's complement was a pretty sorry-looking bunch, but they would survive. The onboard bulkhead-mounted medibots were working like demented little demons, debriding, cutting, suturing, injecting, hydrating, and dosing. Michael's only contribution to the process was to lift and shift spacers around so that the bots could get in to finish the job. Finally, it was his turn, and it surprised him when the medibots told him in no uncertain terms to strip his skinsuit off so that they could clean and stitch a cut on his back he had thought was just a bruise.

He patched his neuronics into the medibot's holocam to see what was going on and winced when he saw the jagged, shallow gash across his back running down from his shoulder. "I didn't even feel that," he murmured. He should pay more attention to his suit integrity alarms, he thought. Canceling them without checking for damage was probably not a life-extending strategy.

Corporal Yazdi looked impressed. "Nice one, sir. You know what?"

Michael rolled his eyes. "What?"

"Should have been a marine." Yazdi grinned. "Not a scratch on either one of us."

"Hmmph!" Michael winced as a suture went in too deep. "That hurts. Tell you what, Corporal Yazdi. Stand behind Marine Murphy; that's the moral of the story. He'd stop a tac-nuke at forty paces."

Yazdi smiled. "He bloody well would. You ready for an update, sir?"

Bugger, Michael thought. He had forgotten: Once an officer, always responsible, or so the saying went. The time had come to display the leadership qualities three expensive years at Space Fleet College had ground into him, even though all he really wanted to do was to curl up in a corner and go to sleep.

His hyperexcited, adrenaline-fueled high was beginning to drop away. The full impact of what had happened had sunk in, dragging his spirits down as it did. He could not see how more than a handful of *Ishaq*'s crew could have gotten away, and that meant a lot of people he knew might be gone. Stone, Fellsworth, Ichiro, Bettany. "Christ," he muttered aloud. That was for starters. How many more would there be? The list would be meters long.

"Sir?" Yazdi prompted gently.

Michael started as he came to earth. "Shit. Sorry. Daydreaming again. Fire away, Corporal."

"We're in trouble, sir."

"Trouble? Of course we're in trouble." Michael looked baffled. Talk about stating the blindingly obvious.

Yazdi shook her head. "I don't mean it like that, sir," she replied patiently. "Have a look at the holovid. I've slaved it to the external holocam."

Michael did as he was told. He stared at the holovid, but it did not make any sense. "Who is that?" All he could see was a single merchant ship closing in on them. He looked closer. "Who is he?"

Yazdi shrugged. "Don't know, sir. It looks like he doesn't want us around. Here, sir."

"Stand by one." Overriding the lifepod's automatic pilot, Michael frantically spun the pod to point its armored nose at the unknown attacker. It was not much, but every little bit helped. "Right, Corp. Sorry. Go on."

"No worries. Here, sir. Have a look." Michael looked on intently as Yazdi zoomed the holocam in as close as it would go. For a moment, what he was seeing did not make sense. The ship was using chromaflage to conceal something, but what? An icy hand clamped itself around his heart as it came to him.

"Oh, Jeez! Are those what I think they are?"

"They are, sir. Those are rail-gun ports. That's what took the *Ishaq* out. That's—"

The holovid flared with the brilliant flash of a rail-gun

broadside. An instant later, the lifepod was slapped backward, the hull screeching in protest, a massive crunch announcing a rail-gun slug strike. It was over in an instant, so quickly that Michael did not have time to feel any fear. Desperately, he checked for damage.

"Lucky, lucky, lucky," he muttered as he ran the pod's diagnostics. The slug had punched into the lifepod's bow and ripped its way along the outer skin without penetrating the inner hull, leaving only a blazing white-hot furrow spewing ionized gas to record its passing. They had survived by pure, blind chance; a hit dead center would have gutted the pod. He took a deep breath. A lifepod was a small target, but even small targets got hit. His stomach knotted at the thought.

"Christ! Now it all makes sense. Those are the bad guys, Corporal."

"They sure as hell are, sir."

"Hang on a moment. Let me have a look at something." Michael patched his neuronics into the *Ishaq*'s event log he had downloaded in the awful near-panicked rush to get to the lifepods before the ship blew. The data were raw and there were terabytes to look at, so it took a while, but he found it in the end: data from *Ishaq*'s infrared sensors acquired in the moments before the rail-gun attack had hit home. There it was. Michael could not be sure, but it looked to him like the characteristic heat signature of a ship that had lost fusion containment and exploded. He looked again. Not one ship, either—lots of ships. *Ishaq* had not died alone. Other ships had died that day. Why? None of it made any sense.

"Shit. This changes things bigtime." Michael sat back to think. "Right, this is what we need to do, Corporal. First, I'm going to comm you and Murphy here a data file—a big data file. It's the *Ishaq*'s event log, and if we live long enough, we'll need it to convict these people of piracy. I'm going to put a neuronics block on it, so whoever these people are, you can't tell them it exists. Okay?"

The two marines nodded. "Good." There was a short pause as the transfer went through. "Right! Now we need to get our escape kits tucked away and then our skinsuits back on in case they get lucky and punch a hole in us. Anything else?"

Yazdi shook her head. "No, sir. Got to say, I don't fancy our chances. They're either going to blow us to hell or it's some damn prison camp somewhere."

Michael nodded. Yazdi was right. If they were going to be blown to hell, there was nothing he could do to stop it. And if they were about to be captured, they would need the little escape kits tucked away safely under synthskin patches: two under the upper arms, one low on each buttock, and one behind each thigh above the knee. Neuronics blocks made it impossible for any Fleet spacer to reveal the kits' existence to anyone not positively authenticated as serving Fleet personnel, so their captors would never find out. Whoever they were.

"Right," he said forcefully as a quick check of the holovid showed their attacker closing in. "Let's get the escape kits out and make a start. We may not have much time." He stood up to reach a small panel high on one bulkhead, pressing his finger down on the access control. A small prick signaled that his DNA had been sampled, and then the panel clicked open, revealing a tightly packed mass of small white packets.

They were in business.

Commodore Monroe looked at his chief of staff in frustration. "What do you mean we can't eliminate them? They're only damn lifepods, for Kraa's sake. Rail guns, lasers, machetes, baseball bats, sticks. I don't give a damn what you use. Get rid of them. No survivors, remember?"

"I do, sir, but these are military lifepods with hardened, self-sealing hulls. They are damn tough. We're only fitted with standard mership lasers. They are taking far too long to break into them, and even then we're only depressurizing them for a second or two. They'll go to skinsuits and wait until the hull reseals. We could be all day."

"Rail guns, then."

"Sir," Monroe's chief of staff replied, a touch impatiently. "They're too small. We can't get them all. We've had two hits, neither fatal. It'll take too long. Sir, I strongly advise that we move in and scoop them up. We can work out what to do with them later."

Monroe thought about it for a moment. His chief of staff

was right. He knew now that he had made a mistake. He had sent the rest of his ships on their way without thinking the problem through. According to the traffic schedule, the next merchant ship was due to arrive in less than half an hour. The window of opportunity he had taken to destroy twenty-seven FedWorld merchant ships and one heavy cruiser was closing fast. He was confident that his false identity would hold up to scrutiny, but not if he was sitting in the middle of an expanding cloud of ionized gas, firing lasers and rail guns at defenseless lifepods. Then there was the FedWorld heavy cruiser *Al-Masu'di* due in fifty minutes to worry about. He was damn sure they would not let him go without asking the hard questions.

"Right, I agree. Let's do it." He watched as his chief of staff gave the orders to move *Quebec-One* in close. Its two shuttles would launch as it approached to round up the strays.

"Okay, sir. That's done."

"Good. How long?"

"Twenty minutes, sir. Unlike ours, their pods are programmed to close in on each other to make recovery easier."

Monroe grimaced. It would be close. "How kind of them. Such caring people, the Feds." He sniffed. "How many pods?"

"Twenty-five, sir."

Monroe's eyebrows shot up. "Twenty-five? That all?"

"Twenty-five, sir. That's it."

Monroe blinked, still struggling to understand the full magnitude of the loss. "Kraa! So few."

"We didn't give them much time, sir. We caught them napping. When the fusion plant powering the aft rail-gun batteries lost containment . . . Well, that was pretty much it for most of them. The rest would have gone when the main engines went up."

"So how many spacers are we talking about?"

"FedWorld heavy cruisers carry twelve-man lifepods, sir. So at most, let's see . . . Three hundred? Probably less allowing for casualties."

Monroe turned away. For a brief instant he felt sick, his

adrenaline-fueled compulsion to eliminate the pods gone. He might be a Hammer. He might hate the Feds—and he did—but he was a spacer, too, a human speck alone in the appalling vastness of space. Three hundred survivors from a crew of—what?—well over a thousand spacers. That was hard.

Monroe turned back to his chief of staff. "One more thing."

"Sir?"

"They will have seen *Quebec-One.* Nothing we can do about that, but they must not know who we are. I want standard mership skinsuits worn, visors down. Nothing obviously Hammer, nothing military-issue, and stun-gun anyone who's not already unconscious. Once we've got them locked down on board, we'll work out what to do next."

"Understood, sir!"

Monroe watched as the man fired off the necessary orders. He did not have to ask his chief of staff what he wanted to do with their three hundred or so unwanted guests. It was bloody obvious. He could see it in the man's eyes. But somehow he could not see himself ejecting defenseless spacers into the void. Killing at a distance was one thing. Killing people you had just rescued, well, that was quite another—he smiled grimly—even for a Hammer who had commanded an operation that had killed twenty-eight ships and close to two thousand spacers.

Monroe sat back; he was well satisfied with the day's work. The Feds would be shitting themselves when the news broke, he thought. The loss of twenty-seven merships would be bad enough; the impact on their interstellar trade would be nothing short of a disaster. But the loss of the *Ishaq* would be ten times worse. For the Feds, it would be an absolute catastrophe. Monroe had been to staff college. He knew how the Feds saw themselves. The power of their Space Fleet was the foundation on which the safety and security of the entire Federated Worlds was built.

He smiled again. For once, things were going the Hammer's way. It was a good feeling.

Michael could not work it out.

Why would that damn dog not leave him alone? All he wanted to do was sleep; the warm, fuzzy, welcoming darkness kept pulling him down to a safe place away from all the pain and disappointment of the world. The dog was persistent; it kept licking his face, its cold wet tongue dragging him back from the warm, safe depths toward a cold light burning fiercely far above him. And the dog was winning; bit by bit, the light got stronger and stronger.

He opened his eyes and screamed in agony. Blinding white light drove red-hot slivers of pain into his skull. He dropped back into the darkness, but not for long. Slowly, the darkness seeped away, the cold and light returning until he was fully conscious again.

This time he opened his eyes slowly. The overhead lights were searingly bright, and a blue-white glare hammered into a head suddenly splitting with pain. He closed his eyes and lay still for a moment, his entire body jangling and fizzing with little shocks of pain. Shit. He remembered now. Stun guns; the bastards had stun-gunned him, but who were they, for God's sake? He could not even remember what they looked like.

Cautiously, he opened his eyes again. Standing above him was a shipsuited figure, black against the blinding brightness overhead, his face covered by some sort of mask. Michael's eyes hurt. He could not make the man out. Where was he? He started to turn his head.

"Ah, ha, you little Fed wart. Awake, are we? Get up. Now!"

Michael did his best, but nothing would work properly. His legs collapsed under him as he tried to struggle to his feet.

"You idle piece of crap. Get the fuck up," the shipsuit ordered, reinforcing his words with a full-blooded kick to the ribs.

Michael screamed as the boot hit home, the pain almost overwhelming him as something inside his chest tore with a crackling rip. The agony was almost unbearable. He could barely breathe, but at least it had cleared his head. He could think now. He commed his neuronics to dump painkillers into his system. Instantly, the pain receded; after a huge effort, he managed to get to his feet, hand clamped to a pipe to keep himself upright. He stood swaying in front of the anonymous shipsuited figure. He stared at a pair of pale blue-green eyes, the only thing visible through two slits in the hood, a crudely made piece of cloth like a small bag draped loosely over the man's head. I'm going to call you Shithead, Michael decided.

"Good," Shithead said. "Walk!" He waved Michael toward a hole in a wire cage crudely erected across one corner of what looked like the empty cargo bay of a merchant ship. "I'll tell you where to go."

Michael began an unsteady shuffle out of the cage. Apart from the two of them, the huge bay was completely empty, an echoing shell. Where in God's name were the rest of his lifepod? Where were Yazdi, Murphy, and the rest? While he walked, Michael carefully checked himself out. He had been searched roughly; his shipsuit had been left a tattered wreck, pockets torn off and badges gone. His boots had gone, too, but a furtive check confirmed that his escape kits were still in place, thank God. Something told him he was going to need them.

Once he was out of the cage, Shithead waved him on; they came to an airtight door. "Go through, turn left. Keep going and don't stop until I tell you," Shithead called from somewhere close behind his right shoulder.

Michael turned to him. "But who—"

He had barely opened his mouth when Shithead whipped a short club from behind his back. Stepping to one side, he smashed the club backhanded into Michael's stomach. It was so quick, so unexpected, Michael could do nothing to avoid the blow. The club drove the wind out of him, doubling him over with an *ooooffff* as the air in his lungs exploded out of his mouth.

Shithead stood back, watching in silence. Michael slowly recovered, his mouth working desperately as he fought to re-fill lungs screaming for air. It took a while, but eventually he was able to stand upright with great difficulty, the pain in his lungs, stomach, and ribs coming and going in great searing waves.

Shithead put the tip of the bat into Michael's face. "You don't talk unless I ask you a question. Got it?"

Michael stood there, not saying a word. Shithead could go screw himself.

"Well? You understand?" Shithead swung the bat back, but this time Michael was ready for him. He ignored the pain from his ribs and stomach as the simple routines drilled into him by Corporal Yazdi kicked in. Michael's arm went up. Half turning under the oncoming blow, he deflected the club away from him. Shithead lost his balance as he followed through. As he twisted, Michael stepped behind him and with delicate precision kicked the man hard in the crotch, the arch of his foot hitting home with a deeply satisfying crunching thump. Dropping the club, Shithead collapsed to the deck, screaming in pain. Michael grabbed the club off the deck. He was going to beat the son of a bitch to a pulp.

He never got the chance. A stun shot on full power hit him square in the back, dropping his body to the deck alongside the moaning Shithead. He writhed in a futile attempt to escape from the exquisite agony of tortured nerve endings, the club slipping from his fingers to clatter away across the plasteel deck panels.

Michael lay in a twisted heap, lungs heaving as he struggled to breathe, the aftereffects of the stun-gun shot driving bolts of molten pain up and down every nerve in his body. A second shipsuited figure appeared over him, this one a fat, dumpy man with pitiless eyes. He looked down at Michael through the slits in his hood. "I don't suggest you try that again, sonny. If you do, I'll ask the boss if I can space you. And you know what? I'm sure he'll agree. Understand?"

Michael's mouth tried to shape the words, but nothing in his body seemed to be working properly. His brain was, though; he was going to call this one Porky.

Porky leaned down. "I think you understand," he whispered. He stood upright, stepped back, and kicked Michael casually in the kidneys for emphasis. He waved over the men who had followed him into the cargo bay.

Porky pointed at Michael. "Right. Two on this one. Interrogation room for him," he ordered. "And two on this sad fucking apology for a spacer," he sneered, pushing the toe of his boot into Shithead, who by then was lying flat on his back, legs drawn up against his chest, whimpering softly. "Take him to the sick bay. I think he's going to need to have his nuts iced." He prodded Shithead in the ribs with the muzzle of his stun gun. "Oh, yes. Iced nuts for you." He laughed.

In a flash, the joke took root and started to flower. "Iced nuts," Porky bellowed; the laughter turned to hysteria as the men around him joined in. "My favorite! Iced nuts," he roared, slapping his thighs, tears beginning to run down his face.

His captors staggered about, to a man overcome by demented laughter. Michael lay there, wondering what the hell was going on. These were seriously dangerous people, he decided. So who were they? Idiot, he told himself after a moment's thought. Run the damn voice analyzer and see what it says. Even as he put his neuronics to work, a new voice cut across the raucous laughter echoing around the cargo bay.

"What the hell is going on here?"

Nerve ends jangling with pain, Michael twisted his head around to have a look at the latest arrival. He might have known it: yet another hooded, shipsuited figure, but this one was different. He radiated a dangerous calm, an almost hypnotic authority, and in an instant his captors fell silent. He would call this one Snake, Michael decided.

"That's better." Snake walked over to Michael. "Name, rank, and serial number," he demanded.

"Helfort, Michael Wallace," Michael mumbled. "Junior Lieutenant, Federated Worlds Space Fleet, serial number FC0216885, and that's all you're getting from me, you murder—"

Snake's boot flashed out, catching him under the ribs, the kick strong enough to lift him bodily off the deck. It was as much as Michael could do to roll away, a scream whistling out through clenched teeth as pain swamped him.

"Ah, yes, I see the problem now." Snake looked thoughtfully down at Michael. He bent over to pick up Shithead's club. "I think we've got a smart-ass on our hands." He squatted down next to Michael, prodding him with the club for emphasis. "Your daddy should have warned you to be more careful with that mouth of yours, young man. It'll get you into trouble one day. Now, here's the deal." Another poke, a hard one this time, into ribs already begging for mercy. "You behave, you answer my questions, and you stop the backchat. Do all that, and I won't space you. That's the deal, and it's the only deal on offer, so I suggest you take it. Understand?"

Snake's arm started to take the club back, so Michael nodded, flinching away. The man was right. His mouth would get him into trouble, and this was getting him nowhere. He also had a feeling that dropping Shithead to the deck, deeply satisfying though it had been at the time, might be something he would live to regret.

"Understood," he conceded reluctantly.

Snake hit him anyway. Michael saw the blow coming but was too slow to move out of the way. The club slashed down onto his left cheek, opening a gash, his mouth filling with the coppery taste of blood. Michael stifled a scream; even dulled by the painkillers in his system, the pain was almost too much to bear.

Snake stood up. "Good. Now I think you see where I'm coming from. You two!" He waved two men over. "Take this one to interrogation. Now!"

Hands went under his armpits to drag him away. Michael's neuronics pinged softly. The voice analyzer had a preliminary result. Michael's heart turned to ice as he read the report.

The men were Hammers.

Michael was hustled through a bewildering succession of corridors.

His escorts probably enjoyed the trip much more than Michael did, bouncing him off anything that caught their eyes along the way; Michael hissed with pain as new insults overlaid old injuries. By the time they got to the interrogation room—a small, brilliantly lit compartment—Michael was beginning to wonder how much more abuse he could take. His body was now one huge mass of pain, and the long gash on his back had opened up; he could feel it leaking blood again.

The two Hammers dragged him through the door and slammed him into a simple metal chair bolted to the deck. Michael screamed as the pain from his damaged ribs overwhelmed him. In seconds, they had his arms and legs plasticuffed to the chair. Immobilized, Michael sat there trying to recover, comming his neuronics to dump more painkillers into his tortured system. Trying to move was pointless, so he did not bother.

The painkillers cut in, a cool, soft wave washing through his body. Soon he was able to straighten up a bit and look around. The brilliantly lit compartment was bare except for a steel table behind which was an empty seat. No doubt it was intended for yet another hooded, shipsuited anonymity, Michael thought.

He did not have to wait long. Someone new appeared, this one a tall man, his shipsuit hanging down loose over a thin and stringy frame. Staying well clear of Michael, he made his way around the table. He stood there for a moment and looked down, his eyes beady, glittering in the harsh light. Michael decided to call this one Stork.

"So," Stork murmured softly as he sat down, rearranging the old-fashioned paper pad in front of him. Has to be the Hammer, Michael thought. Who else could it be? The rest of humanspace had stopped using paper centuries earlier. Stork looked him straight in the eye as he pulled out a pen. A bloody pen! Michael almost laughed. He was in some bizarre time warp.

"Right," Stork said finally. "Let's get started. Name, rank, and serial number."

"Helfort, Michael Wallace. Junior Lieutenant, Federated Worlds Space Fleet, serial number FC0216885."

Stork looked up at him in surprise. "Say that again!" he barked.

Michael sighed. This was getting tedious. His body was seriously damaged, his head felt like it had been hit with a shovel, he was exhausted, he felt sick inside at the thought of how many of *Ishaq*'s spacers must have been lost, and all this Hammer pig wanted was stuff he had already told them. Didn't they talk to each other?

"Helfort, Michael Wallace. Junior Lieutenant, Federated Worlds Space Fleet, serial number FC0216885."

"What ship?"

Michael shook his head. "Can't answer that."

Stork nodded and sat back. He looked at Michael for a long, long time. He nodded again before leaning forward to write out Michael's details in longhand on the paper pad. He then ripped the top sheet off. He put it carefully to one side and wrote something else. Michael struggled to read it, but he could not see well enough. It was too far away, and his eyes refused to focus. Stork got up and went to the door. There was a murmur of conversation, and then Stork was back, but without the paper. He's sent a message to someone, Michael said to himself; that's what he's done.

Stork stood over him. He shook his head slowly.

"Helfort, eh? I remember you. You had some part to play in what you Fed pigs call the Battle of Hell's Moons. I remember you from the holovid news. Bit of a fucking hero, I seem to recall. Well, that won't help you now, you sad sack of Fed shit. Not one little bit." With another shake of the head, Stork was gone, leaving Michael alone in the bleak plasteel compartment.

Michael's heart sank. If they thought for a moment he was important, they would watch him like a hawk. Goddamn it, he thought. Any chance he might have of escaping had gone up in smoke. He had a terrible feeling that the Hammers were going to be more than a bit interested in him, but what use could he be? He had been a small cog in a huge machine. More than that, the Hammers were taking great care to conceal who they were. That meant they did not want anyone to know that they had been behind the attack on *Ishaq*. That meant . . . An icy-cold hand took Michael's heart and squeezed it hard. Oh, God, he thought. That means we are dead. That is why they were trying to hard-kill the lifepods. No survivors meant no witnesses. No witnesses meant no exposure of the Hammers' part in whatever crazy game they were playing.

Michael found it hard to think straight but forced himself to go on. There could not be much time, and he had to work out a way to save himself and those few of the *Ishaq*'s crew lucky enough to have made it this far. He took a deep breath to steady himself, ignoring the pain beginning to burn back through the painkillers. There had to be a way. There must be a way. He thought and then thought harder, harder than he had ever thought before. His life depended on getting this right.

A buzz of voices announced the arrival of whoever it was Stork had called down. The new man, dressed like everyone else Michael had met, walked in quickly. Slamming the door, he sat down. The body language screamed senior officer, Michael thought. The man had that indefinable something that all brass projected. His eyes did, too. Startlingly blue, they were old eyes, the lines radiating out from them visible through the crude slits. They were the eyes of a man who had seen too much, who had watched death and destruction all his life. Suddenly, Michael felt very frightened. These were the eyes of a man to be afraid of.

The silence dragged on. Unaware he was even doing it, Michael pulled back from the man. His embryonic plan, which had looked so good only a moment before, appeared to be distinctly shaky. Well, he thought philosophically, it was all he had. Maybe the new man—Kingpig he was going to call him—would go for it.

Kingpig leaned forward. "So," he hissed venomously, "you're the famous hero of the Battle of Hell's Moons?"

Michael sat silently. Even if he had largely ignored it up to now, FedWorld training was emphatic on many things, especially on how to behave when under interrogation. Stay quiet as long as possible. Speak only when the level of physical duress becomes unbearable, and then say as little as possible.

Repeat ad nauseam until the cavalry came over the hill, shot the bad guys, rescued the good guys, and everyone lived happily ever after.

Yeah, right, Michael thought cynically. Somehow, he did not think the cavalry would get there in time.

He decided to throw the accumulated wisdom of the Fed-World's interrogation experts into the bin. He had to take the risk.

He nodded, then wished he hadn't. Christ, his head hurt. "I am, sir, though I think hero is overdoing it. I did my duty, just like you do yours."

"Ah, duty." Kingpig sat back. "Duty. It is such a convenient word. Duty—it covers so many sins, don't you think?"

Michael shook his head carefully. "I don't agree, sir. Not for us Feds. Maybe where you come from."

A narrowing of Kingpig's eyes warned Michael not to push too hard. Never forget this man is dangerous, he reminded himself. He took a deep breath. The time had come for the first roll of the dice.

"By the way, sir. We know who you are. You're Hammers. You're—"

"What? No, we are not!" Kingpig cut him off, his voice flat with barely controlled anger, his hands curling into fists pushed down onto the table. No, not just anger. There was something else there, Michael thought. Fear? What could this man be afraid of?

Well, Mister Kingpig, you are a bad liar, Michael thought, a really bad liar. He fought to keep his voice calm, even businesslike. He was not fighting for his life. His body was not a bruised, battered wreck. No. He and Kingpig were talking about the next flame-tree harvest. Businesspeople. Man to man.

"I'm sorry, sir," Michael insisted, "but you are Hammers. We know you are. First, your accents are a dead giveaway. It's pretty hard to mistake, you know." He paused to see how Kingpig would respond. The man did not move, but his eyes did, closing to narrow slits. Slowly, Michael cautioned himself, slowly. It was time for the big lie.

"Second, sir, the *Ishaq* got an intelligence report a few

weeks back. I must admit, it was pretty vague, but it did raise the possibility of a Hammer operation against allied traffic. Converted merchant ships fitted with rail guns. I don't remember the rest, but Fleet did not rate the report highly, so it was pretty well ignored. In retrospect, that was one big mistake, I think." Michael forced an angry bitterness into his voice. There may well have been such a report floating around the bureaucratic back blocks of Fleet, not that he or anyone else on board *Ishaq* had ever seen one. The only thing *Ishaq* had been given was all that crap about the Karlisle Alliance.

Michael watched Kingpig closely. His eyes had opened a fraction as Michael spoke. Bull's-eye, he thought. The man had bought it, he decided, so it was time for the next big lie.

"So you see, sir," Michael said, keeping his voice matter-of-fact, "it's only a matter of time before Fleet connects the dots, puts the Hammer in the frame for what's happened, and then I would say it's probably all over. Stand by to receive boarders, and they won't be coming for a chat over coffee and biscuits," he added cheerfully. He did not feel cheerful at all. His heart was pounding. If Kingpig believed him, it would be in his personal interest to look after Michael and the rest of the captured *Ishaq*s. The Feds took an extremely dim view of Hammers who spaced prisoners of war, pursuing those responsible to the ends of humanspace with a relentless, cold-burning fury, and every Hammer knew it. But if Kingpig did not believe him, his prospects were not good.

Kingpig sat unmoving.

Say something, you Hammer asshole, Michael thought. For Christ's sake, say something. But Kingpig was silent. Without another word, the man got to his feet and left the compartment, slamming the door behind him.

Michael was left alone for a long, long time. Unwilling to use the few painkiller drugbots he had left, he allowed the pain to return to his shattered body, wave after wave rising up until he began to drift in and out of consciousness. The Hammers must have done more damage than he realized, he thought as he started to slide into darkness.

He was jolted awake by the crash of the door opening. Three hooded men entered. His heart sank. He recognized two of them: Porky and Shithead. Without a word, the men cut away the plasticuffs before dragging him out of his seat and across the floor and then slamming him hard against the bulkhead. Michael's mouth was dry with fear as his arms were forced over his head, new plasticuffs pulled brutally tight to lock his wrists to the pipework. Then his legs were forced apart and tied off. He was defenseless. All he could do was hang there as the three men stood in front of him. Oh, no, he thought. They all held what looked like baseball bats, and his old friend Shithead, his eyes closed to the thinnest of thin slits, did not look like he was there to offer Michael batting tips.

Michael slowly emerged out of the darkness into a world of agony. His eyes would not open. Everything hurt badly except for the parts he could not feel. His left leg was dead. His groin was numb. The left side of his face was not there. Pain was everywhere else.

Slowly he got himself back under control. Comming the last of the painkillers into his system, he waited until the blessed wave of cool softness worked its magic. That was good, he thought. The only problem was that that was the end of them, and the way things were going, he would need a truckload more, and soon. With a huge effort, he started to put his hands up to his face. He had to see.

"Sir, sir!" The voice was urgent, demanding. "Sir, sir!" There was a muttering of voices; he could feel hands working on him. He could not make out what they were saying. Goddamn it! Why could he not see?

Another voice, much closer. "Sir! Lie back. We're just cleaning you up." Someone was shouting in the distance. Something about water. It made no sense.

"Mmmphhthh," he tried, but he could not speak. His mouth was full of something foul. It tasted coppery, metallic. His tongue was thick; the damn thing would not do what it was told. Michael lay back. God, he was tired. He slipped back into the darkness.

When he awoke, he felt better, though not much; everything still hurt like hell, but at least his head was clearer.

Cautiously, he opened his eyes, the sudden bright light making him wince with pain. He lay there for a moment. All he could see through slitted eyes was a distant deckhead hung with the usual confused mess of pipework, cables, lights, and gantries. That did not tell him much. One deckhead looked much like any other. He was in a hangar or cargo bay probably. Suddenly a face appeared. Michael's eyes would not focus properly, and so he had no idea who it was. The face was a blur.

The face spoke. Thank God, Michael thought. It was not another damn Hammer. "Ah! Good, you're awake. How do you feel?" the man asked.

"Uuurghhh." Michael tried to get his tongue to move properly. It felt thick, like an old wool sock. "Water," he croaked.

"Here you go," the face whispered gently.

Michael drank greedily. The water was cold, and there was plenty of it. It felt good. "Thanks," he mumbled gratefully.

"Tell me if you want more. You want more?"

Michael shook his head.

"So how do you feel?"

"Run over," Michael croaked. "By a truck. Hurts everywhere."

"Where mostly?"

"Ribs. Face. Bad."

"Okay. Lie there while I have another look at you."

Michael nodded weakly. Whoever the man was, he knew his stuff as he quickly and expertly checked Michael over, his fingers probing, prodding, and manipulating. When he was done, he leaned over.

"I know you won't believe me, but you're going to be fine, well, eventually. The damage is mainly superficial. So far as I can tell, no concussion, eyes and vision okay, no major bones broken, though your left cheekbone is in a bad way. Might be broken; can't tell. Nothing too serious internally that I can see. Plenty of cuts and bruises, a lot of ligament damage, especially to the ribs, and some broken teeth. Oh, and someone kicked you in the groin. There's a lot of swelling down there in all the wrong places, but that'll mend."

"Shithead."

"What?" The man sounded baffled. "Who? Me?"

Michael shook his head. "No, no. Not you. Shithead did that. After I did it to him. One of the Hammers."

The man looked confused. "Hammers? What Hammers?"

Michael struggled up into a sitting position. He quickly wished he had not; his ribs responded to the insult with a vicious stabbing wave of pain. "Holy Mother of God!" he whistled through clenched teeth. He waited until the pain receded a bit. "The men who've taken us. They're Hammers."

The man looked like he had been kicked. "Hammers. Oh, fuck!"

Michael nodded. " 'Oh, fuck' is right. What's your name?"

"Kaufmann, sir. Leading Spacer."

"Medic?"

"Not exactly, sir. I'm a comm tech, but I do have emergency first aid training."

"Ah, good. Thank God for that."

Michael looked around carefully for the first time, struggling to get his eyes to focus properly. It seemed he was one of about fifty spacers being held in a wire cage. Most looked okay, though some clearly were not. A couple in particular looked to be in a bad way, each with a small group around him doing what they could to help. He turned back to Kaufmann. "Who's senior here?"

"You are, sir. A couple of cadets are the only other officers; the rest are all spacers."

"Shit." The last thing Michael felt up to was doing the senior-officer-in-charge bit. "Okay. Who's the senior spacer here?"

"Warrant Officer McGrath, sir, but we don't think he's going to last. The ship's doctor has had a look. Severe head injuries, third-degree burns, internal injuries. He's in a really bad way. We're trying to keep him comfortable until, well, until . . ." Kaufmann looked down at the deck as his voice trailed off.

The rage roared up in Michael, obliterating everything else. "What!" he shouted, ignoring the screams of protest from his ravaged body. "The fucking doctor says he's dying, and he's just left him here? Get a guard here. Now! You and you!" He pointed to two young spacers sitting against the wire of the cage close to him, their faces white with the shock of it all. "Get me up."

With their help, Michael stood at the gate, hands locked into the wire to stay upright. "You," he shouted at one of the guards, "get over here. Get over here now or by God, you'll regret it." To Michael's surprise, the man, shipsuited and hooded like all the rest, did not need much persuading; he slouched over to see what Michael wanted.

"Yeah? Waddya want?"

"Right, you fucking piece of Hammer filth," he shouted furiously, "listen to me. You go now and get whoever's in charge of this circus. Tell him Helfort wants to see him. Now!"

The man stepped back in astonishment. Without another word, he spun on his heel and was gone.

Kaufmann was impressed. "Bugger me, sir. Don't fool around, do you?"

"Yeah, well. What has to be done and all that," he whispered as he slid down the wire and onto the deck.

When Michael shuffled painfully out of the interrogation room, he felt a brief moment of elation.

He did not know who Kingpig was, but the man was not all bad even if he had allowed him to be beaten to a bloody pulp. It turned out that the doctor had not bothered to inform Kingpig that some of his unwilling guests were dying and that more would die without proper medical attention. Kingpig had been visibly angry when Michael told him. Michael was glad he was not the doctor. It looked like the man's casual attitude toward his duties would cost him dearly. Even better, it seemed that Kingpig had bought the story that the Feds could soon be on to them. Michael did not know who they were, but there must be other officers in other cages, and they would have run the same analysis as Michael, and so they must know it was the Hammers they were up against.

The only flaw in Michael's hastily constructed position was the fictitious intelligence report. Kingpig had told him that all the other officers he had interrogated had flatly denied that any such thing existed. Kingpig must have attributed that to their unwillingness to reveal classified information; the possibility that they actually might be telling the truth did not seem to have occurred to him. So they were safe, for the moment at least.

When Michael was pushed back into the cage, he was pleased to see the Hammers already stretchering away the worst of the casualties. It seemed that Kingpig really was the man in charge or at least a man who could make things happen. Michael was exhausted. He had to sleep. He waved Kaufmann over.

"Sir?"

"Tell whoever is next senior after me that they're in charge. I can't do this mu . . ."

With that, Michael slumped to the deck before rolling slowly onto his side. Two seconds later, he was asleep.

Sunday, September 5, 2399, UD
HWS Quebec-One, *pinchspace*

Michael felt much better despite the fact that he was one huge ache shot through with sharp stabbing shards of pain from a brutally mistreated body. A good night's sleep made a huge difference, even if he had to sleep on the bare metal deck like all the rest of the spacers in his cage.

Things could have been a lot worse, he thought philosophically. The ship's doctor, now seemingly convinced that Michael was not a man to be trifled with, had taken great care to fix him up. To Michael's surprise, the lack of AI-controlled medibots made Hammer medicine no less effective, slower than he was used to but good enough. Now, wounds stitched and what turned out to be a fractured cheekbone operated on, Michael was happy to sit back and let the handful of remarkably effective painkillers he had been given work their magic. On top of that, the rest of his cage had been checked out; they had been fed and watered properly and given access to a crude but effective pair of heads installed in the cage behind a screen.

Arguably better than all of that, they had established a makeshift communication system with the rest of the *Ishaq*s captured by the Hammers. Under the cover of some suitable noisy diversion—singing badly at the top of their voices was popular—tap-code messages could make their way up the pipework that ran vertically through all the cages. Primitive it might be, slow it certainly was, but the system worked, and that was all that mattered.

Amid an ocean of bad news, there was some good. Fellsworth and Chief Ichiro both had survived; they were up two decks from Michael's cage in what the *Ishaq*s now called Cage Bravo, along with the rest of the women prisoners, 142 in all. They had gotten out of the warfare training department ahead of Michael, and their lifepod must have left the ship only seconds before his. Aaron Stone had made it, too, though he was badly injured and now in the ship's sick bay; nobody seemed to know if he would make it. Corporal Yazdi and Marine Murphy were okay, of course, the pair having survived the ordeal without so much as a scratch. Yazdi was in Cage Bravo. Murphy was up in Alpha. Leading Spacer Petrovic, Matti Bienefelt's classmate from basic training, was injured and still in the sick bay but would pull through. Sadly, so were a few people Michael would have traded for one of his friends in a heartbeat, Constanza supporters all of them.

Fellsworth appeared to be the ranking officer, so onto her shoulders fell the dubious honor of being senior officer. He wondered how that would sit with the Hammers. They had rigid views on the role of women in society. Cooking, cleaning, sex, babies, and deferring to men on all matters pretty well summed Hammer attitudes to women. Up against a set of prejudices a tacnuke could not shift, Fellsworth was not going to find being senior officer easy. Michael worked his way through the survivors one more time. "Bugger," he muttered. If the Hammers bypassed Fellsworth, the next in line was a Lieutenant Commander Hashemian and then his old friend, Xing. Hashemian was very bad news; from the moment they had met, the man had made no attempt to conceal a bitter resentment of Michael. He and Xing were soul mates of the worst sort. If the Hammers refused to work with Fellsworth and one of those useless timeservers ended up as the man in charge, God help them all, Michael thought.

There was bad news, of course, and much too much of it. Only 286 *Ishaq*s had gotten clear before the ship blew. Petty Officer Bettany had not made it. Word was that rail-gun slugs had caught him. Michael felt awful. His probably had been one of the bodies Michael had climbed over on his way to the lifepods.

Constanza, Morrissen, and the command and sensors teams had all died when a rail-gun salvo had hit *Ishaq*'s aft quarter, the slugs penetrating the armor up into the combat information and sensor management centers, both of which were packed for the ship's drop into normalspace. He did not give a damn about Constanza, but Morrissen and all the rest deserved better. *Ishaq*'s marines and air group were all pretty well gone, too, lost when the ship's mine magazine on 8 Deck went up, triggering a sympathetic detonation in the aft missile magazine.

Michael had sat in a corner as the full import of the news sank in. Head in his arms, he had wept silently as the enormity of what had happened hit home. Most of the people Michael had been close to on board were gone, their deaths fueling the white-hot flame of hate that burned deep inside him. When he ran through the list of survivors, he swore he would do whatever it took to destroy the Hammer.

The moment of weakness did not last long. Michael buried the grief deep inside and got on with surviving. Enduring was all that mattered. He had to survive long enough to make the Hammers pay in full for the pain and suffering they seemed determined to inflict on the rest of humanspace.

His second in command, Chief Ferreira, dropped to the deck beside him.

"How are things, sir?"

"Ripping along, Chief, ripping along. How are the troops today?"

"Oh, you know, sir. They're all pretty shell-shocked by it all but otherwise okay. They're starting to complain about things, so that's a good sign."

Michael smiled. Fleet folklore said the time to worry about spacers' morale was when they stopped complaining about things in general and the food in particular. His dad had always sworn by the old adage; he reckoned he should, too.

"Good. I'm going to ask Kingpig for exercise time. I'm going to suggest another cage. We can play futbol or something."

"That'd be good. Another few days and this lot"—Ferreira waved an arm at the cage's occupants—"will be getting antsy. Be good to head that off."

"I agree. I'll have a go today. Apart from that, anything?"

"Nothing serious. Nelson and Khurtsidze are due to go back to sick bay to have dressings changed at 10:00. That's about it." Ferreira paused for a second. "Sir?"

"Yes?"

"Well . . ."

"Come on, Chief. Spit it out!"

"What do you think we're in for?"

Michael shook his head. "Honestly, I don't know. I think I've managed to convince Kingpig that Fleet knows the Hammers are responsible, so I don't think they'll space us. Even the dumbest Hammer knows they'll be hunted down if they do. That means a prison camp somewhere. But beyond that?" He shook his head. "I have no idea. It's what, three hundred plus light-years from Xiang Reef back to the Hammer Worlds? If that's where we are going, we'll be dropping sometime during the afternoon of the twelfth. Say a week from today." Michael shrugged his shoulders. "If we drop earlier or later than that, then your guess will be as good as mine."

"Shit." Ferreira leaned back against the wire and thought about it for a while. "A week. Long time. Any chance of taking the ship?"

"I wish." Michael shook his head sadly. He looked around. "No, don't think so. Christ, a baby with a teaspoon could get us out of these cages. The problem is that the Hammers know that. Notice how they keep us covered all the time from the main access lock with stun guns anytime we go in or out of the cage? We could rush them, but I don't think we would get far. Anyway, as of last night, word from on high"—Michael pointed up to the women's cage two decks above—"is to sit tight and protect the escape kits. Sorry, meant to tell you, but you'd crashed out."

"No prob, sir. Much as I would like to think we could take this sucker and swan on home, I don't think we could. I would put good money down that Kingpig is too smart."

"So would I, Chief. So would I."

Sunday, September 12, 2399, UD
HWS Quebec-One, *pinchspace*

The week dragged on interminably, and the pressure of sitting around doing nothing was beginning to tell. The only thing that broke the monotony was an endless round of interrogations, in Michael's case more than all the others in his cage put together. The Hammer interrogators were very good, and Michael thought they were sounding less and less convinced by his fictitious account of intelligence linking them to the mership attacks. Not that it mattered much anymore, though. The lie had served its purpose. The Hammers had not killed the survivors from the *Ishaq,* and Michael did not think they would.

The inactivity was hard to take. Despite Michael's best efforts, Kingpig had rejected his idea of a cage for futbol out of hand. Worse, Michael's authority was beginning to wear thin as he chivvied his troops to stay active and positive.

Tempers were beginning to fray. Fights, sometimes bad ones, were all too common. The Hammers did not seem to care. Safe behind their stun guns, they watched from a distance as Michael, Ferreira, and anyone else who could be bothered to help broke up the fights.

Michael sighed. In another few hours, they should know their fate.

Michael sat bolt upright as the characteristic hum of the ship's main broadcast being switched on cut through the desultory buzz of spacers talking among themselves. It had never been switched on before. Michael was sure he knew what it meant. Here we go, he thought. This has to be the drop.

"All stations. Stand by to drop in five minutes. Five minutes. Out."

For a moment, the cage was silent. Then it erupted in a welter of excited talk, the boredom and ennui that had blanketed the spacers for days gone in a flash. Michael shouted for silence.

"Okay, guys. Get ready for the drop. Let's hope these Hammer filth are taking us somewhere nice."

It was a pretty sad joke, Michael thought as laughter, almost hysterical in its intensity, engulfed the cage.

The excitement of the drop out of pinchspace had evaporated long before.

Michael stood by the wire, hands jammed into the pockets of his tattered shipsuit. Behind him, the occupants of his cage lay sprawled across the deck, awake but silent. Michael cursed the Hammers. What in God's name were they doing? Probably fighting over who would get their hands on the *Ishaq*s, he thought. Utterly depressed, he slumped to the deck; with nothing better to do, he was asleep in a matter of seconds.

A violent crash jerked him awake and onto his feet. What now?

It was Porky, smashing his club on the wire to get their attention; hooded or not, Michael would recognize the man anywhere.

Porky came to the wire where Michael stood. Behind him,

two more spacers stood, well back, stun guns leveled at the cage and its occupants.

"Get your men on their feet, Helfort."

"What's happening?"

"Helfort"—Porky sounded utterly uninterested—"if there's anything I think you should know, I'll tell you. Now, get your men on their feet."

Michael shrugged his shoulders. "Okay." He turned to his men. "On your feet, everyone. Come on," he said to the laggards, "on your feet."

Porky waited until all the *Ishaq*s were standing. He stepped away from the crude gate cut into the wire. "Right," he ordered with quiet authority. "When I call out your name, leave the cage, turn forward, and go through the air lock door. Leading Spacer Järvinen, let's be having you."

One by one, Porky called out the occupants of Michael's cage. The numbers thinned quickly, but Michael was not too concerned. Rank had its privileges, after all, and being last to leave was one of them. When the only remaining spacer left the cage, Michael stepped forward and made to follow the rest of his men.

"Where the fuck do you think you're going, Helfort?" Porky hissed venomously.

"Leaving, like the rest," Michael said, puzzled. "Why?"

"No, you're not. Get back from the gate, you piece of Fed scum."

Michael stepped backward, his confusion total.

After locking the gate and without another word, Porky and his backup left the compartment. Michael stood unmoving for a long time. He was alone and very afraid.

The men who appeared at the cage door were something new.

They did not wear hoods, for a start, and a quick search through his Hammer information base told him they were dressed in the black uniforms of the Hammer's Doctrinal Security Service. Two chevrons woven in silver thread into the black fabric marked one out as a corporal. The other was a trooper. Shit, Michael thought. DocSec; that was all he needed. He had heard a lot about DocSec, none of it good. If half of what he had heard was true, DocSec was a truly nasty organization, the Hammer's internal security force and secret police rolled into one.

Michael made his way to the wire.

"Yes?" He put as much authority into his voice as he could muster. "What do you want?"

"You, sir," the corporal replied. "I want you. Junior Lieutenant Helfort, right?"

Michael nodded.

"Good. Come with us, sir," the corporal ordered, his voice polite but firm. "Stand away from the gate, please."

The DocSec trooper unlocked the gate and stepped back. "Come through, sir."

Warily, Michael stepped through. Pleasant though the two men were being, they were still DocSec. The two black-uniformed men plasticuffed his hands behind him before taking him by the arms and hustling him out of the cargo bay, their footsteps echoing through the huge empty space.

The instant the air lock from the cargo bay shut behind them, the two DocSec troopers stopped being polite. The trooper took Michael by the hair on the back of his head. The corporal stepped in front of him; with vicious deliberation, he hit Michael heavily three times across the face. With his hands secured behind him, Michael could do nothing to protect himself except twist his head to one side in a frantic bid to escape the attack. It was futile. He grunted in pain as the first blow smashed into his face, a ring on the corporal's right hand opening up a deep cut across his forehead to drop a curtain of blood down his face and onto his wrecked ship-suit. The second was worse, his newly repaired cheekbone absorbing the full impact of the backhander. Michael screamed in agony. He did not even feel the third as it turned his mouth into a bloody wreck.

The corporal put his mouth to Michael's ear. "Now, Helfort, let me explain something," he hissed. "We don't give a fuck whether you live or die. So do as you are told and don't talk until you're ordered to. Got it?"

Michael could barely speak, the pain was so intense.

"Yes," he mumbled, fresh blood frothing up into small bubbles across his battered mouth. "Understood."

"Good. Right, Helfort. I've got good news. You're going dirtside. There are some people who really, really want to talk to you."

Michael did not much care anymore. They could put him in lead boots and drop him into thirty meters of liquid pig shit for all he cared right now. Dripping blood, he was half dragged, half pushed along yet more corridors, down two levels in a drop tube, and along another set of corridors until finally they got to a lander for transfer dirtside. He had screamed with pain most of the way as his tortured body was driven into every hard projection they passed. The troopers' only response had been to backhand him again and tell him to shut the fuck up before smashing him into the next door frame they came to.

Dragged through what looked like a lander's air lock, Michael was pulled down a short corridor and into a small compartment. He was thrown bodily onto a metal rack, his plasticuffs quickly and efficiently replaced by a single plasfiber wrist strap secured to the lander's hull. Then, with a parting slap to the head, the DocSec troopers left him alone.

Michael lay barely able to move, searching desperately for the last of the painkillers he had been given by the Hammer doctor. Digging them out, he swallowed them gratefully. When the pain finally started to subside, Michael had a look around through blood-gummed eyes. What he saw did nothing to improve his morale. The lander had been stripped down to absolute basics. There were no seats, only open-meshed metal racks layered deck to deckhead, one of which he now occupied. Frankly, he did not much care. Being left alone was more than enough for him.

Bit by bit the pain receded. Encouraged, Michael experimented. He could move, but not without protest from his badly battered body. He resigned himself to an uncomfortable trip dirtside.

He made a promise to himself: He was going to get out of this one way or another. He had no idea how, but he was not going to give up. Buoyed by his new resolve, he waited until shock and tiredness started to push him under. He made himself as comfortable as the metal rack and limited headroom allowed and did his best to sleep.

He had almost succeeded when, with no warning, the lander unberthed to start its long drop down the gravity well to the planet below. Which planet, he had absolutely no idea. The DocSec pilot clearly did not care too much for his passengers, and the entire journey down seemed designed to make life as miserable as possible, every maneuver so violent that Michael began to wonder how the lander's airframe could take such abuse. To Michael's relief, the lander finally thumped down, but with such casual violence that his aching head was whipped from side to side. He could not wait to get off. The brutal trip had made him lose his breakfast, but at least he now understood why the inside of the lander was bare metal. It was obvious, really; it made hosing it out that much easier. God knew what it must be like with a full complement of prisoners. He could only hope that he would never have to find out.

The moment the lander came to a halt, bobbing on its landing gear, the two troopers were back, seemingly unaffected by the state of the compartment Michael had been held in and apparently untroubled by the rough trip dirtside. Unstrapped, pulled unceremoniously down from his rack, he was half carried, half dragged off the lander and down the ramp into the hot, humid air of what looked like early evening. Michael had only a few seconds to look around before he was bundled carelessly into the back of a small van with blacked-out windows and plasticuffed to the seat frame. The whole routine was as cruelly rough as before, to the point where Michael began to think—when he could think between bouts of agonizing pain—that inflicting pain had to be a trade skill taught wherever DocSec troopers were trained to be the vicious thugs they all obviously were.

Two hours and two more rounds of gratuitous brutality later, Michael was thrown bodily into a small cell. A single small window set high in one wall lighted the bleak plascrete box; the light recessed into the ceiling was off. Michael sat looking up at plasglass-filtered sunlight dappling one wall of the cell an orange-red. Suddenly, it was all too much, and he began to cry. He could not stop, his tears washing tracks down through the dried blood caking his face.

He had never felt so alone in all his life.

Sunday, September 12, 2399, UD
Chief Councillor's residence, city of McNair,
Commitment

Fleet Admiral Jorge stood unmoving as Chief Councillor Polk's rage washed over him, the relentless torrent of invective like nothing he had ever been subjected to before.

"Sir!" he said, rather more firmly than he had intended—a lot more firmly, in fact.

Polk stopped dead, staring at Jorge, his face an angry red mask.

"Sir," Jorge continued gently. "What's done is done. Can I remind you that it is a long time since any Hammer ship took on and beat a Fed heavy cruiser? In fact, sir"—Jorge was warming to his task now—"I will be submitting a recommendation that Commodore Monroe be awarded the Star of Kraa for his leadership of Operation Cavalcade to date. I will also—"

Polk's hand went up. Polk stared at him for a long time. To Jorge's surprise, the man smiled for an instant. Then, to Jorge's utter astonishment, the bloody man was laughing, his chest heaving until tears began to run down his cheeks.

"By Kraa, Admiral, you really are something else," Polk sputtered finally, getting himself back under control with an obvious effort, wiping the tears from his eyes. He shook his head in disbelief. "You are unbelievable. Absolutely unbelievable. I wanted to have the bloody man shot. Kraa's blood, I wanted to have you shot, too, but no! You want me to give him a medal! Not any old medal, either. Oh, no. You want me to give him the Star of Kraa, no less!" Polk's voice rose in disbelief. He took a deep breath and waved a hand at Jorge. "For Kraa's sake, sit down, Admiral. Sit," he said resignedly.

"Thank you, sir." Jorge sat, praying as hard as he could that the storm was over.

"So if I accept your proposition that Monroe did the right thing," Polk went on, to Jorge's relief sounding much more relaxed, "then what the hell am I going to do with Kraa knows how many damn Fed spacers? I don't suppose you'll let me have DocSec shoot them?" Polk asked hopefully.

"Sir, we have that under control, and"—Jorge's voice hardened noticeably—"with all due respect, having them shot by DocSec is not a good option. On behalf of Fleet, I must point out that our spacers get captured, too. If the Feds find out we have shot almost three hundred of theirs—and they will—then . . . well, let's just say it makes things very difficult all around." Not to mention the fact that the Feds will pursue me to the ends of humanspace and beyond, he thought despairingly.

Polk stared at Jorge bleakly, all traces of good humor gone. "You know, Admiral, I don't think I will ever understand spacers. Kraa! The things you get worked up about! I really don't give a rat's ass what the Feds do to Hammer prisoners of war." Polk snorted dismissively. "The cowardly losers should not have let themselves be captured in the first place. They're no damn good to us anymore, that's for sure, so the Feds can make meat pies out of them for all I care."

The look on Jorge's face—a mixture of horror and disgust—stopped Polk dead. "All right, Admiral, all right. I'll let this one go," he conceded reluctantly. "I know these things matter to you, but I'm sure I don't have to warn you what happens if the Feds find out about Cavalcade before we decide to let them in on the secret."

"No, sir," Jorge agreed stiffly, trying extremely hard to keep the relief out of his voice, "you don't."

"Good. Let's get on with it. So, these Feds. If I can't have them shot, what in Kraa's name are you going to do with them?"

"That problem's been solved, sir. They're in transit to one of Fleet's old camps from the last war, the most remote my staff could find, on Maranzika. Nobody will know they even exist. The camp is so remote that escape is pointless, I have imposed a complete communications blackout, and an air exclusion zone is now in force around the camp. Supply and security have been taken over by Operation Cavalcade personnel, so operational security will not be compromised."

Jorge held his breath. Polk had to be reassured that Cavalcade operational security really was safe; if Polk was not, he was dead. After a lifetime's thought, Polk nodded his head.

Jorge breathed out slowly—the man did not look happy, but then again, neither was he tearing his head off, so maybe he had gotten away with it—before continuing. "There is one exception, though, sir. One of the Feds is an officer called Helfort, Michael Helfort."

Polk looked puzzled "Helfort? Who the hell is Helfort? Remind me."

"Well, sir. According to the Feds, he's one of the heroes of what they like to call the Battle of Hell's Moons. Quite a celebrity, I understand."

Polk scowled. "Ah, yes. Helfort. A smug little man. I remember him now. Bloody Feds. What about him?"

"DocSec's Section 22 has him in custody. They think he might be useful. He might be, er, well, persuaded to put a different spin on the *Mumtaz* affair." Jorge did his best to keep a straight face; privately, he thought DocSec had lost the plot, but if they wanted Helfort, he was happy to oblige. But there were some things he did not want Polk finding out about; the fact that he had horse-traded Helfort to DocSec in exchange for the right to keep the rest of the Feds under Fleet control was one of them.

Polk grunted derisively. "Admiral, why in Kraa's name would I care? The *Mumtaz* affair is history. If DocSec wants to play with him, that's fine by me. At least Section 22 can be trusted to keep their mouths shut."

Jorge nodded. Polk was right. By Kraa! If there was one thing DocSec was really good at, it was keeping secrets, and Section 22—the section responsible for VIPs—was the best.

"So," Polk continued, "whatever. Have DocSec brief me if anything of value comes up. That'll be all, Admiral. You can go."

Monday, September 13, 2399, UD
Secure Interrogation Facility Bravo-6, Commitment

Michael awoke with a start as the door to his cell crashed open with a bang. He had fallen asleep where he had been sitting and was stiff and sore. Sometime during the night he had toppled over without waking up, ending up curled into a fetal ball on the cold plascrete floor.

Oh, no, Michael thought as he looked up through sleep-fogged eyes still clogged with blood, cringing away from the black-uniformed figure towering over him. Not another beating. Please, God, not another beating. He was not sure he could take much more of this.

"Hello, Helfort. I'm Colonel Erwin Hartspring, Section 22, Doctrinal Security Service," the man declared pleasantly, tapping his thigh with what looked like a short riding crop held in his left hand.

The man was tall, his body lean, muscles whipcord taut under an immaculately pressed tight black uniform with woven silver badges and a small row of medal ribbons on the left breast. His face was long and gaunt, with wrinkle-cut skin stretched tight over prominent cheekbones, windburned to a reddish-brown and sharpened by a straight nose dropping to a fine pencil mustache above thin, bloodless lips. His hair was cut down to a fine black stubble. It was the man's eyes that made Michael's heart sink. They were a pale, washed-out amber. They looked empty, pitiless. They were the eyes of a man who had seen too much to care about the battered, blood-soaked body at his feet. The man was a trash-press parody of a cold-blooded killer.

Michael shivered.

Hartspring leaned forward, the better to look at Michael, poking him with his riding crop. He winced, nose wrinkling in disgust.

"Oh, dear!" The man stepped back. "You are a bit of a mess, and to say you smell bad is an understatement. Really," he added conversationally, "I keep telling my troopers to be more careful, but you know what?" Michael looked up at him suspiciously.

Hartspring paused.

Michael was obviously supposed to answer, so he shook his head. "No, sir," he mumbled.

"I tell them, Michael, not to damage the goods, but you know what? I don't think they listen to me." He shook his head in mock despair. "Very coarse people, you know, these DocSec troopers. Most of them are not very bright and much too fond of the sight of blood for my liking. Other people's blood, of course. They hate seeing their own. Oh, well, can't be helped, I suppose." He sighed in resignation.

He turned and shouted through the open cell door. "Sergeant!"

A well-built, powerfully muscled man a good head and a half shorter than Hartspring appeared in an instant. "Sir?"

"This is Sergeant Jacobsen, Helfort. Sergeant Jacobsen?"

"Sir?"

"Say good morning to Junior Lieutenant Helfort. He's the hero of the Battle of Hell's Moons, you know. If Fed holovids are to be believed."

Jacobsen's face was completely blank. He did not look at Michael. "Good morning, sir," he barked at the far wall of the cell.

Hartspring smiled. "See how polite we can be, Helfort? Remember that, won't you."

He turned back to Jacobsen. "Now, Sergeant. This is what I want you to do. Doctor first. Tell that lazy scab-lifting son of a bitch that this is one of my Class A prisoners. Tell him that if I find that my very important Class A prisoner hasn't been fixed up properly, then I'll be fixing him up. Permanently. Got that?"

"Sir!" Jacobsen's face was impassive.

"Good. When the doctor's finished, take Helfort to Suite 517. I want him stripped, searched again, and then cleaned up. Bath, clean clothes, something to eat. You know the routine. When he's done, give me a call."

"Sir."

With that, Colonel Hartspring was gone. Jacobsen reached down. Taking Michael by the collar of his tattered shipsuit, he lifted him effortlessly to his feet and bundled him out of the cell.

The whole business was completely unreal.

Without warning, Michael had risen from a living hell into a bizarre fantasy world, a world a million light-years away from the squalid brutality of plascrete cells and sullen thugs seemingly committed to making his every conscious minute a pain-filled nightmare.

In front of him were the remains of breakfast, probably the best Michael had ever enjoyed despite the pain eating involved. Michael, his appetite more than restored by the fact that some DocSec thug was not about to give him a good kicking, had demolished the spread as fast as his wrecked mouth and face would allow.

Comfortably bloated, he sat back. To all intents and purposes, he was in a luxury suite that would not have disgraced a five-star hotel. In fact, it was better than anything Michael had ever stayed in. Well, up to a point. The place was a luxury suite only if one ignored the fact that the door was plasteel and locked, the windows were plasglass and sealed, and his every move was watched by holocams covering every cubic centimeter of the suite. He could not even take a crap without being watched, for God's sake. He laughed mirthlessly at the thought he might become a star of Hammer holovids. Michael Helfort takes a dump, now live on Channel 43!

Oh, and there was not a single thing in the whole apartment he could use to commit suicide. Nothing. He knew. He had looked everywhere.

Not that he planned to commit suicide, but it was always an option if things got too tough, he supposed. He could break out one of his escape kits, the one with the handy length of monofil line, but the thought of it slicing his head off if he tried to hang himself was more than he could bear. Worse, if he did, the Hammers would know about the kits, and that would screw things up big-time for everyone else. A sudden shiver ran up his spine. For all he knew, the Hammer had shot the rest of the *Ishaq*s out of hand. Maybe they were all in the lime pits. Maybe he was the last—

Michael forced himself to stop. Wondering what might have happened to the rest of the *Ishaq*'s crew would get him nowhere. He had done what little he could. What he should be thinking about now was himself.

Things were going to get tough again. He knew that. Michael was no fool. He knew what Colonel Hartspring was up to. He knew why Sergeant Jacobsen had been paraded in front of him. Good cop, bad cop. Soft man, hard man. Pampered one minute, beaten half to death the next. Michael shivered. It was all so clichéd; he knew exactly where this was all heading, and if he could not find a way out, he might end up so badly damaged that he would be better off dead.

Some Hammer genius had decided that he had something to offer. Clearly, the Hammers being the Hammers, they would do whatever it took to get what they wanted. That much was for sure.

He did not know if he could hold out long enough to convince them he would never, ever cooperate. Would they stop before they killed him in the process? Would they even care? Probably not, he suspected.

He shivered, the sudden rush of sour fear turning his stomach over and over and over as he bolted out of his chair. He just made it to the toilet, where he lost the breakfast he had enjoyed so much, his ribs screaming in pain as spasm after violent spasm racked his body. Jeez, he thought, slumping to the floor to recover, that was fun.

Cleaning himself up, Michael came out of the bathroom, and there he was. Colonel Hartspring stood silent in the middle of the room, a half smile on his face, riding crop in hand. Sergeant Jacobsen, face as inscrutable as ever, stood half a pace behind him and to one side.

"Not feeling too well, Michael?"

Michael stared for a second. Then he snapped. "Fuck you, Hartspring!" He did not stop to think, his body speaking for him, his system suddenly fear-charged with enough adrenaline to get across the gap to Hartspring in an instant. If he was lucky, he might rip the colonel's eyes out before Sergeant Jacobsen beat him to death.

Hartspring did not move, though his eyes narrowed in a sudden flash of anger. Michael took a deep breath, fighting to get himself back under control. Careful, Michael reminded himself, careful. Hartspring was a DocSec colonel, and they came in only one variety: lethally dangerous.

When Hartspring finally spoke, his voice was gentle and conciliatory. "Come on, Michael. No need for that," he urged patiently, as if Michael were a wayward child. "Come on, sit down," he said, pointing to a chair with his little cane. "We need to talk."

Without a word, Michael did as he was told, watching Hartspring warily as the man settled himself into a chair opposite him.

"Now." Hartspring leaned forward. "Listen to me, Michael. We can do this the easy way or we can—"

Astonished, Hartspring stopped as Michael lost it completely for the second time in as many minutes, but this time there was no anger. This time his head went back, and he laughed hysterically, chest heaving despite the pain, tears pouring down his face, hands slapping the arms of the chair. "Oh, Jesus! That hurts," he sobbed, half laughing, half crying, near hysteria. "Really, Colonel Hartspring." He paused to wipe his face, carefully avoiding the latest repairs to his shattered cheekbone. "Colonel . . ."

Michael put his hands up, palms out, in an attempt to pacify Hartspring; by now the man looked pretty pissed. Michael decided he had to go for it. He had to take the chance.

"Colonel," he apologized, "I'm sorry, really I am. Please

forgive me, but save the corny trashvid stuff. I know how you guys do things. I know all about DocSec. You're going to be nice to me, make me an offer, God knows what about. I'll refuse, then your tame gorilla here"—Michael waved a dismissive hand at Jacobsen—"will beat the shit out of me, then you'll be nice again. Around and around we'll go until I drop dead or you get what you want."

Hartspring sat mute, refusing to respond.

Michael plowed on. "So, Colonel, let's cut to the chase. Why don't you tell me exactly what you want. I'll think about it and let you know if I can do what you want or not. If I can, then fine, I will. If I can't, then I'll tell you straight up."

Michael took in a slow, deep breath. The moment had come for another big, big lie. He was getting good at them. He stared Hartspring right in the eye, face fixed in what he fondly hoped was a convincing look of earnest good faith.

"But here's the catch, Colonel. If you lay a hand on me after that, I'll order my neuronics to put me into a coma, a terminal coma. Your Doctor Whatshisname out there will never get me back. No Hammer doctor will ever get me back. Doesn't matter how good they are. If you don't get me to a Fed doctor inside sixty days, I'll slip away quietly, and that'll be that. You can feed me to the pigs. You can have me stuffed and mounted on a pedestal. You can chuck me into one of your damn lime pits. I won't know, and I sure as hell won't care."

For a moment, Hartspring sat there. In an instant, he was out of his seat and, blindingly fast, reaching across to Michael, his riding crop slashing down backhanded. The crop sliced down across Michael's face, reopening the cut across his forehead before a second slashing blow added a new cut to the side of his head. Thank God he's not left-handed, Michael thought through the blinding pain, forcing himself not to respond. If Hartspring had been, his left cheekbone would have gone for the third time.

With obvious effort, Hartspring got himself back under control. He stood back.

Michael looked up at him, ignoring the blood running down his face. "I think you heard me, Colonel," he said through teeth clenched tight with pain. "So do we have a deal?"

Hartspring half turned to Jacobsen. For one awful moment, Michael thought he was going to call his bluff and put Jacobsen to work. His heart began to pound, but Hartspring had other plans.

"Sergeant! Take Helfort to the doctor. Get him stitched up. I want him back here within the hour. Understood?"

"Sir."

Hartspring turned and left.

A long and painful hour later, Hartspring returned.

"Right, Helfort. Sit down. I'll make this quick. In exchange for your life, resettlement under a new identity anywhere in humanspace, and a one-time payment of five million Fed-Marks, the government of the Hammer of Kraa requires you to sign this affidavit"—Hartspring pushed a single sheet of paper across the table—"testifying to the fact that the Battle of Hell's Moons was part of a wider Fed campaign to destroy the Hammer of Kraa and that the hijacking of the *Mumtaz* was nothing more than a convenient excuse for an illegal act of military adventurism."

Michael's eyebrows shot up as Hartspring sat back. What a load of bullshit, he thought. The man was barking mad.

"Thank you, Colonel." Michael kept his tone businesslike. "That's clear. May I think about what you're asking me to do?"

"You do that, Helfort. I'll be back at 09:00 tomorrow for your answer."

"Thank you, sir. I don't suppose you'll let me talk it over with someone from the FedWorld embassy?" he added.

"Don't push your damn luck, Helfort. Remember where you are," Hartspring replied viciously. "I'll see you at 09:00 tomorrow."

"Fine by me, sir."

Michael watched Hartspring leave. He stared at the door as it shut with a heavy thud, locks closing with metallic thunks.

Grabbing a big glass of fresh orange juice, he sat down to

think through Hartspring's offer, not that it needed any thinking, really. He already knew the answer—it would be some
variation or other on the time-honored theme of "go fuck
yourself"—but he needed to be sure he had no better options.

He shook his head in bewilderment. Why the Hammers
thought putting him up on the stand would help improve
their image was a complete mystery. Now, if they could get a
Fed admiral to turn over, that would be worth the effort. But
a humble junior lieutenant? It was complete bullshit.

Michael realized that what he was seeing here was a textbook example of a culture that believed its own propaganda.
Well, he decided, that's what you got when dissent was ruth-
lessly suppressed, when reasoned argument was impossible.
After all, arguing with someone who had the power of life
and death over you was probably a good way to end up in a
DocSec lime pit.

Well, be that as it may. He could not change what a bunch
of dumb Hammers might think, and he was not going to try.
He had rolled the dice. He had told the big lie. Either the colonel believed he could put himself into a coma at will or he
did not.

If Hartspring did not believe him, he was completely
screwed. The Hammers would soft-soap him one minute and
beat the crap out of him the next until he either gave in or
died. Michael shivered, the fear coming out of nowhere to
grab him, turning his bowels to water. He was scared, more
scared than he had been looking out at an oncoming Hammer rail-gun salvo.

He cursed silently. It was going to be a long, long day.

Michael started as the door banged open. It was Colonel Hartspring, on time to the second, followed by the ever-watchful Sergeant Jacobsen. Michael searched Hartspring's face for clues, but the man was impassive as he waved Michael into a chair and sat down himself.

"So, Michael. What's the answer? Do we have a deal?"

Michael shook his head. "No, we do not. I cannot do what you want me to do. I'm sorry."

Hartspring put his head back and sighed. It was the sigh of a patient man coming to the end of his tether. Nice acting, you Hammer pig, Michael thought as his heart sank. Hartspring leaned forward and looked straight at him.

"I know you think we're fools, Michael." His hand went up as Michael started to protest. "No, let me finish." He paused to regather his thoughts. "We're not, you know. Well," he said, tapping the table with his riding crop—Michael had never seen him without it—for emphasis, "I'm not. Now, personally, I happen to think you're a damn liar. All that crap about comas and so on."

Michael's heart headed for his boots. Oh, shit. Here we go, he thought, instinctively bracing himself for the inevitable onslaught from Jacobsen.

"Now, those set above me by the power of Kraa, while they agree with me that you are a damn liar, aren't willing to take the chance that you might be telling the truth. They think a dead Helfort might be more of a problem than a live Helfort even if the little fucker won't do what we want him to. But let me tell you something else, Helfort." Hartspring spit contemptuously. "I always thought you weren't worth the trouble, Helfort, and I was right. You're just another piece of useless Fed crap. So, the bad news is this. I'm going to ignore my bosses and take the chance that you might just be telling the truth."

Michael's spirits crashed. Hartspring got to his feet and looked down at him for a moment, his face a mix of scorn and anger.

"Filth." He nodded, the riding crop pointed right into Michael's face. "Lying Fed filth, that's what you are. Well, you had your chance. No more Class A privileges for you," he said, waving his arm around at the luxurious suite. "Effective immediately, you're a Class D prisoner. Sergeant Jacobsen!"

"Sir?" Jacobsen stepped forward.

"You know what to do," Hartspring said, turning to leave. "And for Kraa's sake, Sergeant! Try not to kill him."

"Sir!"

Jacobsen stared at Michael. A small smile ghosting across Jacobsen's face crashed Michael's spirit even further. This did not look good, and he was pretty damn sure Class D prisoners did not count for much in DocSec's perverted, psychopathic scheme of things.

Michael stood up. "Sir?"

Hartspring turned back, looking irritated. Obviously, Class D prisoners weren't worthy of a DocSec Colonel's attention.

"What?" he barked sharply.

"What happens now? Where do—"

That was as far as he got. Jacobsen, taking a half step back, whipped out a small stun pistol. Casually, he stun-shot Michael in both legs, dropping him to the floor screaming, his back arching up off the floor, his mouth a rictus of agony.

Jacobsen stood over him, waiting patiently until Michael recovered. "New rules, Helfort. One, you're not Helfort anymore. You're 419963-Q now. Second, you talk only when I tell you to. Understood?"

"Yes, Sergeant."

"That's sir, you Fed maggot!" Jacobsen shouted, stamping his boot hard into Michael's stomach. Michael rolled away in agony, his mouth open wide as tortured lungs fought for air.

"Understood, sir," Michael whispered when he finally regained his voice. God's blood! When would it end?

With great care, Jacobsen leant forward and spit into Michael's face. "Good. I hope you do understand, 419963-Q. I really do, but to make sure . . ."

The door to Michael's cell smashed open, dragging Michael out of nightmare-racked sleep.

Two DocSec troopers burst in. Wordlessly, one grabbed him, pinning him hard against the wall. The second put what looked like a gas-powered inoculation gun against his neck. That was what it was. There was a brief *pffftt* and a short, sharp, stinging pain, and then Michael was dragged out of the cell along an endless series of corridors to a loading dock, thrown into a van, plasticuffed, and left alone.

He sat slumped, too stunned even to think. It all had happened so quickly. Since Sergeant Jacobsen had dumped him, battered to the edge of unconsciousness and bleeding all over the floor of his new cell, he had not seen or spoken to anyone. If not for his neuronics, he would not even know what day it was. The light had never gone off, and meals had come seemingly only when some damn DocSec guard could be bothered to sling the filthy slop that passed for food in through the tiny slot at the bottom of the cell door.

With a start, Michael realized with mounting horror that whatever he had been injected with was attacking his vocal cords. An icy-cold paralysis starting at the base of his neck was creeping up his throat until, no matter how hard he tried, he could not make a sound. There was nothing. Not a croak, not a gasp, not a wheeze, nothing. All he could do was breathe, and even that was hard work, his lungs on the very edge of suffocation.

It absolutely terrified him, the cold sweat beading on his forehead running down into his eyes, the salt stinging viciously. He started to panic, losing his tenuous grip on reality until with a desperate effort he took control, beating the panic back where it had come from. Slowly, he recovered, resigned to whatever fate the Hammer had in store for him.

After a long wait, the van set off. The ride was short. Only a few minutes later, the van slammed roughly to a halt, and the two troopers reappeared. After they cut the plasticuffs, he was dragged bodily out of the van and into the evening sun. They stood alongside the huge bulk of a lander carrying DocSec markings. His escorts were muttering something about a problem with the access door. Michael did not care; the pain of old injuries, reactivated by the short trip, almost overwhelmed him.

Finally, the door problem was fixed, and the troopers hustled him up the short ramp and into the lander. He waited again, plasticuffed to a metal bench in the shuttle's single large passenger compartment. Passengers! You idiot, Michael thought despairingly. DocSec prisoners, the lowest of the low in the brutal, vicious system that administered the Hammer Worlds, were a million kilometers from being passengers. Feeling worse than he had for a long, long time, Michael sat there as the lander slowly filled up. Prisoners in crude plasfiber boots, dressed in the standard DocSec prison uniform of orange overalls crudely marked with their new identities, arrived in a steady procession, maybe two hundred of them in the end. They were all men, their pain and fear filling the shuttle with an acrid, sour smell. Without exception, they were a sorry-looking bunch, their faces liberally marked with bruises and cuts. Harried by DocSec troopers wielding short clubs with cruel efficiency, they were beaten, pushed, and shoved onto the racks. Michael winced as a particularly vicious blow caught one of the new arrivals across the side of the head, dropping him to the deck like a sack of potatoes. Ignored, the man lay still, blood from the gash in his scalp pooling slowly around him.

The racks got fuller, but that did not bother the troopers. They simply jammed more prisoners in, indiscriminately laying about with their clubs to make space.

Eventually, one of the troopers deigned to notice the man lying unconscious on the deck. Waving a second trooper across, the two men picked the unconscious prisoner up and smashed him onto a rack. The terrible wound to his head was ignored. After securing the unfortunate man, the troopers made a final cursory check that all the prisoners were secured. Then the troopers left, slamming the compartment door shut behind them.

The compartment was quiet, but only for a moment. A gentle buzz started, a mixture of cursing, moaning, and sobbing, the noise rising and falling like crickets on a hot summer day. Michael could do nothing except lie there—he could not do any cursing, moaning, or sobbing of his own because his vocal cords were completely dead—and hope that all this soon would be over. The waking nightmare he was trapped in had already lasted a lifetime; he was beginning to wonder if it would ever end. If death was the only way to end it, why wait? This was a life not worth living.

When the shuttle's engines started, Michael gave himself a mental shake. It was not over until it was over, and while he still lived there was always a chance.

After a short taxi, the shuttle ran its engines up to full power before accelerating up and away. Michael could only hope that things would get better. It better be soon, he thought as he slipped into an uneasy, pain-filled sleep.

Curious, happy to have something—anything—break the monotony of another empty day, the occupants of Camp I-2355 stopped what they were doing to look at the truck.

It had appeared out of the blizzard raging across the sorry-looking collection of huts set around a muddy, ice-puddled parade ground before pulling up in a screech of brakes. With a crash of gears, it reversed to put its tailgate right up against the outer of the two gates leading into the prison compound and stopped. Camp guards in bulky cold-weather gear formed up around it, stun guns at the ready.

Two guards dropped the tailgate and climbed inside as others opened the inner gate. Moments later, the guards reappeared, dragging out an orange-overalled man between them. Climbing down, they pulled him out and dropped him carelessly to the ground. Hands under his armpits, they dragged the prisoner through the icy slush until, twenty meters inside the gate, they dropped the man, turned, and left.

The first of the camp's occupants to reach the man spun him over onto his back. His mouth dropped open. With desperate urgency, he shouted for help. "It's one of ours. It's Helfort! For God's sake, give me a hand."

In seconds, Michael had been cradled in the arms of four prisoners and was being rushed to the nearest hut. Once they were through the door, orders flew in quick succession. Michael was blue with hypothermia, and if they did not move quickly, they would lose him.

Soaked to the skin, Michael lay unresponsive as his orange DocSec overalls were stripped off. The hut filled with gasps of outrage as his battered body was revealed, its tapestry of bruises, welts, and cuts, old and new, all overlaid by crusts of dried blood, provided stark testimony to DocSec's enduring commitment to inflicting pain.

Only vaguely aware of what was going on, Michael did not care. He was happy. Even though he was barely conscious and tired beyond belief, he knew he was safe. He was no longer alone. He was back among friends. Gratefully, he slipped into unconsciousness, the welcoming blackness pulling him down to safety.

Michael awoke with a start. Where in God's name was he? He stared up in baffled confusion. This was not a cell. It was some sort of rough wooden hut. So where? Lifting his head off the pillow with an effort, he looked around, catching the eye of a man at the back of the hut sitting at a crude wooden desk.

"Aha!" The man smiled broadly. "You're back. Excellent. Wait there a second." The man went to the hut door and disappeared, the blizzard roaring outside driving a wedge of cold air and snow into the hut.

"Sorry about that," the man said when he got back, leaning over him. Michael did not recognize him, but he had to be a Fed. Too good-looking to be a Hammer, that was for sure; the man's classical good looks were all too obviously the product of generations of cosmetic geneering.

"Right, I'm Leading Spacer Kostas. You're in the camp hospital. How are you?" the man asked.

Michael started to speak. His mouth opened and closed in

a desperate attempt to get something intelligible out, but the words refused to come no matter how hard he tried.

Kostas frowned. "Oh, shit," he muttered. "We've heard about that nasty little DocSec trick. Bunch of fuckpigs! Hang on while I connect."

Michael felt a sudden rush of relief as Kostas connected his neuronics to Michael's. They might not be able to speak, but at least they could communicate.

"How are you?" Kostas commed.

"Better, thanks, Leader. Where am I?"

"Camp I-2355. It's an old Hammer prisoner of war camp. We think it's about 8,000 kilometers south of McNair City. We're all here."

"Everyone?"

"Everyone! Now that you're here, that is." Kostas's face clouded over for a moment. "Well, not quite everyone. There are 283 of us in all. We lost a few from injuries along the way," he said bitterly. "Anyway, Lieutenant Commander Fellsworth's on her way over to see you, so you can . . ."

He stopped. Michael was no longer listening.

Michael had passed out, a small smile on his face.

Michael was desperately frightened, afraid that it had all been a dream, that he would wake up to see the grimy, plascrete wall of a DocSec cell. He was so afraid, his eyes had been screwed shut ever since he had woken up. Trembling, he forced himself to open his eyes. If it had all been a dream, he could close them again and pretend he was back among friends.

It was not a dream. It was not a DocSec cell. It was the wooden hut. With a sudden burst of energy, Michael dragged himself upright, ignoring the protests from his battered ribs. The instant he did, he wished he had not been so eager. Head spinning and heart racing, he felt like throwing up.

"Oh, shit," he muttered. Christ, he felt weak as piss. Closing his eyes, he lay back. After a minute or two he felt better, and he reopened his eyes to see where he had ended up. The place was spartan but immaculately clean. Eight beds in two rows, all empty apart from his. A couple of tables, two chairs, a desk. Toward the back, a screened area, cupboards, and a partitioned-off area—obviously the heads, Michael thought. The hut had small windows—no curtains—looking out onto a gloomy, snow-riven day. Day? For a moment he was confused. According to his neuronics, it was almost midnight. Then he remembered Commitment and its forty-nine-hour days. Local planetary time was actually early afternoon.

The hut's inner door opened with a bang; Michael jumped. A tall, lanky, sandy-haired man in a badly worn Fed shipsuit underneath a bulky cold-weather jacket hustled in, brushing off the fresh snow that powdered his shoulders. He smiled to see Michael sitting up.

"Oh, hello, sir! Remember me?"

Michael shook his head. "Sorry, Leader," he croaked. "I don't." His throat was sore, and his voice sounded like gravel being crushed.

"That's all right. Leading Spacer Kostas, part-time officer in charge, Camp I-2355 hospital, also known as Hut 10."

"Nice to meet you, Leading Spacer Kostas."

"You, too, sir. Notice anything different?"

Michael could not think of anything. His head was all mush. He shook his head.

"You're talking! You couldn't do that twelve hours ago." Kostas looked pleased. "We got the camp doctor to fix you up. Not a bad bloke for a Hammer."

"Bugger me," Michael croaked. "You know what? I'd bloody well forgotten. Christ, it's good to be able to talk again, I can tell you. That little stunt of theirs is scary. Like suffocating in slow motion."

"Bastards." Kostas spoke with quiet anger. "One day, one day. Right! Enough of that. Now, my orders are to keep you in bed until tomorrow. So do I have to chain you up, or can you do that?"

Michael laughed. He felt good, better in fact than he had for a long time. Common sense told him that any attempt to walk would have him measuring his length on the floor, so he was not going to try. "No. I'm not going anywhere," Michael said awkwardly, "but I really do need to take a piss."

"Uh, okay. One piss bottle coming up."

"Make sure the bugger's warm, Leader, and big."

Theatrically, Kostas rolled his eyes up to the ceiling. "God help me. I've got a delusional smart-ass for a patient . . ." A long pause followed. "Sir."

Michael laughed. His body was a battered mass of cuts, bruises, and raw pain, but he felt good. This might be a prison camp, but it was *Ishaq*'s prison camp and he was with *Ishaq*'s people. Compared with where he had come from, it was more than good enough.

Monday, September 27, 2399, UD
HWS Quebec-One, East Yuan Reef

"Dropping, sir."

With the usual stomach-turning lurch, *Quebec-One*, now masquerading as the mership *Marta Jacovitz*, dropped out of pinchspace precisely into the center of the drop zone for the transit across East Yuan Reef. Its hull flared from gray to yellow and purple and back again in the flash of its brilliant orange anticollision strobes.

Commodore Monroe nodded in satisfaction as the ship's sensor team quickly rebuilt the command and threat plots, the holovids in front of him painting the thin spread of green vectors tracking the few merships crossing the East Yuan. Two red vectors marked the positions of two FedWorld Skipjack class light cruisers, the *Seadevil* and the *Nautilus*. Monroe's pulse sped up a bit as he watched. He could not help himself. The *Seadevil* and the *Nautilus* might be two of the oldest warships in the Fed's order of battle, but they were still a force to be reckoned with. One of their sister ships, the *Bonito*, had given his ship, the heavy escort *Jaguar*, a hell of a mauling at the Battle of Cord's Deep the last time around, a mauling he had been lucky to survive. Still bitter, he remembered the many who had not.

The *Seadevil*'s officer in command appeared on the command holovid, the flat tones of his heavily accented Standard English interrupting his thoughts. The man in the gray shipsuit looked bored; he sounded bored.

"Merroneth system mership *Marta Jacovitz,* this is the FedWorld Warship *Seadevil.* Good morning. Chop vidcomm channel 67. Over."

"*Seadevil, Marta Jacovitz.* Roger. Going to 67. Out."

Monroe braced himself. If they wanted to board and search, *Quebec-One*'s captain had only seconds to alter vector away from the East Yuan to jump into the safety of pinchspace before a rail-gun salvo took them out. With one eye on the plot, Monroe watched as the duty officer in command ran through the formalities with *Seadevil* as the ship's false registration details squirted by laser tightbeam across to the Fed warship.

The *Seadevil* obviously was not in the mood to worry about a ratty tramp ship from some obscure system out galactic west. With an offhand good-bye, Monroe's ship was dismissed. "Enjoy the day while you can, my Fed friends," Monroe muttered, "because things are about to get a whole lot worse."

Monroe turned back to the command plot. Leaving the drop zone and heading across the reef ahead of them was a FedWorld mership, *Liberty of Man.* Monroe snorted. *Liberty of Man!* Watch this space, you Fed pigs, because any minute now *Quebec-One* will be taking a few liberties of her own, he thought.

"Commodore, sir?"

It was *Quebec-One*'s captain, a depressingly young-looking lieutenant commander. The man made him feel a million years old. "Yes, Captain?"

"On vector, sir. Target positively identified as the Fed mership *Liberty of Man.* Closing on target at 1,000 meters per second. Rail guns have a valid firing solution. I intend to fire as soon as we are clear of the reef."

Monroe smiled as he stood up. It always felt good to send

another shipload of Feds to the damnation of Kraa. "Roger that. I'll be in my cabin. Call me thirty minutes before we leave the East Yuan."

"Sir."

The captain of the *Liberty of Man* yawned. It had been a dull trip so far. Sadly, he had more of the same to look forward to. He yawned again as the navigation plot ran off the seconds until their next jump. Once safely in pinchspace, he would do his daily walk around the ship in an attempt to find out what his first officer—the laziest and most dishonest spacer he had worked with in over thirty years as a mership officer—had been up to behind his back.

He did not get the chance. A single tightly grouped rail-gun salvo from the Merroneth system mership that had been behind them all the way from the Delfin Confederation 200 light-years back ripped into the *Liberty of Man*'s hull.

The *Liberty of Man*'s captain did not have time to think before the massive fusion plants powering his main engines lost containment, vaporizing his ship into a huge ball of incandescent gas. Cursing, the officer in command of the *Seadevil* belatedly sent the ship to general quarters, but it was much too late.

Quebec-One had jumped into pinchspace, with only a fading flash of ultraviolet left to mark her presence.

Tuesday, September 28, 2399, UD
Camp I-2355, Branxton Mountains, Commitment

With infinite care, Michael swung his feet out of the bed and onto the floor. After a struggle, he was on his feet, swaying from side to side.

Watching anxiously, Leading Spacer Kostas stood back, but Michael had told him in no uncertain terms that he was going to the head under his own steam and nothing short of a direct order from the president herself was going to stop him. He still ached all over, and the nagging, stabbing pain from his repeatedly broken cheek and grossly abused ribs was a constant reminder of his time with DocSec. Not that he needed much reminding. The memories of that awful time would stay with him as long as he lived.

Michael took a deep breath before shuffling off in a swaying drunkard's walk. Even if he had to crawl, he told himself sternly, he was going to use a proper toilet instead of one of Leading Spacer Kostas's damned bottles. After that, he was going to have a decent shower, and then he was going to put on the clean shipsuit procured by Kostas from God knew where. Once that was all done, he would be ready for anything, including Fellsworth.

Twenty minutes later, refreshed in both mind and body, Michael sat in bed waiting as Fellsworth arrived. The door banged open as she barged her way in out of the blizzard raging outside.

It was good to see her. Pulling up a chair, Fellsworth sat down next to Michael's bed. She looked at him for a moment, smiling.

"How do you feel, spacer?"

Michael took a long time to answer. He stared at her. "Well, sir, not the best, I have to say. I, er . . ." He stammered to a halt, unable to speak.

Fellsworth waited patiently. It was not like she had anything more important to do, after all. The boy—and he was only a boy, for God's sake—looked awful, and it was not just the physical injuries so shockingly on display. There was something about his eyes that was hard to describe, a desperate emptiness that spoke of the horrors he had been through more than the man himself ever could.

"It's been a bit rough, you know," Michael said after a while.

"I think I do. Do you want to tell me about it or leave that for another time?"

"Got a better idea, sir. I put my neuronics to full recording whenever . . . whenever the Hammers started anything. I would like to dump the complete data file across to you."

Fellsworth blinked in surprise. She had never known anyone willingly give another human the window right into the soul that full neuronics recordings provided. Well, apart from pornovid stars, of course, but they did it because it made them money, lots of it. If she downloaded the data file into a virtsim machine, she would be able to go through exactly what Michael had gone through, every last excruciating second of it. If she wanted to? She was damn sure she did not.

"You really want to do that?" she asked dubiously. "You don't have to, you know. You've got time to edit your recordings back to the key facts we'll need if we ever get to prosecute the Hammers responsible."

Michael shook his head. "No, sir," he said firmly. "I don't think I could, anyway. I don't think I'll ever look at the file again. In fact, I'll probably delete it. So please, take it."

"Fine, as long as you're sure. I'll archive it with two or three other people to be safe. It'll be locked. That okay?"

"That's fine, sir. I would love to think that we can use it one day, but—"

Fellsworth's hand on his arm stopped him dead. "Michael! You listen to me. We are getting out of here one way or another. You can trust me on that. Still got your escape kits?"

Michael nodded. Despite all the attention he had gotten from DocSec, the little kits patched to his skin were intact.

"Good. We've all got ours, and suffice it to say there's no damn Hammer prison that can keep 283 Fed spacers armed with their escape kits locked up. Right? You sure?"

Michael nodded. He was.

"Okay. Let's do the transfer."

Paralyzed by an uneasy mix of confusion, doubt, and fear, Michael started as Fellsworth's voice shattered the long silence.

"So, to sum up: We're leaving. Those of you who thought we would simply sit here waiting for the Hammer to decide what they would do with us, think again. We're leaving, and that's a direct order. By the end of next month, we will be out of here. It will not be easy, but I don't think I have to remind you we have a duty to escape, and it is a duty that I as senior officer intend to see honored. Now, before I distribute the draft work plan, are there any questions?"

Michael watched Fellsworth closely as she scanned the hut. It was packed tight; apart from the sentries posted to keep an eye on the guards, every one of the survivors from the *Ishaq* was there. The silence was long and drawn out; the group was struggling to come to terms with the bombshell Fellsworth had dropped on them. Michael could hardly believe it, and judging by the stunned-mullet looks on the faces of all the spacers present, everyone else was having the same trouble.

Chief Ichiro got to her feet. "Sir?"

"Yes, Chief?"

"Not a question, sir. Just to say that I don't think I've heard anything quite so good in a long time. I can't speak for anyone else here, but the end of November can't come soon enough," Ichiro declared emphatically.

The instant she sat down, the hut erupted into a storm of cheering, stamping, and clapping. The sudden wave of optimism and commitment from every spacer present was almost overwhelming.

No, hang on, Michael thought, not every spacer. Hashemian, up at the front of the hut alongside Fellsworth, stayed seated, his face wooden. Damn, Michael thought, what is he up to? He looked around. Hashemian was not the only one. Xing and a small group off to one side sat unmoved and unmoving. This is not good, Michael said to himself. Hashemian was Fellsworth's second in command; his duty to support his senior officer was as clear as his implied insubordination was unmistakable. Michael wondered if Fellsworth had even noticed.

Eventually the hut settled down. Fellsworth, face flushed with emotion, cleared her throat.

"Thanks for those kind words, Chief. The check is in the mail," she said drily.

"No problem, sir," Ichiro shot back as the hut erupted again, this time in laughter.

"Anyway, let's move on. I'll get a draft work plan to all of you today. Actually, it's more a list of who's in what team, an outline of what each team's objectives are plus the arrangements for progress reviews, and so on. When you get it, please go through it carefully. Any problems, talk to your team leader in the first instance. Team leaders can talk to me at any time. Right, that's it. Officers and senior spacers, stand fast; all the rest back to work."

Fellsworth waited patiently as the hut cleared. When the door closed behind the last spacer, she waved everyone into a circle.

"Right, folks. First, let me welcome Michael to the group. Sorry you weren't kept in the loop, but I wanted you to concentrate on getting better."

"No problem, sir. I'm fine now. Point me in the right direction and tell me what needs doing."

"Good," Fellsworth said briskly. "Now—"

"One second, Karla." Hashemian's hand went up to stop her.

Fellsworth frowned at the interruption, or was it Hashemian's failure to call her "sir" as tradition and her position dictated he should? Michael could not work out which it was as she waved at Hashemian to continue.

"I am going to say it again," Hashemian continued. "This escape plan of yours is madness, and I cannot go along with it. I cannot allow you to risk our lives in some harebrained scheme that will never work. More to the point," he added menacingly, "I know I am not the only one here who thinks so."

Oh, shit, Michael thought. He was no lower-deck lawyer, but this smelled horribly like mutiny.

Fellsworth looked at Hashemian levelly for a long time before leaning forward to look the man full in the face.

"I know what you think, Max. I know because we have discussed your objections at great length. I have taken those objections into account, but my decision still stands. You know that, too. So when the time comes to leave I-2355, we all leave. That is an order, a direct order from me as your lawful superior. Now," she said quietly, "which part of my direct order do you not understand?"

"Karla, please"—Fellsworth's lips tightened at the deliberate insult, but she said nothing—"do me a favor. We're caught up in some crazy Hammer scheme, but we are not at war. There's no reason to risk my life or anyone else's. We need to be patient, and we'll get home. It may take some time, but I'm confident that it will happen. So let's forget the direct orders, shall we?"

"Fine," Fellsworth said icily. "I'll take that as a no. Who else agrees with Lieutenant Commander Hashemian?"

Lieutenant Xing broke the long silence. "I do, sir. I'm with Lieutenant Commander Hashemian. I'm not going to be part of this scheme. It's madness, so count me out. I won't be part of it."

Hashemian nodded. Michael thought his air of self-righteous satisfaction was probably a bit premature.

"Noted, Lieutenant Xing. I think you've made yourself perfectly clear. Anyone else?"

Two hands went up: an ordnance warrant officer and a comm chief; Michael didn't know either of them, but he was surprised. In his experience, admittedly limited, non-commissioned officers had a finely developed sense of self-preservation.

Fellsworth nodded. "So, Max, there are four of you. Have you discussed this among yourselves? I ask only because it helps me know that you've really thought this through," she inquired in a tone of such utter sincerity that Michael was fooled, but only for a second. He watched in amazement as Hashemian walked straight into the trap Fellsworth had set, dragging his fellow mutineers with him.

"Yes, of course, Karla," Hashemian said impatiently. "I would not want to go off half-cocked on something as important as this."

You fool, Michael thought, you bloody fool. The game's over. That's mutiny, and you stand convicted out of your own mouth.

Fellsworth nodded casually. She looked unconcerned. Hashemian sat back in his chair. He looked utterly confident, self-evidently sure that Fellsworth was about to capitulate.

"Fine. Michael!"

"Sir?" Michael replied, surprised. What did he have to do with any of this?

"Go to the door. Outside you will find Corporal Yazdi. Tell her to come in, please."

Michael could tell from Fellsworth's tone of voice that this was not the time to ask what the hell was going on, and so he did as he was told. To his surprise, Yazdi, together with Murphy and ten or more spacers—all leading spacers, he noted in passing—were drawn up in readiness. He was shocked to see every one of them holding a small homemade club.

"Inside, Corporal Yazdi," he said curtly. "Fellsworth wants you."

"Yes, sir!"

Yazdi did not wait for Michael to step back. Waving her team to follow, she pushed past him into the hut, with Michael coming on behind. When they entered, Yazdi's team spread out in a half circle.

"Corporal Yazdi!" Fellsworth's tone was unmistakably the tone of the officer in command.

Yazdi snapped to attention. "Sir!"

"Arrest Lieutenant Commander Hashemian, Lieutenant Xing, Warrant Officer Kobach, and Chief Petty Officer Mondavi."

"Sir!"

Yazdi's team wasted no time; they were so quick, Fellsworth must have briefed them on what to expect, Michael thought.

Yazdi had known what was coming. In seconds, the four mutineers, their faces white with shock and disbelief, had been dragged from their seats and stood up, their hands tied efficiently behind their backs.

"Prisoners secure, sir."

"Thank you, Corporal Yazdi. Right, pay attention," she said, looking at the four men ranged in front of her. The rest of her officers and senior spacers, all clearly taken by surprise, watched in openmouthed amazement.

"Lieutenant Commander Hashemian, Lieutenant Xing, Warrant Officer Kobach, and Chief Petty Officer Mondavi. By the powers vested in me as senior officer, you are charged with mutiny in the presence of the enemy. A detailed charge sheet will be provided to you shortly. You will be held under close arrest pending preparation of the brief of evidence. Corporal Yazdi! Take the prisoners away."

"Sir."

"Oh, Corporal Yazdi."

"Sir?"

"Try not to let the Hammers see what's going on."

"Sir."

When the door closed behind the alleged mutineers, Fellsworth sat back in her seat, rubbing her face. For the first time, Michael realized the stress she must be under. She had a lot on her plate: the escape, Hashemian and his crew, dealing with the Hammers, keeping the *Ishaq*s motivated and focused, and more. It was a lot.

Fellsworth recovered quickly. "Okay, team," she said emphatically, "let me apologize for not bringing you in on what was going on, but . . . well, let's say that what happened here shouldn't have, and I certainly didn't expect it to. Anyway, it has, so let's deal with it first before we turn to the escape. Let me see; provided the brief of evidence stands up to the investigating officer's scrutiny, I will be convening a court-martial . . ."

Michael lay in his bunk. Around him, the inhabitants of his hut coughed, farted, moaned, and snored their way into sleep. Outside, the mother of all blizzards lashed the plasfiber building, driven snow skittering scratchily onto the glass of uncurtained windows.

It had been one hell of a day: Fellsworth's extraordinary plan to escape, Hashemian's act of reckless stupidity, his own unexpected appointment as investigating officer. He had protested, of course. Too junior, he complained. No problem, Fellsworth replied; that's allowed by the extraordinary-circumstances provisions of the Courts-Martial Manual. Too inexperienced? Ditto. Too involved? Ditto. At that point, Michael gave up and accepted his fate. He checked later; she was right, of course. Given the circumstances—and they did not get much more extraordinary—Fellsworth could pretty well do anything she liked.

Michael yawned. One thing was certain: Things were going to get busy for the occupants of Camp I-2355. He turned over and was soon asleep.

Wednesday, October 13, 2399, UD
Camp I-2355, Branxton Mountains, Commitment

A wayward swirl of snow chased the young spacer into the hut, the door slamming behind him as he hurried through the tightly packed ranks to the rear of the room. Morosely, Lieutenant Commander Fellsworth watched his approach. It had been a very long day; an unusually keen Hammer officer of the guard had insisted on turning over the huts twice that day without, needless to say, finding anything he shouldn't have. Why today? Fellsworth wondered. Most days the occupants of Camp I-2355 were left alone, troubled only by morning and evening roll calls. The Hammers were supremely confident that escape, though always possible, was utterly pointless, a slow death from starvation and exposure guaranteed by I-2355's position deep in the Carolyn Ranges of South Maranzika. Privately, Fellsworth thought the Hammers had a point: The wilderness surrounding the camp was brutal in the worst possible way, and one could go north for close to a thousand kilometers without meeting another human being. Going south was no better: The weather got worse and the mountains steeper, and there were still no people; if you got through, you had only a sheer drop into the icy waters of the Great Southern Ocean to look forward to.

The spacer skidded to a halt in front of Fellsworth. "They're gone, sir."

"Outside the wire?"

"Yes, sir."

"Thank God for that. Maybe the jokers will leave us alone for the rest of the day. All right, people," Fellsworth called. "The court is called to order."

Fellsworth crashed her makeshift gavel down onto the table, and the low buzz of conversation filling the hut stopped instantly. One eyebrow raised, she looked across at Michael; he stared back at her with a "what have I forgotten now?" look on his face. With a start, he remembered and came to his feet.

"Uh, sorry, Your Honor. Yes, let me see," he stuttered, frantically checking to see what came next. "Yes, all parties, including the court members, are present as before."

"Thank you so much," Fellsworth acknowledged drily. For all his inexperience, Michael had performed the role of trial counsel almost flawlessly, though he did have a tendency to let his mind wander at times. If the matter at hand had been less serious, it would have been funny. She turned to the members of the court-martial seated to her right.

"Lieutenant Commander Akuffo, have you reached a sentence?"

"We have, Your Honor," Akuffo replied, her voice stiffly formal.

"Is the sentence reflected on the sentence worksheet?"

"It is."

"Please fold the worksheet and pass it to the trial counsel so that I can examine it."

Michael took the sheet of paper and passed it to Fellsworth. Opening it, she studied the sheet for a long time. At last, she nodded.

"I have examined the worksheet, and it appears to be in

proper form. You may return it to the president. Defense counsel and the accused will rise. Lieutenant Commander Akuffo, please announce the sentence of the court."

The hut was silent as the four mutineers rose to their feet, their faces tight with fear.

Akuffo cleared her throat. She looked nervous. "Lieutenant Commander Maxwell G. Hashemian, Lieutenant Charles W. Xing, Warrant Officer Morris P. Kobach, and Chief Petty Officer Julia J. Mondavi. This court-martial unanimously finds that the following aggravating factor has been proved beyond a reasonable doubt. Proven: that you committed the offense of mutiny in the face of the enemy. This court-martial finds that any extenuating or mitigating circumstances are substantially outweighed by the aggravating circumstances, including the aggravating factor specifically found by the court and listed above."

Akuffo paused to clear her throat again. She held the sentence worksheet in both hands. It trembled slightly.

"Lieutenant Commander Maxwell G. Hashemian, Lieutenant Charles W. Xing, Warrant Officer Morris P. Kobach, and Chief Petty Officer Julia J. Mondavi. It is my duty as president of this court-martial to announce that the court-martial, all of the members concurring, sentences you to be put to death."

An audible intake of breath ran around the hut. Michael's heart started to pound. He always had known that it might come to this, but now that it had, the extent of what had happened struck home fully for the first time.

"Accused and counsel, be seated. Trial counsel, retrieve the exhibit from the president. Now," Fellsworth said formally, "members of the court, before I excuse you . . ."

Fellsworth ran through the closing formalities, and Michael tuned out for a moment. He had been so frantically busy with the court-martial that he had given little or no thought to what came next. He hoped Fellsworth had. Legally, she could carry out the sentence of the court—the rules governing court-martials held under extraordinary circumstances provided for it—but Michael suspected that she had other ideas. In any case, it was all academic; he would bet his pension that the Hammers would never allow her to hang four of her crew from a convenient tree. The mutineers would end up appealing to the FedWorld Military Court of Final Appeal, assuming they all made it back home safely, of course. In that case, and if the convictions were upheld, the sentence probably would be reduced to neurowiping. Fleet had not executed a death sentence in centuries, though that was no guarantee. Fleet had come close more than once.

He turned his mind back to the proceedings. He wondered what Fellsworth was going to do.

Michael stepped out of the hut as the four convicted mutineers were hustled away. For once the sky was clear, though a bitter wind from the northeast promised snow later in the day. Some day! It was not even midday, and the sun was sinking fast into the west. It would be dark soon. He started toward his hut, wondering what delicacies the galley crew would have on offer for lunch.

"Michael!" Fellsworth called after him. "Hold on a second."

Michael turned. "Sir?"

"Come with me," she ordered. "I need you to witness what I sincerely hope will be the last chapter in this sorry saga."

"I don't—" Michael said, puzzled.

She cut him off. "No questions. Just come with me. I need a full neuronics record of what comes next."

Puzzled, Michael followed her through the snow. Fellsworth's destination soon became obvious, and before long they were alone with the four mutineers. They stared at Fellsworth, their faces a mix of fear and bravado.

"Come to tell us when we get turned off, have you, Fellsworth?' Hashemian said bitterly.

"Actually, no. I'm here to tell you how you don't, so—"

"Yeah, yeah, right," Hashemian sneered. "Why don't you—"

Xing did not let him finish. "Shut the fuck up, Hashemian. You've done enough damage, so listen for once."

"That's very good advice, and I suggest you take it, Hashemian," Fellsworth said emphatically. Hashemian's head went down in defeat. "Good. Now, I have a simple proposition. All I need is a yes or a no. So listen up. Okay?"

The group nodded reluctantly.

"Good. If you give me your word that you will do everything in your power to ensure that we escape successfully from this damn camp, I will guarantee that your sentences will be set aside."

"You can do that?" Xing asked, hope splashed all over his face.

"I can, and I will. On my honor as a commissioned officer, I absolutely guarantee it," Fellsworth said. Her confidence was justified; although the Hammers were undoubtedly their enemy, it was a nearly certain bet that the appeals court could not agree without a formal declaration of war. That meant no death sentence. A technicality, true, but enough to get the four spacers off death row. "So, what's it to be?"

There was a short pause as the four spacers looked at one another. First Xing nodded, then the rest.

"Good," Fellsworth said, "but let me hear you say it."

There was a chorus of agreement. Fellsworth was satisfied. "Michael, you got all that?"

"I have it, sir."

"Fine." She turned back to the mutineers. "Helfort will comm each of you a copy of the recording. Right, we are done here. I am releasing you on bail on your own recognizance pending appeal. That's all. Michael, brief Corporal Yazdi so she knows what the situation is."

With that she was gone. Michael sat, stunned by it all, as were the mutineers. They looked shell-shocked.

"Corporal Yazdi!"

Corporal Yazdi and Marine Murphy watched in silence as the four mutineers left the hut.

"Do you think they believed me?" Murphy whispered.

"Well," Yazdi replied, stretching up to pat Murphy on the shoulder, "I would. I think it was the bit about ripping their arms off that did the trick. So yes, I think they did. I don't think they'll be talking to the Hammers."

"They better not," Murphy muttered darkly.

Fleet Admiral Jorge got to his feet to make his way to the lectern. He nodded at the grim-faced man seated at the head of the Council table. "Thank you, Chief Councillor. In the interests of time, I'll give a quick overview of q-ship operations to date and then take any questions."

"Fine," Polk muttered, waving at Jorge to continue. He had heard it all before, but to keep the Council up-to-date, he would have to hear it again.

Jorge nodded to his flag lieutenant, who flicked on the holovid projector. A three-dimensional model of human-space bloomed on the holovid that filled an entire wall of the room.

"You can see here, gentlemen"—Jorge flicked a laser pointer across the display—"following the success of the Xiang operation in which the Feds lost twenty-seven merchant ships and the heavy cruiser *Ishaq,* the ships of Commodore Monroe's task unit have dispersed and are now acting independently. So far, Monroe's ships have destroyed a further eleven Fed merships without incident, in some cases right under the noses of Fed patrols. The flashing red icons on the plot show these—here, here, and here."

Jorge paused, pleased to see the smiles of approval on the faces of everyone present—even the usually sour-faced Polk—before continuing.

"Our intelligence sources confirm that Operation Cavalcade is on track; the Federated Worlds are being forced to redeploy forces away from planetary defense to protect their trade routes."

"And the follow-on operation?" Polk asked.

"Damascus, sir. As I said, the Feds are being forced to do

what we want them to do, so it's looking good. At this stage, I am confident that the preconditions for Operation Damascus will be met. Its objective is to convince the Feds that an attack in overwhelming force on their home planets is imminent, an attack they cannot counter thanks to our development of antimatter warheads for our missiles. If it can do that—and I am convinced that it will—then the Feds will be forced to the negotiating table. At which point"—Jorge looked pointedly across the table at the councillor for foreign relations—"the Hammer Fleet will have done everything it has been asked to do."

"Any change to the timing?"

Jorge shook his head. "No, sir. Unless things change, I will be seeking formal approval from the Council in March to initiate Operation Damascus effective April 1."

Polk looked pleased. "Good. Now, turning to other matters . . ."

Thursday, November 25, 2399, UD
Camp I-2355, Branxton Mountains, Commitment

It had been two months to the day since Michael had arrived at I-2355. Now, finally, the long hours of laborious preparation were finished. He was outside the wire and clear of the camp. Michael still did not believe it; his heart pounded and his chest heaved as he lay under his chromaflage sheet waiting for the rest of his stick of escapees to make it out.

With Hashemian's short-lived mutiny safely contained, the pace had been relentless. Outwardly, the occupants of I-2355 did the little that had to be done around their camp, mainly clearing the snow dumped by endless blizzards, performing household chores, and turning out in the cold for the Hammers' twice-daily roll calls.

Inwardly, well out of sight of the Hammers, the camp was

a hive of furious labor as geneered bacteria from the escape kits were broken out and put to work. Soon the camp's kitchen was organized into the production lines that would manufacture all the essentials needed to support an escape from I-2355 in the middle of winter. The bacterial brews all smelled like camp stew, but eating their product, though not fatal, was not recommended.

One produced a gray-green slime that when dried would become concentrated high-energy biscuits. A second produced a clear mix that could be drawn out through a thin hole to produce meters and meters of monofil line strong enough to carry the weight of two men. The third was a wood-based cellulose mix that could be poured into crude molds for final shaping into hiking staffs, snowshoes, tent poles, backpack frames, and lightweight snow shovels. The fourth, another unholy cellulose-based brew, could be poured onto any clean flat surface; two hours later, the brew would have cured into thin sheets of tough but flexible waterproof material, perfect for making crude but serviceable tents. The fifth produced the resinous glue needed to hold everything together and waterproof seams. The only items not made on site were the escapees' chromaflage ponchos; good though Fed geneering might be, it was not up to the job of making ponchos out of bacteria. Those were supplied by the kits, ready-to-wear. As for cold-weather clothing, the *Ishaq*s had the Hammers to thank; the gear they had supplied had been good quality, and there had been plenty of it.

Aided by the Hammers' total lack of interest in what the *Ishaq*s were up to, the manufacturing process had gone well, though to Fellsworth's horror, the glue brew had been tested by the camp commandant during one of his rare tours inside the wire. Strolling through the kitchen, tureens of geneered bacteria in full view everywhere, he had to try the glue. Well, it certainly smelled delicious. A spoon was called for, and the mix was tested. Needless to say, the vile taste and gummy consistency of something he was assured was a FedWorld favorite left him shaking his head even as he discreetly parked the unwanted morsel in his handkerchief. He would never understand those Feds, he said to his second in command as they left the hut to inspect the latrines. What strange people they were to eat such vile food.

Finally, from the kitchen, the materials went to small manufacturing groups set up in each hut. From there the hundred and one items the *Ishaq*s would need to survive in the bitterly cold wilderness that surrounded the camp flowed in an endless stream, to be taken out and buried in caves cut into the five-meter-high snowdrifts that filled the lower part of the camp compound.

Fellsworth was not simply planning to survive. She meant to get the *Ishaq*s home. She had allocated three months for the group to get clear of the worst the Carolyn Ranges could throw at them. That meant a lot of walking each day, every day, and for months. It was a huge task at first sight, but a close look at the high-resolution maps loaded into every *Ishaq*'s neuronics showed that it could be done.

Fellsworth had picked the Hammers' weak spot, a weakness that showed up every day in their complete indifference to what actually was going on inside I-2355. The Hammers had a simple view of things. They thought that there was no point escaping. That was why the prisoner of war camps from the last war were where they were.

I-2355 had been built deep in the heart of the Carolyn Ranges, the mountains at the southeastern end of Maranzika, a 16,000-kilometer-long landmass and Commitment's largest continent. Apart from the isolation camps used by DocSec to lock away its prisoners, the nearest civilization was the small fishing village of Penrhyn, more than 1,200 kilometers away in a direct line across snow-covered mountains, their serried ranks reaching up past 10,000 meters. Safety in the form of the FedWorlds embassy in McNair was a truly demoralizing 7,000 kilometers north of Penrhyn.

As far as the Hammers were concerned, escaping was just another way of dying, slowly and painfully. If hypothermia did not do the job, starvation surely would, and only a fool would risk that.

Fellsworth took a different view. She had set up a small working party as soon as she had arrived at I-2355. Working in secret, their job was to find a way to get everyone out of the camp and a way for the escapees to survive long enough to get clear of the Carolyn Ranges. Once clear, the main group would go to ground, living wild off the plentiful game that roamed the northwestern foothills of the Carolyn Ranges; smaller groups would strike out toward McNair. All they needed was a computer with access to the Hammer's public net. Twenty minutes was more than enough time to post a message on the right public bulletin board, and their job would be done. In theory, at least, the embassy would pick up the message and decrypt it. The decryption would tell them where the *Ishaq*s were and how many of them there were. How the embassy got them out safely was another problem, but that was their problem, and Fellsworth was not going to worry about it.

Fellsworth and her planners also believed the Hammers would expect them to head for the coast; God knew, only a lunatic would head deeper into the mountains. She relied on the Hammers looking coastward—to that end, an elaborate false trail had been constructed running in the wrong direction—as she led the *Ishaq*s up the narrow valley that cradled I-2355 and across a 4,300-meter-high pass before dropping down into the valley of the Upper Gwyr River as it ran down to the O'ksander Valley, a thickly wooded temperate rain forest rich with game. That was Fellsworth's initial target. There the group would rest until the Hammers had given up looking for them before embarking on the next and most dangerous part of the plan: leaving the O'ksander Valley to travel down the Gwyr and disappear into the untracked vastness of the Forest of Gwyr.

It was at this stage in Fellsworth's briefing that Michael had come close to admitting that the doubters might have a point. It was not much of a plan. Taking advantage of Commitment's long nights and the invariably foul weather that prevailed across the Carolyn Ranges to screen them from surveillance satellites and marauding landers was one thing. Cutting down trees to make crude rafts before floating, huddled under chromaflage ponchos, down a river thick with broken ice and rock-strewn rapids did not look like a recipe for success. It was more like a recipe for mass drowning in his opinion.

But Fellsworth's was the only one they had. To Michael's way of thinking, anything but anything was better than being a prisoner of the Hammer. If the plan worked, they would be down out of the Carolyn Ranges well below the snow line, safe in the Forest of Gwyr, where ten million Hammers would never, ever find them. God knew, they had all the time in the world to get there.

So here he was, safely through the shallow tunnel, one of two laboriously cut by hand under the razor wire–topped fences that surrounded I-2355, belly down in a deep snow-drift overlooking the camp, well clear of security holocams and movement detectors. Michael shivered as he waited for the rest of his stick, trying to ignore the cold slowly seeping into his body, only his eyes showing under the thin chromaflage poncho. To the casual observer, there was nothing to see. Only snow, snow, and more snow, the slowly drifting flakes warning of the coming blizzard.

Michael whistled softly with relief as the last three spacers in his stick finally appeared, the three spacers squirming and wriggling past him to follow the rest of the stick already on their way to the rendezvous point one kilometer up the small creek that cut down past the camp. Once they were safely clear, they would have at least eighteen hours of darkness to press on hard, ten before the Hammers discovered they had no takers for morning roll call. Michael intended that his stick would be at least fifteen kilometers away from the camp by then. He would push until two hours before dawn, and then they would dig in to sit out the long Commitment day before moving off again. It was going to be tough. The snow was deep, and more was due. But they had little choice, and Michael was confident they would hit their initial objective. Fellsworth's training regimen had been brutally tough, and the *Ishaq*s were as ready as they would ever be.

Well, things were off to a good start. They were safely outside the wire, and he had his full complement of seven spacers, well, spacers and marines. To his surprise, Fellsworth had allowed the leaders to pick their own teams, figuring that they would perform better than would complete strangers thrown together at the last minute; she changed people around only if she thought the teams were seriously unbalanced in some way. Michael had gotten the people he wanted: Stone, Yazdi, Murphy, Ichiro, and Petrovic, plus a couple more he had not met, including a junior spacer named Jamie Piccione, possibly the youngest and most frightened of all the *Ishaq*s he had come across. His slender form made him look like a baby up against Murphy's massive bulk. Fellsworth had had a quiet word with Michael before they left, making it clear that even if he did not make it, she expected Piccione to. One of the privileges of leadership, she had said, and she was not joking.

With a deep breath, Michael set off behind Murphy as he bulldozed his way into the worsening blizzard, the rest of the stick falling in behind. It was going to be a long, hard night.

Tuesday, November 30, 2399, UD
Koenig's High Pass, Carolyn Ranges, Commitment

Above 4,000 meters, the wind was a maelstrom of vicious, stabbing knives. The cold sliced through weatherproof clothing as if it were made of rice paper.

Michael had not felt his feet or his hands for well over an hour. He assumed they were still there; he was able to walk, and every time he fell forward into the snow—which was often—he was able to push himself back up. His eyes were beginning to freeze, and the tiny amount of exposed skin around them was dead to his gloved touch. The rest of his stick trudged ahead of him, heads down, hunched shapes disappearing into the snow-driven darkness. Only the monofil guideline laid by Fellsworth's advance party kept them on track, with each member of the stick secured by a single safety strap clipped to the line. It was their only protection against a fall into the howling black void that dropped away from the narrow path that wound its way along the foot of a sheer black wall, disappearing up into the night.

There was no going back. Michael did the only thing he could: He struggled on, chest heaving in the thin air, and prayed that the nightmare would be over soon.

They were close to the top now, thank God. It had been a long climb up to Koenig's High Pass from the complex of caves they had sheltered in to escape the Hammer aircraft scouring the mountains for the escapees. Every step of the way, the wind had ripped and torn at them like a howling animal. He knew that his stick could not take much more punishment.

He climbed on. Suddenly he almost lost his footing as the path turned sharply down. The snow had been scoured off the track by the wind, leaving only rough broken rock; the dim light from his chemstick showed him where to put his feet as he accelerated downhill. They had made the crest, but if anything, conditions had worsened. With every meter he climbed, the wind had strengthened, battering at him, threatening to pick him up and throw him bodily down the mountain. Now it seemed to have a mind of its own, a demented, malevolent creature determined to rip him off the path, out into the emptiness, and down to his death on the rocks far below.

Michael had to force the pace. He had to get his stick into shelter soon or he would have severe frostbite to deal with on top of all the other injuries his team had picked up in the relentless climb to get clear of Camp I-2355. Ichiro had fallen heavily, a greenstick fracture of her forearm the result. Piccione had a badly gashed forehead but fortunately, in spite of an impressive amount of blood, no concussion. Stone, the weakest of the team, still not completely recovered from the injuries he had suffered in the Hammer attack on the *Ishaq,* had twisted an ankle early on; he now relied on Marine Murphy's massive strength and seemingly limitless reserves of stamina to keep going. The rest of them were hanging in but would not be for much longer. They had to get out of the wind, get their boots and gloves off, and start getting some warmth back into their hands and feet.

Making his way down the hill, Michael uttered a small

prayer of thanks. The wind had begun to ease at last. Even as it did, the snow began to deepen, the track ahead of him a well-beaten furrow in the soft white surface. Michael cursed softly. The track was a mixed blessing—good for getting off this damn mountain quickly, bad because it would show the Hammers which way their missing charges had fled. He could only hope that the blizzard lasted long enough to cover it over. Otherwise, they were probably dead. There were only two ways in or out of Camp I-2355; if their tracks were spotted, even the dumbest Hammer commander would have no trouble bottling them up until they starved to death.

A faint gray tinge marked the start of a new day by the time Michael's stick hit the tree line. They came off the rock-strewn slope into the protection offered by increasingly thick forest, the wind dropping away almost to nothing, a shocking, snow-deadened silence falling like a blanket over the group. By Michael's calculations, another few hundred meters would see them at the control point. Once he had checked in, another kilometer would bring them to their lay-up point, a deeply cut ravine that was thickly wooded overhead. Once there, they would have a good chance of finding a deep, dry cave where they could recover in safety.

The control point was around and underneath a huge boulder tucked away out of the snow that still was falling heavily. The tracks left by Michael's stick already were disappearing. Fellsworth and her small command team stood motionless as Michael made his way over, signaling his stick to take shelter.

The pale green light from the chemstick made Fellsworth look shockingly worn, her face a mask of exhaustion. Even so, she was smiling. Michael's was the third from the last group across. Sixteen more spacers to come, and she would have led the *Ishaq*s across one of the highest passes on Commitment in weather so appalling that nobody in his or her right mind would have thought of trying to cross.

"Michael," she said, her voice hoarse with tiredness. "Good to see you. Not much fun, I know."

"You can say that again, sir."

"Your stick looks good. No casualties?"

"Some minor stuff. Nothing serious."

"Good. Any sign of the sticks following you?"

"None, sir. Sorry. Couldn't see the proverbial red barn at ten paces."

Fellsworth laughed. "Not to worry. They're two of the strongest teams, so hopefully we'll see them soon. On you go. Lay up until first light tomorrow. Whatever you do, set a fire only if you can find a cave, a deep one. And keep it small. No bonfires. Got it?"

"Sir."

"Good. Stick commanders' conference at point Bravo Golf one hour after first light."

"Roger that, sir. See you then." Turning away, he moved downhill, waving his stick into line behind him.

Wednesday, December 1, 2399, UD
Upper Gwyr Valley, Carolyn Ranges, Commitment

Even though he had slept well, Michael was exhausted. He had been completely drained by the enormous effort it had taken to get his stick away from the camp and safely across the brutal nightmare that was Koenig's High Pass.

Michael lay back against a rock while he waited for Fellsworth to get things going. His feet hurt, his hands hurt, and parts of his face had the bluish-white patches of early frost damage. Even so, he had gotten off lightly. Apart from his face, he had avoided any serious damage even if the process of rewarming had been a painful one. A few days and he would be fine; happily, so would the rest of his stick.

He looked around at the group, counting heads. He sat up; something was wrong. Another quick check confirmed it: It looked like they were one stick commander short. With the blizzard still howling over the treetops high above them and the snow falling relentlessly through the trees, Michael knew that anyone not off the mountain by then had no chance. He shivered, and it was not just from the cold. The mountainside fell steeply away from Koenig's High Pass in an uninterrupted sweep of icy, wind-scoured snow, dropping hundreds of meters down into a boulder-strewn, snow-choked ravine. Anyone who came off the guideline would fall. Unable to slow down, let alone stop the fall, they would have smashed into the ravine too fast to have any chance of surviving.

Michael closed his eyes at the awful thought. He had been less than half a step away from the same fate for all those long hours, a perverse and vindictive wind toying with him as he struggled to keep his feet along a path that was only thirty icy centimeters wide in places.

"Okay, folks. Listen up." Fellsworth's voice was tired, but her underlying strength showed through the fatigue. Nobody listening to her could have any doubts that she was going to make a success of what inevitably had become known as the Long March.

"Right, first the bad news, though I'm sure most of you have worked it out already. Lieutenant Kamarova's stick is lost. They were last to cross the pass, and no one saw them go. We think they may have cut the guideline too early, someone slipped, and that was it." She stopped for a moment, the pain of losing eight of her spacers clear in her eyes. "We won't forget them. I've sent a team to check out the bottom of the ravine below the pass in the hope that someone made it. There's a faint chance, but I don't hold out much hope. I've given the search party until last light, and then they'll come back in, earlier if the blizzard looks like it's easing."

She took a deep breath in. "Right," she declared firmly. "First up, there's a small change of plan. I am concerned that Lake Schapp could be a trap. Here, have a look."

With a few strokes from her staff, she drew a quick mud map of the Gwyr River as it ran northwest toward the Forest of Gwyr. A small circle in the middle marked the position of the moraine-dammed Lake Schapp.

"By now, the Hammers must have worked out that we did not head for the coast. That is," she said with a grim laugh, "as long as they don't think we're all dead in a snowdrift. So, putting a blocking force in is their best next option, and the lake is the obvious place to do so. In fact, it's the only place they could get landers in and out safely given the shitty weather in these parts. The rest of the Gwyr Valley is too steep-sided. If they have troops in place, I don't want to run into them. The bad news is that those of you with marines and spacers with covert ops experience in your sticks will have to hand them over. They will become my recon unit."

A small groan went up from those affected, Michael included. Yazdi and Murphy had been the rocks on which his team had been built. To lose his two marines now would be a real blow.

"Yeah, yeah, I know," Fellsworth acknowledged patiently when the muttering died away. "I would not want to lose them either, but not crashing into a Hammer patrol is a higher priority. Anyway, where was I? Oh, yes. The recon patrol will leave four hours before dawn. They will check the route to Lake Schapp. If the Hammers are there, they'll pull back, and we'll have to sit and wait them out. If it's clear, the plan remains unchanged, but we'll go a day later. I'll get you the precise departure schedules sometime today when we've had a look at the injury list. The most mobile sticks will leave first, cut down to the Gwyr River, turn downstream, and continue on to set up camp past Lake Schapp tomorrow night. Bivouac there two days before pushing on. Any questions?"

After a brief flurry of questions, none of any significance, the briefing broke up. Michael got to his feet, pleased that he would have an extra day to recover. A day's break would be wonderful. He had not gotten far when Fellsworth waved him over.

Michael's heart sank. He smelled a new assignment, and he would bet his life that it would not be counting the rations. Michael walked over to where Fellsworth was sitting.

"Job for you, Helfort. I want you and Corporal Yazdi to make for McNair. We need to get word to the embassy there that there are survivors. And before you ask why I chose you, it's because you're both small enough to pass for Hammers. A few weeks of half rations and a decent layer of dirt and they'll never pick you out as Feds," she said confidently.

"Fine, sir," was all Michael could say in reply.

"Good. Now, find Yazdi, get a plan together, and brief me in . . . an hour's time. Okay?"

Michael nodded. He shivered as he walked away to find Yazdi. It was easy for Fellsworth to be so sure; he wasn't. Pushing on alone, just the two of them, against the most ruthless police state in all of human history, without money or identity cards, without the security and support the rest of the *Ishaq*s provided—all of that was bad enough.

But the thought of falling into DocSec's hands again was a hundred times worse. It absolutely terrified him.

Wednesday, December 15, 2399, UD
Lower Gwyr Valley, Carolyn Ranges, Commitment

Michael woke from an uneasy half doze with a start. "What the *mmmppphh*!"

Corporal Yazdi's hand was clamped firmly over his face. "We've arrived. Civilization," she whispered into his ear.

Michael was awake in a heartbeat. Taking great care to stay under his tattered chromaflage poncho, he rolled over carefully to make sure their crude log raft did not capsize into the icy water of the Gwyr River.

"Where?" he hissed, scanning the darkness. He could not see a damn thing, only the black of a moonless Commitment night.

"Not that way," Yazdi hissed. "Downstream."

Despite the predawn gloom, it was obvious what Yazdi had seen. In the distance, a single white cottage stood close to the riverbank, a thin bar of warm yellow-gold light spilling from one window and smoke curling out of a squat chimney. The sight almost overwhelmed Michael. Inside would be food, warmth, clean clothes, sleep—all the things he craved after those terrible days hurtling down the Gwyr's viciously rock-tipped rapids. Even when they were clear of the worst the river could throw at them, there were two nerve-wracking days spent negotiating marine positions set up across the Gwyr Valley where it debouched into the O'k-sander Valley. Senses dulled by fatigue, hunger, and cold, they spent one long Commitment day holed up only thirty meters from a marine company; Michael and Yazdi had all but stumbled into the marines' position before realizing their mistake, saved only by a sentry more interested in taking a piss than in doing his job. Unable to retreat, they had been trapped, the marines' fire, their food, and their warm dry tents mental torture of the most exquisite sort. Eventually, the marines had broken camp and moved on, leaving only a few pathetic scraps of food for Michael and Yazdi to scavenge in a desperate attempt to keep their never-ending hunger at bay.

Then there had been the endless hours spent in the darkness drifting along, lying under their ponchos, invariably wet and cold, always tired and always hungry, until the eastern sky lightened with the promise of dawn and forced them to steer their awkward craft into the riverbank to hide until night fell again.

"So what do you think?" Michael muttered. "Go past or lay up?"

"Lay up, I think."

Michael nodded. "I agree. If we get reasonably close, we may be able to pinch some food." His mouth watered at the thought.

"We should be so lucky. Still, let's hope. Come on. Let's get ashore."

Yet another long Commitment day later, Michael and Yazdi pushed the raft back into the water. The river was black and oily in the darkness.

It had been a bad day. Despite Michael's best efforts, their prayers had not been answered. They had caught no fish, their rabbit traps were empty, and the occupants of the house had refused to cooperate by leaving long enough for Michael and Yazdi to ransack it.

Michael's head dropped in despair. The raft drifted slowly past the cottage unseen, to the casual observer just a clump of branches drifting aimlessly in the current. Slowly, the cottage fell away behind them, and the riverbank reverted back to endless forest.

"Corp?"

"Sir?"

"We can't go on like this much longer. We've got to get off this damn river before it drowns us or freezes us or we starve to death. Or all three at once," Michael added with a grim laugh. "Now, I've had a look at the map, and there's a small town coming up on our left. Baboushan; it's an old mining town. We should dump the raft, and then do a bit of breaking and entering. I think we're far enough away from the camp. They won't make any connection between a break-in this far from the camp and the *Ishaq*s. And God knows, we can't go on like this."

"I agree." Yazdi's voice betrayed her exhaustion. Michael nodded. It had been a long, cold, dangerous ride down the Gwyr, and it could not go on much longer. They had to bite the bullet. They had to get off the river. If they stayed on the damned raft, they eventually would drift out to sea, and what was the good of that?

"Good," Michael said. "Let's do it."

Michael could not contain himself. The smile on his face stretched into a broad grin, and then his head went back, his laughter almost hysterical in its intensity. Corporal Yazdi, freshly washed hair bundled up in a towel, looked at him like he was a madman. Then she lost it, too; the sheer joy of getting off the river and into somewhere warm was too much to bear.

"Fuck." Michael finally got himself back under control, his face wet with tears of pure happiness.

"Thanks for the offer but no thanks," Yazdi replied. That did it; they were off again, the isolated house outside Baboushan ringing with shouts of laughter.

"Oh, Christ," Michael wheezed when he finally got himself under control. "I can't do that too often." He wiped the tears from his eyes. "My ribs don't appreciate the joke."

"Not surprised," Yazdi said. "Right. I'm going to have another snoop around. Back in a tick."

Michael nodded. They had eaten well but carefully; their stomachs were so shrunken that both had difficulty putting away even the meager amount of food Yazdi had scrounged from the house. The place obviously had been empty for a while, but Yazdi had found some canned soup, and the freezer had had bread in it. So soup and bread it would have to be. One thing was for sure; that was a damn sight better than an emaciated rabbit half cooked over a tiny fire.

Michael was still getting rid of the evidence of their visit when Yazdi came back, her eyes sparkling with excitement. "Sir," she called, "come and have a look."

Michael followed her out into the darkness and around the side of the house. Fifty meters down a rough track was a ramshackle garage. Triumphantly, Yazdi flung open the doors to reveal a small truck, battered and well used. "You're kidding." Michael stared at the thing, wide-eyed. "Jesus! It's an antique. Does it work?"

Yazdi shook her head. "Dunno yet. Only one way to find out." Climbing in, she scratched around inside. Michael had a look in the back; it was empty. Judging by the smell, it was used for carrying timber, and not that long ago, either. They needed to get away, and soon.

Yazdi snorted. She had climbed out; the hood was up. She was staring into the engine compartment in disbelief. She leaned in and sniffed. She shook her head. "It's diesel. Unbelievable. Should be in a museum."

"I don't care. If it moves, that's all that matters. Can you start it?"

"Think so. Trusting lot around here." Yazdi waved a key. "Let's try this. Found it in the glove box. Might save me hot-wiring it."

Michael smiled. Yazdi was a woman with hidden talents. Climbing into the driver's seat, she put the key in and turned it. After only the slightest hesitation, the little truck's engine burst into life. Yazdi let it run for a minute and then turned it off. It sounded pretty healthy. There was an awkward silence. Michael and Yazdi looked at each other. With no money and no identity cards, their plan had always been to keep a very low profile until they lucked out and found a computer with access to the Hammer public net. Not much of a plan but good enough for Michael, not least because it kept the chances of being picked up by DocSec to an absolute minimum.

The truck had changed all that.

They could stick to their plan and leave the truck where it was, rusting slowly in its shed. Or they could roll the dice and use it to go north, to get as close as possible to McNair and the safety of the FedWorld embassy. And even if they did not make it to McNair, there had to be a computer he could get at somewhere along the way. He hoped. Michael sighed despairingly. To keep faith with Fellsworth, all he needed was twenty minutes, for God's sake. Twenty minutes on a computer to tell the Fed embassy that close to three hundred spacers had survived the destruction of the *Ishaq*. But how best to do that? Keep the risk of capture to a minimum by working their way slowly north? Or jump in the truck and go for it, ignoring the risk of being stopped at a DocSec roadblock?

"So what do you think?" Yazdi asked softly.

Michael took a deep breath. He had to decide. They could not sit around forever while he agonized over what to do. He took another deep breath and made his decision.

"I'll get our stuff," he said quietly. "We'll use the truck. So let's get going. I'm sick of this creeping around shit."

Yazdi looked relieved. "Couldn't agree more. I'll make sure I can drive the damn thing."

Michael ducked back into the house. Picking up the two packs, he was making a final check to make sure they had not left anything incriminating when something made him look again at a cheap simwood-fronted cupboard.

Later, Michael cursed himself long and hard for not having been more inquisitive earlier. Finding food, warmth, and clean clothes had been enough to make him forget the mission Fellsworth had given him. The cheap cupboard he had ignored was not a cupboard at all. It was a door into a tiny office. There, sitting on a plain wooden desk surrounded by dusty papers, was the oldest computer he had ever seen.

His breath caught in his throat.

If it worked, if he could log on, if it was connected to the public net, if he could find the right public bulletin board—that was one hell of a lot of "if"s, he thought—he could post the message, alerting the embassy that at least some of the *Ishaq*s had survived, had escaped from the Hammer, and were waiting to be rescued.

Thirty long, anxious minutes later, Michael sat back, sick with relief. He was done. He had found the website he needed, a public bulletin board for people with problem pets; lost animals was a popular thread. Bunch of sick comedians, those escape-and-evade planners, he decided as he keyed in the coded message for help and pressed the Submit button. For what seemed like an age, nothing happened. He was beginning to panic by the time he got confirmation that the post had been accepted. He shook his head as he logged off and shut down the computer. It was all so damn primitive. It was like being back in the Dark Ages. No wonder the Hammers were screwed if this was the level of technology they depended on.

He was finished. He had done what Fellsworth had sent him and Yazdi the best part of a thousand kilometers to do. It was up to the embassy now. There was nothing more he could do.

Making his way outside, he pulled the map of Commitment out of his neuronics. A quick search brought up Barkersville. That looked like a promising place. It was a small farming town, so stealing diesel for the truck should not be a problem, and the road in from Baboushan ran through open country with only a handful of tiny hamlets along the way. If DocSec or the local police were stopping traffic to run identity checks, maybe they would see the roadblock early enough to get away. Not much of a plan, he would have to say, but without money and without valid Hammer identity cards, it was probably the best they could do. Their original plan—to live rough while they worked their way north on foot to McNair in the hope that they could contact the Fed-World embassy and arrange a pickup—no longer appealed to him. It was too slow, too uncertain, and besides, he had debts to repay.

Yazdi looked up from her study of the truck's engine as he approached. "Saw you found a computer. You've done it, haven't you?"

"Sure have," Michael said with a huge grin; he could not help himself.

Yazdi breathed out hard. "You have no idea how happy that makes me. Shit. Mission accomplished and all that. Jeez, Fellsworth would be pleased. Wish we could tell her."

"Yeah. I wish we could." Michael stopped for a moment; he hoped the *Ishaq*s were okay. "Anyway, I've been doing some thinking."

"What we do next?"

"Yes. Here's how I see it. We've done what Fellsworth sent us to do, and there's nothing more we can do to help the *Ishaq*s. They're on their own until the embassy gets our message and works out a way to pull them out. How the hell they are going to do that, I have no idea. I wish we could do more, but there's nothing we can do."

Yazdi nodded but said nothing.

"Well, nothing directly," Michael continued. "But indirectly, there is a lot we can do."

Yazdi looked up, her face suddenly alive.

Michael smiled. "Thought that might get your attention. It seems to me that creating a bit of confusion, a bit of mayhem, here and there will do a lot to divert the Hammers' attention from our people. It's a long shot, but apart from hiding in the bushes, what else can we do?"

There was a long pause as Yazdi thought about that. She nodded. "I agree. It's simple, really. Sit around or do something to hurt the Hammers. If that takes some of the heat off the *Ishaq*s, even better."

"Exactly. Now, pull up the map. I think Barkersville should be our first port of call."

The thought of action had transformed Yazdi. She looked positively cheerful as she gunned the battered truck down the long road leading away from the isolated house. Michael smiled. Of course Yazdi looked cheerful. Mayhem was her business, and there was every chance she would be back in business before much longer.

He smiled grimly as the truck turned north onto the main Barkersville highway. Yazdi was humming softly to herself as the truck built up speed.

Michael settled down to get some sleep. The Hammers had had their turn. Now it was his, and he was going to do his level best to make them regret going anywhere near the *Ishaq*.

Thursday, December 16, 2399, UD
Federated Worlds Embassy, city of McNair,
Commitment

Insistent chiming announced an incoming priority comm; it dragged Amos Bichel out of the blackness of sleep. The man responsible for FedWorld field intelligence and covert operations on the Hammer Worlds shook himself awake. Head more or less clear, he answered the comm.

Seconds later he was out of bed, pulling his clothes on with frantic urgency, ignoring sleepy complaints from his wife. No matter how hard he tried, he simply could not believe what he had just been told. He shook his head in disbelief. Survivors from the *Ishaq?* Unbelievable. What on earth would the Hammers do next? They must have a death wish because one thing was for sure: The brown stuff was really going to hit the fan now.

He commed the duty officer back.

"Marty! Are you sure about this?"

The duty officer's voice left no room for doubt. "Boss, I've been through it ten times," he explained patiently. "It's clear as day. There are survivors from the *Ishaq*, and they're here on Commitment."

"How did they get the message out?"

"Followed standard operating procedures. An officer

called Helfort did the job. Posted a message on a public bulletin board, using one of our accounts. We check regularly in case there's anything, but this is a first, I have to say."

"Right. I'll be over in five. We'll go through it one last time to be one hundred and ten percent sure. Then I'll call the ambassador. Jesus! I don't think he's going to be too happy about all this."

Friday, December 17, 2399, UD
Town of Barkersville, Commitment

"Ready?"

"As I'll ever be, sir," Yazdi replied, her voice betraying a barely controlled mix of excitement and nerves. She held up the knife she had stolen from the house, its edge honed razor-sharp after hours of effort. "Let's get it on."

Michael held up his knife and put on a voice laced with solemn pomposity. "Right. By the powers vested in me, blah, blah, blah, I hereby declare war on all Hammer fuckpigs who get in our way. Let's go."

Yazdi carefully engaged the clutch and rolled the truck out of the small copse in which they had been hiding. Slowly, she drove down the lane into the outskirts of Barkersville. If it had been quiet when they had driven through the day before, it was completely dead now; the entire town was in bed, asleep, they hoped, despite the fact that it was broad daylight. Yazdi slowed the truck to a stop on a side street one block short of a grim one-story plascrete building and parked in the shadows. Michael had a good look around, pleased to see that there was not another living soul in sight. No surveillance holocams either.

Yazdi patted Michael on the shoulder. "Right. Stick to the plan and we'll be fine. Let's do it!"

Climbing out of the truck, she turned the corner and

walked briskly into the Barkersville police station. Michael waited the minute Yazdi had asked for before he followed her in, nerves jangling and hands wet with sweat. He pushed through a grubby plasglass door and into the reception area. The place could have been any police station on a thousand worlds. Old and tired, it smelled of defeat and beaten-down people. The bare concrete room, its walls broken by pin boards papered with drooping and tattered notices, was dominated by a single counter behind which stood Yazdi with an evil smile on her face, a finger to her lips. Waving him on, she turned and went through a door Michael assumed must lead to the back of the station.

He followed, swallowing hard as he stepped over the body of a middle-aged police sergeant facedown on the plascrete floor, a thin dribble of blood slowly winding its way out from underneath his body, stun-gun holster empty.

Michael had guessed right. Beyond the door was a corridor that ran clear through to the back of the station. Yazdi had not wasted any time. Two policemen manning radios—a worn sign above the door said this was the incident control room—were slumped forward on their desks, and the only sound was the desultory chatter from bored officers out on patrol. Yazdi was moving quietly back down the corridor, checking each office as she went.

"Gotcha," Michael heard her mutter as she ducked into one of the last rooms on the left before a cross-corridor. He followed her in. The room was small, with a shelf on one wall holding a single multichannel holocam recorder, the machine laughably antique to look at.

"We'll come back when we're done," she whispered. "Prefer not to have any holovid of what we've been up to."

Michael could only nod. He could not speak; his stomach was heaving in protest. He felt awful. If he showed it, Yazdi either did not care or had better things to think about. She waved him to check right while she looked left. Heart in mouth, knife held tight in a hand slippery with sweat, he moved silently down the corridor, checking each of the offices in turn.

Empty. Empty. Empty.

Then his heart sank. The last one was occupied. Taking a deep breath to steel himself, he walked straight in. The man behind the desk, a youngish officer, looked up in baffled surprise. A small engraved sign on the desk read DETECTIVE SERGEANT H. K. KALKOV.

Michael moved around the desk and extended his right arm as if to shake hands with Kalkov. Taken completely by surprise, the man sat unmoving, mouth slightly open. Michael stepped in close. With no fuss or bother, he slipped the knife in his left hand under the man's ribs and up into his heart. With a soft *whoooof,* the air rushed out of Detective Sergeant Kalkov's lungs. His eyes bulged and then rolled up into his head, and he slumped back in his chair, head falling back, mouth open in surprise. Michael tried not to look. Quickly, he relieved Kalkov of his stun gun and small handheld radio before spinning on his heel and running from the room. The man's face was seared into his memory now, and Michael knew with sickening certainty that it was something he would never be able to forget.

The rest of the corridor was still clear as Michael rejoined Yazdi. "Five more minutes, no more," she whispered.

Michael nodded. He did not want to think about what he had done, what he probably would have to do again. Then all doubt vanished. A black jumpsuited DocSec trooper appeared, his back toward them as he turned to lock his office. Michael beat Yazdi to the trooper, his hand pulling the man's head to one side, his knife slicing up deep into the throat. It was too easy. The man twitched for a second, then dropped to lie crumpled awkwardly on the floor. It was messy; there was blood everywhere, a pool spreading fast, red-black and thick, the air filling with a sickly copper smell.

Stepping away, Michael felt ill, his self-control crumbling under waves of nausea. He forced his body back under control, stepping back to take the trooper's weapon, a compact machine pistol worn in a thigh holster, and two spare magazines.

They moved on. More offices and then a corridor leading on to the cells. Yazdi shook her head. They were running out of time. It would have been good to find the armory wide open, but even provincial Hammer policemen were not that slack. She circled her finger. With a brief detour to grab the holocam recorder, they were through and out of the reception area. Yazdi stopped only for a second to take a pair of battered binoculars off a low shelf, and they were back on the street, walking sedately back to the truck. There was not a soul in sight.

Safely around the corner, Michael almost made it to the truck before he lost control of his stomach. In a spectacular series of gut-wrenching heaves, he dumped every gram of food he had eaten in the last few hours onto the pavement.

Yazdi grabbed him and hustled him into the truck. "Time for that later," she whispered. Seconds later, they were on their way, just another old truck passing through a quiet country town.

Pale and shaking, skin clammy with ice-cold sweat, Michael was still in shock when Yazdi finally got the truck's antique holovid to work. She found a news channel, and they listened as a stunned commentator described the awful scene that had greeted the early arrivals for the day shift at the Barkersville police station. The local police commander came on and in a voice that was equal parts shock, horror, and bafflement admitted that they had no idea who might have caused the carnage. He could not comment further. Because one of their troopers had been killed, the matter was being handed over to DocSec for investigation.

"Got away clean," Yazdi said laconically. She flicked off the holovid.

Michael grunted. There had been nothing clean about it at all. He was ashamed to admit it, but he had enjoyed knifing the DocSec trooper. The fierce burst of exhilaration exploding through his body as the knife went home had been pure ecstasy. But not the rest. They were ordinary coppers, with wives, kids, dogs, houses, mortgages, all that sort of stuff. He felt soiled by the sheer brutality of what he and Yazdi had done.

Michael got out of the truck and walked a little deeper into the woods in which they were hiding. He needed to be alone. He needed to get away from Yazdi. The realization that a large part of Yazdi was an utterly ruthless, totally amoral killing machine had come as a huge shock. He never had thought of her that way. Up to then, she had been only another marine, another green uniform, another reliable NCO. Yes, they needed guns, but did those guns have to come at the cost of five lives?

The life of one DocSec trooper would have been enough, surely.

Ten minutes later he made his way back. Yazdi looked at him sympathetically. "I know it's not easy, but they are the fucking Hammer. So tuck it away, sir, and let's start thinking about what comes next."

Michael nodded. Yazdi was probably right. Christ, she had better be, though he knew he would never be able to tuck it away.

Saturday, December 18, 2399, UD
Outside Kraneveldt Planetary Defense Force Base,
Commitment

With a screech of ancient brakes, Yazdi stopped the truck safely under the cover of a thick stand of trees, its nose rammed firmly into a clump of bushes.

"This'll do," Yazdi declared after a good look around. "I'll cut some branches to screen us from the track."

"Okay. I'll take a look at the base." Michael climbed stiffly out of the truck. It had been a long and tense drive up from Barkersville, but surprisingly, they had not been stopped once. A small convoy of DocSec trucks that had ignored them completely while racing south had been the only evidence of a response to their attack on the Barkersville police station.

According to Michael's neuronics, they were on the far

side of a small rise overlooking Kraneveldt Planetary Defense Force Base. He stood for a moment to enjoy a rare sense of peace, the last rays of a slowly setting sun warm on his back, the western sky a lurid mass of gold and scarlet slashes shot haphazardly across a blue sky deepening slowly to black. He had left the stolen police handheld in the truck; it was quiet now except for an occasional laconic report. However hard the Hammers were looking for what they were calling the Barkersville terrorist gang, they were not looking anywhere near Kraneveldt. Until they kicked the Hammers again, Michael reckoned, he and Yazdi were safe.

Crawling up to the crest of the rise, he turned his attention to the Hammer base. The place was enormous, an ugly mass of ceramcrete that sprawled out across the shallow valley in front of them, orange floodlights coming on all across the huge Hammer base to mark the end of another interminably long Commitment day. Nothing moved; the base was quiet to the point of being dead. Weekends were weekends, Michael thought, even for those godless Hammer sons of bitches.

He settled down to have a long hard look at what he thought might be their next target.

The flight lines lay beyond the clutter of hangars and plascrete buildings of all sizes that infested the airbase. There, two long rows of aircraft were tucked away from the weather under open-sided plasteel-roofed hangars that stretched down one side of the runway. Most were ground attack aircraft, together with a squadron of air superiority fighters. Michael dismissed them as of no interest. He was confident he could fly a lander; Hammer planetary defense aircraft were an entirely different matter. Toward the far right-hand end of the runway was a small collection of dark gray lumps parked out in the open, seven of them in all. Aha, Michael thought.

Hoping to find an easy way in, he studied the base's defenses at length. In the end, he gave up. The Hammer knew how to build fences, that was for sure. He rolled onto his back and handed the glasses back to Yazdi.

"You have a look. I can't see any obvious way in."

Taking the binoculars, Yazdi looked long and hard before

shaking her head. "Nor me. We'd need an assault lander to get through."

Michael nodded. "So, if we're going to get in . . ."

"It's through the front gate."

"Thought you might say that. Let me have another look."

In the fading light, Michael studied the landers with interest. The binoculars Yazdi had stolen were not much good, but they were enough for him to see that at least two were ground attack landers. Judging by the slight flare in their after hulls, they were Hammer Space Dynamics LGA-44's; Fed intelligence had codenamed them Lanyards. Introduced into front-line service just in time for the Third Hammer War, the Lanyards had been the backbone of Hammer ground attack forces ever since; even now they were regarded with respect by the FedWorld military. The Lanyard might be crudely engineered by Fed standards, but it was simple, tough, reliable, and heavily armored.

Michael grunted in satisfaction. The Lanyards, with their massive blunt noses and brooding bulk, might be obsolescent, but they were all business. They were brutally capable machines, and Michael was happy to see them. He handed the binoculars to Yazdi. "Give me a moment, Corp. I want to look at something." Closing his eyes, he started to look through everything the TECHINT knowledge base in his neuronics could tell him about the Lanyard ground attack lander.

He had an idea.

Saturday, December 18, 2399, UD
Outside the city of McNair, Commitment

Four little flybots that had been thrown out hours earlier from a fast-moving Fed embassy people mover sat unmoving in a rock-littered field.

At last, with infinite care, one of the flybots, lying upside down against a large tree stump, got to work. First, a tiny wand barely a centimeter long emerged from a belly port, the tip a microvid camera no bigger than a pinhead. Moments later, a second wand appeared, this one tipped with a tiny radio frequency sensor. After a short pause, the two sensors began an excruciatingly careful scan of the area. Then, for good measure, they repeated the entire process one more time, the onboard AI programmed to make absolutely sure that nothing remotely man-made was watching. There was another short delay before the flybot, happy now that the coast was clear, began the painful process of getting itself right side up. Extending its rotor blades, it slowly levered itself first onto its side and then, with the tiniest of pushes, onto its belly, the two sensor wands snapping back below its skin as it did.

There was another long pause before two more wands emerged to carry out another painfully careful scan to make sure nothing had changed. Reassured, the flybot bent the tips of its lower rotors down until they touched the ground and, lifting itself up, crawled the meter or so it needed to be clear of the tree stump for takeoff.

A final check was followed by another pause as it signaled to its brothers that the coast was clear. Then, without warning, the rotors ran up to speed, and the flybot was up off the ground. Accelerating hard, its rotors bit deep into the late morning air, driving the bot low across the broken ground before it climbed steeply to track southeast at a steady 120 kph. Seconds later, it was followed by its three partners.

The little flybots had a rendezvous with the survivors from the *Ishaq* to make.

If Saturday had been quiet, Sunday was even quieter. So far, only four cars and a pickup had passed them in almost an hour.

Michael began to worry. The eastern sky was lightening by the minute; the plan he and Yazdi had worked out depended on their getting inside the base well before the day shift arrived. Michael did not want some smart-ass pointing out that truck and driver did not belong together.

Binoculars trained down the long stretch of empty road, Yazdi stiffened beside him. "Might have something here. Stand by."

It was something: a gray Planetary Defense Force truck, heavily loaded judging by the labored way it managed the gentle slope up toward them. Beyond the truck, the road stretched away empty into the distance.

Yazdi scanned the vehicle carefully. "Perfect. Driver's alone. No passenger. Road's clear both ways. Let's do it."

The truck ground its way up the slight slope toward them. At the last minute, Yazdi stepped out into the road, waving her arms frantically. The driver took the bait, bringing the truck to a stop with a screech of overworked brakes. While Yazdi ran around the truck to the driver's side, Michael ripped open the door and climbed up into the cab, one hand lunging for the distracted driver's throat, the other grinding his pistol into the terrified man's ribs. Michael did not hesitate, dragging the man bodily across the cab and out onto the verge, throwing him into the low scrub that bordered the road. Standing back he looked down. This was no man. He was more a boy, a skinny boy trembling in shock, eyes frantically hunting for help, hands up to keep Michael back.

"What do you want?" the boy stammered, voice trembling with shock. "Please don't hurt me. Please."

Michael ignored him. The plan called for a quick shot to the head to make sure no blood got onto the driver's gray fatigues, but all of a sudden Michael knew he could not—would not—do it. It would be cold-blooded murder.

"What the fuck's going on?" Yazdi hissed. "Why haven't—"

Michael's hand went up to stop her. "Pull the truck off the road while I tie him up, Corp. Then we'll hide him in the back. That way they'll find him eventually."

"Hey! That's not the—"

Michael turned on her. "That's a fucking order, Corporal," he whispered fiercely, "so do it. Now!"

For one heart-stopping moment, Michael thought Yazdi was going to call his bluff, her hand starting down to the gun in her pocket. But she did not. She stopped, nodded slowly, and went to move the truck.

Michael squinted into the lights that flooded the security post, the peak of his stolen cap pulled well down over his face. Heart pounding, he struggled to keep control as he handed his identity card and the card containing the truck's movement order out the window.

He had every right to be nervous. His plan for getting into the base was so riddled with flaws that it was barely a plan at all. It was more a series of gambles, with his and Yazdi's lives at stake. And the biggest gamble of all was that a stolen identity card would be enough to get them into Kraneveldt.

Michael did not care. He had rolled the dice so many times in the past few months, why not do it again? If it did not work out, the fallback plan was simple: They would shoot their way in or die in the attempt.

Michael was relieved to see that the young lance corporal on the security gate looked like a sack of shit. He stood, swaying gently, as he studied the movement order Michael had shoved under his nose; the identity card he ignored. Black bags under reddened eyes spoke volumes about the young man's lack of sleep. The stupid jerk probably had done back-to-back shifts to give one of his mates a decent long weekend. Well, that act of generosity was one this particular lance corporal would live to regret.

The lance corporal yawned as he waved the movement order and the stolen identity card under a scanner. Satisfied that both were genuine and passing up the opportunity to use what looked like a serious biometric scanner to confirm Michael's identity, he handed them back.

"Know where to go?" The man obviously did not care.

Michael nodded. He had no idea but was not going to admit it.

Thankfully, the lance corporal told him anyway. "First right, keep going. On your way."

The boom went up, and the crash bollards sank into the road. Michael eased the truck forward, desperately fighting not to stall the damn thing and trying not to look down at Yazdi. She was jammed down into the footwell on the passenger's side, mostly—but not completely—concealed by a casually thrown jacket.

"Not far now," he whispered to Yazdi.

"Thank fuck for that," she grumbled. "I'm dying down here."

Michael grinned. "Hang on. Won't be long."

He turned the truck into a gap between two hangars, stopping before he came out onto the dispersal area proper. The landers were directly in front of him now; with a sense of relief, he saw that the lower access hatches on all of them were wide open, with the stairs down. Even if they had been buttoned up tight, he still could have gotten in, but it would have taken time; standing around in the open in the middle of a Hammer airbase struggling with a recalcitrant lander door was not how he liked to start his day.

A quick look around confirmed that they were alone.

"Okay, Corp. Out you come."

Yazdi struggled out of the cramped footwell. "Thank Christ for that. I've got no legs left."

"Ready?"

Yazdi nodded.

"Stick close, and if we're challenged, keep moving. No running. We're going for that lander there." Michael pointed out the nearest lander, its massive shape towering over them, its hull a dirty gray-black. It looked well used.

"Got it. Let's go."

Praying that nobody got close enough to see that Yazdi was dressed in civilian clothes, Michael climbed out of the truck. He walked smartly across the dispersal area into the shadow of the ground attack lander he had picked, Yazdi following close behind. The instant they were in, he slapped the door controls to retract the stairs and shut the hatch behind them. Breathing heavily, he and Yazdi stood there waiting while the armored hatch thudded home, the interlocks going in with a reassuringly solid *thunk-thunk,* two green lights above the door coming on to show the hatch had a good seal.

"Fuck! What a way to make a living." Yazdi laughed nervously. "I'm really glad that's over."

Michael could not agree more. The short walk across the tarmac to the lander had taken five lifetimes, his back rigid with tension as he waited for the challenge that never came.

"Me, too," he replied. "Come on, we've got work to do. Check every compartment. I don't want to be interrupted. I'll see if we can fly this thing. Oh, and Corp."

Yazdi turned. "Yes?"

"If there is anyone, stun-shoot them, then tie them up. Okay?"

Yazdi looked long and hard at him.

"Stun-shoot only. Got it?" Michael said firmly.

Michael took an agonizing, nerve-wracking hour before he was ready to make his move. Sitting in the command pilot's chair, he worked methodically to match the assault lander's controls and instrumentation with the intelligence summaries provided by his neuronics. While he did that, Yazdi, who was ransacking the lander for survival gear, kept an anxious eye on the airbase around them, but a Sunday was a Sunday, it seemed. Apart from an occasional vehicle, nobody even came close to the landers, let alone took any interest in them. As for the truck, it was ignored totally.

At last, he thought he had it. He had yet to touch a single control or switch on the old-fashioned panels ranged around the command pilot's seat, worried that the lander's control system would lock him out. But by now he was pretty sure the lander would do as it was told.

He turned his attention to the weapons station; it was much simpler and largely matched the intelligence summaries provided by his neuronics. It was the work of only a few minutes to get on top of it. Calling Yazdi over, Michael sat her down and commed her what his neuronics thought were the correct operating procedures for the lander's twin cannons. He told Yazdi to ignore the rest of the lander's weapons systems. His orders were simple—answer the voice prompts and, once the system was live, put the laser target designator's lozenge on the target and press the trigger. If all went well, the system should do the rest. There was one more thing, he added as an afterthought. Speak very, very deeply. Hammer women did not operate lander weapons systems.

Michael took a deep breath to steady himself; he could not put the evil moment off much longer. If they were going to get the lander operational, he would have to bite the bullet.

"Time to go."

Yazdi smiled, a smile tight with tension. "Too true. Can't sit here all day, anyway. Eventually someone's going to wonder what that truck's doing there."

Michael nodded. Yazdi was right. They were on borrowed time. Happy that Yazdi was ready, he picked up a headset and plugged it into a spare socket. Without the benefit of neuronics, the Hammer relied heavily on voice-activated systems with touch screens as a backup, and so he was going to have to talk to the damn thing nicely and hope it cooperated.

Ten minutes later, he breathed a huge sigh of relief. Things definitely were going their way. Not much had changed since the last war, and when he had made a mistake, the lander's control system had prompted him helpfully to do the right thing. Best of all, when it came to security, there was none. Not a damn thing. No identity checks, no password protection, nothing. If one knew what to do, the lander was wide open, and if one did not, the system would supply a prompt. The Hammers clearly assumed that their landers were secure enough behind walls of razor wire protected by dopey, half-asleep lance corporals.

Well, they were about to find out that was a bad mistake, Michael thought, a really bad mistake.

Michael took a deep breath. The assault lander was flight-ready. He scanned the command holovids one last time. Propulsion, flight control, navigation, weapons, threat warning, target management—all systems were ready to go.

He brought the lander's two fusion plants online, the lander trembling slightly as cooling pumps kicked in. "Okay to go?" he called across to Yazdi.

"Much as I'll ever be," she replied with a nervous smile. Michael grinned. He knew she hated landers. She only tolerated them, she said; they were a necessary evil, useful only for getting marines down dirtside quickly so that they could get on with what they did best—killing people.

"Off we go, then."

Tapping the brakes off, Michael nudged the lander's main engine throttles forward gently. Slowly, reluctantly at first, the lander eased onto the taxiway. Once it was clear of the other landers, Michael turned the lander to face along the length of the flight line and stamped on the brakes.

"Right, Corporal Yazdi." Michael's command overrode the safety interlocks that prevented the cannons from operating when the lander was on the ground. "Let them know we mean business! Weapons free."

"Roger that."

"Let's go."

Michael mashed the throttle levers forward, the lander shuddering as raw power ripped the air behind it apart. He released the brakes, and the assault lander accelerated hard down the taxiway past the flight lines and their neatly parked aircraft. Yazdi opened up, the fuselage shaking as depleted-uranium rounds ripped away, the high-pitched buzz-whine of the rotary cannon filling the lander's command cabin. Michael glanced at Yazdi as she methodically hosed the cannons up and down the flight line. Her teeth were bared in a rictus of sheer animal ferocity. For an airbase that had been empty only a few minutes before, there were suddenly a lot of people around; everywhere, desperate airmen scrambled to get clear of the blizzard of death falling on their heads.

It was carnage, and Michael loved it.

Michael's headphones were screeching, the panicked voice of the duty controller trying to find out what the hell was going on. Michael ignored him, concentrating hard on keeping the lander's enormous bulk on the narrow taxiway.

He smiled in grim satisfaction. They were rolling fast now; Yazdi was busy shredding a long line of air superiority fighters, their gleaming plasfiber wing and fuselage panels disintegrating under a vicious hail of cannon fire. One by one, they fragmented into shattered wrecks, their fusion mass driver plants losing containment to explode into vicious white balls of incandescent energy roaring up into the morning sky.

"Kind of them to keep their fusion plants online," Michael murmured. "Must have planned to go flying today." They were coming up the serried ranks of ground attack aircraft. Confident that Yazdi knew what she was doing, Michael concentrated on getting the lander safely in the air.

With the end of the taxiway approaching fast, Michael ran the main engines up to emergency power. The lander's warning systems screeched in protest as its main engines kicked him in the back, the lander climbing sluggishly across the inner perimeter fence. It took Michael a few anxious moments to get used to the sidestick controller, with the lander staggering and wallowing into a shallow climb, but he was relieved to find that it handled much the same as the ones he had trained on. It was heavier and slower to respond, but it did what it was told.

Then things got busy. Michael's headphones screeched; somebody was awake out there. The radar warning receivers were telling him that Kraneveldt's close-in air defense radars were coming online. Michael did not hesitate; a voice command launched radar-homing missiles, the radars exploding in plumes of dirty black smoke. A confused and bewildered Hammer air defense command and control was locked into a fatal paralysis of uncertainty and indecision.

Michael accelerated the lander hard but kept it low, bringing it around in a wide turn to run back across the airbase. A second salvo of antiradar missiles raced away to sterilize the base's remaining air defense sites.

"Hit anything you like, Corp," Michael urged. "Give them a good hosing. This is our last pass, then we're gone."

"Roger that, sir."

Michael looked quickly across at her again. She was totally focused on the laser designator screen in front of her, teeth bared in ecstasy. A killer doing what she did best, Michael realized. He eased back on the main engines to give Yazdi more time. He lined the lander up for its last run across the base, boiling clouds of dirty gray-black smoke from destroyed aircraft climbing in front of him. Michael flew the lander low across the perimeter wire, the massive machine only meters off the ground. Yazdi opened up again. Twin streams of metal followed the laser designator across the base complex; he could see buildings disappearing in clouds of shredded plasteel, small explosions boiling up and out of the wreckage, men diving desperately for safety as the lander roared past, its fusion-fed main engines ripping the air apart over their heads.

"That's it," Michael called, reefing the lander around in a hard left turn, launching another salvo of antiradar missiles to streak away and deal with the latest missile sites to wake up. "See if you can get the base fusion plant on the way past. Should be five clicks, starboard bow. Hundred FedMarks says it's not protected." That's what centuries of beating the crap out of your own people makes you, Michael thought—arrogant, careless, always taking things for granted. Well, the Hammers were about to find out what a mistake that was. A quick check confirmed that the plant's air defense radars were not even online. He pushed the throttles forward. It was time to go.

The lander roared past the base power plant, and Yazdi did what she had to do. The plant's ceramcrete outer skin and inner ceramsteel shell were no match for the hypervelocity depleted-uranium slugs laid down by the lander's cannons. For a moment, nothing happened. Then, with a blast that threw the lander violently onto its side, the plant went up in a huge white flash. A towering column of superheated gray-white smoke shot through with writhing, swirling red flames climbed hundreds of meters high, urged on by the plant's auxiliary systems as they, too, succumbed to Yazdi's cannon fire. Finally, they were past and the cannon fell silent.

"Waaah!" Yazdi hissed breathlessly, engrossed in the holovid from the lander's aft-facing holocam. What once had been a fully operational Hammer airbase fell away behind them, a shattered, smoking ruin. "That was awesome."

"Good work. Now let's see if we can get away with it." Michael pulled the nose up sharply, the lander's enormous power driving it through the sound barrier and well beyond, passing through the clouds and up into a brilliantly blue sky. Finally he leveled off and eased back on the power. If he did not, the lander would be in orbit and . . .

Michael cursed out loud as he shoved the lander's nose down hard, the sudden negative g-force shoving him hard against his safety harness.

"Oh, Jesus. What the hell are you doing?" Yazdi protested.

Michael ignored her and kept cursing. He had completely forgotten the Hammer's battlesats. Climb too high and the lander would be easy meat without the planet's atmosphere to take the edge off the enormous power of the battlesats' ship-killing lasers. They had not been hit yet, which he could only attribute to confusion in the Hammer command hierarchy. Initiative was not a trait much encouraged in Hammer subordinate commanders, and Michael thanked God for that, driving the lander in a plunging dive to safety below the thick gray mat of cloud.

The lander punched through the cloud, and the ground reappeared, closing at a truly frightening rate. Michael chopped the power and pulled the nose up sharply to aerobrake the lander to a more reasonable speed, the violent maneuver bringing yet more protests from the long-suffering Yazdi. She was not the only one who was upset. The lander's flight management system was beginning to get pissed, too, and the endless warnings—terrain, overspeed, wing loading, hull loading, engine overthrust, vectored thrust nozzles overtemp—were getting to be a real pain in the ass. Even as

Michael reminded himself that there was no point going so fast that he'd hit an object bigger and stronger than the lander, he flinched. Something extremely large—it looked remarkably like a rocky, snowcapped mountain peak—had flashed past below the lander's port wing. "Ouch, that was close," he muttered. Maybe he should listen to some of the warnings the lander was throwing at him.

He pulled the lander up to a safe altitude, tucking it just below the layer of thick cloud that protected them from orbiting battlesats and their ship-killing lasers. Easing the throttles forward, he settled the lander down to run fast, straight, and level on a course direct for McNair. The good news was that the lander's long-range search radar was working faultlessly. So far, apart from commercial traffic, there was not one military aircraft in the skies around them.

Barely a minute later, that changed in a hurry. First one, then five more contacts popped onto the holovid display, his headphones warbling to report multiple search radar intercepts. Damn, Michael thought, squinting at the command pilot's primary holovid. Judging by their speed and rate of climb, they had to be air superiority fighters, probably Kingfishers from the O'Connor Marine Base south of New Berlin; an instant later, the lander's threat management system confirmed the intercepts as Kingfisher search radars.

Tough as the lander was, it would be no match for a Kingfisher's heavy long-range air-to-air missiles. What he needed now was speed. He needed to keep the buggers as far away as possible for as long as he could. Slamming the throttles hard onto the stops, he pulled the lander up into a shallow climb, the speed picking up rapidly as clouds swallowed the lander.

"Corp!"

"Sir?"

"Okay. They're on to us. Air superiority fighters. Six of them. By my reckoning"—Michael did a quick bit of mental arithmetic—"they'll be close enough to launch missiles in a matter of minutes. So hang on. This is going to be rough."

"Roger that," Yazdi replied without enthusiasm.

Anxiously, Michael watched the hostiles closing in from

the west. They were joined minutes later by four more coming from the north, probably from one of the bases that ringed McNair: more Kingfishers probably.

Things were getting tricky. The lander was about to become a flying death trap; the only safe place for them was on the ground. They would be cold and hungry, true, but at least they would be safe. For the moment, that was all Michael cared about.

"Hang on. I'm putting down," he shouted. He pitched the lander downward, the negative g-force setting off a barrage of alarms. He ignored them as the lander drove down hard in a desperate dive for the safety of the sheer-sided valleys that cut through the mountains below. Then, as Yazdi closed her eyes, unable to look at the awful sight of rock walls screaming past only meters from the lander's left wingtip, Michael cut the power and pulled up the nose sharply. Holding the lander on its tail, he fired belly thrusters, and the lander, protesting loudly at the appalling way it was being treated, began to lose speed rapidly as it came into a hover.

They almost made it, but Michael had left it a minute too late.

The instant he got the lander stable above the only flat piece of ground he could find and lowered the undercarriage, the first Hammer missile, swooping down on them at hypersonic speed, smashed into the lander aft of the port main engine. The shock of the impact hammered the lander's tail down, with the missile's boosted high-explosive warhead and residual kinetic energy ripping most of the lander's port quarter to shreds. Desperately, Michael struggled to regain control, the lander sagging and wallowing, a hairbreadth away from rolling over, the mountainside now dangerously close to their left wing and getting closer by the second. With the shock-damaged port main engine struggling to stay online—Michael had diverted what little power he could get out of it down to the lander's belly thrusters—he somehow got enough control back to walk the lander away from the mountainside. He did not mess around; he did not have the time to. Chopping power, he let the lander drop like a stone for a second before ramming the throttles back up to full power, the efflux from the belly thrusters incinerating the ground below them. Great clouds of rock and steam billowed up around them in a massive roiling column.

Probably it was the cloud of ionized rock and water that saved them. In its terminal dive, the second missile lost lock only seconds away from impact, enough to drift fractionally off target to slice through the base of the lander's port wing. The warhead exploded in a huge ball of flame on the ground below, the blast smashing the lander into an uncontrolled roll to starboard and into the ground. Michael winced as the armored hull absorbed the impact of the explosion.

Then the lander hit hard. The impact was much harder than Michael had expected, the shock whipping him violently from one side to the other, his unprotected head slamming back into the headrest with sickening force as the lander bounced one last time before coming to a stop. Blood from a new cut to his head ran down the side of his face. For a moment he teetered on the edge of unconsciousness, waves of foggy blackness threatening and then receding. Head spinning and ears ringing, he struggled out of his harness, slapping the emergency button to blow out the lander's doors and hatches. Yazdi was slumped forward in her harness. She looked half-dead, a long gash in the side of her head gushing blood all over the place.

Michael ripped her harness off. Grabbing her, he half dragged, half carried her to the ladder. With one hand on her collar, he pushed her through the hatch, hanging on as long as he could before her dead weight took over. He dropped her—he did not have much choice—and she fell with a dull thud to the main cargo deck below.

Pausing only to retrieve their packs and the long-dead DocSec trooper's gun, Michael dropped into the payload bay. Somehow he got outside, the air stinking of burned rock and acrid with explosive residue, hot gas and steam still rising from the glassy black patch of flame-scorched ground below the lander. Michael looked around in frantic, heart-pounding desperation. Kingfisher air superiority fighters might not have been built for ground attack, but they carried cannon. He and Yazdi had to get clear—now.

Michael found what he was looking for: a small copse up-
stream, a wind-battered collection of pines clustered around
a large boulder-strewn outcrop. It would have to do. With
strength born of desperation, he heaved Yazdi over his shoulder, thanking God that she was so small as he struggled one-
handed to get his chromaflage cape across them.

With a deep breath, he set off in an awkward shuffling run,
head down, with one hand holding Yazdi firmly on his shoulder, the other gripping their packs and his gun. His lungs were
heaving as he forced himself to keep going. The terrible fear
of falling into the Hammer's hands again drove him on.

They barely had made it to the copse when the first Kingfisher howled overhead. The rest followed a minute later, the
air above ripped into ear-shattering shreds as one after another they climbed under full power over the smoking wreckage of the lander. Trusting that his chromaflage cape would
keep the two of them safe from the Kingfishers' optronics, he
staggered on, heart pounding and legs burning, scrambling
and scrabbling over broken rocks up into the heart of the
copse. A massive slab had split off to form a shallow, flat-
roofed cave, its entrance protected by the huge boulder keeping it off the ground. It would have to do, and Michael
gratefully dumped Yazdi's dead weight onto the ground, sliding around her to pull her inert body into the cave.

He could not see the lander, only a small patch of sky; he
watched the Kingfishers run up the valley in line ahead. One
after the other, they raked the lander with withering cannon
fire until, with a blinding flash of ultraviolet and an earth-
shattering crump, the lander's fusion plants lost containment
and the entire craft went up in a towering pillar of gray-white
smoke. For one awful moment, Michael thought the huge
slab of rock would drop onto their heads, as the shock wave
lifted the slab up a few centimeters before dropping it back.
After one last pass and more cannon fire for good measure,
the Kingfishers left, climbing nearly vertically under full
power, their sound and fury fading slowly into the distance.

For a full two minutes—it seemed like a lifetime—he lay
still. He did not want to leave, and only the nagging fear of
being recaptured got him moving again. He turned to see

how Yazdi was doing. She groaned; her eyes opened, unfocused and glazed, as she struggled to get a grip on reality.

"Corp, Corp!" Michael hissed urgently. "Corporal Yazdi! We've got to go."

Slowly, Yazdi came to. She stared up at him, her face a waxy gray under a thin sheen of sweat cut through by red-black trails of blood from a badly gashed forehead.

"Fuck," she croaked, "you look like I feel."

"Welcome back, Corp," Michael whispered. He struggled to keep the concern out of his voice. Yazdi did not look good. "Don't worry about me. Only a few cuts. How do you feel?"

Yazdi took a long time to reply, her voice slurred and faltering when she finally spoke. "Piss weak. Headache. Can't see too well. Ribs bad. Feel sick. Give me a minute. I'll be okay." She tried to sound confident but failed miserably.

"Let me check." He accessed her neuronics, then wished he hadn't. Her vital signs were all in the red. A brain bleed probably, Michael thought. Yazdi needed a regen tank, and soon. Michael smashed a fist onto the ground. There was not a damn thing he could do to help her.

"Corp," he said. "We can't stay here. We're too close to the crash site. We have to go. Can you walk?"

"Probably not," Yazdi said, a crooked smile breaking through her pain, "but I am a marine, so I will, anyway. Help me out of this stinking rat hole."

A few minutes later and after a drink of water, Yazdi was as ready as she would ever be. Leaning heavily on Michael, she started to walk.

They almost made it out of the valley.

Yazdi struggled from the start. Approaching the shallow saddle that led away from the crash site, her body sagged heavier and heavier against him. Michael could feel her strength ebbing away with terrible speed. He pushed on, desperate to get clear.

Without warning, Yazdi slipped out of his grasp and slumped to the ground. The climb had been too much for her. "Sorry," she said softly. "Sorry, can't do this. Got to . . ." Her eyes closed, her head rolling to one side.

A quick look and Michael knew they could not go on. Yazdi's face was a dirty gray death mask, her breathing shallow and ragged as she drifted in and out of consciousness, mumbling incoherently.

Michael cursed savagely under his breath as he dragged her into the shelter of a hollow protected by two creeper-draped boulders.

Quickly, with Yazdi settled, he pulled his cape off his shoulders. Dragging Yazdi's cape out of her pack, he lay down beside her, pulling the two chromaflage capes across their bodies. A quick check confirmed that the capes looked like the dirty gray dirt below them. He lay back. There was nothing more he could do now—not for Yazdi, not for himself. Michael did not like their chances. If they were found, they would not see another Commitment day; after the humiliation they had inflicted on the Hammer, a quick shot to the head was probably the only offer they would get from DocSec. He smiled grimly. Truth was, a shot to the head probably would be for the best. He could do without another meeting with Colonel Hartspring and his sadistic sergeant. What was his name? Oh, yes, Sergeant Jacobsen, may he rot in hell. He closed his eyes and tried to doze off.

All too soon the sound of heavy-lift transporters began to fill the valley.

Sunday, December 19, 2399, UD
Branxton Ranges, Commitment

"What a waste of fucking time." The DocSec trooper's voice was bitter.

"Don't tell me." The second trooper sounded equally pissed. "Tell that useless moron in charge. What in Kraa's name does he think we're going to find? For Kraa's sake, just look at the damn lander. How the hell does Major Dickwad think anyone could get out of that alive? Asshole."

There was a long pause. One of the troopers, clearing his throat of a troublesome obstruction, spit down into the delicately flowered creeper that was Michael's only protection.

"Yeah, what an asshole."

Another long silence.

Michael could hardly breathe. The two DocSec troopers had been standing on the rock directly above the hollow hiding him and Yazdi for a good five minutes. Go away, he urged them silently.

The troopers' radios crackled into life. "All units, this is Eagle One. End of search. Return to crash site. All units, acknowledge. Over."

Michael allowed himself to hope as, one by one, the DocSec search units responded.

"About time." The trooper spit again. "What a clusterfuck. Come on, let's go."

"Yeah."

The two troopers jumped down to make their way back to the crash site, accompanied every step of the way by a vociferous and unflattering commentary on the doubtful ancestry of all DocSec officers in general and the major in charge in particular. As they walked away, Michael offered up a small word of thanks. The on-scene commander had not been well briefed. The man clearly thought that the lander had exploded on impact and had concluded, not unreasonably, that whoever had hijacked the lander had died in the crash. More important, so had his troopers. The search was a token effort; it was an exercise in ass covering, nothing more, nothing less, and the DocSec troopers forced to walk their overweight and unfit bodies up and down the hillsides knew it.

At long last, heavy lifters carrying the DocSec search teams away climbed into the evening sky, and Michael and Yazdi were safe. Well, Michael thought, for the moment at least. It had been a close thing.

By the time DocSec finally had left, Michael had fallen asleep, the stress of the long day demanding that he rest. He woke with a start an hour later, lying absolutely still as he listened for anything unusual. There was nothing. The only sound was the wind, whistling softly as it moved through the grass and scrubby vegetation. Reassured, he slipped out from under the chromaflage cover and crawled to the mouth of the hollow for a look around. The valley was empty, and the light was fading fast. The Hammers had not put guards on the wreckage, but that happy state would not last. They had to be back to clean up sometime. Michael had no doubt what he and Yazdi had to do: get clear of the area and then hole up until she was well enough to resume their desperate push north. After a final long, careful look around, he decided they really were alone. DocSec had gone. Even better, there was no sign of any surveillance drones, and he doubted the idle bastards would have bothered to deploy remote holocams. If all went well, they should be able to get clear unseen.

Michael crawled back into the hollow and pulled back Yazdi's chromaflage cape. He shook her gently. She had been asleep for hours. Michael could only hope she had recovered enough to be able to walk out.

Michael frowned. He shook Yazdi again, but she seemed strangely unresponsive, her head drooping to one side, hair falling down across her face. When he shook her one more time, something terrible, something icy, took his heart in its hand and squeezed it hard. Desperately, he shook her again before putting his face down to hers, praying he would feel a faint warmth as she breathed out. There was nothing. He felt her face. She was cold and clammy, her skin a waxy gray. He swept her hair back off her face, and all he could see was her eyes. They were wide open, staring at something Michael could never see, empty and accusing. Frantically, praying that he had gotten it wrong, he checked for a signal from her neuronics. There was nothing.

Corporal Yazdi was dead.

Michael rocked back on his heels, barely able to take it all in, the terrible realization that he was now completely alone crushing the last faint hope that he might make it off this god-forsaken shithole of a planet. He had always known their chances were slim to nonexistent, but Corporal Yazdi's unwavering confidence that they would make it home one day had kept him going, her quiet strength fueling his determination to hang in no matter what the Hammers and a hostile planet threw at them. Now he would have to do it on his own. How, he had absolutely no idea.

For a long, long time he sat there mourning her loss.

At last he knew it was time to go. With great care, he closed Yazdi's eyes and crossed her arms on her chest. He pulled the chromaflage cape up to cover a face now strangely peaceful. He hated the thought of some damn wild animal tearing her apart, so patiently and methodically, he collected stones and rocks to cover her body, small ones to start with, then larger and larger until the hollow was filled in and she could sleep undisturbed. Finally, he took his knife and, using a stone, slowly and with great care hammered out her epitaph in crude uneven letters on the rock.

MR0854771 CORPORAL NOORANGIZ YAZDI FWMC
KILLED IN ACTION DECEMBER 20, 2399
A TRUE COMRADE

An age later his fingers were in agony from the hammering, but he was finished. He sat back to have a look. He nodded. It was good. It was not much, but it was all he could give her.

Picking up packs and gun, and putting his chromaflage cape over his head, he crawled out of the hollow. Standing up, and with a quick look to make sure the valley was still deserted, he turned and walked away a few meters before stopping. Turning, he made absolutely sure he would know where to come back to. Then, as he looked down at Yazdi's grave, its headstone another rock on a lonely hillside, he swore an oath.

He would not rest until the Hammer was destroyed. Completely and utterly.

"Sleep well, Corporal Yazdi," he said softly, his eyes filling with tears. "We will be back to take you home. I promise."

Michael turned and climbed on. He never looked back. Five minutes later, with the rain that had been threatening all day finally settling into a thin sleeting drizzle, he crossed the saddle Yazdi had died trying so hard to reach and dropped into the next valley.

He was going north to McNair. How he would get there, what he would do if he did make it, he had no idea. He could not think of anything better to do, so McNair it was. Head down to protect his face from rain that was slanting down hard and cold, he set off.

Thursday, December 23, 2399, UD
Branxton Ranges, Commitment

Ripped from nightmare-riddled sleep by a callused hand clamped across his mouth, Michael started violently. The knife held to his throat was already drawing blood.

"Move and you die," a voice hissed in his ear.

With an effort, Michael made himself relax.

"That's much better," the voice whispered, the hand lifting slightly. "Who are you?"

"Who's asking?"

Michael winced as the point of the knife went in deeper.

"Smart-ass! Who are you?"

Suddenly Michael was too tired to care anymore. Whoever owned the voice, it did not sound like a DocSec trooper.

"Junior Lieutenant Helfort, FC0216885, Federated Worlds Space Fleet. And who the fuck are you?" he added belligerently.

The man laughed softly. "Aha!" he whispered. "Now, Junior Lieutenant Helfort, there's a Hammer marine recon patrol due to walk right across you in about thirty minutes, and I strongly suggest you don't want to be here when that happens. So get your stuff and follow me."

"But who—"

"Later. Just call me Uzuma. Come on!"

Still groggy, Michael stumbled around, picking up the gear he had scattered around the small hollow the previous night; his gun had gone. He'd barely had time to eat the meager meal he'd allowed himself from his fast-dwindling reserves before passing out. The effort of a long forced march over broken hilly ground had been too much for his overworked, underfed, and badly abused body. He had started at last light and had kept going throughout a long Commitment night until he could walk no more. Even with some sleep, a desperate tiredness still threatened to overwhelm him, the grinding fatigue evidence of how hard he had pushed himself.

Moments later, they were off, and Michael had to struggle to keep up with the relentless pace set by the vague chromaflage-shrouded shape ahead of him. With a shock, he realized as he looked around that the man was not alone. In the gloom, he could see more dark shapes, mostly armed with what looked like standard-issue Hammer assault rifles. But there was one with a heavy machine gun slung casually over one shoulder and another carrying what was unmistakably a small missile launcher with a four-round reload pack on his back.

Who in God's name were these people?

Endless hours later, Michael collapsed onto the ground as his captors finally called a halt. The group holed up in a cave Michael had not spotted until they were right on top of it.

To Michael's surprise, they had not stopped at dawn. They had marched on well into the day, seemingly unconcerned about being caught in the open in broad daylight. Apart from two brief halts, one to eat and one to wait as a wandering surveillance drone meandered slowly past overhead, they had not stopped. They did not stop even when a battlesat's laser incinerated something high on the hillside above them, the splitting crack making Michael cringe; his captors' confidence in the effectiveness of chromaflage capes was not something he shared.

Now, finally, they had stopped. Michael did not bother with food. A quick drink, and then, crushed by fatigue, he found a quiet spot at the back of the cave and without a word lay down. He was asleep in seconds.

Warily, Michael opened his eyes.

Without moving his head, he looked cautiously around. Except for a single dim chemstick, the cave was dark, its floor covered by huddled sleeping shapes. Michael got up slowly, trying to ignore the pain in overworked legs as he crept carefully down the cave. Ducking past a blanket screening the cave from the outside world, he almost fell over a man crouching over a small holovid linked to a couple of low-light holocams that had been set up to watch the approaches to the cave.

The man looked up. It was Uzuma.

"Not thinking of leaving, are we?"

Michael shook his head. "State my legs are in, I wouldn't get far. No. I need to take a leak."

Uzuma pointed back into the cave. "Go back in as far as you can. Come out here when you're done. We need to talk. I'll get you something to eat and drink. It's going to be another hard day."

Hooray, Michael thought. Just what he and his tortured body needed: another hard day to add to the endless stream of hard days that had started when he had banged out of the dying *Ishaq*.

Five minutes later, Uzuma watched silently as Michael, suddenly ravenous, tore into the food in front of him. Surprisingly, it was good and not at all what he had expected the raggedy-assed mob he had fallen in with to be eating: some sort of spiced flatbread stuffed with meat and peppers washed down with a thick, slightly sweet drink that seemed to recharge his body instantly. It was better than anything he had had in a long time. Hunger finally sated, he sat back and belched softly. Uzuma laughed.

"Feeling better, I take it."

"Oh, yeah," Michael responded gratefully. "Much, thanks."

"Well, Michael, make the most of it. We don't often eat that well. Now, down to business."

"Shoot."

"We've been following you for a few days. For a skinny little runt, you sure work hard. Must be that fancy Fed geneering we hear so much about," Uzuma offered with a grin.

Michael nodded even though geneering had nothing to with anything. Every waking moment he had thought about the oath he had sworn over Yazdi's grave. That and a slow-burning hatred had driven him relentlessly on.

"How do you know I'm a Fed?"

Uzuma laughed. "You're too good-looking to be a Hammer even if you are half-starved and a bit frayed around the edges. Lot of scars. Who've you upset?"

Michael nodded, fingering the scar put across his forehead by Sergeant Jacobsen a lifetime earlier. "DocSec," was all he said.

"Aaah. We wondered. Anyway, let me tell you a few things," Uzuma said softly, his eyes not leaving the holovid screen in front of him for more than a second or two. "We're with the New Revolutionary Army." His hand went up as Michael started to speak.

"No questions, okay? Now, we hoped there were survivors from the lander, and we've had patrols out to pick you up before the bad guys did. There were two of you, right?"

Michael nodded.

"And your partner?"

"She's dead." Michael's voice was flat, unemotional. "Head injury when we crashed. Internal injuries, too. She didn't make it."

Uzuma nodded sympathetically. "Pity. If we'd gotten to you a bit earlier . . ." His voice trailed off into silence. "Anyway, it was not to be. You were too far away. You've done well. The Hammers are pretty upset. You gave Kraneveldt a good going over, and the Hammers still can't work out who it was."

Michael looked surprised. "Surely they've got us on their security holocams."

"Apparently not. You kept your head down, which was good. That cap—nice touch. There's holovid of you getting into the lander, but from too far away to identify you. They're blaming us, which is good because I really, really wish we'd done that job."

"So glad to be of help," Michael said ironically. "Since you haven't beaten the shit out of me despite having me by the balls, I'm happy to accept that you're the good guys—"

"Trust me, Michael," Uzuma interrupted emphatically, "we are the good guys."

"Fine. So what's the plan?"

"Ah, well." Suddenly Uzuma was evasive. "The plan. Umm, well, let's say the plan is for you to trust me. There are some people who want to meet you."

"That's it?" Michael asked incredulously. "Trust you? Meet some people? That's the plan?"

"Yes, Michael. Trust me. Believe me when I say that it's the best plan. In fact, it's the only plan, so I suggest you go with it." Uzuma stopped for a second. "You know, I quite like you, Michael. So I would hate to have to kill you, which I will if I have to. You can trust me on that, too."

Michael flinched.

His face softening, Uzuma leaned forward and patted Michael on the knee. "Enough. Two days will see us at the drop-off point. We move out in an hour."

Saturday, December 25, 2399, UD
Branxton Ranges, Commitment

Michael blinked as the black hood was removed. The sudden glare made his eyes water.

"Sit down, Michael. Please."

Michael did as he was told, sitting in a battered old chair. The man opposite him was in his late twenties, though his eyes were the eyes of a man twice that age, bottomless and dark brown, set deep under dirty black hair. Michael's nerves jangled. There was something about the man that was deeply unsettling, a barely concealed intensity. No, it was not intensity. It was ferocity, a single-minded purpose to which everything would be sacrificed. This was not a man to cross; this was a bad man to have as one's enemy, Michael decided.

Michael waited. He had learned. Asking these people questions was a waste of time. If there was something he should know, he would be told.

The man looked at him thoughtfully for a long time before

speaking. "I'm Mutti Vaas, Michael, and I'm happy to see you. Luckily for you, you're now in the hands of the NRA."

"Ah," Michael said, "the New Revolutionary Army. Your man Uzuma said that's what he belonged to. No details, though. So what the hell is the NRA? Didn't feature in any intelligence summary I've ever read."

"Later," Vaas said brusquely. "Now, some friends of yours asked us to look out for you, and when we heard about the Kraneveldt business . . ."

Michael's mouth sagged open in astonishment. If Vaas and his men had been asked to look for him, his message to the embassy in McNair must have gotten through! A tiny seed of hope began to grow somewhere deep inside.

"Who? Who asked you?" He had to know.

Vaas put his hands up. "Don't ask, can't tell. Sorry. But I do have some good news for you."

"I hope so. What news?"

"Well, we're going to get you out of here. Next week probably. We're going to hand you over to your own people. They'll arrange to get you off-planet."

Vaas's words were so understated, his voice so matter-of-fact, that nothing registered at first. When it did, Michael's heart pounded as he absorbed what he had been told. Hardly daring to breathe, he looked Vaas right in the eye.

"Off-planet? You're kidding me, right?"

"No, I'm not." Vaas's voice brooked no argument. "Off-planet. That's what they say. How, I don't know. Not my business."

"Oh, oh," Michael stuttered. "Can I ask some questions?"

"You can ask, but I have some first," Vaas said drily.

"Go ahead."

Vaas's face hardened. "Were you responsible for the attack on the Barkersville police station?"

Michael tried to swallow, his mouth suddenly dry. He had hoped that whole foul business would be forgotten. He certainly never intended to admit to it now that Yazdi was not there to bear witness against him. "Er, well," he foundered, taken by surprise. "I . . ." He trailed off into silence. What could he say?

Vaas whistled softly through pursed lips. He nodded. "I thought so. I'll take that as a yes, shall I? Look, Michael." His voice softened. "To some extent I don't blame you; we have a pretty good idea what you've been through. But you need to understand something about us, about the New Revolutionary Army."

Vaas paused. Michael sat there silent, the knowledge that he had failed a test he should never have failed gnawing at him. Vaas looked at him for a while before continuing.

"The NRA is not a bunch of psychopathic killers like those DocSec perverts. Chief Councillor Polk calls us terrorists, but we're not. We have rules, and when you get home, when you get debriefed, make sure your people understand that. We are Hammers, true, but we're not like the rest of them out there. Got it?"

Michael nodded his agreement.

"Good. We have rules, and believe me, I enforce them"— one look at Vaas's face and Michael was quite prepared to believe him—"and our rules are these. Our enemy is the Hammer government, not the Hammer people. Any Hammer the NRA comes up against in combat is fair game. Don't care who they are. If they shoot at us, if they attack the NRA, we shoot back. But we don't kill the wounded, we don't kill ordinary policemen just doing their jobs, and we don't kill civilians." Vaas paused for a moment. "There is one exception. We kill every DocSec trooper we get our hands on. We kill DocSec anywhere, anytime, even if they're wounded. They get one bullet because that's all the filthy swine are worth. So at least you got one right," he said with a faint smile. "But Michael, we do not kill police."

Michael felt ashamed, unclean, the guilt flooding back. He could not say anything. There was nothing to say. What he had done would stay with him forever. With a cold, sinking feeling he realized that the deaths back at Barkersville had placed a burden on him that he could never, ever put down.

Vaas sat back. "Okay. That's enough from me. You have some questions?"

Michael nodded, taking a deep breath to help push the

puzzled face of Detective Sergeant Kalkov out of the way. "Well, who are you for a start?"

"I'm the leader of the NRA's Resistance Council. We're the only effective opposition to the Hammer government, and you'll get no prizes for guessing we want to change the way the Hammer Worlds are run."

"Oh."

Michael must have sounded unconvinced because Vaas laughed. "I know," he said. "It sounds like bullshit. It's not. The NRA is a guerrilla army. How big doesn't concern you. We're having some success. This part of Commitment, the Branxtons, is ours. Despite all their fancy fliers, landers, drones, survsats, battlesats, and all the rest of their damn technology, the marines and those fucking DocSec psychopaths have learned to stay well away. Took a while and a pile of bodies to convince them, but they got the message in the end. We own the Branxtons, and they know it."

Michael still looked unconvinced.

Vaas stared at him hard. "Your neuronics working?"

"Of course. If I'm alive, they work."

"You can record everything you see?"

"Yes."

"Good. If you make a recording, then nobody can say we staged it, right?"

"No." Michael was completely baffled. "But what?"

"A little operation we've got planned. I would like to send you along as an observer. I need a living witness to the fact that the NRA is an effective force, that we are not a bunch of psychopathic heretics. So will you record it?"

Michael shrugged his shoulders. "Of course. Why not? Provided I get out of here, I don't much care what I do."

"Good. That's settled, then." Vaas stood up. "Michael, I'm sorry, but I have to go. We won't meet again before you leave, so good luck. I hope you get home safely. Remember one thing." Vaas leaned forward, his eyes blazing with a sudden, frightening intensity. "Not all of us are bad. All we want from people like the Feds is help. Give us the tools and we'll finish those Hammer scum off."

Vaas stepped back; Michael was shocked to see how tired

the man was. He looked exhausted, his face gray and drained. He waved a man forward. "Michael, this is Tabor. Please do exactly what he says. We don't have time for games. Make the recording I want and take it with you. You'll know who to give it to. Good luck."

With that, Vaas was gone. Silently, Tabor signaled to Michael to follow.

Thursday, December 30, 2399, UD
Branxton Ranges, Commitment

"Right, Michael. Briefing time."

Michael sat up. About bloody time, he thought. He was tired of sitting around waiting for something to happen.

"You recording?"

"I am now," Michael replied.

"Good. Okay, here's what's going down." Quickly, Tabor scratched a mud map in the dirt floor of the cave. "This is the road from Cordus—here—up to Merrivale—here. Merrivale is the Hammers' forward base for operations in the northern part of the Branxton Ranges. The road is pretty narrow, and here"—he stabbed his stick into the map midway between the two towns—"where the valley closes in, is the killing zone. This is where we are going to ambush a DocSec convoy an hour after first light tomorrow. Ten heavy trucks escorted by four DocSec armored personnel carriers. Your job, Michael, is to watch and record what happens. Then we'll move to the handover point, here"—another stab—"about twelve hours' hard march west of the ambush site. We move out well before first light. Any questions?"

Michael sat with his mouth half-open. He had a hundred questions.

"Yes. How on earth do you know that a convoy—"

Tabor cut him off. "Can't answer that, sorry. Next question."

"Um, okay. Why are DocSec running resupply convoys by road? Why not resupply Merrivale by air?"

Tabor nodded thoughtfully. "Good question. Several reasons. Arrogance mostly. We pulled our 2nd Regiment out of this area months ago, and we think DocSec has convinced itself that things are back to normal. The heretic NRA is finally on the run, defeated, demoralized, and dispersed; you know the sort of thing."

Michael looked skeptical. "Even so, trucks? Escorted by thin-skinned APCs? They must be mad."

"No, not mad," Tabor said with a shake of his head. "Stupid, yes, though it's not all DocSec's fault. Keeping Merrivale supplied by air has been a real problem for them. It's a big base, and supporting it by air alone has been a nightmare. This is the third convoy they have run and the biggest; if it gets through, they will resume road resupply to ease the load on their air assets. We intend to show them that would be a really bad idea."

"Sounds good to me. But why no proper armor?"

"Lack of armor's not their only problem. This convoy ought to have close air support, but it will have neither, and that's because of politics." Tabor grinned fiercely. "Kraa, I love the Hammer sometimes. We'd be screwed if the military didn't hate DocSec more than they hate us."

"Sorry, Tabor, what do you mean, politics?"

"When DocSec needs heavy armor or close air support, they have to ask the military: the Planetary Defense Forces usually, the marines sometimes. The powers that be won't let DocSec have their own. Kraa knows," Tabor added bitterly, "DocSec's dangerous enough as it is. Anyway, the PDF hates DocSec and vice versa, so DocSec finds it hard to ask for help, and even if they do, the PDF finds it real easy to say no. This time, they asked, and guess what? PDF said no."

Michael shook his head despairingly. What a way to run military operations. No wonder the NRA was flourishing, and long may that prevail, he thought.

"So the convoy's on its own?" Michael tried not to sound incredulous.

"Not quite. When the shit hits the fan, even the PDF has to get off its ass. The nearest PDF base is Perkins, a bit over 200 kilometers away. If they had aircraft on Alert 5, we'd expect a response within twenty minutes. But"—Michael could see that Tabor was enjoying this—"that won't happen."

"Go on, then," Michael said resignedly. "Tell me why."

"Lieutenant General Portillo is the commanding general of the PDF. He hates . . . no," Tabor added after a moment's reflection, "that's not right. Portillo loathes DocSec. Seems like the dimwits shot one of his brothers out of hand. Big mistake. Turned out an informer fingered the wrong Portillo. Another family altogether, it seems. What a shame." Tabor did not look sorry at all. "Anyway, Portillo refuses to keep aircraft on Alert 5 just to bail out some incompetent bunch of DocSec troopers stupid enough to get themselves in trouble. All Portillo will allow is Alert 15, so we will get a response from Perkins, but it won't be quick enough to save DocSec and its precious convoy."

Michael was impressed. For all its shortcomings, the NRA's intelligence seemed remarkably good. He could only hope the intelligence matched reality.

"One last question, Tabor."

"Go ahead."

"Are you sure this is not a trap, with the convoy as bait."

"No, we can't be sure. But we're pretty certain it's legit. Let's just say we have good sources. Now, I've got things to do, so is that it?"

"That'll do for now, thanks."

"Good. Remember, we move out well before first light, so be ready."

"I'll be ready."

"And remember, Michael. This is our ambush, not yours. Your job is to record what happens and get away safely. That's all. You'll have a gun, but you are not to get involved. Understand?"

Michael nodded. "Understood."

"I really hope so."

Michael watched Tabor disappear into the darkness. He hoped the man was right when he said the convoy was not a trap. If it was not, he could not even begin to imagine what the hell DocSec thought it was doing. Everything he learned about the Hammer reinforced his growing view that never had there been a bunch of people more willing to believe their own propaganda. They seemed to have developed self-delusion into an art form, a fatal art form.

Why DocSec had decided to be so stupid he did not much care about one way or the other. Michael had not been completely honest with Tabor. Yes, getting a good neuronics recording was his priority, but he had sworn an oath over Yazdi's grave, and he meant to honor it irrespective of what Tabor or Vaas or anyone else from the NRA might have to say. He had a score to settle with those black-uniformed DocSec rabble. He could only hope he got the chance to make a start.

The lead armored personnel carrier appeared from around the corner, its speed quite slow, exactly as Tabor had said it would be, as the green-and-black camouflaged vehicle slowed to negotiate the tight, nearly right-angle turn. Michael watched as the APC crawled up the road, the rest of the convoy following it, tucked in tightly behind. The trucks were like nervous sheep, Michael thought, and the APC was leading them to the slaughter.

The lead APC closed in on a small chalk mark on the road. The instant the APC hit the mark, two missiles streaked across the valley to smash into its lightly armored sides. A microsecond later, the vehicle, spewing smoke, swung off the road, toppling in slow motion down the slope and coming to a rest with a sickening crunch against a huge boulder.

The flat ripping crack of heavy machine gun fire as it flayed the rest of the convoy signaled the next phase of the operation. Chips of basalt splintered off the cliff and were whining viciously overhead. The task now was to pick off the DocSec troopers as they struggled to get clear of vehicles slamming to a halt in confusion behind the second APC, which was now a smoking ruin slewed across the road.

The DocSec troopers spilling out of the trucks had nowhere to run. Every direction they turned, they faced a lethal blizzard of carbine and heavy machine gun fire. In minutes it was all over. The convoy was jammed nose to tail in an untidy, crumpled line of smoking, ruined wrecks strewn along the road, with the bodies of the DocSec troopers lying where they had been cut down. NRA troopers were walking down the line, the flat crack of a single shot now and again ringing out as any DocSec troopers still left alive were consigned to Kraa.

Beyond the carnage, a thin plume of smoke marked where the surveillance drone had plunged to earth.

Michael lay there, any temptation to join in completely negated by the brutal, ruthless efficiency of it all. The whole business was over in a matter of minutes; the ambushers already were beginning to pull back. The NRA might be a bunch of raggedy-assed guerrillas, but they could fight, by God. He was no expert, but it all looked pretty textbook to him, with the Hammers first caught between the jaws of the ambush and then, unable to reach cover, butchered where they had been pinned down.

After the echoes from the last shot had died away, the silence was broken only by the sounds of the river and the metallic clicking of rapidly cooling engines. As Michael panned slowly across the ambush site, he noticed that something was wrong, something was missing. He had not noticed it before, but there were only three DocSec APCs: two at the front of the convoy but only one at the rear, where there should have been two. Before he could ask Tabor where the missing half-track was, the man stood up.

"Time to go," Tabor ordered.

Michael decided that the question of the missing APC could wait for another day. Tabor obviously had forgotten about it. He had turned and, in a half run, was making his way down to the river. Without hesitating, he plunged in and was across, climbing up to the road. He paused to make sure Michael was close behind.

"One klick that way." He pointed down the road. "Ravine to the right will get us off the road. Let's go. Fast."

They took off. Michael knew that the surveillance drone would have gotten a contact report out even as it plunged to its death on the rock-strewn slopes below. That meant ground attack aircraft from Perkins Planetary Defense Base would be on their way any minute now.

They had crossed the river and were on the road when proof that things did not always go the NRA's way turned up. The missing DocSec APC, clearly in a hurry to catch up, came around the corner, bearing down on them almost before they were aware of it. Acting on instinct, Michael, with Tabor close behind, leaped for the safety of the shallow ditch even as the APC succumbed to a single missile launched by the downstream cut-off group. Michael flinched as the backblast from the explosion battered his ears. A second missile drove the APC off the road, the shattered wreck coming to a crunching halt against the rock wall. Michael offered up a quick prayer of thanks that someone in the ambush force was paying attention even as he cursed the ambush commander for not warning Tabor that there was one more APC on the way.

Tabor waved Michael up and out of the ditch. "Come on, Michael. We've got people to meet."

Michael scrambled out of the ditch and onto the road. As he and Tabor ran past the smoking ruin of the APC, the rear doors banged open and a black-jumpsuited DocSec trooper half crawled, half fell out of the APC onto the road.

Tabor did not hesitate. He reacted first, but Michael was only a half second behind, the two men pouring a hail of fire into the hapless trooper. Michael grunted in satisfaction at the sight of the bullet-riddled body sprawled awkwardly across the road.

Tabor peered into the APC. Reaching in, he effortlessly dragged out a bulky DocSec officer, black woven rank badges on his combat jumpsuit marking him out as a major. Dumping him on the road, Tabor reached in and dragged out a second officer, this one a lieutenant.

"Convoy commander," Tabor grunted. "Must have gotten held up. Should have turned around and run, stupid man." The major suddenly moaned, his eyes opening, glazed and unseeing.

Tabor did not hesitate. He stepped back a meter and carefully put a single shot into the man's forehead. "DocSec trash," he hissed, leaning forward to spit with great care into the dead man's face. He waved Michael forward. "Check the other one while I clean out this one's pockets."

Michael did as he was told. The DocSec lieutenant was still alive. Michael did not hesitate. "That's for Corporal Yazdi, you piece of DocSec filth," he whispered viciously, his gun coming up to fire two shots in quick succession.

"You're learning," Tabor muttered approvingly as he stood up. "Come on. We need to go."

Michael nodded. Two DocSec down, millions more to go, but it was a start.

Tabor unclipped a grenade and casually underhanded it into the APC. By the time the grenade blew the inside of the vehicle apart, Michael and Tabor were safely down the road on their way to the safety of the scrub-filled ravine.

After a lung-burning climb, Michael and Tabor cleared the ravine and were across the saddle on their way down the other side when the two ground attack aircraft belatedly arrived from Perkins. Michael and Tabor dived for cover as first one and then a second howled overhead before disappearing up the valley to begin their search.

"That's good"—Tabor struggled to refill oxygen-starved lungs—"235s with full loads. Klaxons, I think you Feds call them. They'll beat the area up a bit and then piss off, hopefully well before DocSec can drop in a ground force to pin us down. If they even try, which I doubt." Tabor had to fight to get the words out between gasps. "DocSec has no stomach for a fight. They'll take their time; they'll wait for PDF or marine armor to secure the road first. Gutless pigs." Tabor spit, his contempt for DocSec obvious.

For a good forty-five minutes the Klaxons circled over the ambush site. Michael hoped that the sustained bursts of cannon fire and the dull thudding whump of fuel-air bombs going off were more in hope than in expectation. Twice, one of the Klaxons, obviously convinced it had located a cave full of heretics, climbed to 10,000 meters before dropping a bunker buster, the rocket-powered, case-hardened projectile going hypersonic before driving deep into the rock, the ultra-low-yield tacnuke warhead exploding deep underground with a sharp crack that made the earth shake. Michael shook his head; only the Hammers would use nukes on their home planet.

"Those clowns will claim they've wiped out an entire heretic brigade by the time they've finished, I suppose?" Michael asked.

Tabor nodded. "They will. If you believe Portillo, his ground attack fliers have wiped out more NRA soldiers than there are people living in McNair." He spit dismissively.

Tabor tipped his head to one side and listened intently for a moment. "Sounds to me like they're moving east. Shit, I hope the team got away. Anyway, it's good news for us. When I'm sure, we'll move out."

"What about drones? Surely they'll have those over the top of us."

"They will, but we're going in the wrong direction. Safety for the NRA is that way"—Tabor pointed southeast—"and the Hammers know it, so that's where the drones will go. We're going that way," he said, pointing northwest, "but we do need to get below the tree line as fast as we can. So keep your eyes open. Remember, if they come over the top of us, lie still, and I mean still. Let your chromaflage do the work." He paused. "Right, I think they've gone."

With one last check that the Klaxons really were gone, Tabor was on his way, Michael in hot pursuit.

Saturday, January 1, 2400, UD
Branxton Ranges, Commitment

Tabor shook Michael's hand.

"Good luck," he whispered. "Your pickup team may take some time, so be patient. Getting here is not easy, even for you Feds and all your smart-ass technology. But don't worry. They will be here." Without another word, he vanished into the darkness.

Michael lay under his chromaflage cover, stifling an unexpected urge to call Tabor back. All of a sudden he was absolutely terrified, his chest heaving as fear threatened to panic him into running after the man.

A tenuous shred of self-control kept him together. Bit by bit his breathing slowed until he got himself together. He was still scared shitless, but the overwhelming urge to bolt had passed, thankfully.

The hours dragged past, and despite still being scared shitless, Michael had begun to doze off when a rustle in the grass in front of him snapped him fully awake, his senses straining to work out what the noise meant. He tightened his grip on his assault carbine, slowly working it forward, ready to fire. Barely able to breathe, he looked intently out into the darkness from under his cape but saw only the dim outlines of starlit bushes and trees.

"Helfort!" a voice hissed softly.

The voice was so close and so unexpected that Michael jumped. He had not seen a damn thing. Before he could do anything, a hand had clamped itself onto his wrist and a whispered voice was in his ear.

"Lance Corporal Jamal, FedWorld Marine Corps. Time to go, sir."

Heart racing, Michael put his head down onto the earth and lay there for a moment. This was going beyond a joke.

He looked up to where the voice had come from.

"Good to see you. I can't tell you—" He choked on the words.

"Later. We need to go. But first let's get you properly dressed."

Jamal quickly stripped him of all his Hammer clothes, waiting patiently as Michael struggled into a marine-grade active chromaflage skinsuit complete with battle helmet and short-range laser tightbeam comms. With quiet efficiency, Jamal checked that everything worked.

"Good," he said finally. "We're ready. Now, follow me but not too close. Stay ten meters behind me. If anything happens, drop to the ground and stay there until I come back to get you. No heroics, and for God's sake, use that damn carbine only as a last resort. Got all that?"

"Yes," Michael said meekly, his confidence growing by the minute in the face of Jamal's quiet self-assurance.

"Right. Let's go."

While they walked, Jamal tightbeamed him the plan. Michael studied it carefully. The plan seemed pretty simple. Heading for Bretonville, they would work their way down through the forests that covered the flanks of the Branxton Ranges until they reached the main McNair–New Berlin motorway. They would cross the motorway south of Bretonville, using one of its many underpasses, and, once clear, would turn west to head for the fishing town of Piper. The pickup point was two kilometers outside Piper. When Michael asked how the pickup would work, Jamal refused to tell him. "You don't need to know," he said. "Trust me and do as you're told."

Michael did the only thing he could. Head down, lungs burning, he followed the marine toward Bretonville, praying every step of the way that Lance Corporal Jamal knew what he was doing.

The Federated Worlds ambassador to the Hammer of Kraa Worlds felt physically ill as he looked down at the emaciated body in the sick-bay cot. Michael Helfort was sleeping the sleep of the dead. The embassy doctor had commed him the results of his exhaustive medical. It made distressing reading.

The ambassador shook his head again. Helfort's body could be fixed—there was no doubt about that—but what about his mind?

He left Michael to sleep. He commed Amos Bichel. He needed to know two things: How were they going to get Helfort home? And what were they going to do about the rest of the survivors of the *Ishaq,* who, despite the Hammers' increasingly desperate efforts to recover them, were still at liberty somewhere deep in the trackless wastes of the Forest of Gwyr?

The ambassador sighed. What a bloody mess. Since the Hammer was involved, it was a mess that could—no, definitely would—only get worse.

Michael's heart was hammering, his mouth bone-dry. He could not help himself. The prospect of leaving the safety and security of the FedWorld embassy compound absolutely terrified him. He took a deep breath to stiffen himself and stepped forward. He was about to climb into the secret compartment slung under the embassy people mover when the ambassador's hand on his arm stopped him.

"Good luck, Michael."

They shook hands. "Thank you, sir."

"Look after Marine Shinoda. The marines want her back in one piece."

"I'll make sure they do, sir." Michael tried hard not to think about Corporal Yazdi lying alone in a shallow grave on some godforsaken mountainside.

Five minutes later, the people mover cleared the embassy compound and, with its DocSec escort falling in close behind, was on its way south.

Later that morning, a young couple—poor country people to judge from their clothes—made their way into Bretonville Station. Tickets clutched in hand, they boarded the maglev express to McNair. A passing DocSec patrol did not bother to check them out. They were just another pair of country bumpkins going up to the big smoke, so why bother?

An hour later, the couple stood in the impressively ornate lobby of the state lottery office, models of embarrassed indecision. Eventually, one of the staff deigned to notice their predicament and waved at them to go inside to the counter.

A bored clerk looked up at them as they approached. "Yes?"

Michael cleared his throat. He hoped that the vocalization

reprogramming that had been dumped into his neuronics would work as advertised. If it had not given him the flat, crushed vowels of a native-born Hammer, he and Marine Shinoda would be in a lot of trouble.

"Umm, yes. Er, we, we have a winning ticket in last night's lottery and I, er . . . I would like to collect that, please, if you could, um, help us, please," Michael gibbered. Christ, he was nervous, which was probably a good thing. He did not have to work too hard to look like the hayseed his clothes and identity card declared him to be. And speaking of identity cards, he had been hugely impressed with Bichel's technical team. He and Shinoda were now fully paid-up members of DocSec's Section 4 Knowledge Base, something Michael never would have believed possible. Apparently it was. If that wasn't impressive enough, Bichel's team had hacked into the state lottery to give him a winning ticket. It was the simplest way to give them a sizable lump of untraceable local funds without creating a public profile, Bichel had said smugly.

An elbow in the ribs from Shinoda brought him back to reality.

"The ticket, husband. Give the man the ticket," she whispered, a paragon of the wifely deference so prized by Hammer men.

"Oh, yes. Hang on." Michael fumbled in a pocket. "Here it is."

The clerk checked the ticket painstakingly before running it under a scanner. After a short pause, he nodded.

"It's for 250,000 k-dollars," he said, "and no publicity." The clerk, elevating bored disinterest to an art form, did not even ask for Michael's identity card before handing over an anonymous stored value card loaded with their winnings. Michael held the small plastic card tightly and marveled at the inconsistency of it all. On the one hand, the Hammer was the most tightly controlled society in human history. On the other hand, they still used anonymous stored value cards; Bichel had told him there was no limit to the amount they could carry. Michael suspected he knew why. Corruption on the massive scale that infected Hammer society could flourish only if huge amounts of money could move untraced, hence the anonymous stored value card clamped in his hand.

Five minutes later, his confidence rising by the minute, Michael and Shinoda were on their way to get exit visas for Scobie's World from the downtown DocSec visa office. That, too, happened without any fuss. The visa clerk, openly impressed by their lottery win and surprisingly unresentful, downloaded the visas they needed into their identity cards in a fraction of the time Bichel had warned it might take. They made two more stops—to buy tickets on the first starliner for Scobie's World and to find new clothes—before they were finally on their way to McNair spaceport, a pair of exuberant, blow-it-all lottery winners.

For Michael, the tension was finally easing. He had one last DocSec check to get through, and then he would be off this goddamned planet, never to return, he hoped. No, that was not right; he would happily come back as long as he was piloting a FedWorld assault lander. His newfound belief in Bichel's technical team was growing to a point where he was beginning to enjoy the whole business even though the suicide pill he had asked for—which, somewhat to his surprise, he had been given—was a constant reminder not to get too confident.

Things that could go wrong often did.

Not this time.

With mounting excitement, Michael, his hand tightly locked in Shinoda's, stood at the floor-to-ceiling plate of armored plasglass that formed an entire wall of the first-class lounge. He was watching something he had not dared dream about: the planet Commitment receding slowly away from them as the liner *Councillor Vladimir Spassky* began its slow acceleration out-system. He gave in to a sudden wave of impulsive happiness and picked Shinoda up, folding her into a bear hug of an embrace, the relief swamping his body madly intoxicating.

"Watch it, sailor," she whispered into his ear as he swung her around. "We may be Mr. and Mrs. Benoit to those shit-sucking Hammers, but . . ."

Michael laughed out loud as he put her down. "Sorry," he whispered back. "It's been a tough few months."

"I know," Shinoda said.

Afterward, Michael realized that he should not have been surprised at what had happened. Nature had its own ways of helping broken minds mend. Falling into bed with Marine Shinoda a day out from Commitment, overwhelmed by a wave of physical desire that he was not going to argue with, was probably one of them.

Try as hard as he might, he did not feel the slightest bit guilty at betraying the promises he had made to Anna.

That was then. This was now. Against all the odds, he was alive. He was battered, he was bruised, he had injuries he would carry for the rest of his life, but he was alive.

"Good afternoon, ladies and gentlemen. We have docked, and you may now disembark. We trust you had a good trip. We look forward to seeing you all again on board soon."

Not a chance, pal, Michael said to himself, not a chance in hell.

He and Shinoda hung back. Around them, excited Hammers, voices raised at the prospect of shaking off the petty repressions inflicted on them back home, poured off the *Councillor Vladimir Spassky* straight into the milling line piling up at immigration control. But even there they were not out of the Hammer's reach. Officially, Scobie's World was an independent, sovereign system, a fiction cruelly exposed by the DocSec trooper sitting behind the clerks processing the new arrivals.

Michael shivered at the sight of the hated black uniform. He knew as well as anyone that it took a delicate balancing act to maintain Scobie's independence. On the one hand, Scobie's World tried extremely hard not to upset the Hammer. On the other hand, it tried equally hard not to be classed as a Hammer vassal system with all the economic restrictions that would bring. But in the end, most of what Scobie's World did was on the Hammer's terms, and one of those terms was ceding de facto control to DocSec over everyone arriving on or leaving the place. That was not surprising. The

Hammer was well aware that many of its citizens would never return home given the chance.

The line began to shrink. The time had come for Mr. and Mrs. Benoit to disappear.

Michael and Shinoda, waved through immigration without incident, took the first shuttle heading dirtside for the capital of Scobie's World, New Dublin. Once they had passed through the spaceport, a mobibot took them into town and dropped them off right in the heart of the city. New Dublin's mixture of the garish and the shabby was expertly tailored to the Hammer tourists who infested every souvenir shop, every wedding chapel—Doctrine of Kraa ceremonies a speciality—every bar, every casino, every strip club, every massage parlor, and every brothel. Michael shook his head in disbelief. How anyone with half a brain could enjoy a shithole like New Dublin was beyond him. He would be glad to get off-planet, and the sooner the better, even if it meant the end of his unplanned relationship with Marine Shinoda.

It took two more mobibots before Michael started to feel safe. "What do you think?" he asked.

Shinoda's head had not stopped moving from the moment they had left the *Councillor Vladimir Spassky*, her neuronics working overtime to make sure the faces of the people they met did not reappear around the next corner, that the pattern of movement around them was that of Scobie's Worlders going about their everyday business.

"Well," she said, "I think it's safe to say that I don't think anyone is even the slightest bit interested in two Hammer tourists wandering around this back-blocks shithole."

Shinoda grinned as Michael folded her into a fierce bear hug.

"God, I hope so," he whispered into her ear.

Shinoda laughed. "Put me down, sailor. Come on. We've got work to do. This way."

Michael followed Shinoda past endless giant holovid screens pulsing with light and color. He shook his head. From what he could see, nothing was off-limits. If it could be bought, someone on Scobie's World would sell it to you. Shinoda made a quick final check as they turned down a narrow street. Michael winced as he laid eyes on their final destination. Crass did not even begin to describe it. Twenty meters from the corner was the Leprechaun's Retreat Irish Bar and Restaurant, its exterior festooned with enough virulently green shamrocks and gold harps to leave even the dumbest Hammer in no doubt that this place was a genuine Irish bar.

Michael and Shinoda plunged inside, the noise deafening as a small band struggled to be heard over the determined efforts of hundreds of Hammers to have a good time, an exercise that largely appeared to mean getting blind drunk in the shortest possible time. There, toward the back, was what they had come so far to find: a small, disheveled, and extremely drunk Hammer doing a bad job of singing along with the band.

Michael flicked a glance at Shinoda. She nodded. The logo on the T-shirt—-an obscene cartoon of a pig doing something unspeakable with a large cucumber—identified him as the man who would give them the new identities and clothes they needed to get off-planet.

Twenty minutes later, Michael and Shinoda were in a mobibot on their way back to the spaceport.

Michael sat silently, savoring the wonderful feeling of connectedness that enveloped him as he let his neuronics hook into the net. He had been out of touch for a long time, and even if he could not talk to the AI-generated personal agent who managed the routine details of his life, it was good to be able to find out what was going on in humanspace without having to watch the turgid bullshit that passed for a Hammer newsvid.

The news was not good.

The Hammers clearly were having some success with their campaign against Fed merchant shipping. From the look of it, Fleet was having a hard time coping with hit-and-run attacks that had spread right across humanspace. The government was paying the price; most commentators were confident in their predictions that the New Liberal government of Moderator Burkhardt was finished.

Michael stopped scanning after a while. It did not make sense, any of it. He could not even begin to understand why the Hammers were doing what they were doing. The elaborate scheme they had concocted was unraveling badly. When the Fed government saw his neuronics records, the Hammer's days had to be numbered. After the *Mumtaz* affair, the government would rip the heart out of the Hammers and nail it, bleeding, to the nearest wall.

He smiled, a smile utterly devoid of charity, the smile of a man watching his bitterest enemy swing on the end of a rope. Well, if it came to that, he would be there. That was for sure. He was in the mood to rip out a Hammer heart or two.

"Spacer Torrens, Spacer McArthur. Returning to the Fed-World Courier Ship *Spacerunner.*"

Michael's mouth was bone-dry. He could not help it. This was the tricky bit. Hacking into the Hammer's knowledge base to create false identities for him and Shinoda was one thing. Hacking into Scobie's immigration control systems was quite another, not least because unlike the Hammers, they would use purpose-built security AIs to manage their system audits. In theory, that should make a successful hack next to impossible, though if that had been the case, he and Shinoda would not be standing there. Michael could only hope that the unknown hackers had done a proper job. Fingers crossed, he stood waiting.

"Comm me your entry permits and full identities. Finger in the scanner for DNA matching." The immigration officer did not bother to conceal his lack of interest. Nor, to Michael's relief, did the inevitable DocSec watchdog.

Michael and Shinoda did as they were told. An anxious pause followed as they waited for the system to confirm that they were legitimate crew members of the *Spacerunner.*

With a flick of the wrist, the officer commed them the clearances they needed. He waved them through. Ignoring a sudden desperate urge to break into a run, Michael walked into the access tube.

Then he was through *Spacerunner*'s air lock and back on sovereign FedWorld territory. He got only another meter before his attempt to confirm his identity to the ship's staff crumbled to dust. All of a sudden, it all became too much, the accumulated stress of the past months driving him onto his knees.

He was safe.

"Feeling better?" the *Spacerunner*'s doctor asked.

Michael nodded. He certainly was. His body never missed an opportunity to remind him of some old injury or other, and deep down inside he was far from all right, but as long as he did not think too much, he felt pretty good. He had slept well, breakfast had been as good as anything the first-class restaurant on the liner served, and the young doctor standing in front of him was no more a commercial spacer than he was. She was FedWorld Space Fleet from her regulation haircut right down to her fleet-issue boots, and Michael felt all the better for it.

The doctor smiled. "Good. Now, I have some people who have been on my back from the moment you arrived on board. They want to talk to you. You okay with that? Because if you're not, they can wait."

Michael shook his head. No matter how much he wanted to forget the past, he had to tell the debriefing team everything he knew—good and bad—if he was ever to come to terms with what he had done, what he had been through.

"No, no. I'm fine. Where do they want me?"

"Conference 2. Ship's AI will show you the way. You can contact me any time if you need a break. Got that? Call me any time at all, and I'll put a stop to it."

Michael nodded as he got to his feet. "Thanks."

The doctor took his arm. "Michael."

"Yes?"

"Don't let them push you around. When you've had enough, you call me. Is that understood?"

Michael bobbed his head. She would never understand that he wanted to unburden himself, and now.

The doctor watched Michael as he made his way out of the sick bay. She shook her head as she began her draft report to Fleet's surgeon in chief.

"Thank you, Michael. You've been most helpful. You understand how sensitive this all is, so I'm going to put a neuronics block on it for the moment. Once the Hammer's part in all this is in the public domain, then it'll be lifted. Until then, I've classified it as top secret—no foreign eyes. Okay?"

Michael nodded. "Fine by me, sir." He had expected to face a Fleet debriefing team, but he was pretty sure that neither of the two men who had sat patiently listening to his account of what had happened since the *Ishaq* had been destroyed was Fleet. He thought they were spooks, Department 24 most likely.

"Okay. That's it. We'll be dropping soon, so you can go and get ready for that bit of fun and games."

"Thank you, sir." Michael was gone in a flash.

The two men waited until the door hissed shut behind Michael. The older of the two got up and started to pace up and down. "What a bloody mess," he said.

"More than a mess," the second man replied. "I'm no lawyer, but the Barkersville police station attack is a problem. Legally, it's murder. No argument."

"I'm afraid it is. Anyway, that's for someone else to sort out. I would hate to be the person who puts Helfort in the dock for murdering two Hammers, even if it was in cold blood. The great unwashed would have me hanging from a lamppost in no time flat. Christ! The pollies are going to shit themselves when this little mess comes home to roost."

"They are, by God. You know what? I don't think I would have done anything different."

"Nor me. Bloody Hammers. Come on, enough navel gazing. We've got a report to write."

For some reason, Michael felt more nervous than the last time he had faced DocSec. He was so nervous, he could not stay still, standing up and then sitting down and then standing up again.

Finally the door opened. In quick succession, his mother, his father, and his sister Sam rushed into the room, and in seconds he was enveloped in all their arms, the tears running uncontrollably down all their faces.

"Christ, son, but you're a worry," his dad said when he had gotten himself back under control. "Any chance of your transferring to the Parks and Wildlife Service?"

Michael smiled tightly. He knew his dad would pressure him to leave the Fleet. Who could blame him? First the *Mumtaz* business, then the Battle of Hell's Moons, and now all this. His dad should pressure him. Michael could see what it was doing to him. His father looked ten years older than he had when Michael had left to join the *Ishaq*.

"Dad, Mum, Sam, sit down. We need to talk."

When his parents left, Michael sat down heavily. Things had not gone well. His parents had refused to see that his promise to Corporal Yazdi meant something, and Sam had agreed with them. Let someone else deal with the Hammer, she had cried. Why you? You've done enough.

For Michael, it was very simple. A promise to a fallen comrade was a promise that had to be kept.

And he had not begun to do enough. He had not even started. He had debts to collect, debts payable in blood, the blood of the Hammers responsible for the spacers killed on board *DLS-387* during the Battle of Hell's Moons, of the

Hammers responsible for the spacers and marines killed when *Ishaq* blew, of the DocSec thugs who had nearly killed him, of the Hammers who had killed Corporal Yazdi.

Oh, yes. He would collect no matter what his family and friends argued.

Tomorrow the doctors would start repairing the physical damage the Hammers had done to his body. Three days of back-to-back operations, they had said. Then it would be the shrinks' turn, though Michael had no intention of letting them anywhere near the flame of hate that burned deep within him. Nor would he let them see the part of him that wanted to give up completely, to let it all go, to find somewhere quiet, dark, safe. Maybe somewhere to end it all before the hate and fear and guilt drove him over the edge, chased every step of the way by the ghostly face of Detective Sergeant Kalkov, a face that pursued him through the twists and turns of every nightmare-filled night.

No, that was too easy.

He was physically scarred, but the shrinks would not see the emotional scars. He would not let them. They would assess him as mentally bruised but basically okay. He had no doubts of that. By the time he recovered, he would be passed A-1, fit for frontline Fleet service. When that happened, they could not stop his return to active duty. The day of reckoning for the Hammer was approaching fast, and he had every intention of being there when it came.

Saturday, January 22, 2400, UD
Base hospital, Federated Worlds Space Fleet College,
Terranova

Michael struggled to sit upright in bed as a tall, lanky officer walked in, gold shoulder badges flashing in the light of the late afternoon sun.

"Afternoon, Helfort. Feeling okay?" the man asked cheerfully.

"Better, sir. Thanks." It was not quite true. The doctors and their damn nanobots had spent a long time inside his body over the previous three days, and he had the aches and pains to prove it.

"Good. The doctors seem pleased. You've come through well, and they assure me that you will be one hundred percent physically by the end of next month. We need to talk. Let me close the door and grab a seat."

When Michael's visitor was settled, he looked Michael right in the eye.

"I'm Captain Vitharana, deputy Fleet advocate general."

Michael nodded. "I know, sir. I remember you. Space College. Two lectures on the laws governing the conduct of war."

"Ah." Vitharana smiled. "Gripping stuff, no doubt."

"Certainly was, sir. Every minute."

"Well, I'm glad someone was awake." Vitharana laughed. "As I recall, cadets can sleep with their eyes open, and most probably did. Anyway, we digress. I need to talk to you about Barkersville."

Michael's heart sank. He was not stupid. He had seen how the debriefing team had reacted when he had described what had happened that awful night. Since then, it had been nagging at him, the nightmares starring Detective Sergeant Kalkov making damn sure not a day went by without his reliving the moment when he had slid his knife into the man's heart. He knew Kalkov's death was wrong—completely and unforgivably wrong. So how would the powers that be see it? He had a sinking feeling that he was about to find out.

Michael took a deep breath. "I think we do, sir," he said levelly. "I've been thinking a lot about Barkersville."

"Well, Helfort, here's the problem. We've looked in detail at your debriefing report as well as all the downloads you provided, and so has the attorney general."

Michael's eyebrows shot up. "The attorney general, sir?" Michael looked confused. What was she doing getting involved? Surely this was a Fleet matter.

"The attorney general, yes. Unlike your attack on Kraneveldt—well done, by the way—the Barkersville incident involved nonmilitary personnel outside the defense force chain of command. It falls to her to decide how the matter should be handled. So let me cut to the chase." Vitharana took a deep breath. "The attorney general believes she has grounds to indict you for the murders of, of . . . now let me see. Ah, yes, a Detective Sergeant Kalkov, Commitment Planetary Police Service, and Trooper Askali, Hammer of Kraa Doctrinal Security Service."

Michael lay there propped up on his pillows, a shocked look on his face, as Vitharana plowed on.

"So that's what she thinks. Now, before you get too concerned, let me tell you what we think, and when I say 'we,' I mean everyone above me in the chain of command up as far as the president. It's pretty simple, really. Irrespective of the merits of the attorney general's views, Fleet cannot—will not—allow one of its officers to be tried for murders committed in the circumstances in which you found yourself. Which is fine, except Fleet cannot alter the facts of what happened. Nor can Fleet tell the attorney general what to do or what not to do. Legally, nobody can. Now, we have to find a way around this problem, and so I have a proposal for you to consider. I'm going to give you twenty-four hours to think it over. I'll be back to talk to you tomorrow to see what you think. Understand?"

Michael nodded. "Sir!" What else could he say?

"Good. Now, here's what we propose. In a nutshell, we intend to bypass the attorney general by petitioning the president to pardon you for the Barkersville matter. If she grants the pardon, the attorney general can proceed with the indictment if she wishes. But if she did get the matter into court, you would enter a plea of pardon, and provided of course the pardon was valid—and let me assure you, Helfort, it most certainly will be—then the court would have no alternative but to throw the matter out on its ear, so to speak."

"That's a lot of 'if's, sir," Michael said dubiously.

Vitharana shook his head. "No, not really. Suffice it to say that the commander in chief has every confidence that this matter can be resolved. With the president's assistance, of course, and I think you can have every confidence in the commander in chief. It's generally a good habit for junior officers to get into," he added wryly.

Michael thought about it. It all sounded too easy. There had to be a catch. There always was.

"Fine, sir. That's clear. So what's the catch?"

"Ah!" Vitharana had the decency to look faintly embarrassed. "The doctors told me there's nothing wrong with your faculties. Yes, there is a catch, I'm afraid." Vitharana paused.

"Yes?" Michael asked. He wanted this business over with.

"Sorry, yes. The catch is that you must plead guilty before the pardon is even considered by the president."

Michael did not like the sound of that, not one bit. "And let me guess. That plea is admissible in later proceedings? If the pardon is not granted, for example."

Vitharana nodded. "Yes, that's right."

"So I put my head in the noose and hope like hell that the president cuts the rope? Sir, that's an awful lot of trusting!" He shook his head. Suddenly, Vitharana's plan was not looking too attractive.

"Helfort," Vitharana said sternly, "listen to me. I can promise you this: Fleet will not let you down. One way or another, this matter will be resolved in your favor. So yes, there is an awful lot of trusting needed, as you put it, but sometimes that is what's required. So that's the decision you need to make. Do you trust Fleet or not? Simple as that."

"Understood, sir."

"Right. I'll comm you the detailed proposal. Have a good look at it, talk to the Space College legal AI if you need to, and believe me, I really think you should. If you have any questions the AI can't help you with, then you call me at any time. Any time. Okay?"

"Got it, sir."

"Good. I'll see you tomorrow."

Captain Vitharana had been gone a long time, but still Michael lay thinking through the extraordinary proposal the man had put to him.

Quite how Fleet could persuade the president to cooperate, Michael had no idea. He was not even sure it could. But Vitharana had sounded awfully sure of himself, so he could only assume that the president must have been briefed already; somehow—a wink, a nod?—she must have convinced Fleet she would go along with its plan to get him off the hook. He still had to plead guilty, and for him to do that would not be easy. It might even be impossible. Talking about what had happened in Barkersville was one thing, but entering a formal admission of guilt? That was different.

He would have to sleep on it.

Saturday, January 22, 2400, UD
Forest of Gwyr, Carolyn Ranges, Commitment

Lieutenant Commander Fellsworth moodily poked at the small fire she had coaxed into life, its flames throwing splashes of yellow-gold onto the walls of the huge limestone cavern that had been her home for what seemed like a lifetime.

Cursing the fate that had posted her to the *Ishaq* in the first place, she spit into the fire and got up. Time to walk around her little empire. No sooner had she started to climb up the mound of broken limestone that nearly filled the mouth of the cave than a figure burst in, the spacer's excitement plain to see.

"Got a tickle; my neuronics got a tickle!" the woman shouted. "We've been found!"

Looking back later, Fellsworth would swear that her heart stopped for a moment. For so long she'd wanted to believe that somehow one of her spacers had gotten a message through to the embassy in McNair. Now, when proof finally had arrived, she could not believe it.

"Show me," she ordered, scrambling out of the cave into the open air.

Five minutes later, she sat watching in disbelief as a little flybot maneuvered with exquisite precision down through the forest canopy before setting down on the ground right in front of her.

"Fuuuck," Fellsworth hissed through clenched teeth. They had been found. They really had been found. The *Ishaq*s around her erupted into cheers, laughter, shouts. Spacers and marines in tattered shipsuits were dancing around the little bot in an uncontrolled frenzy of joy, the noise rising as word spread, the rest of the *Ishaq*s pouring in to see what all the fuss was about.

It took a while, but finally Fellsworth restored order. She commed into the bot and, her identity confirmed, waved one of the spacers to flip the bot over, its belly opening to reveal the payload of comm gear. To whom it would connect her, she had no idea, but as long as it worked, she did not care. It sure as hell would not be to the Hammers.

Amos Bichel terminated the voice call from Fellsworth.

Finally, he thought, he had something to plan around, though how in God's name they were going to get the *Ishaq*'s crew off-planet was completely beyond him at the moment. There was no obvious answer to that problem. At least they now had absolute, incontrovertible proof that the Hammer had been behind the destruction of the *Ishaq*. Helfort's testimony was good but, on its own, not good enough. This was. It pinned the whole mership campaign on the Hammers; now they were on borrowed time.

Comming the ambassador, he started to put together his report. If he was quick, he would get a courier away in time to catch the next flight out.

It had been a long night and an even longer day, but finally Michael had decided what he would do.

It was simple in the end. He had done what he had done despite knowing it was wrong because he had not had the balls to stand up to Yazdi. So he was going to come clean, admit his guilt, and hope that Vitharana's plan worked as advertised. The alternative—indictment, courts, a trial, the trashpress in overdrive—just did not bear thinking about.

The door opened to admit Captain Vitharana. A woman wearing the distinctive gold gorget of a registered observer followed him. Christ! Things were getting serious, Michael thought, if he merited one of them.

Vitharana wasted no time. He did not even bother to introduce the observer.

"Right, Helfort," he said briskly. "Have you made a decision?"

"Yes, sir. I have."

"You've taken advice, I hope?"

"I have, sir, from the college legal AI. She was very helpful."

"Good. So?" Vitharana asked.

Michael did not look at Vitharana, staring instead at the registered observer. He wanted every second of this recorded and recorded properly. He took a deep breath to steady his jangling nerves. This was not easy. "I take full responsibility for what happened at Barkersville. For the murders of Detective Sergeant Kalkov, Commitment Planetary Police Service, and Trooper Askali, Hammer of Kraa Doctrinal Security Service." His voice hardened. "I take full responsibility for all of it, sir, including those that Corporal Yazdi, you know . . ." He faltered, turning back to Vitharana. He could not say the words.

Vitharana got it, anyway. He nodded.

"I was the senior officer present, sir," Michael continued, his voice firm again. "I had the command authority to stop what happened. I could have, should have stopped the murders, all of them, but I did not. For that reason, I take full responsibility for my actions and those of Corporal Yazdi. That's what I want to say. I have a detailed statement prepared that I would like to comm to the registered observer. That'll cover it all."

"Let me read it first."

Michael shook his head. "No, sir. I don't want anyone to say that it was not entirely my statement. I've stuck to the facts, so I can't have gone too wrong. If you don't mind."

Vitharana looked surprised and more than a little discomfited. He was obviously not used to junior lieutenants telling him what he could and could not do.

"Go ahead, then."

The registered observer had gone. For a while there was silence, the two men happy to let things slide for a moment.

Vitharana broke the silence. "You've done the right thing, Michael. You know that?"

Michael nodded. He thought, hoped he had.

"Good. Let's leave that for a moment. Now, I've spoken to your doctors. They say you are making good progress and it's okay for me to take you out for the day as long as you don't do any walking. So I've set up a meeting, which I would like you to attend." Vitharana got up to leave. "I'll pick you up here tomorrow at 10:00 sharp. Dress blacks."

Michael looked puzzled. The only clothes he had were hospital-issue pajamas. Apart from his shipsuit and boots, he had lost everything else when the *Ishaq* blew. "Dress blacks? Why—"

"Ours is not to reason why, Michael. A brand-new set will be delivered first thing tomorrow."

Michael almost shook his head as Vitharana left. The whole world had gone nuts. Where in God's name would he be going in dress blacks?

Despite the best efforts of generations of politicians to persuade them otherwise, the citizens of the Federated Worlds held an unshakable belief that their public servants, however important, should not be glorified by the construction of elaborate buildings.

So it was that the president's official residence was an unassuming if sprawling affair of pink-gray Terranovan granite spread across a few hectares on the lower slopes of the New Tatras on the western side of Foundation. Around the residence, gardens showed off the best FedWorld plant geneering had to offer, the long winding drive passing through a riot of vegetation, plants with leaves and flowers of every possible color, shape, and size, before it delivered visitors to a wide porch that led into the president's offices.

That was where Michael, totally bewildered, found himself being wheeled out of a Fleet mobibot and into the reception hall. It was a beautifully proportioned room floored in dark red-blond rain forest timbers taken from the tropical rain forests that covered much of the planet of Nuristan.

They did not stop. With Captain Vitharana close behind, Michael's chairbot hurried him through the hall past walls hung with holovids of past presidents gazing down with magisterial authority. There was a short pause in front of floor-to-ceiling double doors. Then the doors opened, and Michael, with open-mouthed astonishment, found the president herself getting up from her desk and bearing down on him at an alarming rate.

He started to struggle to his feet, but she put a hand up to stop him. She looked down at him for a moment, her strikingly deep brown eyes set wide under a sweep of white hair. An aide brought over a chair, and she sat down in front of him.

"Well, Michael. I expect you're somewhat confused?"

"Yes, Madame President, I think I am." What an understatement that was, he thought.

President Diouf laughed warmly, her mouth opening to show teeth perfectly white against ebony skin.

"Well, let's unconfuse you then, shall we?" she said gently.

"That would be good, Madame President," Michael replied gratefully.

"Right. Let's deal with the Barkersville business. You've taken advice, I understand."

Michael nodded.

"Good. So you'll know that a presidential pardon doesn't require a conviction in a court, though that's usually how it happens. It doesn't even require an indictment. You've been dirtside only for a matter of days, so an indictment is weeks away, and a court case months, but I am disinclined to wait that long. With me so far?"

"Yes, Madame President."

"Okay. Now, I can issue a pardon in this matter if I want to. If it is in the public interest to do so, which I can assure you it most definitely is. There's another hurdle, though. To issue a pardon, I have to believe that the person seeking the pardon not only admits guilt freely but also genuinely regrets what he has done to the point where there is no chance that the offense would be repeated. Now, that's harder than it seems because words are cheap. We all know that. You know that. But in your case it hasn't been hard, and I'll tell you why. It's because you took responsibility not only for your actions but also for those of your subordinate, Corporal Yazdi. That was the thing that clinched it. Let me just say, then, for the record"—her voice hardened—"that I am completely satisfied on the basis of the evidence presented to me that you admit your guilt freely, that you regret your actions, and that you will not repeat the offense. Right!" she said firmly. "That's the formal bit. So unless you have any questions?"

Michael shook his head. He just wanted this to be over.

"No? Good. Let's give you that pardon, then, shall we?"

President Diouf's voice changed into what Michael would

always think of afterward as the president's official voice, a voice stiff and formal, every word enunciated with careful precision.

"Junior Lieutenant Michael Wallace Helfort, Federated Worlds Space Fleet . . ."

While the president droned through the obscure and archaic legalese of a presidential pardon, Michael tuned out. Somehow an enormous weight had been lifted from him; he felt purged. He would never stop feeling guilty, but it was not going to be the burden it had been.

". . . Signed, Reshmi Diouf, President, Federated Worlds and dated the twenty-fifth day of January, two thousand four hundred, Universal Date."

The president waved an aide over. He hurried forward and handed her a single sheet of heavy cream paper carrying a large red seal. She took the document and studied it intently. She nodded, satisfied.

"Michael, this is the formal document. We will hold it on file here for you. A copy will be commed to you for your personal records. Remember, the entire affair has been classified top secret, so I suggest you forget about it. I'm certainly going to. Now, there's one more thing I want to do, so listen up . . ."

There were only two entries in the *Government Gazette* under "Presidential Notices (Honors and Awards)" for January 26, 2400. They were short and to the point:

The President today presented a member of the Federated Worlds Space Fleet with the Conspicuous Gallantry Medal for bravery in the face of the enemy.
For reasons of operational security, the member cannot be named, nor can the circumstances leading to the award be described.

The President today presented a member of the Federated Worlds Marine Corps with the Conspicuous Gallantry Medal for bravery in the face of the enemy.
The Conspicuous Gallantry Medal has been awarded

*posthumously. For reasons of operational security, the
member cannot be named, nor can the circumstances
leading to the award be described.*

Wednesday, March 15, 2400, UD
The Palisades, Ashakiran Planet

Michael hated to admit it, but he was bored shitless.

He sat, feet up on the railing, looking out across the upper
Clearwater Valley as it faded away into the haze of another
long, hot day. The family retreat in the mountains was one of
the best places in humanspace, but for Michael it rapidly was
becoming a prison, one he had been confined to ever since he
had been discharged from the hospital almost three months
earlier.

Visitors were strictly forbidden, even Anna, much to his
frustration. He was not even allowed to tell her that not only
had he survived the loss of the *Ishaq,* he was back home. He
effectively was being held incommunicado under house arrest, and that was no fun.

His emphatic refusal to resign from the Fleet was now a
major source of friction within his family, to the point where
he barely talked to his parents anymore. With little else to do,
he was watching so many trashy holovids that he was beginning to go slowly nuts, and, he reminded himself as he tossed
an empty beer bottle into the bin before comming the house-
bot to bring him another, he was definitely drinking too
much. Hell with it, he thought as he put another bottle of ice-
cold Lethbridge pilsener to his lips, what did it matter?

"Michael. In here, now!" The note of urgent alarm in his
dad's voice got him out of his chair and running into the
house in no time.

"What's up, Dad?"

His father waved an arm at the holovid, his eyes filling
with tears. He tried but could not speak as he and Michael

watched the grave face of President Diouf as she laid out in chilling detail how the Hammer had been waging a covert campaign against the Federated Worlds. Michael stopped listening. All he could think about was the fact that survivors from the *Ishaq* must have been found. Thank God for that. He hoped the people he cared for—Fellsworth, Stone, Murphy, and all the rest—had survived.

". . . and so, my fellow citizens, it is with the deepest regret that I have to tell you that as a consequence of what is little more than a sustained campaign of piracy intended to cripple our economy, the Federated Worlds Chamber of Deputies today approved the issue of a notice to the government of the Worlds of the Hammer of Kraa. That notice informs them that a state of unrestricted war is now in force. I signed that notice one hour ago."

She paused, looking directly at the holocam.

"Let me say this in closing. It will take time. It will take treasure. It will take lives. But we will utterly destroy the current government of the Hammer of Kraa. Until that happy day, the Federated Worlds cannot and will not rest. From now on, one simple phrase will show us the way forward, and it is this: Whatever it takes."

She paused again. With eyes filled with a sudden, terrible sadness, she continued.

"May God watch over us this day. Thank you for listening."

Michael's father sat there unmoving as Michael turned off the holovid. Eventually, a long time later, he spoke, his voice filled with the dying embers of hope destroyed.

"Michael?"

"Yes, Dad?"

"I can't stop you from doing what you think is right. Promise me that when it's all over, you'll come home. Please, promise me!" he said, his voice breaking.

Michael pulled him close and hugged him tight. They stayed that way for a long time.

Wednesday, March 15, 2400, UD
Offices of the Supreme Council for the Preservation of
the Faith, city of McNair, Commitment

Fleet Admiral Jorge sat down opposite an impassive Polk. Jorge's heart was racing, and his stomach churned with a sick dread. He only had one chance left, and if he did not take it, he would finish the day facedown in the bottom of a quicklime-filled trench. Polk had not needed to threaten him. Jorge knew how things worked. He did not wait for Polk to open the proceedings.

"Sir, as you instructed, we've looked at the implications of the Feds' declaration of war, and my staff and I are agreed that it changes nothing. We—"

Polk's impassivity collapsed. "Changes nothing?" he hissed venomously, smashing the flat of his hand onto the desk, the sharp crack making Jorge jump. "Changes nothing? By Kraa, you had better pray that I believe that, Admiral."

Jorge's hands went up as if Polk were about to launch himself across the desk to rip his throat out.

"Sir. Bear with me, please," Jorge pleaded. "Fleet has never, ever worked on the assumption that we could keep the Feds in the dark until we launched Operation Damascus. That would have been unforgivable. There are simply too many points of failure to be sure. So, while we hoped they would never find out, we have always assumed they might, and for that reason Rear Admiral Keniko and his planners have long had a fallback plan in case."

Polk's eyes narrowed in suspicion. This was news to him; it all sounded rather convenient.

Jorge plowed on. "Sir, I have Admiral Keniko outside. I think the best thing would be for me to have him explain the changes. I think you will see that far from setting us back, the Feds' declaration of war may play straight into our hands.

In a nutshell, we believe we can achieve all the operational objectives we set for Operation Damascus and possibly more. Our plans will change, but our objectives won't. If anything, our chances of success are much improved. So may I bring Keniko in?"

Polk nodded, trying not to encourage the little germ of hope that had sprung to life.

Jorge returned, followed by an extremely anxious-looking Keniko. Polk was not sure why Keniko was looking so worried. Kraa's blood, he was the only man in the room without a death sentence hanging over his head.

Polk did not waste time. "Let's hear it, Keniko," he growled, "and you'd better pray that I'm convinced."

"Sir!" Keniko was quite unable to conceal the tiny tremble of fear in his voice.

Friday, March 17, 2400, UD
Transit officers' quarters, Space Battle Station 39,
in orbit around Jascaria planet

Without a moment's hesitation, Michael was on his feet, folding Anna into his arms the instant she walked through the door into his cramped cabin.

"Anna," he murmured, face buried in her neck. "Oh, Anna, Anna, Anna . . ."

He stopped. Something was terribly wrong. Anna was not responding; she stood there stiff and unresponsive, arms by her side.

Michael pushed her back. "Anna?" he said, a sudden sliver of panic stabbing at his heart. This was not how it was supposed to be. "What's up?"

Anna pulled his arms from her shoulders. With a firm shove, she pushed him away, eyes filling with tears as she sat down heavily on his bunk. Michael made to sit next to her, but her hand went up.

"No, Michael," she said, her voice breaking. "No."

"Anna!" Michael said desperately, stepping back, confused and afraid. "What's the matter? For God's sake, tell me!"

She stared at him for a long time before answering, making no effort to wipe away the tears that poured down her cheeks.

"Matter?" she said finally, her voice subdued. "What's the matter? I'll tell you what's the matter. You think you can disappear for months on end? We thought you must be dead. Missing, presumed dead; that's what they told us. And now—poof! You suddenly reappear like some sort of genie?"

"Anna," Michael said, "that's all in the past. That's—"

"Shut up!" she hissed. "For once, just shut up. I don't care what you think, I don't care what you want, I don't care what you say. And you know what?" She lifted her head defiantly.

"No, what?" Michael muttered miserably.

"You're right. It is all in the past." Her voice hardened. "It's over, Michael. It's over. You're a damn fool. You can't just walk back into my life and expect things to be back where they were. You can't, you can't," she said, her voice breaking. She took a deep breath to steady herself, hands going to her face to wipe away the tears. "And I won't let you. I thought you were dead. God help me, I thought you were dead. Far as we all knew, the *Ishaq* was lost and every one of her crew with her. You included. But you weren't, and here you are again, trying to pretend that nothing has really happened."

"Anna—"

"Don't, Michael. Don't say a thing. There's nothing you can say. We're heading for another fight with those damned Hammers, and I can't, I won't stand around wondering if I'm going to lose you all over again. I can't go through that. I can't. I just can't."

With that, without giving him a chance to say anything, Anna got to her feet and was gone, the cabin door hissing shut behind her with an awful finality. Stunned, Michael could only stand there openmouthed, staring at the door as his entire world crashed around him, every fiber of his body seared by flames of despair and loss, the pain so bad that he did not know how he would survive.

*   *   *

Two days and one massive, sanity-threatening alcoholic bender later, Michael had rationalized the pain away, even though deep inside losing Anna hurt more than anything had ever hurt before. With a mental shrug of the shoulders, he had consigned her to life's out tray. He had made a promise to Corporal Yazdi, and he was going to keep it.

That was what was important right now.

Monday, March 20, 2400, UD
FWSS Eridani, *pinchspace*

Michael felt at home the minute he walked on board his new ship. The deepspace heavy scout *Eridani* had the same sense of closeness he had enjoyed in *387,* a feeling of coherence, of common purpose that the poor *Ishaq* had never enjoyed. Even better, he was able to talk to the ship's master AI—called Mother, just like in *387.*

The best news of all was the cheery presence of Matti Bienefelt. Michael had last seen her more than twelve months earlier, when the battered wreck of *DLS-387* was being loaded for its journey down to its final resting place in Braidwood National Cemetery, from where it would watch over the last remains of the spacers it had not been able to bring home safely. Here was Bienefelt again, fully recovered from the injuries she had sustained during the Battle of Hell's Moons and newly promoted to petty officer to boot. Somehow—Bienefelt refused to explain exactly how—she had wangled a posting to the *Eridani,* where she was now second in command of the heavy scout's surveillance drone team. Michael did not care how she had gotten there. It was really good to have her around again.

He settled back into his seat. He had the watch, but there was not much to do now that they were in pinchspace except keep a careful eye on the ship's automated systems to make sure their embedded AIs did not get any silly ideas and do something stupid. Around him, the on-watch command team was quiet, the sensor holovids blank except for system status reports, the soft buzz of idle conversation barely audible over the ever-present soft hiss of the ship's air-conditioning.

Despite the events of the last few days, Michael was more or less happy. Not ecstatic, he had to admit, but feeling okay. Considering how dumb he had been, that was not too bad a result.

With time on his hands, he commed his neuronics to patch into the sim of *Eridani*'s forthcoming patrol. Although not quite as terrifying as *387*'s forays into Hammer space before the Battle of Hell's Moons, this operation—a tiny cog in the enormous machine tasked with the invasion of the Hammer home planet of Commitment—looked as if it might have its moments. Even though the thought of dropping back into Hammer space sent shivers chasing up and down his spine, things had changed. He welcomed the risk, welcomed the fear, because without them he would not be doing all he could to destroy the Hammer.

With Anna gone, even though he would never give up on her, and with his family barely speaking to him anymore, he was well and truly on his own. Well, apart from the always-comforting presence of Petty Officer Matthilde Bienefelt, that was. At least she would always be there for him, though somehow he did not ever see her displacing Anna. He grinned at the thought. No doubt about it, a life with Matti, who towered over him by close to half a meter and outmassed him by a good fifty kilos, all of it pure muscle, would be an interesting experiment in interpersonal relationships.

Sunday, March 26, 2400, UD
FWSS Eridani, *pinchspace*

"All stations, command. Stand by artgrav shutdown in ten seconds . . . artgrav shutdown now. All stations, final suit checks. Dropping in two minutes."

Ignoring the sudden heave from a stomach deprived of its gravitational frame of reference, Michael flicked his visor down. He waited as his suit's AI ran final diagnostics, a row of green lights confirming that he had a good suit. Flicking his visor back up, he looked around at *Eridani*'s combat information center. With *Eridani* at general quarters, the place was jammed with spacers. Even so, it was quiet, an obvious tension showing in the way the command team concentrated intently on the holovids, the command plot running off the seconds until the ship dropped.

He looked at his team of sensor operators. He knew their names and service records but not much more than that. He hoped they were as good as his new captain had assured him they were, because this time the Hammers would be on their guard, and although the chances were small, there was always the possibility they might drop straight into the arms of a waiting heavy cruiser.

That thought made Michael's stomach turn over; he remembered the shock and terror he had felt when *Ishaq* was destroyed. She had been a heavy cruiser up against a damn mership armed with obsolete rail guns, for God's sake. And compared to *Ishaq*, *Eridani* was tiny, less than one-thirtieth the size, with flank and stern armor that would have trouble keeping out a kid armed with a slingshot.

Then *Eridani* turned the universe inside out and dropped into normalspace. In an instant, the combat information center was a mass of furious but disciplined activity as the command team worked frantically to make sense of the mass of data pouring in from the ship's passive sensors. Michael watched his team monitoring the assessments being made by the sensor AI; now and again, one of them stepped in to correct a mistaken classification, making his confidence grow. His captain had been right. This team was good. Calm, focused, and extremely competent, they quickly and efficiently put together an accurate threat plot, the mass of red high-threat vectors marking Hammer contacts being downgraded one by one to orange.

When the last red vector on the plot changed to orange, Michael allowed himself to relax a little. For the moment at

least, they were clear of any immediate threats, the space between the deepspace heavy scout and the Hammer home
planet of Commitment almost completely empty. Michael
shivered. Even if they were 90 million kilometers away,
Commitment felt way, way too close, the memories of that
awful place all of a sudden crowding in on him.

He gave himself a mental kick. He had a job to do, and allowing the ghosts of the past to distract him was not going to
help. He focused on the threat plot, his team stepping methodically through each contact, tightening classifications
to a point where track numbers started to have names put to
them. Michael's breath caught in his throat as track 445311
was classified as the Hammer heavy cruiser *Bravery*. That was
the son of a bitch that almost had gotten him and the *387* the
last time out. Talk about close shaves. The light scout *387*
had jumped only five seconds before *Bravery*'s rail-gun salvo
would have ripped them apart.

Finally, the process of mapping the billions of cubic kilometers around the *Eridani* came to an end. They were clear.
Time to call it in.

"Command, sensors. Threat plot is confirmed."

"Command, roger."

Having taken formal responsibility for the information
now up on the threat plot, Michael sat back. Apart from the
familiar pattern of traffic flowing to and from Hell's Moons
showing up clearly as a tangled mass of orange vectors running off the right-hand side of the holovid, there was not a lot
to see. There was a heavy concentration of units around
Commitment, its planetary nearspace thick with everything
from space battle stations and heavy cruisers to light scouts,
circling in a web of Clarke and polar orbits. Farther out, there
were three task groups largely made up of heavy and light
cruisers with a sprinkling of smaller units. Beyond them,
Commitment farspace was empty, with not a single Hammer
starship.

The more Michael looked at it, the more puzzled he became.
He would have expected patrols at least out to the 4-light-
minute mark to stop intruders like the *Eridani* from having too
easy a run in, but no. There was nothing. It was odd.

"All stations, this is command. Revert to defense stations. Stand by artgrav in ten seconds . . . artgrav on now. Stand by to launch surveillance drones."

The moment the weight came back on his body, Michael felt better. He had always wondered if a career as a Space Fleet officer was such a smart idea considering how badly he tolerated zero-g, not to mention the horrors of jumping into and out of pinchspace. Around him, the combat information center burst into life as half the command team stood down, the inevitable buzz of conversation bringing the equally inevitable order to keep it quiet. Michael waited until the rush was over before stripping off his space suit and changing seats. When the ship was at defense stations—its second-highest alert state—he was one of the two warfare officers in the combat information center, and it made more sense to be sitting close to his partner, in this case Lieutenant Tanvi Kidav, *Eridani*'s senior warfare officer.

Michael liked Kidav a lot. At first, her implacably taciturn exterior had put him off. But after a few days, he had discovered that there was much more to Kidav than met the eye. It turned out she was an engaging woman with a quiet, dry sense of humor allied with an ability to deliver one-liners to devastating effect. Her speciality was deflating the more pompous of *Eridani*'s crew. Michael knew. He had seen her do it to the ship's senior engineer, Pavel Duricek, a pompous windbag who clearly believed he was the most important person on board, a view that, needless to say, Kidav did not agree with. Pope Pavel, she called him. Duricek hated it.

Kidav smiled as he sat down. "Hi, Michael. Nice and quiet out there, thank God."

Michael nodded. "Way I like it."

"Me, too. Right. You keep an eye on the drone launch; I'll watch the rest."

"Sir."

Truth be told, launching surveillance drones and a pair of pinchcomm satellites was not the most difficult task in *Eridani*'s mission inventory. Michael was pretty sure that *Eridani*'s drone team would do it with the smooth efficiency he was beginning to expect from everyone on board. He could not speak for Carlos Galvan, *Eridani*'s drone officer, but with Petty Officer Bienefelt to back Galvan up, he knew things would go as they should. *Eridani*'s captain, Lieutenant Commander Dana Lenski, seemed to have something that the late and unlamented Captain Constanza did not: the ability to get the best out of her people.

"Command, drones." Galvan's voice was matter-of-fact.

"Command."

"Ready for drone deployment."

"Command, roger. Stand by." Michael did a quick final check of the threat and command plots to make sure nothing had slipped past him. Nothing had. "Deployment approved."

"Roger."

Michael watched intently as the drone handlers spilled out of the forward upper air lock, their chromaflage space suits dialed down to a dirty gray-black all but invisible in the miserable light coming from Commitment's orange-red dwarf sun more than 150 million kilometers away. Bienefelt's huge bulk was easy to spot. Michael nodded appreciatively as he watched the team.

The drone team knew what they were doing. Splitting into two, they quickly had the massive cargo bay doors open, and a steady stream of drones started to appear. Finally, two much larger pinch comsats appeared, and the cargo bay doors were closed. Michael heaved a sigh of relief. The *Eridani* was hard for Hammer radar or optronics to see, but only when fully stealthed with her skin chromaflage activated. Two bloody great sharp-edged cargo bay doors rather spoiled the effect, increasing *Eridani*'s radar cross section dramatically.

Now the handlers were pushing the drones clear of *Eridani,* and Michael watched as one by one the drones' diagnostics confirmed they were ready to go. The two pinchspace comsats were following close behind like two sheepdogs.

"Command, drones."

"Command."

"Ready to launch. Passing control to Mother." Michael did another check. The threat plot was unchanged. A quick look at the drones confirmed that they were ready to go. There was no need to keep the handlers out any longer, and with *Eridani* slipping through space at more than 40 kilometers per second, they should be back inside, where bumping into a piece of dirt no bigger than a pinhead was not a life-threatening event. Michael knew. He had been there.

"Roger. Recover teams."

"On our way."

From the first time he had seen her working, Michael knew Bienefelt was good, but *Eridani*'s handlers were every bit her match. With economical elegance, they swarmed back to the air lock, stopping precisely with only centimeters to go before dropping neatly back into the ship. Well, not all of them, Michael noted with a smile. Carlos Galvan was as clumsy as Michael had been when he had been the drone officer in *387*. Even so, it took only a minute and they were all back, the air lock closing behind them.

"Surveillance, command. Nicely done. Thank you."

"Roger that." Galvan sounded pleased. He should, Michael thought. Surveillance drones had minds of their own, and once they started to get out of control, things could get dicey in seconds.

Michael turned his attention back to the drones. Mother was happy with them, her own checks confirming that she had good birds.

"Captain, sir, command."

"Captain."

"Drones and pinchspace comsats deployed, sir. All nominal. Ready to launch." Michael half smiled. Lenski knew all that or she was not the skipper he suspected. But tradition was tradition: AIs were not to be trusted, so keep humans in the loop and all that.

"Launch authorized."

"Sir."

Michael watched intently as Mother drove the drones slowly clear of *Eridani* before methodically aligning each one along its intended vector. The pinchspace comsats followed, leaving *Eridani* coasting along alone. Then, as one, engines powered by hypercompressed nitrogen came to life, thin whiskers of gas driving the drones away from *Eridani* and toward Commitment, the comsats angled away to take up their positions well outside Commitment nearspace, where a wandering Hammer ship on antidrone patrol was unlikely to trip over them.

Three hours later, the captain slid into her seat between Michael and Kidav. "Ignore me, guys," she said. "How's Mother going on Phase 2?"

"Another two hours, sir," Kidav replied. "We've got a short list of possible targets, but I agree with Mother. We should watch things a bit longer. There's no rush."

"Agreed." She turned. "So, Michael. An old friend of yours over there, I think." Lenski waved a hand in the general direction of the plot.

"The *Bravery* you mean, sir?"

"The same." Lenski leaned closer. "You did well, Michael," she said softly. "Hell's Moons. Must have been hard."

It was not a question; Michael just nodded.

"You know," Lenski said conversationally, sitting back, "I think we underestimate the Hammer sometimes. *Bravery* is a good example. I went through the Hell's Moons after-action reports. The *Bravery*'s skipper knew what he was doing. Her drop in-system was as good a piece of work as I've seen. Quick to set up, quick to get salvos away."

"It was; I'll give them that," Michael agreed. "Though five seconds too slow, thank God. And yes, I do think we underestimate them. Much as I hate the fuckers"—Michael's voice hardened noticeably—"they aren't all corrupt, incompetent fools. That's something worth remembering."

The depth of emotion in Michael's voice did not surprise Lenski. His service record had left her stunned; there would be few in the Fleet who had been through what he had been through. She had also talked at length to Bienefelt when the petty officer—the largest woman Lenski had ever met—had joined *Eridani*. Bienefelt and Michael, not to mention the rest of *387*'s crew, had done it tough, topped off in Michael's case by having *Ishaq* blown out from underneath him, followed by surviving a stay with DocSec and then waging a one-man war against the Hammer before somehow getting off-planet and

safely home. He had paid a price for surviving. That much
was obvious, a price that was part survivor's guilt and part an
intense obsession to get even with the Hammer.

Whenever the Hammers came up in conversation, Michael's
eyes spelled out what he really thought of them. The burning
hate was obvious, the intensity impossible to hide. She needed
to watch him, she reminded herself. A degree of hate was fine;
she had no problem with that. It was necessary to do the job.
God knew, she hated the Hammers, too, but a man who hated
too much could endanger her ship and the lives of her crew.
She was going to watch him closely until she knew where
judgment stopped and blind hatred took over.

"Okay, team. I'm going walkabout."

"Sir."

The insistent demands of *Eridani*'s klaxon as it drove the
crew to general quarters could not be ignored any longer.
Michael reluctantly abandoned the safe, warm, dark place he
had toppled into as soon as he had collapsed into his bunk.

Running on autopilot, he swung himself out of his bunk.
Moving with practiced efficiency, he was into his space suit.
Pausing only to grab his gloves and then his helmet, he was
out of his cabin, pounding along a crowded corridor and then
up a ladder to the combat information center. When he arrived, the place was bedlam as the rest of the command team
arrived, some still struggling into suits. With *Eridani*'s usual
efficiency, bedlam was replaced swiftly by quiet calm.

Michael quickly confirmed that his team was closed up
and online. He sat back as the reports flowed in from the rest
of the ship. Malik Aasha, the *Eridani*'s executive officer, was
hounding and harrying the laggards to their posts. Finally it
was done, and Aasha, an extremely tall, dark man with the
sharp-edged face of his Somali forebears, was satisfied.

"Captain, sir," Aasha reported formally, "the ship is at general quarters in ship state 1, condition zulu."

"Good. Shut down artgrav and depressurize. All stations, depressurizing in one, so final suit checks. Dropping in two minutes. Hold on to your hats, folks. This could be a rough ride."

Hell, Michael grumbled to himself. He understood why

Lenski was depressurizing the ship before they dropped, but that meant being buttoned up in his combat space suit when his stomach did its usual backflip and triple somersault. Oh, well, he consoled himself, better a small accident inside his space suit than a big one outside. Normally, *Eridani* and every other ship in the Fleet maintained an internal pressure of 80 percent of normal with the oxygen levels raised to compensate. Even that translated into 8 tons per square meter pressing on the pressure hull, something one could do without when shoring up battle-damaged bulkheads.

When *Eridani* dropped, Michael and his team did not have time to worry about what lay ahead. They worked frantically to confirm that the threat plot looked much as it had when they had jumped out-system two hours earlier and in particular that no Hammer heavy cruiser was waiting for them as they dropped. Michael sighed with relief, pleased to see that the plot was unchanged and the potential targets they had identified from 90 million kilometers out were still pretty much where they had left them. The only difference was that this time the plot did not revert to a more comforting orange. It was dominated by an uncompromisingly angry mass of red vectors tagged by Mother as hostile force Tango Golf One. Those contacts were the primary threat to the *Eridani,* a mixed task group of heavy and light warships led by a single heavy cruiser, though at 102,000 kilometers, they were too far away to be an immediate problem.

"Command, sensors. Threat plot is confirmed."

"Command, roger. Weapons?"

"Targets confirmed."

"This is command. Launch missile salvo one."

"Roger. Launching missile salvo one."

With the tearing buzz of hydraulically powered dispensers ramming missiles into space, *Eridani* deployed her first salvo of Mambas, the antistarship missiles escorted by a cloud of decoys and active jammers driving away on pillars of searing white-blue light. Ahead lay their targets: four hapless Hammer merships hauling slowly out-system, ships the system commander unwisely had allowed to stray way too far out before jumping to the safety of pinchspace. Lenski had tasked two Mambas to each mership; the rest she kept back. She had other plans for them.

The Hammer task group did not sit back and watch the *Eridani* at work. Even as the Mambas hit home, with the doomed merships erupting into gigantic balls of red-white plasma as their main engine fusion plants lost containment, antiship lasers from the Hammer task group found the *Eridani* and were beginning to flay the ceramsteel armor off her starboard bow. Quick work, Michael thought as he scanned the data coming in from the AI that was monitoring the integrity of *Eridani*'s armor. Good work, too. The lasers were tightly grouped, with the Hammer's master fire controller holding the beams steady on the target point on *Eridani*'s hull, forcing Lenski to start rolling the ship to minimize the damage to her forward armor.

Despite himself, Michael was impressed. The Hammer's laser beam formation and targeting was better than anything Michael had seen reported in the technical intelligence summaries pushed out by Fleet. Not for the first time, he reminded himself not to take the Hammers for granted.

"Command, Mother. Rail-gun launch from hostile Tango Golf One. Target *Eridani*. Time of flight 2 minutes 12."

In an instant Michael's stomach knotted, the taste of sour bile rising up into his throat. He hated rail guns. Christ, with the *Eridani* barely 100,000 kilometers from the Hammer warships, it was going to be tight. He glanced forward to where Lenksi sat flanked by her two senior warfare officers. She did not move as the report was acknowledged. Michael turned back to the job at hand, his team watching intently as the sensor AI sorted through the mass of onrushing slugs in a desperate attempt to eliminate the decoys. To Michael's horror, at one point during the planning, the command team had seriously considered riding out any rail-gun attack if the swarm geometry gave them a good chance of survival. Jesus Christ, he had thought, staring in horror as the idea was batted around. Survive a few Hammer rail-gun attacks and then see how you feel about that idea, he had said to himself.

In the end, Michael had not needed to object. Much to his relief, Lenski had killed the idea stone dead.

This Hammer rail-gun swarm was good. In a matter of seconds, four heavy cruisers from the Hammer task group had gotten a well-coordinated, tightly grouped rail-gun salvo away that left *Eridani* with absolutely nowhere to hide. Her only chance was to jump into pinchspace. Michael counted the clock down as *Eridani*'s missile crews worked frantically to get the next salvo away. The instant the missiles were deployed and on their way, joined by the missiles held back from the first salvo, their targets two 10,000-ton Diamond class light patrol ships running exposed on the edge of the task group, Lenski gave the order.

After barely two minutes in Hammer nearspace, the *Eridani* jumped, leaving behind the ionized remnants of four merships and two Diamond class light patrol ships fighting for their lives as the *Eridani*'s missiles fell on them.

The mood in *Eridani*'s combat information center was upbeat, not that anybody had any illusions about the mission they had just completed. Hit-and-run attacks made little difference to the strategic balance of the war. In truth, all they did was put the Hammer on notice that they weren't going to have things all their own way while preparations for the invasion of the Hammer's home planet moved ponderously forward. But *Eridani* was now officially blooded, and four Hammer merships had been destroyed and two light patrol ships had been attacked and probably damaged. All in all, it was a creditable tally for her first combat patrol.

After a while, with the ship safely in pinchspace, Michael slipped quietly out of the combat information center. He had mixed feelings. Yes, the *Eridani* had performed well; it was always good to hit the Hammer.

But there were some negatives from the day's operation. First, the Hammers he had seen were a step above the rabble that had opposed them at Hell's Moons—a big step, too. Something had changed, but what? Second, where were all the Hammer's ships? If the Feds had come calling in force, it would have been all over in a matter of hours. The Hammers would simply not have had the ships to oppose a full-scale attack. So they were taking a chance—a big chance—and to Michael's way of thinking, there had to be one hell of a big payoff to justify exposing the planet from which all Hammer power flowed.

Michael made his way to the *Eridani*'s canteen. He had promised to buy Bienefelt a beer; the opportunity to have a quiet chat with her was something he never passed up. Over a couple of beers, she would tell him more about what was really going on below decks than ten years of ship's management meetings could. He whistled scornfully. Management meetings! Hot air fests, more like it, another opportunity for the ship's officers and senior spacers to be treated to the latest pompous lecture from the resident gasbag in chief, Pavel Duricek. The man was a pain in the ass.

He would catch up with Bienefelt; then he would sleep on the problem of the missing Hammer warships. If by some miracle he was struck by a blinding revelation, he would talk to Kidav about it in the morning. Otherwise he would bury the problem. After all, it could simply be nerves, and he had plenty of those to go around. He sighed. They were stuck in pinchspace until they got to the mobile forward operating ship positioned in deepspace 100 light-years out from the Hammer system, so there was nothing he could do no matter what brilliant insights he might come up with.

Tuesday, March 28, 2400, UD
FWSS Eridani, *berthed on Federated Worlds Warship*
Koh (SVL-407), *interstellar space*

With the gentlest of bumps, *Eridani* berthed. Hydraulic locking arms pulled her in tight to the huge bulk of the light support vessel.

"All stations, this is command. Hands fall out from berthing stations. Revert to ship state 3, condition x-ray."

Michael hit the ground running. He did not want to waste any time. Lenksi had left him in no doubt that *Eridani*'s error-prone ultraviolet detector arrays were to be working by the time the ship undocked in twelve hours' time. He was on his way to make sure the maintenance team standing by to fix the problem actually was waiting for him as promised. If it was, he could get on with the main business of the day.

To his relief, two spacers from *Koh* were there waiting when *Eridani*'s massive hangar doors opened. Two minutes was more than enough for Michael to be completely convinced that there was nothing he could offer two experienced technicians except gratuitous advice and general aggravation. They did not need either; they would do a much better job without him peering over their shoulders and being a pain in the ass. His conscience was clear. Leaving the techs firm instructions to keep him informed, he told Mother where he was going and set off on his second mission of the day, a mission that he had allowed Bienefelt to talk him into, the nervous excitement beginning to build inside him.

He smiled at the memory. Petty Officer Bienefelt, human-space's only cyborg agony aunt! Now, there was a truly bizarre thought.

Massing over 800,000 tons, the *Koh* was enormous, and getting to berth 4-Lima was an exercise in itself. At last he made it, stopping at the end of the personnel access tube to clear security. With a deep breath, he set off down the tube, wondering as he did whether he was about to make a terrible mistake.

Befitting a heavy cruiser, immaculate spacers infested *Damishqui*'s gangway. Michael was only another anonymous shipsuited junior lieutenant; he was completely ignored. Fair enough, he thought as he made his way to the quartermaster; he was happy to be ignored. In peacetime, he would have been shot for daring to cross the gangway dressed so casually, but wartime or not, some things did not change, and he took great care to salute the ship in the best college style as he crossed the brow, thankfully without stumbling; some considerate soul had synced *Damishqui*'s and *Koh*'s artgravs.

"Sir. Can I help you?" the quartermaster asked, returning the salute.

"Yes. Could you comm Junior Lieutenant Cheung to the gangway, please?"

"Can do, sir. Identity check, please."

The young leading spacer watched patiently as Michael's identity was confirmed. "Thank you, sir. I'll comm her now . . . okay, sir. Done. All right, she's on her way." The quartermaster leaned forward. "Probably a good idea to wait clear of the gangway," he whispered conspiratorially. "Commodore Perkins and enough brass to sink the ship are due any minute."

"Thanks, Leader, will do." Michael grinned. He felt greatly relieved. He would not have been the least bit surprised if Anna had told him to piss off. Tucking himself out of the way, he stood and waited.

Anna wasn't long. Michael caught his breath as she appeared, a slight, shipsuited figure almost lost in the ebb and flow of *Damishqui*'s crew as they readied the ship for combat.

"Hi, Michael," she said flatly. "Follow me. I know somewhere we can talk. But I've only got a few minutes."

"Fine," Michael said to Anna's back as she led the way off *Damishqui,* down the access tube, and into an empty compartment a few meters inside the *Koh.* The door hissed shut behind them as she turned, arms folded across her chest. Michael's heart sank. He knew defensive body language when he saw it. Suddenly, he did not know what to do or say, so he stood silent, unmoving, staring into Anna's eyes, as always lost in their green depths.

Anna sighed despairingly. She shook her head. "God above, Michael. You don't change. What the hell am I going to do with you?"

Michael shrugged. "Um, well, maybe we could, you know, sort of start again . . ." He trailed off as Anna's cheeks flared red with sudden anger.

"Start again!" she hissed fiercely. "What makes you think I want to start again? What makes you think we can start again after all we've been through? Christ, Michael! It's not that simple."

"Look, Anna," Michael said desperately. "I know it's not. But the fact is I love you. Yes, I can live without you if I have to, but I really don't want to."

Anna stared at him in silence for a long, long time before she spoke. "That's not the problem," she said finally. "Problem is whether I want you in my life anymore. You can stand there all you like telling me how much you love me, but it makes no difference. I know all that. I just don't know what I want. I need more time."

"Anna, look—"

"No! Enough! We can talk forever, and it's not going to help one little bit. I've got to work out what happens next, so let me do that and we'll talk again. Now look, I really have to go." She turned to go.

"Anna!" Michael protested. "Can't we sort—"

"No, we damn well can't, Michael!" Anna snapped, turning back. "Oh, shit," she said gently. "Sorry. Look, Michael. Leave things with me. We'll meet up next chance we can, see how we feel then. Promise. Now, I really have to go. You be careful." She stepped close to kiss him on the cheek. Michael's heart pounded as her familiar scent brought memories cascading down. "Very careful. You hear?"

With that she was gone.

Michael stood for a moment, her all-too-quick farewell kiss still warm on his cheek.

He sighed deeply, wearily rubbing eyes gritty from too little sleep and too much stress. The good news was that it could have been a hell of a lot worse. The bad news was that it could have been a hell of a lot better. Still, Anna was talking to him, had agreed to see him again, and had kissed him good-bye. Michael allowed himself to think that maybe, when the latest fracas with the Hammer was over, they could put things back on the rails.

Anyway, he had stolen enough of *Eridani*'s time; with his tame maintainers reporting good progress, he wanted to be there when they did their final tests on the recalcitrant ultraviolet detector arrays. He had learned the hard way that all maintainers had an uncanny knack of making systems work perfectly as long as they were there to twiddle the knobs, only to have everything fall apart the second they left.

If that happened, Lenski would kick his ass from breakfast time to Christmas.

"Any final questions?" *Eridani*'s captain scanned the faces in front of her. "No? Okay. That's all, folks. Go to it."

The mission briefing broke up in noisy confusion around Michael. For a moment, he stared at the command plot with its mission summary. It all looked so easy, so clinical, he thought, laid out tidily like that. In theory, *Eridani*'s upcoming mission should be no problem at all.

He suppressed an involuntary shiver.

Remassed, rearmed, they were going back into Hammer space, this time as part of a task group—four heavy cruisers and four heavy escorts supported by light patrol ships—and it was no quick dash-in, dash-out job this time, either. The task group had orders to take out one of the battle stations in orbit around the planet Faith, the third planet of the Retribution system. According to the Einsteins responsible for planning Fleet operations, the mission was intended to demonstrate the Fed's ability to operate freely even against targets as hard as a battle station, and Hammer battle stations were hard targets. Massing millions of tons, they were not quite as large as the Fed version, but in Michael's humble opinion they were quite large enough and heavily armed. No rail guns, though, thank God. He was beginning to get a real bee in his bonnet about rail guns, to the point where he did not even want to think about the damned things, let alone jump into Hammer space to face them. He smiled ruefully. He would be packed off to the shrinks if Lenski ever found out.

He looked again at the mission summary and shook his head. How many times had he seen mission briefings end up so neatly packaged? He shook his head again. Things were never that easy—he should know—and there was no reason why this mission should be any different.

Doing his best to ignore a sudden twinge of fear that twisted his stomach into a ball, he turned his mind to the things he had to get done before the *Eridani* unberthed.

Twelve hours after the *Eridani* had arrived, *Koh*'s hydraulic rams pushed it gently clear. The minute the ship fell out from berthing stations, Michael headed straight for his bunk. He would be on watch in less than six hours, and his sleep deficit was beginning to get out of hand.

Thursday, March 30, 2400, UD
Defense Council Secretariat, city of McNair,
Commitment

"Now let me turn to FedWorld force dispositions." Fleet Admiral Jorge cued the next holovid slide, this one speckled with red icons marking the estimated positions of every Fed warship identified by Hammer intelligence and endless reconnaissance missions.

"In general, what we can see is the same trend we have observed for some time," Jorge continued. "Apart from ships tasked with operations against our home planets, the Feds have been progressively building up the forces around their Fleet base at Comdur. Here." He stabbed a marker down into a thick mass of red icons 10 or so light-years galactic west of Terranova.

"We now know for certain that these are the forces assigned for the invasion. We do not know which planet they have selected as their primary target, but our assessment is that it is almost certain to be Commitment."

A small shiver ran through the men around the Defense Council table. The consequences of a successful Fed invasion of Commitment did not bear thinking about.

"Now, in addition—"

"Forgive me, Admiral," interrupted Tobias de Mel, councillor for internal security.

"Sir?"

"How can we be sure that planetary invasion is what these ships are for?"

"Well, sir," Admiral Jorge replied, "in part, it's because of the nature of the forces assembled. The last reconnaissance drone fly-by of Comdur positively identified the planetary assault vessels *Cheng Ho, Jefferson, Al-Fayed, Adams,* and *Yamamato.* We also have unconfirmed intelligence reports that the planetary assault vessels *Shrivaratnam, Nelson, Washington, Tourville,* and *Monroe* have been tasked to Comdur, though we don't yet know when they will drop in-system. All told, we estimate these ships have close to 400,000 marines embarked."

"Kraa!" de Mel hissed. "That's one hell of a lot of marines. Are we sure we can stop this, Admiral?"

That is a damn good question, Jorge thought. "Absolutely, Councillor," he replied, his voice emphatic, confident. "When we launch Operation Damascus, all the ships tasked with the invasion will be in orbit around Comdur. When we have finished with them, the Feds will have barely enough warships left to protect their home planets. They will not have the ships they need to conduct offensive operations. They will also have suffered massive losses of experienced spacers and marines. So yes, I am sure we can stop this," he said flatly, even though it was a lie. Anyone who believed that there was any such thing as an absolute certainty when it came to space warfare was a fool. These were politicians, and in Jorge's book at least, that automatically made them fools when it came to all matters military.

"Now, in addition to the planetary assault vessels, the latest reconnaissance fly-by shows the bulk of the Fed fleet's heavy units in orbit at Comdur station. We have also . . ."

Heart pounding, Michael waited for *Eridani* to drop.

Behind a closed visor, his face was slick with a thin, cold sweat. In two days it would be April Fools' Day, which felt uncomfortably appropriate. Here was the ship of fools about to drop right into the Hammer's lap. If *Eridani* and her crew got out safely, they would be right back to do it all over again. Michael could not help but feel they were pushing their luck.

Eight hours earlier, Task Group 300.1, under the command of Commodore Perkins in *Damishqui,* had dropped well out from the planet Faith. Undetected by the Hammer, the task group had laboriously assembled a comprehensive threat plot, data pouring in by the terabyte from both ship sensors and a far-flung constellation of surveillance drones orbiting on the fringes of Hammer farspace. Eventually, Commodore Perkins had pronounced himself satisfied that things were as they should be. Now the task group was on its way in to attack.

What a way to make a FedMark, Michael thought as he watched the seconds run off the drop timer with glacial slowness.

At last *Eridani* dropped, and the shit hit the fan.

The urgent sound of the threat proximity alarm told *Eridani* that things had changed significantly in the short time it had taken the task group to microjump out-system, reverse vector, and microjump back.

"This doesn't sound good, team. So let's do it properly." Lenski cut off the alarm. "Sensors, don't rush it. I don't want us going off half-cocked."

"On it, sir," Michael replied, grateful for Lenski's reassuring calm. He watched his sensors team working feverishly to distill the threat out of the chaotic mass of blood-red vectors spattered across the threat plot. His eyes tightened in disbelief as the cause of the proximity alarm became all too obvious. "Jeez," he said out loud. The operation was falling apart, and they had been in Hammer space for what? Five seconds? The threat plot was a terrifying sight. Where there should have been nothing but empty space, there were thirty Hammer ships—ten of them heavy cruisers—all frighteningly close and all sitting across the task group's attack vector. Where in God's name had they come from? Stop dreaming, Michael, he chided himself. You have a job to do, so call the plot.

"Command, sensors. Threat plot is confirmed."

"Command, roger."

To his credit, Commodore Perkins did not waste a second. His orders were brutally simple. "Close the enemy and engage."

In an instant, Perkins's carefully choreographed attack on the Hammer space battle station, now safely tucked away behind a solid wall of Hammer capital ships, dissolved into the freewheeling chaos of a close-quarters space battle.

Lenski did not hesitate, either. As *Eridani* deployed its first salvo of Mamba antistarship missiles, she pitched the ship violently down and to the left in a frantic effort to get clear of the rail-gun salvos the Hammers would be launching at any second. Until she and every other ship had opened out, the task force—tightly grouped for what Commodore Perkins had intended to be a single surgical strike through the Hammer's outer defenses—was a sitting duck. Forewarned by gravitronics intercepts, the Hammer ships were working furiously to slew their ships onto the threat axis to allow them to get their rail-gun salvos away; their missiles would be close behind.

Michael's heart was in his mouth. There would be little time to maneuver clear, little time to hack enough rail-gun slugs out of space to neutralize the Hammer attack.

"Command, Mother. Rail-gun salvos inbound. Targets *Damishqui, Resplendent, Renown, Secular.*"

"Command, roger. Sensors?"

"Rail-gun vectors confirmed, sir." Michael's voice was ash-dry. This was looking bad; it felt uncomfortably like

Ishaq all over again. Michael shivered; it was pure luck the Hammer ships had been pointing in the wrong direction when the Fed ships had dropped. If they had been pointing at the drop datum . . .

When it came, the Hammer's opening salvo was a good one and well targeted. It took only seconds to close the gap and smash into the four heavy cruisers at the center of the Fed task group. The slugs punched huge holes in the ships' ceramsteel armor, with their kinetic energy transformed in nanoseconds into enough heat to blow great craters in the bows of the heavy cruisers.

As the clouds of ionized armor cleared from around the ships, Michael checked the status of *Damishqui.* He was relieved to see that she had weathered the storm, though her bows had been deeply scarred by the attack, impact craters still spewing white-hot clouds of ionized ceramsteel armor. Now it was the Hammer's turn to receive; the task group's rail-gun salvo was inflicting serious damage on the Hammer starships. Fed rail guns threw a heavier slug that was almost half again as fast as the Hammer's, each slug delivering energy equal to a ton of TNT onto an area smaller than the end of a little finger. Already, one Hammer light escort was pulling out of line, her hull opened up by a secondary explosion, probably from an auxiliary fusion plant powering one of her weapons systems.

"Command, Mother. Missiles inbound. Estimate 6,000 missiles plus decoys. Targets not known. Time to target eighteen seconds."

Oh, Jesus, Michael thought desperately, this is it. He and the rest of *Eridani*'s sensors team could do no more. They could not keep up with the enormous avalanche of information that was pouring in from the task group's sensors; they were now totally in the hands of the battle management AI in *Damishqui,* totally dependent on its interpretation of the mass of data being processed by the sensor AIs in the task group's ships. Putting one's life in the hands of an AI might be a necessary evil, but it was never something that Michael—or any other spacer, come to that—much enjoyed. When AIs messed up, they tended to do it in spades. Then the tsunami of Hammer Eaglehawk missiles was on them, with the *Eridani*'s close in weapons working desperately to keep out the fifty or so that had picked it as a target. The vibration coming up through the deck shook Michael's chair as *Eridani* let go with everything she had. Defensive lasers, short-range missiles, and chain guns all worked in a last desperate attempt to hack down the missiles that had clawed their way through the antimissile screen put up by the cruisers.

"All stations, stand by missile impact."

Michael braced himself.

The attack hit home. *Eridani*'s last-ditch defenses had smashed most of the Hammer missiles into useless junk, leaving only broken fragments of hardened ceramsteel falling on her bows like iron rain. Even so, six got through, their shaped-charge warheads punching deep into *Eridani*'s forward armor, blowing great gouts of yellow-red gas into space. The ship was bucking and heaving as shock wave after shock wave ripped through it, the artgrav struggling to keep up.

A few terrible seconds later the missile attack was over, and for one awful moment there was complete silence. Then there was bedlam as the damage reports began to flow in. To Michael's relief, there were no casualties; the damage had been limited. The Hammer missiles had all hit well forward, and a quick check with the remote holocams showed Michael that *Eridani*'s heavy frontal armor had done what it was supposed to do. Her bows looked like a mad giant had run amok, pickax in one hand, blowtorch in the other, leaving six gaping craters vomiting white-hot gas into space. Despite the missiles' best efforts, *Eridani*'s inner hull had not been breached, though the Hammer antiship lasers were following up the missile strike by probing the impact sites for any weak spots. Lenksi had already reacted to the threat, ordering *Eridani*'s Krachov shroud generators to full power; the tiny disks designed to shield *Eridani* from laser attack were spewing out in the thousands. Another quick check confirmed that *Damishqui* had weathered the storm, though she, too, had been punished heavily up forward, her bows speckled with red-white hot spots, the remnants of multiple missile strikes;

ghostly streams of ionized gas still were spewing out into space from the impact craters.

The light patrol ship *Marie Curie* and the heavy scout *Kaminski* had not been so lucky. The two ships were finished. Slowly they fell out of formation, spitting lifepods in all directions, their orange strobes double-flashing desperate calls for help. Michael's heart went out to them. He remembered all too well the dreadful thudding jolt as his lifepod was blasted clear of the dying *Ishaq*.

The two Fed ships were doomed. Hammer missiles loitering behind the main attack accelerated hard to finish them off, the ships' hulls carpeted with the red-white flashes of warheads punching deep before detonating. Michael flinched as without any warning the two Fed starships blew up almost as one, searing blue-white flashes announcing the loss of main engine fusion plants. He hoped the two heavy scouts nominated as rescue ships—*Sirius* and *Pavonis*—would have enough time to recover the pods. He checked the relative vectors of the lifepods and the oncoming Hammers. God help them, he thought. It would be a close thing.

"So, team," Lenski said, her tone casual to the point of disinterest. "The big question now is what Commodore Perkins is going to do next."

The combat information center was silent. *Eridani*'s spacers knew a rhetorical question when they heard one. For his part, Michael knew the answer he wanted to hear. He hoped like hell Perkins would jump and jump soon, but what he thought did not matter. All that mattered was what Perkins wanted, and for the next two minutes or so the Feds had the tactical advantage. The Achilles' heel of all Hammer warships was their inferior rail-gun and missile salvo rates. Perkins could get a second rail-gun and missile salvo away well before the Hammers could reply with theirs. During that time, all the Hammers could throw at him would be antiship lasers, and they would not be on target long enough to burn through the ceramsteel armor and breach the inner hulls. If everything went well, the Fed task group's second salvo would hit Hammer ships already severely damaged by the first attack well before they could respond.

Michael kept one eye on the command plot, the other on his team. There was not much for them to do. The immediate threats were obvious, and no other Hammer ships were close enough to be a problem. In any case, the blizzard of jamming and spoofing, all mixed in with clouds of active decoys, made the situation so chaotically difficult to interpret that only the task group's sensor AIs could work out what was going on, and even they were struggling. All he and his team could hope to do was pick up any obvious mistakes and, apart from that, trust to the AIs to do the job without screwing up too badly.

The opening Fed salvos smashed home. It was a well-coordinated and brutally effective attack, missiles and rail-gun slugs arriving so close together that the Hammers' close-in defenses were completely overwhelmed. Ship after ship disappeared behind massive clouds of ionized ceramsteel as missiles and slugs blasted huge holes in frontal armor. Michael was disappointed to see the Hammer heavy cruisers emerge apparently still operational, though their bows and flanks—a mass of white-hot impact craters—bore witness to the rough treatment they had suffered. The light units were not as lucky. A light cruiser, the *Kapali,* started a slow rolling turn out of line, a massive plume of ice-crystal-loaded gas scintillating in the intense sunlight confirming that her hull had been breached. She was followed by a second, the *Berithsen,* also breached, her entire port bow a mass of broken ceramsteel blown outward by what must have been an auxiliary fusion plant losing containment. A string of smaller ships followed the *Kapali* and the *Berithsen* out of the line of battle.

In seconds, Fed missiles held back from the initial attack fell on the crippled ships to finish them off, warheads driving explosive lances of incandescent gas deep into their guts. One after another, the Hammer ships disintegrated in huge balls of blue-white plasma as their main engine fusion plants lost containment. Rapidly expanding clouds of ionized gas peppered with orange-strobed lifepods provided the only evidence that they had ever existed.

Michael forced himself to breathe out through teeth

clenched tight with stress. It was carnage. Surely they had done enough damage for one day.

"Command, Mother. Hammer task force now estimated to be 65 percent effective."

"Roger that. Nice work," Lenksi said dispassionately. "That'll teach the Hammers to fuck with us."

Michael looked across at Lenksi. She stiffened in her chair. Aha, Michael thought, mentally crossing his fingers. That would have to be Perkins calling for a bit of chat.

It was.

"All stations, command. Quick update. We have orders from the commodore. He believes we retain the tactical advantage, so the task group will launch two more salvos, one missile and one rail gun. Depending how that goes, we may jump, but don't bank on it. Command out."

Michael groaned softly, as, he suspected, did most of the spacers packed into *Eridani*'s combat information center. Commodore Perkins was going in for the kill, clearly hoping his antistarship lasers and follow-up missile and rail-gun salvos would disable enough of the Hammer ships to make their task group completely combat-ineffective. Michael sat there waiting for the buzz-rip of hydraulic rams launching *Eridani*'s next missile salvo. He turned his full attention to the command plot, watching in awed fascination as the missiles, thousands of them, streaked across the gap toward the Hammer. With only seconds left to run, the missile salvo was overtaken by the task group's rail-gun salvo, the two carefully coordinated to arrive on target at precisely the same time.

It was a massacre.

The Hammer ships reeled under the sheer weight of the ordnance thrown at them. One after another, they began to fall out of the line of battle. The first to go were the few light units that had survived the first attack, their thinner armor and less capable close-in defenses simply not able to absorb the enormous weight of metal thrown at them. In quick succession, most lost the unequal fight. One ship after another disappeared into huge balls of plasma, leaving behind five units, damaged but still mostly intact, venting gas to space as they struggled to get to safety.

They did not get far before scavenging missiles smashed home and they, too, vanished in searing white-hot explosions.

Then the first capital ship went.

The City class heavy cruiser *Morristown,* its port bow slashed wide open into a tangled mass of metal by a failed auxiliary fusion plant, rolled out of line into a stately, slow corkscrewing turn. The battle management AI in *Damishqui* did not miss the chance, and a handful of missiles that had been loitering in reserve were sent in to finish the job, hitting home precisely where the previous attack had opened up the *Morristown's* bows. For a moment, nothing happened. Then, with a blinding flash, the entire front half of the *Morristown* blew apart, followed a few seconds later by the rest of the ship as missile warheads gutted it from end to end, blowing the main engine fusion plants apart into incandescent balls of blue-white plasma.

In quick succession, four more heavy cruisers followed the *Morristown.* The *N'debele* trailed the *Witness of Kraa,* the *Concorde,* and the *Restitution* as they death-rolled out of the line of battle. Two more light cruisers, the *Williams* and the *Chen,* followed close behind, their battered and broken hulls bleeding long streams of ice-laden air into space as they tumbled planetward. All around the disintegrating Hammer task group, space was thick with orange-strobed lifepods blossoming outward in a ghastly slow-motion fireworks show.

Michael turned his attention back to the threat plot. Every bone in his body told him that the Hammers would be sending reinforcements. God knew, they had the ships, and so it was only a matter of time. His instincts were confirmed when the threat plot erupted; two ugly splashes of red announced the arrival of two Hammer task groups. Immediately, Michael's team was buried in the task of confirming who and what the new arrivals were. Backed by the massive processing power of the task group's AIs, it was a quick process, helped by the fact that the Hammer ships were making no attempt to conceal their identities. Every active sensor they possessed was transmitting on full power. Why? Michael wondered as he confirmed the plot.

Lenksi answered his unspoken question. "They want us to leave, I think."

Michael nodded. That made sense, though the Hammer ships had a lot of space to cover before they posed a serious threat.

He held his breath. The Hammers had been handled roughly, but they were still a sizable force, and now help was on the way. Commodore Perkins had only seconds left to decide whether to jump or stay and ride out the next Hammer attack.

Perkins chose to stay. His orders were brief: "Close and destroy the enemy."

For the first time that day, and much to Michael's surprise, the leaden cloak of fear he had carried into the battle fell away. Perkins's decision made sense. If the Hammer was to be beaten, this was what it would take: standing toe to toe and slugging it out blow for blow, salvo for salvo, until they could not take any more. With a quick prayer asking whoever it was in charge of the universe to look after *Damishqui,* he checked that his team was not allowing another Hammer task force to creep up on them. Satisfied that everything was under control, he turned back to the command plot. Once more, it was the Hammer's turn. Perkins's ships might have inflicted serious damage, but combat-ineffective they were not. Yet.

"Command, Mother. Multiple missile launches. Estimate 2,300 heavy and 500 light missiles plus decoys. Targets not known."

Michael braced himself. This was the moment of truth. If the *Eridani* survived this, she would be in at the kill. If not . . .

"Command, Mother. Rail-gun launch. Targets *Damishqui, Resplendent, Renown, Secular.*"

Michael flinched as he watched the awful sight of *Damishqui* and her fellow cruisers disappearing behind huge, boiling clouds of ionized armor, the ships visibly recoiling as the Hammer slugs dumped massive amounts of kinetic energy into their hulls. He held his breath until one by one the ships reemerged, anxiously watching the *Damishqui* to make sure she was not badly hit. Michael allowed himself to relax a bit. She seemed okay, but it was hard to tell.

All hell broke loose. For the second time that day, *Eridani* fought desperately to keep out the wave of missiles that fell on her. This time around, not a single missile got through. Facing a much smaller salvo, *Eridani* was able to pick off the missiles one by one, a pattern largely repeated across the task group, although by some accident of Hammer fire control, the *Renown* got more than her fair share, allowing two Eaglehawk missiles to make it through. They, too, were defeated by the *Renown*'s immensely thick frontal armor, exploding harmlessly deep in the heavy armor protecting the cruiser's bows.

Perkins now split the task group. The rail-gun-fitted ships were tasked to finish off the last of the Hammer ships. The light units were ordered to dump a last missile salvo and then open out to fall back so that they could protect the ships recovering the lifepods from the *Marie Curie* and the *Kaminski*. Then, Michael thought, it would definitely be time to get the hell out of Dodge; otherwise, the two full-strength Hammer task groups now accelerating hard toward them would have them by the throat. He half turned to look across at the captain. For some reason, she turned at the same time, smiling broadly at Michael before turning her attention back to the command plot, apparently relaxed and unconcerned. Michael wondered how she did it. He had had quite enough for one day, the seconds dragging by until the characteristic buzz-rip announced the launch of *Eridani*'s last missile salvo.

"Thank Christ for that," Michael muttered. "Time to go home."

Thankfully, Commodore Perkins agreed.

"Command, Mother. Commodore to all ships. Stand by to jump."

"Command, roger. All stations. Stand by to jump. Engineering, confirm safe to jump."

"Confirmed. Mass distribution recomputed; model is nominal."

"Command, roger."

Lenksi wasted no more time, bringing the main engines up

to full power to drive *Eridani* to jump speed, the maneuvering jets firing furiously to put the ship on vector for home.

For once, Michael had no problem with the jump. The accumulated tension fell off him as he sat back, conscious for the first time of the sweat that had turned the shipsuit under his combat space suit into a sodden, ice-cold rag.

"Jeez," Michael said. "That was fun."

"I suppose that's one way to describe it," Lenski said laconically. "Okay. All stations, this is command. Secure from general quarters. Revert to defense stations, ship state 2, airtight integrity condition yankee. Engineering, repressurize. Starboard watch has the watch. Command out."

Monday, April 3, 2400, UD
Offices of the Supreme Council for the Preservation of
the Faith, city of McNair, Commitment

"Send him in!"

Polk did something he had not done since becoming chief councillor. He got up and went around his massive desk to shake the hand of the man who entered his office before waving him, more than a little surprised, into a seat.

"Well, Admiral. Looks like we're actually going to do it." Polk went back to his own seat.

Fleet Admiral Jorge smiled. "Well, sir. If you mean give the Feds a damn good kicking they won't forget for a long time, then yes, I think we are. And I think we'll get them to the negotiating table."

Polk leaned back and looked thoughtfully up at the ceiling.

"You know, Admiral, I have to be honest"—You lying jerk, Jorge thought; Polk had never been honest in his life. He would not be chief councillor if he had; that was for sure— "When we started down this road, I really thought that ` would all fall apart. Like so many things the Hammer h tried to do over the years," he added bitterly.

Jorge shook his head emphatically. "We all have doubts, sir. We need to. Our contingency planning would be nonexistent otherwise, but this time, I think Fleet can do what it has been asked to do. We certainly have the means to drive the Feds to the negotiating table."

"Your antimatter warheads?"

"Exactly so, sir. It makes every Fed ship vulnerable and their tactics obsolete. You recall the briefing from defense intelligence?"

Polk nodded. "I do. We have a lead of three, more like five, years over the Feds."

"I've told the planners to work on three. On the warhead front, I cannot see how they can duplicate what took us the best part of thirty years in less time. Think of the production infrastructure alone. Not to mention catching up on the fundamental research. So that's how long we've got to get the monkey off our back. I hope, well, I just . . ."

Polk leaned forward with a smile. "Hope those useless sons of bitches at foreign relations can negotiate the result we need. I think that's what you wanted to say."

"Well, not quite the words I would have used, sir, but close enough," Jorge conceded. "I'm sure we can hold the Feds for three years. I think we can probably hold them for five. After that . . ."

"Kraa!" Polk sneered, his lip curling in disdain. "I'll tell you something, Admiral. If the councillor for foreign relations hasn't wrapped up negotiations with the damn Feds before next year is out, then you'll be seeing a new face at the council table, I can assure you."

Jorge had no trouble believing Polk, just as he had no trouble believing that his own life—and the lives of his wife and only son—would be forfeit if the warships assigned to Operation Damascus did not eliminate the threat posed by the Fed fleet.

"Now, enough of that," Polk continued. "I recall we had some other matters to deal with."

"Well, sir. Let me start with the biggest problem I've got: the admiral commanding the Fortitude system, Rear Admiral . . ."

"Dropping."

With a lurch, *Eridani* dropped into normalspace. The command plot bloomed with a thick mass of green icons as the ship went online to Comdur's battle management AI.

Comdur command center was not taking any chances. By the time it had confirmed that *Eridani* really was who she said she was, the ship had been stood down from general quarters and Michael had taken over the watch. In his opinion, the identification process had taken an inordinate amount of time in that it was only one damned AI talking to another. Finally, *Eridani*'s navplan for its entry in-system was authorized, and she was given her final approach instructions.

It was time to start the slow process of decelerating into orbit around Comdur.

Comdur was not any old system, and Lenski was not taking any chances. The Fleet base's outer defenses were a shell of defensive platforms, each an ugly lattice of plasteel girders festooned with double-redundant fusion microplants, a phased-array radar, and the usual clutter of comm dishes, and armed with Lamprey antistarship lasers backed up by containerized Merlin missile launchers. The gaps between the platforms were filled with clouds of randomly shifting deep-space mines.

Lasers and missiles Lenski could cope with. It was the mines she worried about. The two-meter-diameter black stealthed spheres were equipped with a simple optronics/laser fire control system, a 10-kiloton directed fission warhead, and a liquid nitrogen–powered reaction jet maneuvering system. They were basic, nasty, and extremely cheap. In theory the mines knew how to distinguish between the good guys and the bad guys. Even so, Fleet doctrine was absolutely emphatic:

Under no circumstances was a starship captain to trust the things. After all, contractors bidding wholly on price had made every part of them.

"Okay, Michael. You have the ship. Take her in, and for Christ's sake, stick exactly to the navplan," Lenski ordered as she climbed out of her chair.

"Sir," Michael replied. He would; Lenski could depend on it.

Michael turned *Eridani* end for end. After carefully checking that the ship's vector was good, he fired her main engines in a long burst. She would drop in-system carefully, even if it did add a few hours to the process.

Michael looked around to see if Lenski had managed to get clear of the combat information center without being held up. She had not. "Captain, sir," he called out.

Lenski looked up from what looked like a heart-to-heart conversation with an engineer who Michael knew was in the middle of an ugly divorce. "Yes?"

"Initial deceleration burn completed. Vector is nominal for drop in-system."

"Good." Lenski looked intently at the command plot for a good few minutes. It was as if she were committing the positions of the thousands of space mines that lay between *Eridani* and Comdur to memory. Finally, she seemed satisfied that Michael was not going to run into anything unpleasant. "When I'm done here, I'm off. I'll be in my cabin if you need me." She turned back to resume her interrupted conversation.

"Sir."

Even though Lenski was one of the better starship captains around, there was a tangible sense of relief when she finally left the combat information center. Nobody liked having the captain looking over his or her shoulder.

After ten minutes of intense concentration triple-checking every last piece of *Eridani*'s navplan, Michael began to relax. *Eridani* was precisely on vector, the nearest space mines were comfortably far away, and the projected approach to the ship's assigned slot in low orbit around Comdur was clear all the way. By way of reward, he was not being hassled by Comdur control, which was always a good thing.

He sat back in the command chair, suddenly exhausted. Hard as he tried, he could not shake the feeling that he was using up his store of good luck faster than was prudent. Their third and last foray into Hammer space had been as bad as the first two missions had been good. In fact, *Eridani* had been lucky to survive. In theory, the mission should have been straightforward, right out of the tactical textbook.

Stand off, select a target, drop in a sacrificial lamb thirty seconds ahead of the main force as a distraction; main force arrives, shreds the target, and everyone leaves happy. In this case, *Eridani* had drawn the short straw as the sacrificial lamb, with four heavy escorts acting as the main force. With good intelligence, the mission was a classic right out of the idiot's guide to space warfare.

But with poor intelligence compounded by a hefty dose of bad luck, the mission had become the stuff of nightmares.

Standing well out in farspace, Commander Ho, the mission commander in the *New Horizon,* had picked the Hammer light cruiser *Breuseker,* operating alone in a high orbit around the planet Fortitude, apparently conducting trials on its long-range phased-array search radar. And why not? The sensor AIs in all five ships of Ho's task unit unanimously agreed that it had to be the *Breuseker.* Despite objections from Michael and two of his fellow sensor officers—all of them shared a nagging feeling that there was more to the *Breuseker*—the mission went ahead. *Breuseker* it was.

There turned out to be more to the *Breuseker* than first met the eye, a lot more, and none of it good. For a start, she was not the *Breuseker* at all. She was the brand-new City class heavy cruiser *Jennix;* that explained the mistaken identification. The City class shared active sensor suites with the latest Jackson class light cruisers; both being new, Fed sensor AIs had relatively little data to go on when trying to distinguish between the two. In the end, the whole business turned out to be a textbook example of an AI-assisted screwup, the confidence level assigned by the sensor AIs to their identification completely unwarranted.

That was the poor intelligence. The bad luck had come two parts.

First, *Jennix* was not doing radar trials at all. She was setting up for a live rail-gun firing exercise. Second, *Jennix* had changed vector as the Fed ships were on their way to drop in-system. Rather than ending up off the *Jennix*'s starboard beam, safely clear of her rail-gun batteries, the *Eridani* dropped into normalspace directly ahead of the Hammer ship and much too close—so close, so well positioned, that the Jennix had to do nothing except push the button to fire her rail-gun salvo down *Eridani*'s throat.

When *Eridani* dropped, all hell broke loose. *Eridani*'s command team did not see the attack coming until it was too late. To his dying day, Michael would never know how *Eridani* had survived. Someone on board the *Jennix* had been paying close attention to their gravitronics arrays because her rail-gun salvo, timed to split-second perfection, hit *Eridani* only seconds after she dropped. Nine of the tiny platinum/iridium alloy slugs smashed into her bows, the impact so severe that *Eridani* was thrown bodily backward.

Michael and the rest of the command team looked on in horror while Lenski proved what a great captain she was. Ignoring damage control's reports of major hull penetration around the upper cargo air lock and serious casualties, she did what *Eridani* had been ordered to do: keep *Jennix* distracted. *Eridani* did exactly that, getting a full missile salvo away as the four heavy escorts dropped to join the party. Holding out for as long as she could, Lenski smashed the red Emergency Jump button barely seconds before a salvo of *Jennix*'s Eaglehawk missiles arrived to rip her apart.

Five minutes later, the heavy escorts jumped back into pinchspace. They, too, had done what they had come to do. They jumped, leaving the *Jennix* a twisted, bleeding wreck tumbling slowly end over end, spitting orange-strobed lifepods in all directions. The luckless *Jennix* was headed for the scrap yard, the shortest commission in Hammer Space Fleet history, Michael had suggested at the postmission debriefing with a grim, humorless laugh.

In the end, *Eridani* got off pretty lightly, much better than ‌e deserved in fact. Nobody killed, thank God, but eight ‌cers went straight into regen tanks, with fifteen more walking wounded, one of whom needless to say was Petty Officer Bienefelt, though she was only scratched.

Michael shook his head. It had not been *Eridani*'s finest hour, and even Lenski's heartfelt apology for not taking him and his sensor team more seriously could not obscure the fact that one bad call had put *Eridani* seconds away from total destruction. There was not a heavy scout built that could survive a sustained short-range encounter with a Hammer heavy cruiser. The fact that *Jennix*'s first rail-gun salvo had failed to cripple *Eridani*'s pinchspace jump capability was pure undeserved luck, as was *Jennix*'s delay in getting her first missile salvo away; that delay had been long enough to allow *Eridani* to launch her own missiles and jump clear. Even then the danger had not been over. With her mass distribution model distorted by the ceramsteel armor blasted off by the *Jennix*'s rail-gun attack and only enough time for engineering to do a first cut recalculation, it had been touch and go whether the *Eridani* could ever drop safely back into normalspace. Waiting for the drop had been one of the worst and longest moments of Michael's life, a life, as he had pointed out to Bienefelt, that had seen more than its fair share of bad moments.

Still, they had made it in the end, and the news was not all bad. The damage to *Eridani* had been beyond the *Koh*'s ability to fix, and that meant they would score time off while Comdur's yards repaired the upper cargo air lock.

Even as he relived *Eridani*'s run-in with the *Jennix,* Michael was keeping a close eye on *Eridani*'s slow progress through Comdur's defenses. To his and no doubt Lenski's relief, they were safely through the minefields. They were now passing the massive bulk of one of the nine battle stations that made up Comdur's second line of defense, the space beyond them filled with jump disrupters that would force any attacker to drop well outside the minefields and fight its way in. Michael whistled softly at the thought. In three wars against the Hammer, there had not been a single successful attack against Comdur. God knew, the Hammer had tried. At one point in the Second Hammer War, they had thrown every ship they could scrape together into an attack that had cost them so dearly that they had never tried again.

"Captain, sir, officer in command."

"Yeah, go ahead, Michael."

"We'll be clear of the jump disrupters shortly. Intend initiating final deceleration burn as soon as we do."

"Good. Have we heard from Comdur when we'll be moving into the yard?"

"No, sir, not yet. I'll chase them up."

"Do that. I would rather go straight in than hang around in orbit if that's possible."

"Leave it with me, sir."

When Michael had *Eridani*'s final low-g deceleration burn adjusted to his satisfaction, he contacted control. Much to his surprise, they came straight back with the answer Lenski wanted to hear. There was a berth waiting for them; they were to go straight in.

Three hours later, *Eridani,* its mass firmly held by Comdur's hydraulic docking system, was being lowered slowly down the shaft that led to the repair yards kilometers below Comdur's desolate, airless, gray-black surface.

Monday, April 10, 2400, UD
FWSS Eridani, *berth Bravo-10, Comdur Fleet Base Repair Facility*

The first few hours after they berthed had been frantic.

Michael had kept well clear. Despite the shock loading *Eridani*'s precious sensors had endured when the Hammer rail-gun slugs had smashed home, they were all fully operational. So, he decided, he would tidy up a few loose ends, and unless he was grabbed for some shitty little job or other—he was only a junior lieutenant, after all—he would go ashore to check up on Bienefelt's progress. Needless to say, what she had assured all and sundry was only a minor scratch turned out to be a deep laceration to her left arm. When *Eridani*'s exasperated medic had found out, he had sent her straight to the base hospital on the grounds that the medics there were bigger and uglier than he was and might have more luck getting Bienefelt to cooperate.

Pleased to discover that Bienefelt had actually allowed the medics to fix her injured arm with a minimum of coercion and that she would be back on board later that day, Michael left the base hospital. His next stop was the venerable *Arcturus,* one of only four Regulus class heavy cruisers still operational, berthed across from the *Eridani* in berth Charlie-6.

After being handled roughly by a pair of Hammer heavy cruisers during an abortive attempt to take out one of Commitment's space battle stations, the *Arcturus* was not going anywhere soon, and that meant he would be able to catch up with Charles Mbeki. He had not seen Charles since graduation day, and it would be good to chat with him.

Michael could not get over how much the man in front of him had changed.

The Charles Mbeki he remembered from Space Fleet College had been an easygoing man, always cheerful, never taking life too seriously. This was not that man. Mbeki's face, normally a rich mahogany, had a waxy gray sheen to it, and he had not smiled once since they had sat down in a quiet corner of *Arcturus*'s wardroom.

Michael listened in tight-lipped silence as Mbeki unloaded. Things had been bad for the ship right from the word go, with *Arcturus* living up to her reputation as an unlucky ship. It all sounded horribly familiar to Michael as Mbeki told of a ship cursed with a weak captain, a divided wardroom, an unhappy ship's company, and unreliable systems that were the legacy of eighteen long years of hard service, systems that had failed when *Arcturus* had needed them most.

Finally he was finished. "So there you have it, Michael." He sat back and rubbed a tired face with hands the size of dinner plates. "We were fucked. Completely. The Hammers hit us on the port quarter. Two Eaglehawks, one after the other. Weaps Power Echo. Pow!" He shook his head in despair. "That was that. I suppose we were lucky to get away at all. If the *Seiche* and *Refulgent* had not been there to cover our ass, the Hammers would have finished us off."

Mbeki looked away for a moment, his eyes focused on something a long way away. He looked back at Michael. "Ninety-seven dead, Michael. Ninety-seven! Jesus! I was in the damn power control room only two minutes earlier. None of them made it. Not one. I didn't even get scratched. I knew them all. Every single one."

Michael struggled to work out what to say. What could he say?

"Charles?"

"Yeah?"

"Charles, my friend. Listen to me—"

Michael was cut off by the insistent wail of *Arcturus*'s klaxon. For a second, he and Mbeki looked at each other, their confusion total. The *Arcturus* was berthed, for God's sake, so why would the ship go to general quarters?

"What the hell?" Michael blurted, looking around as he came to his feet.

"Don't ask me," Mbeki said helplessly, a tremor in his voice.

Then the penny dropped. "Shit!" Michael said. "Has to be a Hammer attack on Comdur; has to be. I'm off. See you."

Michael ran hard for the gangway, dodging and weaving through the *Arcturus*'s crew as they rushed to their stations. He barely made it off the ship before *Arcturus*'s massive air lock doors thudded shut behind him. Pausing only to grab a skinsuit from an emergency locker, he pounded down the rock-cut passageway until, after rounding a corner, he finally made it to *Eridani*.

Damn, damn, damn, he told himself. He was too late. The *Eridani* was closed up tighter than a duck's ass, and she would stay that way until the immediate drama was over.

He commed *Eridani*.

Eridani's exec took the comm. "Wait one, Michael," a harried Malik Aasha said brusquely.

Michael did as he was told, trying without any luck to find out what the hell was going on. His security clearance was not good enough to get him into Comdur's BattleNet, so in the end all he could do was stand there and wait. Finally,

Aasha's avatar reappeared in his neuronics. The exec did not waste any time. "Michael! Hammer attack is all we know. Go to the system command center. They may be able to use you. There's nothing we need you for on board. We're not going anywhere. Come back when it's all over."

With that, Aasha was gone. Michael wasted no time, spinning on his heel and setting off at a sprint for the nearest drop tube.

Five minutes later, he skidded to a halt at the marine security post controlling access to Comdur's huge system command center. His heart sank. Behind outer plasglass security doors, the center's plasteel blast doors were closed.

"Shit," he cursed aloud. The doors would stay shut until the attack was over. He did not bother asking the marine security detail if he could get in. He would have to be the president herself to have any chance.

Oh, well, he thought, at least he had tried. Disconsolately, he turned away, only to run right into a small but rather chunky commander, the man barreling around the corner right into him, dropping them both to the ground.

"Shit! Oh, sorry, sir," Michael apologized as the two picked themselves up.

"No harm done, son," the man replied. "We locked out?"

"Afraid so, sir." Michael waved at the doors. "Looks like it'll stay that way. I haven't asked the marines, but—"

The commander put his hand up. "No, don't waste your time. If the command center's buttoned up, then I can't get in, so you definitely won't." He looked at Michael for a moment, frowning. Then light dawned. "Aha," he announced, obviously pleased with himself. "I know you. You're the famous Helfort, aren't you?"

Michael shrugged his shoulders. "Sir."

The man bobbed up and down in delight. "Excellent, excellent. Good to meet you." He took Michael's hand and shook it vigorously.

Michael sighed to himself. Dollars to doughnuts, he knew what was coming next. He was right.

"Knew your parents. Say hello from me when you see them next. John Baker. They'll remember."

"Will do, sir," he replied resignedly. Was there anyone above the rank of lieutenant commander who did not know his parents?

Baker frowned. "Now, we need to know what's going on out there." He pursed his lips and whistled softy. "Ummm . . . let me see. Yes, that should do it. Good, I'm patched in."

Michael's pleading look did not go unnoticed. Baker held up a hand. "Yes, hang on. Okay, right. I've authorized you to access BattleNet as well."

Michael patched in his neuronics. What he saw made his heart stand still. Coming in from galactic north was the largest force of ships he had ever seen. The Hammer must have scraped the bottom of the barrel to get so many hulls into space at the same time. Suddenly it all made sense; this was why the *Eridani* had seen so few ships in Hammer nearspace.

Hundreds of ships or not, it still did not make sense. Comdur's defenses, backed up by the Fleet units now getting under way, would chop the attackers to pieces. It did not matter how many Hammers there were. It was only a matter of time.

He looked again. There was another odd thing. When the Hammer ships had dropped—they had dropped a long way out—the Hammers had launched a missile salvo, but it had been small. The tightly grouped formation undoubtedly was the usual deceptive mix of Eaglehawks bundled with active decoys and jammers, preceded by what looked like a poor copy of the Fed's Krachov shroud. Their version of the Krachov might not be up to Fed standards, but the thick mass of tiny disks was doing a good enough job of deflecting the intense barrage of laser fire being thrown at the missile salvo by Comdur's defensive platforms, encasing the salvo in what looked like a swarm of brilliantly lit scintillating diamonds. Michael looked across at Baker questioningly.

Baker shrugged his shoulders. "Strange. Never seen anything like this before," he muttered, obviously puzzled. "This is something new. Wonder what the rabble are up to now."

They got the answer an instant later. The missiles exploded as one, a single fleeting blue-white flash that was so fast, so transient, that Michael was not even sure he had seen it. The missiles were gone, leaving only thin spheres of ionized gas to mark their passing. Then came the awful sound of radiation alarms, their racket bouncing off the walls of the rock-cut passageway.

Baker went white. "Oh, sweet Jesus. Oh, no. It can't be," he whispered, his voice cracking. Michael stared. The man was beginning to panic. Why? he thought desperately. What was going on?

Then the space mines standing in the way of the Hammers blew, radiation-overloaded fission warheads filling the entire sector with thousands of brilliant blue-white balls of flame shot through with scarlet-red threads. An instant later, they too vanished, leaving only tenuous balls of ionized gas expanding into nothingness.

"Oh, Jesus," Baker croaked to himself as Michael strained to hear what he was saying. "Intense gamma radiation flux. Has to be. Those damn things are supposed to be fail-safe, for God's sake."

Baker's obvious fear was infectious, and Michael felt an ice-cold dread beginning to roll over him. "Sir! What is it? Tell me!"

Baker's hand went up. "One sec. I need to isolate a single warhead detonation from the datastream so I can see the weapon-specific radiation profile, so hang on . . . Oh, Holy Mother. Oh, my God. It is." Baker's voice trembled with shock. "It bloody well is."

"Is what, sir?" Michael asked desperately.

"Antimatter. Shit. Intense gamma radiation, double spike profile. Textbook example. First spike at 84 attoseconds, second one around 6 nanoseconds, but smaller. All gamma radiation. Oh, God help us all. We are screwed. Those clever sons of bitches. Goddamn it, who would have thought?" Baker shook his head, his voice an uncomfortable blend of grudging admiration and shocked disbelief.

"Sir. I don't understand," Michael said urgently, struggling to understand what Baker was talking about.

"Antimatter warheads. They've worked out how to weaponize antimatter. We've always thought it was too difficult."

"Oh, shit!" Michael was stunned, the fear of something he did not fully understand pulling at him. Physics had never been one of his strong suits, but he knew enough about antimatter to know that even a tiny amount coming into contact with normal matter would release a prodigious amount of energy. With a sinking heart, he turned his attention back to BattleNet.

Out in Comdur nearspace, the tactical situation went from bad to catastrophic.

A second Hammer missile salvo followed the first. It was small, too, a tightly packed cluster of Eaglehawk missiles, decoys, and jammers. Ten thousand kilometers short of the nearest space battle station, the only thing left standing between the oncoming Hammers and Comdur, the salvo exploded in a single intense flash. Then, to Michael's horror, the battle station's armor turned white-hot and started to boil off, writhing jets of ceramsteel plasma lancing out into space, the battle station itself starting an almost imperceptibly slow roll out of station. Then the third salvo was on its way in, but this time the salvo was huge. The missile swarm, thousands and thousands strong, drove through the gap blown in Comdur's outer defenses, past the dying battle station, and toward the Fed ships coming out to meet the oncoming Hammer attack.

Michael watched hypnotized by the awful sight. He could barely breathe. Something terrible was about to happen.

The missiles closed in on the Fed ships. One by one, missiles began to die under a hail of defensive fire. Missiles and lasers weeded out the decoys to hack missiles into shattered pieces of tumbling wreckage.

Baker whistled in disbelief as he watched. "How the hell are they doing that?" he muttered.

"What?" Michael asked.

"Maintaining warhead integrity. How do they stop the warheads from exploding even though the missiles have been shredded around them? They should fail, for God's sake. Shit," he added despairingly. "We have got a lot to learn, that's bloody obvious."

Not all the missiles died. Closing in past 10,000 kilometers, the survivors erupted in a single tightly coordinated flash that seemed to vanish even before it appeared. The Fed ships accelerating out hard to meet the Hammer attack began to die as the double pulse of gamma radiation turned their armor first white-hot and then into a seething mass of boiling ceramsteel spewing out and back to envelop the ships in death shrouds of white plasma. Deep inside the ships, spacers followed their ships into death as the wall of gamma radiation punched impulse shock waves through the armor and into the inner titanium hulls, vicious shards of metal spalling off to cut spacers into bloody pulp. Those spared the slashing of razor-sharp metal started to die a slow death from radiation poisoning as their ships' grossly overloaded quantum traps collapsed, gamma radiation sleeting through unprotected bodies.

Then the Hammers jumped.

It was over.

Michael and Baker stood unmoving, silent, stunned by the horror of it all, their neuronics laying it out in pitiless detail. Michael could hardly get his mind around the list of ships dying right in front of his eyes, ships from every class in the Fleet. With them died any hope that this war could be brought to a quick end by an invasion of the Hammers' home planet using overwhelming force.

Hope flared. He was wrong. Not every class in the Fleet was on the rack.

"Sir!" Michael cried urgently.

"What?" Baker replied flatly, all hope ground out of him by the brutally effective Hammer attack.

"Sir! Don't you see? Where are the planetary assault vessels? There's not one in-system. Not one!"

Baker stared for a moment. "By God, Helfort. You are right. How could I have missed it?" His voice rose sharply with excitement. "They've missed them. Let me check . . . yes, by God! They're out doing drop and launch exercises with the marines in deepspace and won't be back until next week. Jesus! Lucky? That's beyond lucky. That's a miracle; that's what that is."

With an obvious effort, Baker got himself under control. "Look. I'd better go. There's work to be done." Baker paused. "Now, Helfort, listen to me."

"Sir?"

"I've said some stuff I shouldn't have said. I'm with the Fleet Advanced Projects Unit, so I know things that most people don't. I should have kept my mouth shut. So I'm going to classify everything we've talked about as top secret and put a neuronics block on it. Okay?"

Michael nodded. He was not going to argue with the man. "Do it, sir." He paused for a moment. "Okay, sir. Go ahead. I've enabled access to my neuronics."

"Thanks . . . right. That's done. Now, get back to your ship. Remember this, Helfort. Helfort!" Baker took him by the shoulders and shook him hard. "Helfort! Listen to me. This isn't over. It's going to take a bit longer than we thought, that's all. Believe that and you'll be fine. Got it?"

"Sir." Michael's voice was ash-dry.

"Good. Get back to your ship. Go. Now!"

Michael turned and ran as though the Devil himself were after him.

Nine point six light-years from Comdur and 75 million kilometers out from Terranova, home planet of the FedWorld system, two Hammer heavy cruisers dropped out of pinch-space. Each deployed a single Eaglehawk missile. Ten seconds later, the missiles were accelerating hard toward Terranova on thin pillars of white fire.

Five seconds later, the two Hammer cruisers jumped.

Hours later, the warheads on the missiles exploded, a wall of gamma radiation driving in toward Terranova, its double pulse the unmistakable fingerprint of matter/antimatter annihilation.

Lieutenant Commander Lenski strode grim-faced into *Eridani*'s wardroom, waving her officers and senior spacers to be seated. She grabbed a coffee from the drinkbot and sat down.

"Okay, folks. First, some good news. The casualty recovery teams have done a great job getting the crews off the ships. Well, those still alive," she added bitterly. "Anyway, the base hospital is struggling, but thank God there are plenty of regen tanks, so we should be able to save most of them. Radiation damage takes a lot of fixing, so we won't see them back in uniform for a long time. They'll start shuttling the survivors back to their home planets tomorrow."

She paused to take a mouthful of coffee and then another.

Michael thought she looked terrible, and it was not from lack of sleep. True, they were all tired. Nobody had slept much since the Hammers had come calling, but it was not that. No, it was something much more fundamental; Michael had seen the same thing on the faces of every spacer he had met since what was now being called the Comdur Disaster. It had taken a while for him to work out what it was, but now he was sure he knew.

It was the awful realization that for all the power, all the technology, and all the wealth possessed by the Federated Worlds, nothing in humanspace was guaranteed. The Federation could be beaten and beaten badly, beaten like they had never been beaten before. Worse, they had been beaten by the Hammers, a people all Feds thought little better than brutal fundamentalists pursuing a bizarre and arcane religion spawned from the deranged mind of an indentured Martian colonist. More than any of that and worst of all, it was the humiliation of losing the Federation's rightful place as the leader of humanspace.

Lenksi continued. "Apart from the fact that the Hammers missed the planetary assault vessels, the other good news is that the ships damaged in the attack are not all write-offs. Some are. My first ship for one, but—"

"That can't be right, skipper. The ark went to the scrap yard centuries ago," a voice chipped in from the back of the wardroom.

"Watch it, Chief O'Halloran, 'cause I know where you live," Lenski called out with a tight smile as laughter rippled around the packed wardroom. "Anyway, as I was saying, most can be recovered, so thank God for radiation-hardened optronics. Again, it'll take time, but a lot less time than building from scratch. Most of the damage is to bow armor, though there's a lot of spalling up forward. Fleet will be calling for ferry crews to get them back to the builders' yards for repair, so stand by for some detached duty."

Lenski took a deep breath. "Now the bad news. The final casualty lists are out, and they make pretty grim reading. The other bad news is that Operation Falcon has been postponed indefinitely."

A soft hiss filled the air. Nobody present could have been surprised to hear that the invasion of Commitment was off, but it hurt to hear the news officially.

"The last thing I have for you is that yesterday two Hammer cruisers dropped into Terranovan farspace and fired two antimatter-armed Eaglehawks. Fortunately, they detonated a long way out, so apart from some spectacular atmospheric fireworks followed by a pretty sizable electromagnetic pulse when the gamma radiation arrived, there was nothing to worry about. There was no damage and no casualties. Nobody knows what the Hammers meant by that little stunt. Some sort of demonstration obviously, but to what end we don't know. So that's the latest. Any questions?"

"What do we do now, skipper? Surely we're not going to give up?" one of the engineers asked.

Lenski shook her head emphatically. "Not a bloody chance," she replied, her voice hardening. "The Hammers have given us a good belting, no argument, but word is that we'll finish what those Kraa-worshipping Hammer filth have started, and by the time this is all over, they'll regret they were ever born."

For a full minute, there was a profound silence. Lenski watched, a grim smile on her face, the faces in front of her taut with steely determination. She nodded. If she had had any doubts about her spacers' willingness, about their ability to take the fight back to the Hammers, they were gone.

Michael stared at the glass of beer Petty Officer Bienefelt had put down in front of him. She was unimpressed. Canteen etiquette was strict: Buyee raises glass first.

"Fuck's sake, sir!" she complained. "You are one hell of a slow drinker, and I'm dying of thirst here."

"Yeah, I know, Matti. Sorry. Here's to . . . well, here's to anything that gives the Hammer grief," he finished lamely, raising his glass.

"Amen to that." Bienefelt downed most of her beer in one swallow. "So what do you think? Captain seemed pretty sure it would be business as usual."

"I don't know, Matti. Wish it was business as usual, but that's hard to see. Things have changed. People say what the Hammer did off Terranova was only a stunt, but it doesn't seem like a stunt to me. Seems more like . . ." He paused for a moment to think.

Bienefelt finished the sentence for him. "A message?"

Michael nodded. "Spot on, Matti. That's exactly right. It's a message."

"Okay, it's a message, but what does it mean?"

"Well, I'm not sure." His frustration showed in hands clenched into fists. "But . . ."

"But what?"

"Well, I hate to think this, but only one thing makes any sense. I think they are telling us to give them what they want or they'll destroy Terranova. Shit! We know they can."

Bienefelt frowned skeptically. "They'd do that? I know they're Hammers, but would they destroy a whole planet? Surely not."

"That's the million-FedMark question, Matti."

Michael was quiet for a long time. He looked Bienefelt right in the eye. "You know what, Matti. I think they might. If we push them too hard, if they think we're serious about invading Commitment, then they might. What have the people who run the Hammer Worlds got to lose? If we invade, all that rotten Hammer of Kraa bullshit comes crashing down; the jokers who run the place all have their balls cut off before being strung up from the nearest lamppost. Jesus, if it was you, would you care too much about Terranova?"

Bienefelt shook her head. "Guess not, but if they nuke Terranova, we can do the same to them, surely."

Michael smiled grimly. "Maybe we can. Then they can. Mutually assured destruction it's called, if I remember my history properly. So a stalemate is where this is all heading." He shook his head despairingly.

"Another beer, sir?"

"Why not?" Michael lifted his empty glass.

Bienefelt shook her head and pushed her glass across the table. "Oh, no. This one's your shout."

"Tightwad!"

Lenski waved Michael into a seat.

"Right. I've got new orders for you. You are to take the *Adamant* back to Terranova for repairs. You're scheduled to leave in twenty-four hours, so I suggest you get your gear together and get across to her. You'll get detailed orders on board."

Michael stared for a moment. "Um, yes, sir. Anyone else from *Eridani?*"

"Yes. I'm giving you Pavel as your chief engineer, plus four techs. Who do you want for coxswain?"

Silly question, Michael thought. "Petty Officer Bienefelt if I can, sir."

Lenski nodded. "Thought you might, but that's fine by me. Have her pick eight spacers as working hands. Not that there's going to be much to do. The AIs will do the work. Any questions?"

"Only one, sir. Who's the skipper to be?"

Lenski's eyebrows shot up. "Jeez, Michael. You're a bit slow today. You, of course, you bonehead!"

Michael's mouth dropped open, "Me? *Adamant*'s a light cruiser. I'm only a junior lieutenant."

Lenski laughed at Michael's confusion. "Let's not get carried away, Michael. Yes, it's a light cruiser, but a pretty battered one, and it's only a ferry trip. Go on, off you go. We'll see you back here Friday morning. Go on, go!"

"Sir!"

When he left Lenski's cabin, Michael tried not altogether successfully not to let the news that Pavel Duricek, the king of pompous windbags, was going to be his engineer get him down. Still, at least it was a short run, and he would have Matti as his coxswain. She would keep things in line.

Wednesday, April 12, 2400, UD
FWSS Adamant, in orbit around Comdur Fleet Base

Accompanied by Duricek and Bienefelt, Michael walked the length and breadth of his new command. The feeling of loss was unnerving. The *Adamant*'s huge mass was echoingly empty, the only sound the steady hiss of the ship's air-conditioning system.

He found it all deeply unsettling.

When the quantum traps that deflected radiation away from the crew had collapsed under the enormous wall of gamma radiation, the ship had been completely sterilized, her crew condemned to months in regen to repair the massive damage that had been inflicted on them. Not a single spacer or marine had escaped serious injury; many would never recover fully. Some had already died, and more would follow.

If not for the AIs embedded in every system on board, their massively redundant optronics completely immune to the effects of gamma or any other form of radiation, the *Adamant* would have been a lump of ceramsteel wrapped around a pressure hull protecting a lot of useless air-filled spaces. But *Adamant* was no empty shell. Apart from the fact that she had no crew, *Adamant* was a fully mission-capable ship.

Michael left the forward compartments for last. It was there that *Adamant* had suffered most of her losses. When the first spike of gamma radiation had dumped huge amounts of energy into the ship's bow armor in less than a billion billionth of a second, an impulse shock wave had smashed back through the armor and into the ship's inner hull. Thousands of those shock waves had hit the *Adamant* in a tiny fraction of a second. In theory, the heavy-duty elastomeric mountings anchoring the ship's armor to the inner titanium pressure hull should have protected the crew from external shock. But under the relentless hammering of successive waves of gamma radiation, the overloaded shock mountings had failed, allowing shock waves to jump into the pressure hull, spalling off lethal shards of metal. Most of the shards had been trapped by the ship's last line of defense—a Kevlar splinter mat bonded directly to the pressure hull—but not all. By the time the Hammer attack was over, far too many of *Adamant*'s crew were dead, their combat space suits no match for shards of high-velocity razor-sharp metal.

Michael followed Duricek and Bienefelt as they made their way forward along the cruiser's central passageway, past the missile batteries, and into the forward rail-gun control room. Michael stifled a shocked gasp as he walked through the airtight door. The compartment was straight out of a horror vid. The cleanup crews and their bots had done their best, but they had a lot of ships to deal with; the aftereffects of the Hammer attack were still plain to see. Every surface was covered in a grisly mix of dried blood and pieces of metal-shredded space suits, all liberally dusted with plasfiber fragments torn from shattered panels and cabinets, bulkheads gouged deep by metal splinters. The three spacers stood in shock.

Bienefelt broke the awful silence. "Mother of God," she whispered.

"Wasn't here to look after these poor bastards. Wish she

had been." Michael's face was grim, white with shock. He checked the ship's AI. Nineteen dead in this compartment alone. "That'll do. Matti."

"Sir?"

"All the compartments like this. Get the bots back in. Let's see if we can do a better job. Use your spacers, too."

"Yes, sir," Bienefelt replied, her normal ebullience buried for the moment.

Michael turned to Duricek. "Chief."

"Yes?"

Michael's eyes narrowed. He had not missed the calculated insult. Duricek might be senior to him, but Michael held a warrant from the president appointing him captain in command of *Adamant*. Duricek would regret ignoring that simple fact, but this was not the time.

"When will the systems status report be ready?" he asked calmly.

"Another hour or so." Duricek's casual tone made it clear that as far as he was concerned, it did not matter when the systems status report would be finished.

Michael's voice hardened. "I'm sorry, Chief. That won't do. Give me a specific time I can work with."

A tiny grain of common sense somewhere deep inside Duricek must have stopped a smart-ass response in its tracks. "Er, right. I'll have it for you in two hours," he mumbled sulkily.

Michael turned to Bienefelt, his face a stony mask. Standing in a compartment drenched in the blood of good spacers, he was in no mood to be jerked around by a pompous, self-important dickhead like Duricek. "On you go, Petty Officer Bienefelt. Get things moving. I can see no reason why we can't depart on schedule, but I'll make that decision once Lieutenant Duricek and I are happy with the state of the ship's systems."

Bienefelt's face was impressively impassive. "Sir."

Michael waited until Bienefelt had gone before turning back to Duricek. "Chief, I'm only going to say this once, so I strongly suggest you pay attention. You may be senior to me in rank, but you are not senior to me by appointment. If you do not show me the respect due by right to every captain in command, I will have you charged. I will not tolerate insubordination. If you have a problem with anything I say or do, let me know, and we'll sort it out in private. In the meantime, you will oblige me by offering the captain in command the proper courtesies. Is that clear?"

Duricek's face twitched as fear and anger wrestled for control, his mouth opening and shutting as he tried to decide what to say.

"Well?" Michael barked, making him jump.

"Yes, sir," Duricek muttered sullenly.

"Good. Get that status report done. We'll reconvene in two hours to go through it. I need to know exactly how fifteen of us are going to operate this bloody great big ship safely."

Duricek gave a quick nod. He left without another word.

What a jerk, Michael thought as he watched the man go. He had enough to worry about without massaging the ego of some pompous oaf. Why had Lenski given him Duricek to be his chief? She must have known the two of them did not get along.

Michael had to keep reminding himself that he was the captain of a real live FedWorld Space Fleet light cruiser. He still had trouble getting his mind around the idea. Junior Lieutenant Michael Wallace Helfort, captain in command, Federated Worlds Warship *Adamant*. It sounded faintly ludicrous. He felt faintly ludicrous.

Michael sat alone, the only occupant of the *Adamant*'s enormous combat information center, as the ship accelerated slowly out of Comdur nearspace and past what was left of the gamma radiation–shattered wreckage of Comdur's elaborate defenses. If all went well, they would jump in a few hours for the five-hour transit to Terranova. Allow four or so hours to decelerate in-system, an hour to berth in the warship maintenance yards of Karlovic Heavy Industries, another hour to hand over the ship, and the job would be done. Sixteen hours, tops. Some command, he thought. Talk about short and sweet. He stretched in a vain attempt to get the ache out of his back.

"Command, engineering." Duricek was unable to conceal the resentment in his voice.

"Go ahead, Chief," Michael replied, careful to keep his voice neutral.

"Sir. Main engines are nominal. Pinchspace jump generators are on line. Ship's mass distribution model is nominal. All other systems are nominal. Confirm we are good to jump."

Better, Michael thought. He did not care for the resentful overtones, but it could have been worse.

"Command, roger. Understand we are good to jump."

"I'll be here in propulsion control if you need me, sir."

"Thanks, Chief. Changing the subject, did you resolve that problem with Weapons Power Foxtrot? God knows, I hope it's the last system we need, but it would be good to have one hundred percent weapons availability."

"The lads are working on it, sir. We found a damaged mount, so I think it's a shock problem. There seems to be a misalignment somewhere. I'm hoping the system AI can work out a way around it because we can't open it up to have a look. At this stage, we don't know when or even if we can get it back online."

Michael could not help smiling. Christ, the man was obvious, his tone making it abundantly clear that he thought worrying about one of the fusion plants that provided power to the *Adamant*'s after weapons systems was a completely pointless exercise. "Okay. Keep me posted on that one. I want it back if at all possible."

"Sir."

Michael settled back. In truth, he was captain in name only. The *Adamant* and all her systems were in the hands of scores of embedded AIs, all working under the control of the ship's master AI. On a small ship like *Eridani,* the master AI would be called Mother. On a ship this size, calling the AI Mother somehow did not seem proper, even if the voice of *Adamant*'s AIs was, as tradition dictated, that of a middle-aged woman.

So Michael stuck to the official title, AI Primary or simply Prime, cold and sterile though it was.

So far, Prime was doing it right. *Adamant* was on vector, and every system she needed to make the pinchspace transit to Terranova was online and nominal. He had rerun the pinchspace calculations off-line; he was pleased to see that his solution and Prime's agreed to the required number of significant figures.

Michael settled back and closed his eyes, his neuronics putting him right at the heart of the *Adamant* to the point where he became one with the ship: His human senses were replaced by *Adamant*'s massive arrays of active and passive sensors reaching out millions of kilometers into space.

It was an awesome feeling.

With only an hour left before they dropped into Terranovan nearspace, the strident ringing of a primary systems alarm jolted Michael upright.

"Prime! Update."

"Command, Prime. We have an intermittent failure reported by the navigation AI. We're getting an unstable pinchspace vector solution. I'm working on the problem and will report back."

Michael's hands were suddenly damp. If the navigation AI was not able to keep *Adamant* on the right vector through the unstable *n*-dimensional probability field that made up pinchspace, things could get bad. His stomach did a quick backflip. He was in no mood to spend the rest of eternity wandering lost and alone somewhere in pinchspace or, if he took the chance and did a blind drop, spending the rest of eternity lost somewhere in normalspace hundreds of light-years from the rest of humankind, unable to jump back to civilization.

Bienefelt appeared from nowhere. "What's up, sir?"

"Not sure, Matti. Problem with the navigation AI. Working on it."

Matti looked worried. "Shit."

"Shit is right. Let the team know I'll brief them when I know something definite. I need to talk to the Chief."

Matti nodded as Michael commed Duricek. His conversation was short and to the point because Duricek and his technicians could do nothing to solve the problem.

"Command, Prime."

"This better be good," Michael muttered. "Command."

"I've been able to reduce the problem but not eliminate it. It seems to be coming from problems with the external pinchspace field sensors; there's instability in the drift compensators. Most likely radiation damage."

"The sensors. Anything we can do?"

"No. That's a yard job."

"So what's it all mean?"

"Our ability to make an accurate drop out of pinchspace has been severely degraded, but not fatally so."

"Okay, Prime. I want a new drop position to make absolutely sure we don't come out of pinchspace inside Terranova."

"Understood. Stand by . . . position computed and uploaded."

Michael checked and rechecked Prime's new drop point. It might be a long way out from Terranova, but at least there was no chance that they would end up trying to share normalspace with something big and heavy. Like a planet.

"Revised drop position command approved." It would be a pain in the ass flogging their way back in normalspace, but at least they would get back alive with *Adamant* intact. "All stations, this is command. We'll be dropping shortly. As you know, we've had a small problem with the navigation AI, but Prime says she's got it under control. To make sure we don't hit anything, we'll be dropping a long way out from Terranova, so we'll be late getting to the pub tonight, guys. Sorry about that. Command out."

Michael watched anxiously as the minutes to the drop ran off with excruciating slowness, but whatever Prime had done to the navigation AI seemed to be holding up. With ten minutes to go, Michael commed Bienefelt to come to the combat information center. The more he thought about dropping well out into Terranovan farspace, the more he realized how alone the *Adamant* would be, how far from help if things went wrong.

"Sir?"

"Matti. Get your guys together. We're going to be hanging around out in deepspace for a long time. If we run into anything, we're going to have to deal with it on our own. So get them up here. I want to know what's going on. That means running full threat and command plots, and I would rather not leave Prime doing the job on its own. Any of them have sensor training?"

Bienefelt checked her neuronics. She nodded. "Yes. One gravitronics, one radar, a couple of electronic warfare types. None current, though."

"Better than nothing. Put the rest on the holocams. Get 'em all up here; find them somewhere to sit. When you've done that, I want you next to me. Two pairs of eyes are always better than one. So move it; we'll be dropping shortly."

"Sir."

"Oh, one more thing. Suit up."

"Sir."

Michael commed Prime. "Prime, this is command. Bring all combat systems online, alert zero."

"Prime, roger. Bring combat systems online, alert zero. Stand by."

Michael commed Duricek. "Engineering, command."

"Engineering." Duricek's tone was as sulky as ever. Michael suppressed a sudden urge to go aft to give the man a good kick in the balls.

"Dropping in three. All set?"

"Yes, sir."

"Good. I've brought the combat systems to instant readiness. I'm not expecting anything, but you never know. So stand by for emergency maneuvering and get your people suited up."

"Sir."

When Michael cut the comm, Bienefelt threw her massive bulk into the seat alongside his; suited up, she was enormous. In a cruiser, two senior warfare officers would sit alongside the captain. How things had changed; a junior lieutenant and a petty officer were now the complete command team for a light cruiser supported by a scratch team of sensor operators badly overdue for refresher training. Well, he said philosophically to himself, it would just have to do.

"Guys all okay?" Michael asked as he struggled into his combat space suit.

"Strapped in, suited up, sir."

"Right. Patch your neuronics into Prime. Make sure I don't miss anything."

"Command, Prime."

"Command," Michael replied.

"All combat systems nominal, at alert zero, all sensors online and nominal."

"Command, roger." Michael knew he was being overly careful, but he would be damned if he allowed his new command to drop into normalspace unprepared for the worst.

Adamant dropped. There was the usual microsecond lurch as the universe turned itself inside out. Michael breathed out slowly as the holovids showed nothing more threatening than curtains of brilliant stars hanging in glorious confusion. For a moment it took his breath away. He quickly identified Terranova's sun, at a rough guess 200 million kilometers away. Not the best drop in Fleet history, but a long way from the worst and close enough to make it home.

He commed his scratch crew. "All stations, command. Sitrep. We're home, Terranova's only 95 million kilometers away, and the threat plot is green. Prime's contacting Terranova control, and I'll let you know what they want us to do. In the meantime, we'll start heading in. Command out."

Michael sat back. The prospect of a long hack in-system was depressing enough. A long hack as captain of a ship with Duricek as chief engineer was even more depressing. Well, he consoled himself, at least they were going home. Maybe he would—

All thought of the pleasures of home leave disappeared in the face of an urgent shout from the operator on gravitronics. Michael was impressed to see the young spacer beating Prime to it by a full second.

"Sir, positive gravitronics intercept. Estimated drop bearing Green 3 Up 1. Two vessels. Grav wave pattern suggests pinchspace transition imminent. Designated hostile tracks

500501 and 502. The vector's all wrong, though, sir. Goes nowhere near Terranova."

Goddamn it, Michael thought. Hammers. Had to be. Without thinking, he commed the ship to general quarters before he remembered that he had no crew to send. He commed the klaxon off.

"All stations, command. Sorry about that. We've got inbound traffic, and the traffic plot from Terranova control suggests it's hostile. So visors down. Prime and I will fight the ship. You guys hold on. Engineering. Stand by to maneuver. Command out."

Michael closed his eyes; he put the command plot up on his neuronics, bringing the range in until the angry red of the gravitronics intercept overwhelmed *Adamant*'s green vector. The rest of the plot was empty, nothing but blackness. Michael's stomach lurched. They were completely alone. If the incoming ships were Hammers—and they almost certainly were—they could only be heavy cruisers, and he could not do what any sane captain of a battle-damaged ship manned by a scratch crew would do: jump, and jump now.

But he could not. Michael cursed his fate. With a suspect nav AI, jumping to safety was not an option.

No, the *Adamant* was stuck in normalspace. She would have to fight it out or die in the process.

"Prime, command. Mission priority is destruction of hostile tracks 500501 and 502, second priority own-ship defense. You have missile and rail-gun launch authority. Fire when ready."

"Prime, roger. Mission priority is destruction of hostile tracks 500501 and 502, second priority own-ship defense."

If responsibility for saving the *Adamant* and her scratch crew weighed heavily on Prime's virtual shoulders, she did not let it show. Her voice was calm and measured. "Prime, roger. I have missile and rail-gun launch authority. Stand by. Command, I have a good drop datum on tracks 500501 and 502. Estimate drop point at Green 2 Up 1, range 40,000 kilometers. Deploying missiles now. Stand by rail-gun salvo."

Adamant's combat information center filled with the racket of hydraulic rams dumping a full missile salvo overboard. Prime throttled the missiles back, the salvo accelerating slowly toward the datum and opening out into a ring so that the Hammer ships would face missiles coming from all directions at once. Michael approved. Quite rightly, Prime did not want the missiles at full power until she was 100 percent sure where the incoming ships would drop. Michael struggled to breathe as Prime refined the drop datum, the seconds agonizingly drawn out into what felt like hours. For God's sake, fire, he felt like shouting, but Prime held on.

The young sensor operator's voice was cracking under the strain. "Sir! Targets dropping. Confirm I have a good drop datum at Green 2 Up 1 at 38,000 kilometers."

"Command, roger," Michael replied calmly.

Still Prime held on.

The ships dropped. Still Prime waited. Michael wanted to scream even though he knew she had to be sure the new arrivals really were Hammers. Hacking two Fed ships out of space would not look good on his service record.

"Command, Prime. Targets confirmed hostile. Stand by rail-gun salvo."

Barely an instant before Michael overrode her, Prime sent the missiles on their way, more than 300 Merlin heavy antistarship missiles buried in a cloud of decoys accelerating up to their maximum speed of 300 kilometers per second toward the unsuspecting Hammers. Three seconds later, *Adamant* shuddered as her rail-gun batteries flung a full salvo at the new arrivals.

It was a textbook ambush; Prime had timed it to perfection. The few seconds she had waited had allowed the Hammer ships to cross *Adamant*'s bow and start moving away. That left their poorly armored quarters wide open to *Adamant*'s attack. The two ships never had a chance; Prime's timing was so good that Michael was not sure they even saw the attack coming.

As the salvos closed in, Michael cursed. Prime's timing had been perfect, but she had closed up the salvo too much. The slugs were too close together; only a few would hit home. Michael held his breath as the edge of the rail-gun salvo, split equally between the two ships, caught the Hammers from below and behind, ripping into the ships around their main engines, where their armor was thinnest. An instant later, the elaborate and complex maze of vulnerable high-pressure pipework disintegrated into a lethal storm of shredded metal. Michael breathed out in relief; Prime might not have designed the perfect rail-gun salvo, but enough slugs had found their targets to do the job.

Then the auxiliary fusion plants in the after section of the ships started to fail. First one blew, then the rest; four blue-white flashes of runaway fusion plants swamped the holocams, with the hulls of the two ships thrashing up and down as massive shock waves ripped forward.

Michael watched intently; he held his breath as he waited for the fusion plants that powered the ships' main engines to blow. The slugs must have gone close enough; he was sure they would go, but nothing happened. He breathed out. The Hammers were lucky Prime had not done a better job. The ships were now slowly spinning wrecks tumbling through space end over end, lifepods spitting out in all directions, their after hulls opened up into huge metal petals festooned with molten metal and plastic fast cooling into grotesquely twisted lumps, shattered pipework, broken decking, and torn cabling trailing out into space. The last icy tendrils of ship's atmosphere were drifting out among small white blobs spinning away into emptiness.

Jesus, Michael thought. Spacers. The white blobs were spacers.

Suddenly, with an irrational stab of panic, he remembered the Merlins now only seconds from impact.

"Missiles abort, abort, abort," he screamed. You bloody fool, he told himself as he sat back. Those ships were finished but not completely destroyed. They could be useful. It had been years since the intelligence guys had seen the inside of a Hammer heavy cruiser, and even two-thirds of one was better than none.

Afterward, Michael would swear that his heart stopped as, with barely 5,000 meters to run, Prime aborted the missile salvo, their warheads firing jets of red-white flame ahead to bounce ineffectually off the Hammer ships' armor. Michael sat back and took a deep breath in. "Christ, that was close," he muttered.

"Prime, command. Confirm enemy contact report passed to Terranova."

"Confirmed."

"Roger." Michael sat back, happy to wait for Terranova to tell him what to do. A bit more than ten minutes later, he had his answer.

"Command, Prime."

"Go ahead, Prime."

"Terranova advises four Fed heavy cruisers have been tasked to assist, designated Task Unit 822.4.1, Captain Xiong, *Seigneur,* commanding. Dropping in five minutes."

That was damn quick, Michael thought.

"Names?" he asked, hoping that one might be *Damishqui.*

"*Seigneur, Select, Ulugh Beg,* and *Rebuke.*"

Damn, he thought. No *Damishqui* meant no Anna. Pity. "Command, roger. Maneuver to take station 100 kilometers behind and between the two Hammers and match vector. Confirm Hammer ship identities."

"The *McMullins* and the *Providence Sound.*"

Michael's eyebrows shot up. The *McMullins* was an old Triumph class ship, but the *Providence Sound* was a brand-new City class heavy cruiser. Fleet intelligence would be pleased.

The minutes dragged past. Michael was content to sit and watch the slowly tumbling remnants of the two Hammer ships, their forward sections the only clue that they once had been fully operational warships.

"Sir, positive gravitronics intercept. Estimated drop bearing Red 45 Up 0. Four vessels. Grav wave pattern suggests pinchspace transition imminent. Vector nominal for Terranova outbound approach."

"Roger." Damn, that boy was good. He was reading the grav arrays well ahead of Prime. Must remember to write him up, Michael thought.

"Sir. Targets dropping. Confirm drop datum at Red 44 Up 1 at 9,000 kilometers."

"Roger that."

"Well, well, well," Michael murmured. The new arrivals had more faith in their navigation AIs than Michael did in *Adamant*'s; 9,000 kilometers was close.

In a brief blaze of ultraviolet, the four Fed ships dropped into normalspace, immediately turning to close in on *Adamant* and her two shattered charges.

"Adamant, Seigneur." Must be Captain Xiong, Michael thought as the command holovid switched to show a Fed captain, her face betraying the same confused mix of fatigue and uncertainty he had seen on Lenski's right after the Hammer attack.

"Adamant."

"I'm Captain Xiong. Effective immediately you're assigned to Task Unit 822.4.1 under my command."

"Roger that, sir." No surprises there.

"We're closing in to send boarding parties across. Then we'll start recovering the Hammer lifepods. Do you need any immediate assistance?'

"None, thank you, sir. My navigation AI is suspect, which is why we were here in the first place, but apart from that all my systems are nominal."

"Roger. Stand by. I'll get back to you when we've secured the ships. Oh, and by the way, well done. Xiong out."

Bienefelt leaned across. "I think she likes you, sir," she whispered, her voice loaded with all the breathy intensity of a teenager sharing the secrets of young love.

Michael leaned over. "Piss off, Matti," he whispered back.

Bienefelt laughed. "I'm going walkabout, sir. See if anything's shifted."

"Fine. Take your guys with you. I don't want them sitting around. I'll patch *Adamant* into the task group's BattleNet. You can keep an eye on what's happening."

"Sir."

After Bienefelt left Michael alone in the combat information center, he sat back. With Xiong and her ships there, there was not a lot for him to do. He patched his neuronics into the helmet-mounted holocam of the marine major leading the boarding party heading for the *Providence Sound*.

There were some privileges to being the captain of a light cruiser, and he meant to make the most of them. The only Hammer ship he had seen the inside of had been some crappy mership conversion, and then only when he was scheduled to have the shit kicked out of him. He was keen to see what the real thing looked like.

Xiong was wasting no time getting across to what was left of the Hammer ships, and the marines certainly looked in no mood to hang around. When the first assault lander got close to the *Providence Sound,* doors port and starboard banged open to release a stream of black-suited marines, the boarding party cutting across the gap with an easy grace. They did not bother knocking. In seconds, a single roll of shaped-charge explosive was fast-glued to an air lock frame and fired, cutting a neat hole deep into the *Providence Sound*'s hull. Two marines dropped into the hole to repeat the process on the inner air lock door, and barely thirty seconds after they deployed, the marines were pouring into the ship.

What Michael saw shocked him. With her artgrav thrown off-line, the inside of the *Providence Sound* was a shambles. The marines' powerful torches picked out a mess of debris and equipment floating in a surreal slow-motion dance backlit by the ship's emergency lighting. The shock wave from the loss of the aft auxiliary fusion plants had ripped equipment, pipework, and cables indiscriminately off their mounts but here and there had left little islands of normality: A workstation with a clipboard still stuck to the bulkhead; a damage-control locker open, its contents still neatly arranged; a holovid still flashing the order to abandon ship in pulsating red and yellow.

Everywhere he could see the bodies of dead spacers, space suits slashed and ripped, visors shattered, red-black scars of blood frozen around hastily applied bright yellow emergency suit patches, evidence of desperate attempts to save the unsavable. Michael watched, sickened. They might be Hammers, but they were ordinary spacers, too.

Something struck him as he watched. Xiong's marines weren't acting like most other boarding parties: spreading out, poking around, seeing if there were any survivors, that sort of thing. They were not hanging around. The slightest problem with a door or hatch, and it was blown open. They did the same with equipment blocking a passageway. Bang. Gone. Move on.

No, these marines were on a mission, and belatedly, as they pushed their way down into the center of the ship before turning to go forward, Michael realized what they were after. When they came to the armored door that protected the forward missile magazines, he knew his guess had been right. These men were after Eaglehawk missiles fitted with antimatter warheads.

The magazine door was the first door the marines did not blow off. A plasma cutter was brought to bear, and a hole big enough to admit a space-suited marine was cut with infinite care. Once they got inside, the doors were opened easily by the emergency override. The marines were in.

Michael had seen plenty of missile magazines. This one looked no different from any other, but it still took his breath away. The magazine was filled with the dull black shapes of Eaglehawk missiles racked from deck to deckhead in hydraulically powered cradles. There were hundreds of the damn things in this section of the magazine alone. Above the racks were the hydraulic rams that moved missiles into the salvo dispenser that sat behind sliding blast doors. Everywhere shock-damaged pipes spawned tiny globules of hydraulic fluid. Little rainbow spheres shimmered, iridescent in the light from the marines' torches as they floated across the magazine.

The major whose holocam Michael was patched into did not waste any time looking around. Once through the door, he was up into the missile racks, looking carefully at the closest missile's warhead. It did not take long for him to find what he was looking for, a small RFID—radio frequency identity—tag fixed to the nose of the missile with a thin plastic tie. He waved up one of his team, who pulled out what looked like a small handgun and put it to the tag. There was a long pause as the two huddled over the missile. Michael prayed that they knew what they were doing. The thought that they might be only centimeters from an antimatter warhead, probably shock damaged, possibly unstable, and potentially liable to explode, taking everything with it—*Adamant* included—made his stomach flip. Thank God he had aborted the missile strike. If he had not . . . Well, suffice it to say, he and his crew would not be watching Xiong's marines stealing Hammer missiles.

Finally, they were done. A thumb went up. Michael's privileges as captain did not extend to being able to patch in to the major's voice circuit, but he did not need to. The man's body language spoke volumes.

The marines had found the antimatter warheads they had been looking for.

Michael felt acutely embarrassed as he crossed the brow to board the *Seigneur.* He had not thought to bring dress blacks for what was supposed to be a simple transit assignment. A shipsuit was all he had to wear. A clean shipsuit, true, but it was still only a shipsuit. He stopped, coming to attention as the bosun's mates piped him on board, the main broadcast announcing his arrival with the traditional "Attention on deck, FWWS *Adamant.*"

The ritual that accompanied the arrival on board of a captain in command completed, Michael stepped forward to take Captain Xiong's outstretched hand.

"Welcome aboard, Helfort, welcome aboard. Meet my officers, and then we'll debrief you on your trip from Comdur."

Duty done, Michael was ensconced in a comfortable chair in Xiong's day cabin, a welcome glass of beer in his hand. There was a moment's companionable silence as Xiong took her own glass from the drinkbot. She put it carefully on the table before sitting down.

Xiong looked across at the young man sitting opposite her. Considering Helfort's reputation, he was not that impressive at first sight. For a Fed, he was small. Probably to compensate, he was heavily built, with well-defined shoulder and chest muscles pushing hard against his shipsuit. It was the face that impressed her. It had the stretched look she had seen in so many spacers fresh from combat. His eyes, a striking hazel color, were sunk deep, framed by a gray-black dusting of fatigue and stress, and were half covered by lanky brown hair falling down across his face, the lines of a much older man beginning to cut their way out from eyes and mouth.

"What made you abort the missile strike, Michael?" Xiong asked.

"Luck, sir, to be honest," he said after a moment's thought. "Aborting the missiles suddenly seemed like a good idea. Can't really say why. I don't know why. Instinct? Fear, maybe."

Xiong's eyebrows went up in surprise. She took another sip of her beer. "You know, Michael, I would have put a million FedMarks down that you would have spun me some yarn or other."

Michael shook his head. "You know what, sir?"

"What?"

"Well," he declared, his voice a crude parody of Pavel Duricek at his pompous best, "between us cruiser captains . . ."

Xiong's head went back as she roared with laughter. "Us cruiser captains. Oh, my . . . us cruiser captains. Now, that's a good one," she gasped, struggling to draw breath. "God's blood, Michael. If you can make jokes at a time like this, maybe there's hope for the rest of us. Sorry. You were saying?"

"Well, the truth is I just did it. But what if I'd been wrong? What if they'd gotten a full salvo away? What if the salvo had been targeted on Terranova?"

Xiong shook her head. "If, if, if. Sometimes I think it's the worst word in the English language. Actually, Michael, it would not have been a problem. Fleet's pulled back most of the heavy units to cover the home planets. A two-ship attack probably would not have gotten through." She sighed heavily. "I'm not sure I can say the same thing for a full-scale attack like the one on Comdur, but . . ." Her voice trailed off. The thought of the Hammer dropping an antimatter attack on the Fed Worlds was too much to think about.

Michael nodded. He looked relieved.

Xiong regathered her thoughts. "Anyway, enough of that. I have new orders for you and your crew."

Michael looked up.

"Yes, Michael. Orders. We're going to keep the *Adamant* here as a temporary base until we've offloaded the Eagle-hawk missiles. Needless to say, our esteemed government doesn't want the damned things anywhere near Terranova. A courier ship is on its way; you'll transfer to that. Now, this may change, but at this stage you'll get some leave, and then it's back to the *Eridani* with another combat command hash mark to add to the one you already have. And that, my boy, is one more than me." Captain Xiong raised her glass in a mock salute. "Fleet has commed me the authorization already, so next time you're in dress blacks, make sure you're properly dressed."

Michael blinked. The thought of hash marks obviously had not occurred to him.

"Oh," was all he could say.

Michael watched the holovid intently as the battered wrecks of the *McMullins* and the *Providence Sound* fell away.

Behind the fast courier, the orange strobes of shuttles transporting captured Eaglehawk missiles across to cargo drones flashed brilliantly against the star-dusted blackness of deep space. Now and again, a searing white flash flared up as a drone and its precious cargo accelerated away to what Michael would have bet his life was, after centuries of will-ful neglect, a seriously reenergized interest in all things anti-matter.

Around the two Hammer ships but pulled well back out of harm's way in case a missile exploded, were the Fed ships, their hulls visible only as bottomless black shapes cut out of the stars. Now they were home to a small team of defense scientists and engineers laboring desperately to try to work out how the Hammers had done what every Fed scientist would have sworn was impossible.

Hope they're dispensable, Michael thought. It seemed to him that poking around antimatter was the quickest way to get a one-way ticket straight into the great unknown.

Michael closed his eyes as a sudden wave of tiredness broke over him. Antimatter was going to change a lot of things, and space warfare would be one of them. What those changes were he would be happy to wait to find out.

Soon he was asleep.

Thursday, April 20, 2400, UD
FWSS Eridani, *berth Bravo-10,*
Comdur Fleet Base Repair Facility

"Well, well, well. Look what the cat's dragged in."

"Lieutenant Kidav, sir!" Michael sounded hurt. He crossed the bow and saluted the ship. "Is that any way to greet the all-conquering hero fresh from his latest triumph over the forces of darkness?"

"Hero, my ass," Kidav replied affectionately, returning the salute. "Lucky is what you are. Lucky, lucky, lucky, and here I am, five years older—"

"Seven, actually."

"Pig!" she conceded good-humoredly. "All right, seven years older, and do I have anything to show for all my years of devoted service? No, not a damn thing."

"Not my fault. You should have stuck close to me. How was your temporary command?"

Kidav scowled, her bantering mood evaporating in a flash. "Well, we got there okay. The poor old *Sunfish* was a mess," she said with a frown. "Really gruesome up forward. Horrible. Those damn ship designers need to take radiation impulse shock a bit more seriously than they have been."

Michael nodded somberly. It had been a bad week, what with the Hammers firing antimatter missiles toward the home planets every few days. The hidden message was so obvious that even the dumbest politician must have gotten it by now. Pretty simple, really: Surrender or we incinerate your home planets.

Michael finally broke the silence. "What's next for us? Any orders?"

Kidav shook her head. "No, not yet. We undock tomorrow as planned. Back up into parking orbit. That's all we know right—"

"All stations, this is command. Stand by for an announcement from the Flag Officer Commanding, Comdur System."

Michael and Kidav stared at each other. "Oh, shit," Kidav muttered. "Please, God, not one of the home planets." Michael could not speak. He stood there, paralyzed by fear.

"All stations, this is Rear Admiral Malhotra. I have received a message from the commander in chief, Space Fleet, which message I am directed to read to you. It goes as follows:

"'To all Fleet personnel. The governments of the Federated Worlds and the Worlds of the Hammer of Kraa have agreed that an armistice will come into effect today at 1200 Universal Time. At that time all military operations will cease, and all forces will disengage and withdraw. Detailed orders specifying how the terms of the armistice are to be met together with revised rules of engagement agreed to by both governments are being sent to all units and commands. The governments of both systems have further agreed that all prisoners of war shall be repatriated together with a full and complete accounting of any deaths in custody by no later than one week from the commencement of the armistice. Upon completion of that repatriation, the two governments have agreed to convene on Scobie's World to negotiate and agree on the terms of a lasting peace, terms that will address the enduring concerns of the peoples of the Federated Worlds and the Worlds of the Hammer of Kraa.

"'Signed, Martha Shiu, Admiral, Commander in Chief, Federated Worlds Space Fleet.'

"That is all."

"Commitment command, this is Federated Worlds Warship *Eridani* with heavy scouts *Van Maanen* and *Groombridge* in company inbound from Comdur system calling on 32, over."

"*Eridani,* Commitment command. All ships maintain current vectors. Transmit vessel identities, approved flight plans, and confirmation that all weapons systems are disabled. Over."

The operator looked bored, eyes looking off-holocam at something much more interesting than the command crew of a Fed heavy scout. His right hand was fiddling absentmindedly with the old-fashioned headset and boom mike perched on his head.

"Roger, Commitment command. Stand by." Tanvi Kidav threw a backward glance across *Eridani*'s combat information center at Michael. She rolled her eyes theatrically.

Michael smiled. "Concentrate, sir," he mouthed silently.

Kidav nodded, squinting for a moment as she commed the information Commitment command had asked for down the link. It took a while. The datastream had been slowed down to comply with the Hammer's antiquated data transfer protocols.

There was a short pause as the Hammers checked and double-checked that *Eridani* and her sisters were not in fact an entire squadron of Federated Worlds heavy cruisers about to drop in-system to lay waste to Commitment.

"*Eridani,* this is Commitment command. Ship identities, flight plans, and weapons systems status confirmed. Maintain current vectors until final approach plan authorized. Contact Commitment nearspace control on vidcomm channel 55, over."

"*Eridani,* vidcomm channel 55, roger, out."

Kidav looked at Lenski, who was sitting silently alongside her. "What do you reckon, skipper? The Hammers are being uncommonly polite, don't you think?"

"They are, Tanvi. I hope it doesn't mean they are saving things up for us. Right, go to 55 and let's see what they've got in store."

"Sir." Kidav commed the channel change.

Michael, tucked away safely out of sight of the holocam and under strict instructions to stay that way, shivered at the sight of the unlovely features of the Hammer's duty controller for inbound traffic. An arrogant-looking man, he had an unblinking stare that was extremely disconcerting. Michael took a deep breath. The high-necked black uniform and the Hammer of Kraa sunburst picked out in gold thread on the left breast brought back memories he had spent a great deal of time burying.

Kidav flicked a glance across at him. "Fuck 'em," she mouthed.

"And the horses they rode in on," Michael mouthed back.

"Concentrate!" Lenski growled.

"Sorry, skipper," Kidav mumbled, turning her attention back to the holovid. "Commitment nearspace control, this is Federated Worlds deepspace heavy scout *Eridani* with heavy scouts *Van Maanen* and *Groombridge* in company inbound to Planetary Transfer Station Zero Three per flight plan. Request approval for final approach, over."

"*Eridani,* this is Commitment nearspace control. Stand by. Transferring final approach plan for PTS Zero Three. Acknowledge receipt."

Kidav and Lenski looked at each other in relief. Michael shared the sentiment. Despite all the agreements and planning that had gone into this mission, it would not have surprised either of them if they had been put into a parking orbit for days on end for no good reason other than some imaginary slight against the might and majesty of the Hammer.

Fortunately, not this time.

The Hammer controller continued. "You are reminded that deviation from this plan without prior approval from

Commitment nearspace control will be met with the immediate use of deadly force. No warnings will be given."

"Commitment nearspace control, noted. Stand by." Kidav nodded confirmation to Lenski that the approach plan had been received, had been passed by Mother as sensible, and was not going to run them headlong into the station or some other large, hard object in orbit around Commitment. "Approach plan received. *Eridani* with *Van Maanen* and *Groombridge* in company commencing final approach to Planetary Transfer Station Zero Three. *Eridani,* out."

Kidav broke the link without waiting for the Hammer operator to acknowledge. Lenski leaned across. "Tanvi, I know this is the first time you've seen them up close, but don't let it get to you."

"Sorry, skipper."

Lenski turned to Michael. "And remember, young man. Stay out of sight. We've got people to bring home."

"Sir."

Michael stared moodily at the holovid as *Eridani* circled endlessly around Commitment, her two companions trailing along behind her like tame dogs.

Below *Eridani,* the planet Commitment was a dramatic sight as the terminator raced across the planet's chaotic mix of whites, blues, greens, and browns. It had been three days since they had dropped into Hammer space, and after a brief stay alongside the planetary transfer station—the ships had been treated as though they carried the Black Death—the Hammers had ordered them to unberth and move into low orbit. So they had, no doubt waiting for some mindless Hammer bureaucrat to decide that the prisoner transfer could go ahead.

"Looks pretty."

Michael swung around. It was Bienefelt. "Oh, hi, Matti. Yes, it is pretty, but so is a well-chiseled tombstone. It's the corruption underneath you've got to focus on." His voice was bitter. He'd seen the list of prisoners to be repatriated together with what the Hammers were pleased to call the nonreturnees list. Nonreturnees! For a very long time Michael had stared at the list, anger never far from the surface.

Aaron Stone. Poor bastard. Even though he had made it out of Camp I-2355 and across Koenig's High Pass to the safety of the Forest of Gwyr, he had not survived; the injuries he had sustained had been way beyond the capabilities of Fellsworth's medics to fix. On top of the stick lost crossing Koenig's, sixteen more had died along the way. Most from accidents, though four had died when their patrol had been caught in the open by two Hammer assault landers.

Not that Michael cared much how they had died. Dead was dead.

What he did know was that they all had died because of the Hammer, and one day there would be a reckoning. Fellsworth had made it. So had Chief Ichiro and the man-mountain himself, Marine Murphy. Leading Spacer Petrovic, too. Even the mutineers had made it; Michael would have traded them for Aaron Stone in a heartbeat. Apart from Fellsworth, they all would be taken home in the *Groombridge,* and so he would have to wait until Terranova to see how they had fared. There had been some good news, but not enough. Not nearly enough.

"Command, Mother. Incoming vidcomm, channel 37."

"Matti, take this, would you," Michael called. "I'm not supposed to be here."

"Sure."

The impassive face of the latest in a long line of black-uniformed Hammers to talk to the *Eridani* appeared on the holovid. "*Eridani,* Commitment nearspace control."

"*Eridani.*"

"Up-shuttle with returnees per manifests will be with you in thirty minutes. Contact up-shuttle call sign Golf Charlie 6 on vidcomm channel 75, over."

"*Eridani,* roger. Up-shuttle call sign Golf Charlie six on vidcomm channel seventy-five. Out."

Bienefelt looked across at Michael. He was silent for a moment. "Matti, tell the skipper while I comm our friends to let them know."

With the *van Maanen* and *Groombridge* duly informed, Michael waited while Bienefelt briefed Lenski before activating the main broadcast. "All stations, this is command.

Stand by to receive shuttle port side in three zero minutes. *Ishaq*s returning."

Michael commed Kidav.

Kidav's cheerful face popped up in his neuronics. "Hi, Michael. What can I do for you?"

"You heard the broadcast?"

Kidav looked pleased. "Sure did. Finally!"

"Yes, finally. Favor to ask."

"Shoot."

"Can you take over the watch from me? I would like to be at the dock when the *Ishaq*s get here."

Kidav winced. "Oh, shit, Michael. Of course. Sorry, I didn't think."

"That's all right. When you're ready."

"On my way."

In the end the up-shuttle had taken more like an hour, but finally it had docked. Michael stayed back, standing apart from the rest of the *Eridani*'s crew. Nobody knew quite what to expect. All they had been given was a list of names.

At last, the transfer air lock swung open with a tiny hiss of air as the two ships equalized. Then two DocSec troopers, a sergeant and a corporal, armed with stun guns and stiffly arrogant in their trademark black jumpsuits appeared. Michael had to hold himself back as red rage ripped into him. He was a hairbreadth away from diving across the brilliantly lit air lock to tear their throats out. By some miracle, he held himself back.

After a cursory look around, the DocSec troopers seemed satisfied. Standing back, they looked on impassively as first one, then another, and then a procession of emaciated spacers half walked, half staggered into view. Their desperation to be clear of their Hammer captors was plain to see, the tattered remnants of shipsuits the only thing marking them out as Feds.

For a moment, the *Eridani*s hung back, stunned by the appalling sight of *Ishaq*'s crew. Then something snapped, and ignoring the DocSec troopers' protests, they rushed forward as one to help the struggling spacers on board, Michael in there with the rest of them. Then he saw her, her smile the only hint that this tattered, limping human being, her grimy face pulled tight across high cheekbones by hunger, was Lieutenant Commander Fellsworth. He snapped to attention and saluted.

Fellsworth shook her head. "For fuck's sake, cut it out, Michael. Give me a hand before I fall over."

Holding her up, he got Fellsworth on board *Eridani* only seconds before she collapsed; a gurney was slid into place hurriedly to catch her. Michael knelt down beside her, his face close to hers.

"I won't ask how it was, sir," Michael whispered, taking her hand in his.

"No, don't. I expect you to buy the vid. It's going to fund my retirement." She smiled, but her eyes did not. "Michael! I must tell you. You did well to get word out. Very well. We would all have died otherwise. We all owe you, and Corporal Yazdi, of course. Is she here?"

Michael shook his head, the pain on his face obvious. "No, sir. She didn't make it."

"Shit." Fellsworth's eyes closed for a second. "Those Hammer pricks didn't tell me that." She lifted her head to look right at Michael, her hand squeezing his hard, her grip surprisingly strong and painfully tight. "You know where she is?"

Michael nodded. "Graves registration found her. She's coming back with us."

Fellsworth's voice was tight with a fierce intensity. "Good. Well, let me tell you something. They'll pay for this. They'll damn well pay."

"They will. They sure as hell will."

Fellsworth held his hand tight for a moment before her eyes rolled up and her head fell back onto the gurney, her arm dropping away. Michael carefully put it back by her side and, unable to speak, waved the medics to take her away.

Eventually, every living *Ishaq* was accounted for, but *Eridani* had one more *Ishaq* to take home. With a heavy heart, Michael and every one of the *Eridani*'s crew not on duty fell in on either side of the air lock, unmoving.

It seemed like a long wait to Michael, though it probably wasn't. Finally, four Hammer civilians in gray shipsuits appeared carrying a narrow rectangular box of cheap gray plasfiber, placing it carefully on the threshold of *Eridani*'s air lock.

Michael stood in silence. Corporal Yazdi was coming home. He had fulfilled that promise at least. As the crew came to attention and saluted as one, four *Eridanis* stepped forward to carry the mortal remains of the little marine back on board.

To his dying day, Michael did not know why he did what he did next. Even as he stepped forward, he knew it was stupid, something Lenski pointed out to him in extremely colorful and un-Fleet-like language later. But stupid or not, he did it. While the *Eridani*'s executive officer checked and signed the clipboard presented to him by the DocSec corporal to confirm that the *Eridanis* had all the *Ishaqs* they were entitled to, Michael slipped unnoticed across to stand alongside the black jumpsuited sergeant.

He stuck his face right up close to the man's. "Sergeant," he whispered, "I have a message I would like you to pass on."

The DocSec sergeant stared at him. "Eh? What?" he mumbled, confused.

"It's for Colonel Erwin Hartspring of Doctrinal Security. Know him?"

"No." The sergeant shook his head. "No, don't think I do."

"Well, not to worry. Colonel Erwin Hartspring. He's a big cheese. Section 22, I think, based in McNair. Now, this is important. Tell him Michael sends his regards and looks forward to seeing him again one day. Got that?"

The sergeant nodded uncertainly. "Michael sends his regards and looks forward to seeing him one day. Yes. Got it," he muttered.

"But," Michael continued, looking around theatrically, "for Kraa's sake, don't say anything to anybody until we've jumped. Otherwise . . ." He drew a finger across his throat, nodding his head back toward the *Eridani*.

"Er, right." By then the sergeant looked completely baffled.

"Got all that? And for Kraa's sake, say nothing until we've jumped. Okay?"

The DocSec sergeant nodded. Bewildered, he watched Michael walk back on board *Eridani,* the air lock doors thudding shut behind him.

Five minutes later, the three heavy scouts and their precious cargo made a high-g departure. Main engines pushed to emergency power punched pillars of white-hot flame planetward, with the Hammers' increasingly strident demands to reduce thrust completely ignored.

Tuesday, June 13, 2400, UD
Korndapp Mountain Resort, Scobie's World

Chief Councillor Polk walked out onto the sprawling deck that fronted his suite. It was going to be a beautiful day, and in more ways than one, he promised himself.

He took a deep breath. The mountain air was pure and cool, the early morning sun cutting long slanting bars of light and dark through the mist eddying up from the valley far below him. In the distance, the Korndapp Range dominated the horizon, its rock faces thousands of meters high. Long tendrils of meltwater dropped down walls slashed by vertical fissures and ravines, unraveling into thin white skeins that twisted and danced in the early morning breeze. Above them, snowfields dusted a soft pink by the morning light crowned impossibly sharp peaks climbing high into the sky, a few stars still bright against the fading blue-black of night.

It was stunning, and in more ways than one.

Polk had to laugh out loud; he could not help himself. The sheer joy of presiding over the final humiliation of the Federated Worlds was as good as any drug. No, it was better, much better, because today was the start of something that would cement his position as chief councillor until the day he died.

There was a wonderful twist to it all, though it was a minor detail, a mere bagatelle. Even so, it greatly amused him every time he thought of it. The Polk clan owned the Korndapp Mountain Resort, home to the negotiations with the Feds. Not that anyone knew that, of course. The endless layers of nominee companies and blind trusts were completely opaque; his many enemies had never found out, and if they could not, the damned Feds never would, either.

Polk laughed out loud. Even he had trouble keeping up with the Byzantine complexities of the Polk clan's business affairs.

Ah, the wonderful, delicious irony of it all, he thought. The Feds were paying the Polk clan for using the Korndapp Mountain Resort, the place where he would make their defeat final and absolute, where the foundations of future Hammer greatness would be laid.

Friday, June 16, 2400, UD
FWSS Eridani, *in orbit around Comdur Fleet Base*

"Come in, Michael. With you in a tick." Lenski waved him into a seat.

"Thank you, sir." Michael sat down. What on earth was going on?

Lenski finished what she was doing and, pushing her chair away from her desk, turned to look right at him. "Well, Michael. All good things come to an end."

"Sir?" Michael said, puzzled.

"Yeah, apologies, Michael. Teasing my officers. Bad habit of mine. Anyway, I have orders for you, a new posting, I'm sorry to say. We're going to miss you."

"A new posting?" Michael looked shocked. This he had not expected. "Where to? Why so soon? I've only been in the *Eridani* for what, two months?"

"Not even that. Anyway, you're posted to leave immediately, and then it seems the Fleet Advanced Projects Unit has need of you, reporting to one Commander Baker care of the Transit Officers Quarters, Comdur base, by no later than 0900, July 3. And before you ask, no, I haven't the faintest idea what the Fleet Advanced Projects Unit actually does, so don't bother asking me. All I know is that they run out of Comdur."

"Baker," Michael said thoughtfully, dredging through his neuronics until he found the recording he had made. "Yes, Commander Baker. I know him. I met him during the Hammer attack on Comdur. Seemed like a smart man."

"That's as may be, Michael. Far more important is your farewell dining out. Don't care what you're doing tomorrow night. Clear your diary and make sure you have your drinking boots on. You're going to need them."

As the dirtside shuttle pulled away from the *Eridani,* Michael had mixed feelings about leaving.

He had enjoyed his short time in *Eridani.* She was a great ship, and he was sorry to be leaving so early. Lenski was one of the better captains around, and leaving Bienefelt behind was a blow. Michael was not superstitious, but he could not shake a deep and growing conviction that the huge woman brought him luck.

However, the Advanced Projects Unit sounded intriguing, and if Commander Baker was anything to go by, it might prove to be an interesting place, though he wondered why they wanted a junior lieutenant. He prayed it was not for some bullshit administrative post.

Anyway, the Advanced Projects Unit was a problem for another day. *Damishqui* was in one of the orbiting shipyards around Paradise for planned maintenance, and after a heart-stoppingly long delay, Anna had agreed to meet up.

Quite where things went from there, Michael could not be sure, but he had put his foot on a nice beachside shack dirtside on Paradise, and if all went well . . .

The only sounds were the soft rustle of palm trees and the gentle intermittent hiss of the surf as it ran up a beach invisible in the darkness beyond the light thrown by a single, guttering candle.

Michael was drowning in Anna Cheung's eyes, the outside world slipping effortlessly away as he drifted down, hopelessly, utterly lost. He could not help himself; he never could. The first time he had met her, a lifetime ago as a brand-new cadet, her eyes had been the first thing he had noticed. Every time they met, they had the same hypnotic effect on him, an effect that made the rest of the world fade away into irrelevance.

"Michael!" Anna said sharply. "For heaven's sake, pay attention!"

Michael came back to earth with a bump. "Oh, sorry, Anna. Honestly, you really should wear glasses. Dark glasses."

Anna laughed softly. Michael's addiction to her eyes was the longest of long-running private jokes, even if it did drive her to distraction at times.

"Michael! Concentrate!"

"Yes, will do. Sorry," he said contritely.

"Thank you so much," she said with exaggerated patience. Screwing up her courage, she took a deep breath before resuming. "Look. I understand you want to, well . . . I know what . . . How can . . . Shit! I'm making a real mess of this, aren't I?" she whispered, putting her head in her hands to hide the tears that suddenly flooded her eyes. "Crap, crap, crap," she muttered. She looked up, wiping her eyes. "Goddamn it, Michael. I know what you want, I really do. Even though in the best part of what, six hours, you haven't actually managed to say it out loud."

Michael looked guilty. She was right. He had been so afraid that Anna would tell him to get lost that his speech—carefully rehearsed a thousand times over—never saw the light of day.

Anna looked right at him, remnant tears dusting her eyes with tiny jewels, gold in the candlelight. "So believe me. If we were anything other than Fleet officers," she said fiercely, taking another deep breath, "I would bloody well ask you to marry me, settle down, get a day job, have kids, the whole nine yards."

She shook her head despairingly. "But damn it, Michael!

We're Fleet officers. Another war with the Hammers is definitely in the cards no matter what those bloody politicians might say. So I'm sorry. It won't work. I can't make that sort of commitment right now. Nor can you, Michael Wallace Helfort. Especially you. God knows, you seem to have a death wish. So . . ." She shook her head again. "Commitment? Marriage? Forget it. It's not possible, Michael. Surely you know that."

Miserably, Michael stared at her. With unerring accuracy, she had picked out the fatal flaw in his position. "So what do we do? Jesus, Anna. Is that it for us? All over?"

"No, you dummy," she whispered fondly, shaking her head. "Of course it's not. Look. I love you. You love me. So that'll have to do until things settle down. Every chance we can, we'll get together. Every leave, every day off, every chance. Okay?"

Michael nodded miserably. "Suppose so," he muttered.

"Bloody hell!" Anna frowned. "Suppose so. Suppose so! Is that all you can say?"

Michael shook his head. "No, it's not." He looked at her for a long time, a small smile ghosting across his face. "There's lots more. So come for a swim, Anna Cheung, and I might give you the benefit of my wisdom if you play your . . . Ow!" he howled. Anna's leather sandalled foot had smacked hard into his shin.

"Pig!" she said, standing up and kicking back her chair. "I might listen . . . if you can catch me!"

She turned and was gone, a fast-fading blur of white muslin disappearing into the night.

Michael looked around the massive Fleet canteen as he waited for Matti Bienefelt to arrive. Under normal circumstances, the place would have been packed with spacers from the hundreds of ships in Comdur orbit, the noise in proportion to the arrogant confidence habitually displayed by Fleet spacers.

These were not normal circumstances. It was still packed, but the place was horribly quiet.

"Hullo, stranger."

"Hullo, stranger, sir, you insubordinate lowlife spacer, Petty Officer Bienefelt."

"Well, up yours . . . sir." Bienefelt banged down a mug of coffee the size of a small bucket before taking his hand in her massive paw. Michael managed to drag his hand away before she crushed it. "And for your information, sir, it's you insubordinate lowlife spacer Chief Petty Officer Bienefelt," she added smugly.

"Well, bugger me." Michael looked in astonishment at Bienefelt. He noticed the chief's shoulder straps only when she dropped her huge frame into a chair. Then again, he would have to be twice as tall to get a decent look at her shoulders in the first place. "Chief? How?"

"Well, the old saying; your misfortune, my good luck." Bienefelt shook her head, her voice suddenly somber. "Lot of people hurt when those Hammers did us wrong. A lot."

Michael nodded sadly. It was true. The Hammers had not killed as many Fed spacers as they had planned to, he was sure of that, but they had badly damaged plenty. "Trust me, Matti. Their day will come."

"Oh, yes. It will. It sure as hell will."

There was a moment's silence. "So," Michael continued. "Chief, eh? What does that mean?"

"One more week in the good ship *Eridani*. Then posted to leave for two months to clear the backlog I've built up. After that, don't know yet. I've asked for a heavy scout running out of Anjaxx."

"Coxswain?"

"Yup."

"Anjaxx, eh?" Michael looked thoughtful. "Now, let me think. Anjaxx? Why Anjaxx? You're a Jascarian." He pondered the problem; then he got it. "Ah ha!" he said triumphantly, wagging his finger in Bienefelt's face. "You are one sly dog, Chief Petty Officer Matti Bienefelt. Now I remember. Isn't there a certain Yuri somewhere on Anjaxx? And isn't he even bigger and uglier than you are? Am I right? Hmmm?"

Bienefelt did her best to look deeply offended. "Good thing you're not just an officer but a runty little officer. Otherwise . . ."

Michael's hands went up in surrender. "Okay, okay, I take it back. Yuri isn't bigger and uglier. Let's just say he's as big and as ugly."

"You are a very rude man," Bienefelt said amicably. There was a long pause. "Sir."

Michael's laugh was cut short by his neuronics. He had an appointment to keep. "Oh, shit, Matti. I've got to go." He got to his feet and put out his hand. "Now listen to me, you big lump. Be careful and stay in touch, okay?"

Bienefelt stood up, towering over Michael as she took his hand. "You're the one who should be careful. So be careful," she said sternly.

"Yes, Chief," Michael said meekly. "See you."

Thanks to his neuronics' timely reminder, Michael made it to the transit officers' quarters with his dignity intact a scant thirty seconds ahead of Commander Baker.

"Helfort." Baker shoved out his hand briskly. "Welcome to Comdur."

"Good to be here, sir," Michael said, taking Baker's hand. The man was just as he remembered him: small, chunky, and radiating nervous energy, though considerably less stressed than the last time around.

"Liar! Comdur's a dump, and we all know it. Now, we have to process you in, and then I've got something I want you to see."

"Sir, what exactly am I posted here to do?"

"Patience, my son. Patience. All will be revealed. Let's go." With that, Baker was off.

Michael, duly processed onto the strength of the Advanced Projects Unit and now the owner of the highest security clearance he had ever seen after a briefing of eye-watering ferocity, had followed Baker at a half trot as the man had led him through a maze of laser-cut rock passageways, his neuronics unable to say where they were going. He was beginning to realize that Baker knew only two speeds: flat out and full stop. To Michael's relief, Baker finally skidded to a halt in front of a marine-manned security barrier. Overkill surely, Michael thought, considering they were a good two kilometers below Comdur's surface and in the heart of the most secure Fleet base in the Federation.

The marines would not have cared what Michael thought. With meticulous care, they cleared first Baker and then Michael through the barrier and into a brilliantly lit lobby backed by steel doors. There was another delay and another identity check with the security AI before the doors agreed to open to reveal a bare plasteel box fitted with simple fold-down seats and red emergency lockers.

No sooner were they in than the doors snapped shut. "Strap in securely. We will depart shortly," announced a disembodied voice. Baker waved Michael into a seat, and they strapped in. The box, vibrating gently, began to move sideways. After thirty seconds or so, it stopped. A recessed red warning light began to flash. "Stand by to drop in five seconds," announced the voice.

Baker looked across at Michael. "Bit of negative g coming up, so I suggest you hang on," he offered offhandedly.

"Oh, right, sir, but—"

The bottom fell away from underneath them as the artgrav cut out completely. Michael struggled to control a heaving stomach suddenly intent on misbehaving. For a moment, he and Baker floated in their straps before a fierce downward acceleration began to build, the negative g pulling the two men out of their seats and tight against their restraining straps.

The complete lack of air noise and the massive acceleration gave Michael all the clues he needed. They were in a drop car in a hard vacuum tunnel heading for the center of Comdur, which lay the best part of 300 kilometers below them. If he remembered correctly, that meant that the drop car, its speed topping out at close to 2,000 kph, would have them wherever the hell it was they were going in less than ten minutes. He flicked a glance at Baker. The man seemed to be asleep, so Michael left him alone.

Baker would give him answers when he was good and ready; there was no point pestering him.

The minutes dragged slowly past. Michael tried hard not to think about the 300 kilometers of solid rock that lay at the end of the tunnel, now rushing toward them at more than 500 meters per second. The disembodied voice returned.

"Stand by for deceleration in ten seconds."

Baker woke up. "Ah, good," was all he said.

Deceleration was an understatement. When it came, Michael winced as the g force in the drop car reversed with sudden brutality, slamming him back into his seat. Jesus, he thought. More like a bloody fairground ride than a passenger conveyance.

Suddenly the g force vanished, and once again the two men floated in their straps. There was a short pause, and then the car began to move, artificial gravity returning to drop Michael back into his seat again. Michael followed Baker's lead as, without a word, he unstrapped and stood up.

The drop car's doors opened to reveal yet another lobby hacked out of the rock. Three tunnels led off the lobby. Baker wasted no time before plunging into the center tunnel; he took off so fast that Michael had to run to catch up. Fifty meters down the tunnel, Baker stopped in front of a bench set up across the mouth of a room the size of a small warehouse and packed floor to ceiling with shelves loaded with orange plasfiber boxes; a sign proclaimed it to be the Personal Maneuvering Systems Workshop. Michael's confusion was now absolute, so he stood there as Baker commed someone out of the back of the workshop.

A crusty old chief appeared, a smile on his face as he saw Baker.

"Hullo, sir. Haven't seen you for a while."

"Some of us have to work for a living, Chief."

"Well, sir, thank God I don't," the man replied cheerfully. "What can I do for you?"

"Two units, please. Oh, I forgot." He waved an arm at Michael. "Chief, this is Lieutenant Helfort. You'll be seeing a lot of him."

"Morning, Chief. Junior Lieutenant Helfort. Nice to meet you." Michael shook hands across the counter.

"Oh, shit, damn, and blast," Baker muttered, shaking his head. "Sorry, Michael. You're improperly dressed."

Michael looked puzzled. It was pretty hard to be improperly dressed in a shipsuit and boots. "Sir?"

"Yes. Improperly dressed. A lieutenant should not be wearing a junior lieutenant's shoulder straps. Fleet Dress Regulations, chapter something or other."

"What? I don't . . ." The penny dropped. "Aaah."

"Yes, sorry. Effective today, you're a lieutenant. Orders only arrived this morning. Should have told you but forgot. Congratulations and all that. Now, where were we?" Baker asked briskly.

"Two units?" the workshop chief asked sardonically.

"Ah, yes. That'll do. Plus stick boots, of course."

Ten minutes later, the personal maneuvering unit heavy on his back and stick boots on his feet, an even more confused Michael followed Baker down the tunnel. He had no idea what they were doing. He had no idea why they were wearing personal maneuvering systems. He had no idea why he had been promoted to lieutenant two years early. All in all, the whole day was turning out to be a complete mystery.

"Good, we're here," Baker said.

They were in front of a plasglass security lock behind which lay a black and yellow striped door marked REPAIR FA-CILITY YANKEE. DOOR M-34. AUTHORIZED PERSONNEL ONLY in emphatic red letters.

"Now, Michael, I'm going to download a safety briefing. While you're going through that, I'll confirm that we can actually get in."

"Sir."

Michael got some answers as he watched the safety vid. Seemingly, behind the black and yellow striped door lay a single enormous space, brilliantly lit by wall-mounted light panels. Quite what the space was for, the briefing did not say. In the vid, it was empty except for a network of spidery bridges running in all directions. The briefing's main purpose appeared to be telling him over and over again that unless authorized by a superior officer, he was to keep his stick boots on the bridges at all times. The rest of the brief was standard stuff for working in a zero-*g* environment. When Baker asked if he was ready, he nodded.

One by one, with their identities confirmed by a skeptical security AI, Baker and Michael passed through the personnel lock.

"Ready?" Baker asked.

Michael could have screamed. Get on with it, he wanted to shout. The suspense was killing him, but he nodded.

Baker commed the door open. It slid back silently. Michael blinked in the wave of harsh white light that flooded out. He followed Baker out onto one of the bridges, the art-grav disappearing as soon as he left the lock. As he looked down, his stomach lurched. They were hanging a good two hundred meters or more above the floor. For a moment, what he saw did not make any sense.

Then it did.

The space was vast, easily big enough to hold five heavy cruisers in a line with room to spare, the massive shapes sitting in cradles anchored to the floor and ceiling. Michael looked closely. The ships showed signs of massive radiation damage, with huge patches of their armor stripped away, in some cases down to the titanium inner hull. There wore orange-strobed spacers and small workbots everywhere, maneuvering units spitting thin white spikes of compressed nitrogen as they wheeled and danced around the ships in an elaborately choreographed ballet. There were heavy bots on the move, too: salvagers, transporters, welders, cutters, hydraulic rammers, and more. Their escorts of safety bots were clearing the way through the endlessly shifting fireflies that infested the place.

Ah, Michael thought. Now he understood. It was a repair facility. No, hang on, that was not right. No repair facility ever had such strict security. After all, the fact that the Federation was fixing its battle-damaged heavy cruisers was hardly the state secret of all time, and why was the facility right at the heart of Comdur? Getting ships the size of heavy cruisers down Comdur's gravity well, small as it was, would take some doing.

So what was going on here?

"Well, Michael. What do you think?" Baker asked.

"Impressive, sir," Michael replied guardedly. "Impressive. But it's not just another repair facility, is it?"

"Smart man," Baker said approvingly. "No, it's not just another repair facility." He paused for a second. "No, Michael. What you are looking at is your next command," he said, waving his arm across the heavy cruisers.

Michael stared at him, mouth open. His next command? What in God's name was the man talking about?

"You got to be kidding, sir!" Michael protested. "A cruiser captain? That's a four-ringer's job. Even if it is to be my job, I haven't got the exper—"

"Stop!" Baker ordered firmly. "Let me tell you something, Michael. You're here because you're the right person for the job. That's my opinion. It's also the boss's opinion and one arrived at after a great deal of thought. So let's go and meet her, and she can put you out of your misery. Now, where is the woman?" Baker asked himself. "Ah, yes. She's inside the *Tufayl,* having an argument with the engineers about something. Right, hold on while I get us clearance from facility control . . . okay, done. Follow me. Oh, and Michael."

"Sir?"

"Please do not crash into anything."

"Sir!" Michael did his best to sound hurt. "As if!"

"Hmmphh," was Baker's only comment. He unstuck his boots and pushed himself into space clear of the walkway. With casual competence, his backpack maneuvering unit spitting spikes of nitrogen, Baker spun on the spot and stopped dead; with easy grace, he accelerated away across the void, directly toward the center of the line of heavy cruisers. Michael was impressed. Baker needed only the briefest of brief jets of ice-cold nitrogen to nudge him back on vector.

With a deep gulp, Michael followed; he tried hard not to look down. When he was more or less lined up, he accelerated after Baker, his trajectory degenerating in seconds into an erratically three-dimensional corkscrew. It was not easy. No, it was bloody well impossible. He'd only worked in zero g wearing a combat space suit complete with life-support and maneuvering systems. Everything was different, and not surprisingly, the result was a mess. He was too light, his center of mass was all wrong, and, not surprisingly, the results were not good to look at. He got there in the end, though it was more a controlled crash than a carefully executed landing as he thumped into the *Tufayl*'s hull in a cloud of nitrogen-chilled ice crystals, frantically trying to compensate for coming in too fast.

Acutely aware that every spacer with nothing better to do must be enjoying the show he was putting on, he bounced heavily off the *Tufayl*'s matte-black armor. A few frantic blips on his thrusters brought him into the cargo air lock, where Baker was waiting to grab him, a huge smile on his face.

"God above, Michael. What a performance!" Baker called cheerfully.

"Glad you liked it, sir," Michael muttered sourly. "I think everyone else did, too."

Baker clapped him on the back. "Don't sweat it. My first time, I managed to break my wrist, so all in all you haven't done too badly. Come on. Park your unit here. The boss awaits."

Michael stuck his boots into the micromesh covering the deck. Arms waving in an attempt to stay upright, he set off after Baker in the awkward motion—push, twist, tug, push—required to move in zero g wearing stick boots. Making their way through the ship, Michael looked around with interest. The *Tufayl* had been one of the ships closest to the Hammer missiles; she had suffered badly in the attack, and it was obvious.

It was a heartrending sight. The ship was a shambles. Evidence of the massive shock wave that had punched its way through the ship was everywhere—machinery big and small, pipework, cabling, lockers, all ripped off their mounts. Here and there, there were dirty black patches he strongly suspected were long-dried blood. He shivered. A lot of good spacers had died here, and he felt their ghosts. Everywhere there was debris from a once-living ship: shipsuits, boots, gloves, tool kits, test equipment, combat space suits, fire extinguishers, emergency cable kits, tables, chairs, holovid screens, mess kits, and more. There was abandoned gear everywhere. The sight was utterly demoralizing.

Baker plowed on. He must be used to all this, Michael thought. He followed Baker down a drop tube, pulling himself down hand over hand.

"Okay, here we are," Baker announced as he pushed himself clear of the tube. They were in a small lobby. Aft lay the *Tufayl*'s combat information center, but Baker went forward to the captain's quarters. He knocked on the door.

"Come!" Michael knew he should recognize that voice. Try as he might, he could not place it.

He recognized the face, though. The long, lean figure of Vice Admiral Jaruzelska smiled broadly as Michael whipped his right hand up into a salute in best Fleet fashion. Well, it would have been if Michael's feet had been better anchored to the micromesh. They were not, and the salute spun his body into a slow turn to the right that, arms flailing, nothing could stop. Doing his best not to laugh out loud, Baker finally rescued him.

Michael, cheeks flaming red in embarrassment, struggled to recover his lost dignity. Jaruzelska made her way over to shake his hand, her face split by a huge grin. "Welcome," she said warmly. "Welcome to the First Dreadnought Squadron, Lieutenant Helfort. Well, what will in time become the squadron when we've made a few alterations."

"Thank you, sir," he replied, wondering what the hell the First Dreadnought Squadron was. He pretty much knew the Fed order of battle by heart; to the best of his knowledge, there was no such beast as the First Dreadnought Squadron.

"How much has Commander Baker told you?"

"Well, sir. Not a lot, really, and what he has told me is, well, is . . ."

"Hard to believe?" Jaruzelska laughed.

Michael nodded. "You could say that, sir. Impossible to believe might be more accurate, though."

"Well, we'll have to put you out of your misery, then. Now, let me explain what this business is all about."

"Sir."

"First things first. My job is simple. I've been given six months to give the Fleet an offensive capability capable of beating Hammer ships armed with antimatter warhead–fitted Eaglehawk missiles."

Michael's mouth dropped open. How in God's name could these battered ships do that?

"Yes, I know, Michael. Hard to see what the *Tufayl* and her sisters can do to take the fight back to the Hammers, but Commander Baker here has convinced me. Commander?"

"Thank you, sir. Well, let's start by dragging a sacred cow out and killing it. The days of the conventionally manned warship are over. Not completely true, but thanks to antimatter weapons, Federation warships cannot carry thousands of vulnerable humans into battle anymore. Now—"

"Hold on, hold on. Sorry, sir"—Michael did not look sorry at all—"but did you just say what I think you said? If you did, that means unmanned warships, and that means the end of the Fleet as we know it. How can that be?"

"Well, Michael, needs must, I'm afraid. Two reasons: a chronic shortage of spacers and the huge amount of mass it will take to make a ship like this safe against antimatter warheads. You can have the crew but not the protection. Or you can have the protection but not the crew. You can't have both, you see. With me so far?"

"Just, sir."

"Good. But you're not completely right. There'll be no un-manned warships, but we can have the extra protection and a much smaller crew. Ten, I'm thinking."

"Ten!" Michael protested. "Sir! I've been there, and I'm not sure that'll work."

"Michael," Jaruzelska cut in, "you may well be right, but we're going to try it. Maybe it'll work. I happen to think it will. All I want from you is an open mind."

"Sir!" Michael replied fiercely. "I'll try anything if it gets us level with the Hammer."

"Good. Go on, Commander."

"Thank you, sir. As I was saying, a heavy cruiser will have a crew of only ten spacers. Not thirteen hundred as now. Every bit of redundant equipment will be ripped out. Any-thing not required to maneuver the ship, to operate its sen-sors, to fire its weapons, and to keep its crew alive—it will all go."

"I get it, sir!" Michael's voice cracked with excitement. "That'll give us a heavy cruiser, but she'd be lighter, faster, and more maneuverable. Jeez, wouldn't that be something?"

"Doesn't stop there, Michael," Jaruzelska said. "Every-thing we take out allows us to give the crew the armor and shock protection they'll need to survive an antimatter attack at very close ranges. And you'll be the first captain in com-mand of what Commander Baker likes to call the new dread-noughts."

Michael gulped. "Shit . . . sorry, sirs, but this is a lot to take in."

"Yes, it is," Jaruzelska said patiently, "but it has to work first, so let's not be counting our chickens. Now, before I hand you back to Commander Baker for a more detailed briefing on what we're up to here, do you have any ques-tions?"

"No, sir . . . oh, wait, just one, if I may."

"Go on."

"Why me, sir? Why have I been picked?"

Jaruzelska laughed out loud. "Thought you'd ask that. I happen to think that experience can be a bad thing sometimes. Every officer with formal command training, and that means every captain of a Fed warship, has been brought up to fight battles with fully crewed ships. By the time they get to command a heavy cruiser, they've had decades of doing business that way, and that's not what I want. What I want is officers trained from the ground up to fight battles with what are—near as damn it—uncrewed ships. I want no preconceptions, no bad habits, no 'this is not the way we do things.' Understand?"

"I do, sir. But why me?"

"You've already done what Commander Baker and I have in mind. You took *Adamant* into battle against two Hammer heavy cruisers and won. Yes, yes"—her hand went up to stop Michael's protest—"I know things went your way that day, but believe me when I say you do deserve a lot of credit. I've been through the datalogs, and it wasn't all luck. That's why you're here." Jaruzelska leaned forward and looked Michael right in the face. "You are the only Fleet officer ever to command what was effectively an uncrewed warship in action," she said fiercely. "You selected yourself."

"Got it, sir," Michael said, a little shaken by Jaruzelska's sudden intensity. "No more questions."

"Good. Off you go. Commander Baker will fill you in on the rest of the plan. We've laid on welcome drinks for you in the unit's mess at six. Oh, and make sure you're properly dressed"—Jaruzelska tapped her shoulder—"otherwise it'll be the most expensive party you've ever been to."

Michael reddened with embarrassment. "Sir."

"Sorry, sir. My fault," Baker said. "Forgot to pass on the news."

"Drinks on you, then."

"You are a hard woman, sir."

Jaruzelska laughed. "Go! I've got work to do. See you tonight."

"We'll be there, sir," Baker said. "Come on, Michael. We've got a lot to see, and then it's into the sims for you. We have to rewrite the Fighting Instructions from the ground up."

Inwardly, Michael groaned. Sims! Why was he not surprised?

It was the end of a long day.

Michael still could not believe it all, and for good reason. What he had been told was close to heresy—no, it was heresy. Baker's proposal not only overturned the most sacred of all of Fleet's sacred cows, it had kicked it to death before chucking it out the window.

Michael shook his head.

Jaruzelska had told him only the half of it. He had discovered that Baker was not a man who thought small. Oh, no. Baker's plans for him went far beyond command of a converted heavy cruiser. For each manned ship, he planned to deploy between four and nine unmanned cruisers—"dreadnoughts" he insisted they be called—operating under the manned cruiser's direct control. In Baker's view, the dreadnoughts would be so tough that they would be able to drive into the heart of any Hammer formation and rip it to shreds, antimatter missiles or not. Provided that he did not screw up in the sims, Michael would take the First Dreadnought Squadron into action when—not if, Michael noted with interest—negotiations with the Hammers collapsed.

The turnaround was incredible. Since its inception, Fleet policy had consistently favored manned warships to the point where the policy was so entrenched in Fleet thinking that to challenge it was a career-threatening move. To be fair, there never had been an AI-commanded warship capable of taking on and beating a manned warship. Endless sims had proved that. Humans made better decisions under the stress and confusion of space war than AIs could; it was as simple as that. Despite the billions of FedMarks invested in AI research and development, FedWorld AI technology, good though it was, had never been able to replicate the human brain.

And there things would have stayed if the Comdur Disaster had not left the Fleet with many more ships than it could find crews for and the Hammers with a weapon those ships could not defeat.

So here he was, Michael thought. Fate had put him at the tip of the sword intended for the Hammer's heart, and he meant to be there when the chance to drive it home came. It would come; he was sure of that. The Hammers wanted much too much and were too sure that they had such an advantage over the Federation that they would not have to make concessions to get it. Well, he might be only a newly promoted lieutenant, but he agreed with Baker: It was only a matter of time before the negotiations collapsed and the Fourth Hammer War started.

He prayed for that day to come—the Hammer had debts to pay.